The Gate to Nowhere

Welcome to the fantastical world of Iltior!

Meet

Runcible Jones and Mariam Orpiment
Two almost normal children stuck at Grindgrim
Academy, the worst school in the country.

Parsifoe and Ulalliall
A shambling magician and her arrogant, age-old transportal.

Thandimanilon and Lars Sparj
The charmingly wicked Dark Lady and her villainous consort.

Sly, slippery Sleeth and sad-eyed Tigris
Two brilliant students of magic, but can either be trusted?

The Cybale
An ancient fanatical cult of wizards about to rise again.

Find out what happens when Runcible and Mariam
are hurled through a gate to Iltior, to become the
children that will change the world's destiny forever.

Other books by Ian Irvine

THE HUMAN RITES TRILOGY
The Last Albatross
Terminator Gene
The Life Lottery

THE THREE WORLDS SERIES
THE VIEW FROM THE MIRROR QUARTET
A Shadow on the Glass
The Tower on the Rift
Dark is the Moon
The Way Between the Worlds

THE WELL OF ECHOES QUARTET
Geomancer
Tetrarch
Scrutator
Chimaera

THE RUNCIBLE JONES QUINTET
Runcible Jones: *The Gate to Nowhere*

RUNCIBLE JONES

The Gate to Nowhere

IAN IRVINE

Puffin Books

PUFFIN BOOKS

Published by the Penguin Group
Penguin Group (Australia)
250 Camberwell Road
Camberwell, Victoria 3124, Australia
(a division of Pearson Australia Group Pty Ltd)
Penguin Group (USA) Inc.
375 Hudson Street, New York, New York 10014, USA
Penguin Group (Canada)
90 Eglinton Avenue East, Suite 700,
Toronto ON M4P 2Y3, Canada
(a division of Pearson Penguin Canada Inc.)
Penguin Books Ltd
80 Strand, London WC2R 0RL, England
Penguin Ireland
25 St Stephen's Green, Dublin 2, Ireland
(a division of Penguin Books Ltd)
Penguin Books India Pvt Ltd
11, Community Centre, Panchsheel Park, New Delhi -110 017, India
Penguin Group (NZ)
Cnr Airborne and Rosedale Roads, Albany, Auckland, New Zealand
(a division of Pearson New Zealand Ltd)
Penguin Books (South Africa) (Pty) Ltd
24 Sturdee Avenue, Rosebank, Johannesburg 2196, South Africa

Penguin Books Ltd, Registered Offices: 80 Strand, London WC2R 0RL, England

First published by Penguin Group (Australia),
a division of Pearson Australia Group Pty Ltd, 2006

10 9 8 7 6 5 4 3 2 1

Text and cover design by Adam Laszczuk © Penguin Group (Australia)
Typeset in 10.5/15 ITC New Baskerville by Midland Typesetters, Australia.
Printed in Australia by McPherson's Printing Group, Maryborough, Victoria

National Library of Australia
Cataloguing-in-Publication data:

Irvine, Ian, 1950–.
Runcible Jones : the gate to nowhere

ISBN 0 14 330158 6.

I. Title.

A.823.3

www.puffin.com.au

CONTENTS

Acknowledgements

Thanks to my agent Selwa Anthony, my tireless editors Dmetri Kakmi and Nan McNab, and everyone else at Penguin Books who has worked so hard and so long on this book. I would also like to thank John, Meg, Angus and Fiona for their comments on the manuscript, and Jane and Jeremy for Runcie's address.

Especial thanks are due to Elinor and Simon for reading the manuscript several times, and for their extensive and thoughtful comments on it, which have improved the book out of sight.

I would also like to thank Simon for the prodigious labour and creativity that has gone into the story images and animations created in support of the work, which can be found on my web site.

The Runcie series is for Elinor

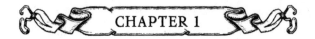

CHAPTER 1

The Prison Visit

As the children's bus turned in to the gates of Hopewell Women's Prison, Runcible Jones felt his panic rising. He'd been rehearsing what to say to his mother, Millie, all the way but, after the hysteria his last visit had caused, he couldn't think of a single safe topic.

The bus stopped at the guard house with a clash of gears and a shuddering jerk, and black fumes puffed up through a rust hole in the floor. Runcie covered his nose. He desperately wanted Millie to talk about his dead father, Ansible Jones, though if Runcie ever mentioned the topic she would have a fit. Ansie's book on magic, his life's work, had caused all the trouble in the first place. Magic was not only illegal; it was a serious crime. Besides, the prison warders listened in to their conversations, hoping to gather more evidence.

The kids scrambled off the bus, jostling each other in wary silence as they formed a queue in the driving rain. Runcie ended up last, as usual, next to the belching exhaust pipe. He was soaking wet and his head was throbbing by the time the line inched up to Security, where it stopped again. At this rate, visiting hour would be over before he got to see Millie. And he still had nothing to say.

Runcie wasn't game to ask her about the break-up, much less the divorce. He'd been just seven when Millie had left his father. That day was burned into his memory, and it was all his fault.

He couldn't bear to question her about the mysterious fire that had killed Ansie and destroyed all his work three years later. Millie had wept for weeks, then refused to mention his name ever again.

And Runcie was too scared to ask his mother why, why, *why*, a year after Ansie's death, she'd been arrested for having a copy of his banned book. Of all the strange events of his unhappy life, that was the oddest.

He already knew the answer to his one remaining question – when are they letting you out, Mum? Seven more years, with good behaviour.

Runcie handed his card to the warder, a stout man with bristling white eyebrows like worn-out toothbrushes and ears covered in a felt of grey hairs. Runcie remembered him from last time; he was the only decent warder here.

He waved Runcie inside but, as he passed through onto the grimy linoleum, he caught his breath. He would have known Hopewell Prison in pitch darkness, for its cold reek of unwashed clothes, sweaty fear and stewed Brussels sprouts would live with him all his days. It was the smell of his mother's despair.

2

He could see her now. Little Millie sat hunched behind wrought-iron bars thick enough to hold back King Kong. She was shivering and her hair, which last year had been as golden as flowing honey, hung over her ears like mouldy straw. Runcie waved, then had to look away. Her grey eyes were fixed on him as if she were starving and he couldn't bear it. Each visit she looked thinner and more tormented. Runcie was terrified that she was going mad.

That left only one good thing in his life – the memory of those times he'd shared with his father, just playing in Ansie's workshop while he told stories, laughed, joked and talked about his work, his passion. Magic! It had been the happiest time of Runcie's life. But later, in her anguish, Millie had attacked his father's work unceasingly. She'd refused to admit that magic existed, and called Ansie a fraud and his book a lie. Runcie felt as though he was expected to deny his own father. Even though he was desperate to find out more about Ansie's work, in his worst moments Runcie found it hard to believe in him.

The line inched forwards. Forty minutes of visiting hour were gone already. Millie's blue fingers were clenched around the bars now, her pale face crumpled like a discarded rag. A whippet-thin warder, standing by the far wall, was watching her, and everything about him shone, from the braid encircling his hat to the metal caps on his black bootlaces and the tip of his bony nose. All but his eyes which, like coal in a cellar, took in everything and reflected nothing.

Now the authorities were blackening Ansie's name, making him out to be a dangerous criminal. It was a lie! His father had been the kindest, gentlest man in the world. He wouldn't even tread on an ant. Why were they doing this to him; to *us*?

The warder with the furry ears tapped him on the shoulder. 'Your turn, laddie. Better hurry.'

Runcie glanced at the clock. Five to twelve, and visiting time ended on the hour. He scuttled across the room, slipped into the seat and his eyes met his mother's. Despite the bone-aching cold, she was sweating. He tried to smile but couldn't.

'You're looking well, Mum,' he lied.

Millie smiled but he wished she hadn't, for it was a ghastly deceit. He clenched his fists under the bench until his nails dug into his palms. She wouldn't last seven more years. What could he say to her? How's the food? What did you do today? Are the other prisoners *nice*?

'Mum,' he blurted without thinking, because thinking did him no good at all, 'please tell me about Dad and the good old days.'

He should have known better. Millie gave a cracked moan then said savagely, almost madly, 'He destroyed our family. Don't *ever* mention his name again.'

'Then why did you have his book?' he whispered. 'Just tell me that, Mum.'

Down the far end of the row, the coal-eyed warder's head whipped around and he leaned forward like a hunting dog straining at the leash.

4

Millie's mad look disappeared and she reached through the bars. 'Runcie, promise me one thing.'

'Of course, Mum.' He took her little freezing hand. Her whole arm was shaking. 'Anything.'

'Promise that you'll *never* have anything to do with magic.'

He stared at her, aghast. How could he promise that? 'Mum?' he whispered.

The minute hand jumped, then the clock began to bong the midday hour. 'Promise, Runcie!' She crushed his hand.

Runcie couldn't make that promise; he just couldn't. He looked up and the warder was stalking towards her, scribbling in his notebook. For the first time, Runcie wanted him to hurry.

Millie must have seen the hesitation in Runcie's eyes, for she hissed, 'Runcible!'

He crossed two fingers behind his back and took a deep breath. He hated lying to her, but he had to. Then he looked into her wet, ravaged eyes and hesitated. Prison was agony for Millie, yet her only thought was how to keep him safe. He couldn't do it.

The warder jerked Millie to her feet. Runcie clung to her hand but it slipped free. It was his chance to say nothing but he couldn't bear to leave her facing that terror. 'I promise,' he whispered, and felt the weight of Hopewell Prison descend on his thin shoulders.

The warder hauled Millie away, still staring over her shoulder at him. The iron door thudded shut.

'Time to go, laddie,' said the kind warder.

Runcie stumbled back to the bus, eyes stinging. He wasn't going to cry. Not a single tear, even in the gloom where no one could see. He had to be the strong one.

What was he supposed to do now? He had to learn about magic. How could he truly know his father, or even believe in him, without it?

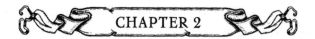

CHAPTER 2

Grindgrim Academy

Runcie's computer, the one thing he'd inherited from Ansie, was acting strangely again. Every so often the screen image spun like a propeller and the whole computer rocked back and forth as if trying to creep off his desk. In between, peculiar pictures flashed across the screen. Presently it was a range of icy mountains but the ice was green, while the sun was huge and red.

Runcie shivered. It was cold in his shabby attic room, and the rats in the roof seemed agitated today. He went to shut down the computer but his hand froze above the keyboard. An eye was staring at him as if peering *through* the centre of the screen. A deep-set, heavy-lidded eye, yellow around the edges and brown in the centre.

The eye went out of focus then snapped back, twice as big and ringed by a brass circle, as if Runcie were being studied through a telescope. His stomach throbbed. Now a bony finger and thumb appeared, ending in sharpened nails that twisted the brass ring; the eye blurred then reappeared, this time filling the screen.

Runcie threw himself backwards off his chair, landing painfully on his elbow. By the time he looked up, the eye had gone and the computer was shutting down, all by itself. He got into bed, turned out the light and pulled up the threadbare covers, but the eye stayed in his mind for hours. What kind of a government spied on kids, anyway?

Runcie, thinking about Millie, let out a heavy sigh. He'd lost hope of getting justice for her months ago. He had phoned every adult in her address book and at least a hundred others, written letters until his fingers were blistered, and pestered people in the street to sign his petition, though few had. He'd even written to his member of parliament, but she hadn't replied.

Though nothing made the slightest difference, he had to keep fighting. He couldn't let them destroy his family. Millie was shrinking with every visit, slipping through his fingers, and one day, soon, he'd lose her completely. That's why he clung so desperately to the magic and the mystery of his father. Those wonderful memories were the one thing that could keep the black fog of despair at bay. It was behind him all the time now, and every day it felt a little stronger, a little closer, but he wasn't going to give way to it. He had to hold out, for if it took him he was afraid his whole family would cease to exist.

If only he could uncover the truth about Ansie.

Thump, thump, thump.

It was six a.m. and still dark, but Runcie slid out of bed at once. Frost made feathery patterns on his grimy window and

8

the floorboards were freezing. He dressed hastily. After Millie's arrest he'd been stuck in an orphanage for months. No one wanted to take in a kid whose mother was in prison for possessing a book about illegal magic, and whose father had died writing it.

It wasn't fair. He'd loved his old school. All the kids there had normal families and normal lives, with mobile phones, high-speed internet and holidays in the sun. And they weren't spied on.

He'd eventually been fostered out to the Nightingales, the strangest couple he'd ever met. They lived at 13 Thirteenth Avenue and they didn't care about his reputation. The only thing they cared about was money – getting it and never spending a penny. Runcie didn't like them much, but he did everything he could to please them, for he was desperately afraid of being sent back to the orphanage.

Lifting the trapdoor, he climbed down the ladder into the upstairs sitting room. That's what Mrs Nightingale called it, though there was nowhere to sit and precious little space to stand. He edged between the leaning stacks of newspapers and magazines that towered two-thirds of the way to the cracked and cobwebby ceiling. She'd collected every newspaper published in the past eighty-seven years and was constantly reading them, though not in any particular order.

Mr Nightingale stood at the bottom of the stairs, tapping fingers as plump, pale and squishy as pork sausages. An odd little man, he wasn't much taller than Runcie, but as wide as he was high. He was as hairless as a garden slug and his flat ears stuck out sideways like fly's wings. His face was red and sweaty, his lips plump, moist and habitually pursed. His body was exactly like a globe – shoulders that were just bumps on top, a belt around his bloated middle long enough to tie up a hippopotamus, and tiny, prim feet that belonged on a plastic doll.

'Good, morning, Mr Nightingale,' said Runcie politely.

Mr Nightingale nodded like one of those puppets whose head is held on with a spring. He handed Runcie two buckets and a knife, then waddled down the junk-filled hall. Runcie followed, yawning.

Two huge sacks of turnips leaned against the back door, grown by Mr Nightingale in an allotment down the street and wheelbarrowed back by Runcie yesterday after school. He took out the first turnip, peeled it and dropped it into a bucket.

'Don't bruise the vegetables, Runcible,' piped Mr Nightingale in an absurd, reedy voice. 'It kills the vitamins.'

'Sorry.' Runcie was always apologising for something. Dropping the peelings into the other bucket, he reached for another turnip. He had to peel both sacks before breakfast. The Nightingales were paid to be his foster-parents but they believed children should work for their living. Runcie could bear that. They treated him well enough, in other respects.

'Waste, Runcible!' Mr Nightingale clapped his flabby hands with a horrid splatting sound, like raw liver plopping onto the floor.

One of the peelings had landed behind the second bucket.

'Sorry, Mr Nightingale.' Runcie picked it up. The fruit and vegetable peelings were used to brew a foul-smelling yellow grog. Mr Nightingale took a small glass of it each night before bed, and each night his wife frowned and muttered about the evils of drink.

Runcie was tired, and his fingers hurt from yesterday's work, but he was determined to do the best job he could. As he peeled, he fretted about that eye in the screen. What could the authorities be looking for?

An hour later, he carried the last bucket of turnips into the kitchen and sat down at the table, rubbing his blistered fingers. He was so hungry that even breakfast at the Nightingales had a certain grim appeal.

Mrs Nightingale was a thin woman with yellow, moss-stained teeth that protruded through her meagre lips. She had the longest neck he'd ever seen, topped by a little, triangular head. Two great round eyes took up most of her forehead, though only the left one worked. Her right eye was covered in a grey growth with its own blood vessels, which bulged out like little balloons when she lectured Mr Nightingale about his grog.

'You're late again, Runcible,' she said from the corner by the fuel stove.

She didn't say it unkindly, for Mrs Nightingale was neither kind nor unkind. It was simply force of habit. She said the same thing every day when Mr Nightingale came back from the allotment, and after each of his forays through the garbage bins, rubbish skips and piles of junk put out by the other house-holders on council cleanup days. The Nightingales didn't do anything with the junk; they just collected it. Every corner of the house was stacked with jars full of bottle caps, used matches, smelly sardine tins and a thousand other worthless items. They didn't even know why they hoarded the stuff. They were like sad robots, doing the same thing over and over.

'Sorry,' mumbled Runcie, looking away. He often caught himself staring at her mossy teeth or her bulging eye veins, and was embarrassed about it. He felt sorry for her, just as he pitied ridiculous Mr Nightingale.

'I should think so.' Mrs Nightingale handed him a glass of celery juice, though judging from the brown colour it had been made from very old, withered celery. 'This'll get your blood pressure down.' She must have been thinking of Mr Nightingale, whose face had gone a sweaty purple from the exertion of watching Runcie work.

'Thank you, Mrs Nightingale.' Runcie drank half the juice, which tasted even worse than it looked, and picked up his knife. Two slices of yellow parsnip bread rested on his plate. He took a careful spoon of marmalade from the bowl and smeared it across the bread. The Nightingales were watching him, making sure he didn't take more than one spoon per slice. There was no danger of that, for it was turnip marmalade and only semi-starvation could induce him to eat it at all.

As soon as he'd spread marmalade on both slices, Mrs Nightingale whipped the bowl out of his reach, just in case. Runcie took a small bite. This batch of marmalade tasted more horrible than usual and the parsnip bread was, well, extremely parsnippy. He picked fibres from between his teeth and took another shuddering bite.

The toaster went *ping* and smoke puffed up from its rear slot in the shape of a tormented wraith, which was strange since the toaster was unplugged. Mrs Nightingale gave her husband an uneasy glance, settled back in the chair and took up her newspaper, which she read with a magnifying glass the size of a frying pan. Today it was a fairly recent paper, only a few months old.

'The problem with the power stations is getting worse,' she said, reading from the newspaper as if it were this morning's. One eye vein swelled and contracted. 'The leader of the opposition is calling for a royal commission to find out the truth.'

'He didn't get one,' said Mr Nightingale, who listened to the radio and knew what was going on. 'The prime minister says it'll be sorted out any day now.'

Mrs Nightingale snorted. 'He wouldn't have a clue.'

There had been a lot of problems with power lately. It was disappearing after the power stations made it, and no one knew why. Electrical appliances were acting up too, all over the world. It was very mysterious.

After breakfast, Runcie did another half-hour's work to pay for the electricity he'd used last night, then got ready for the daily ordeal of school. By comparison, living with the Nightingales was paradise.

Runcie wheeled his bike in through the high wall that sur- rounded Grindgrim Recalcitrants Academy. Before becoming a school it had been a traitors prison for 278 years and, even with most of the razor wire gone, still looked like one. The buildings were soot-stained, windowless stone and the yard was bare asphalt. Holes had been hacked through it here and there, and trees planted, but none had survived. They were like burnt matchsticks.

He looked up at the watchtower on the corner of the wall. It wasn't manned any more, though the playground would have been safer if it had been. Runcie parked his bike in the racks and put the chain around it. Millie would never have allowed him to ride through the traffic but the Nightingales didn't mind. It saved the bus fare and if there was an accident they'd get the Bereavement Allowance.

'Hey, Spoon! Runcible Spoon.'

Runcie darted a nervous glance over his shoulder. The kids often called him Spoon. They thought it was witty. It was a long way to the iron-studded front doors and the bullies were wait- ing for him, as they did every day. They began to chant.

'Runcie runt, Runcie runt, Runcie, Runcie, runt runt *runt*!'

His heart was hammering, his mouth dry. Runcie was the smallest kid in his year and, since he took after his mother, he was always going to be little. He wanted to take them on the way his tall, brave father would have done, but didn't have the courage. He tossed his bag over his shoulder and prepared to look them in the eye. He'd still get a beating but at least he wouldn't have given in. The defiance, tiny though it was, really mattered.

There were five of them today, big thugs all, surrounded by another dozen kids who were just glad it was someone else's humiliation and not their own. The group separated along either side of the path as he approached.

'Runcie runt, Runcie runt, Runcie, Runcie, runt runt *runt!*'

The ringleader stepped out: Jasper Fulk, only twelve but already bigger than most men. He had hard little eyes like slices through a stuffed olive, a twisted nose like a sweet potato and a nutcracker jaw covered in scabs from his father's razor. He was the only kid in Runcie's class who needed to shave and was constantly showing off by rubbing his bristly chin. It sounded as if he were sandpapering a plate.

Fulk was accompanied by Jud Thorp, who took pride in his nickname, The Blob; Stinky Morton the liar; sneaking Ross Pethick, who had front teeth like a weasel and a disposition to match; and white-eyed 'Shylock' Homes, who made a handsome living extorting lunch money from the little kids. Since Runcie never had any lunch money the gang took turns to give him Chinese burns instead. Sometimes he couldn't write for the rest of the day, which generally meant he was put on detention.

'You're late, Runcie runt,' Fulk said. 'Been visiting your witchy mother in prison?' He exchanged grins with his cronies. The Blob's great body quivered with silent mirth.

Runcie didn't answer. There was no point, for they weren't ordinary bullies. School was supposed to be fair but Grindgrim

15

Academy was viciously anti-magic and the teachers allowed, no, *expected* Fulk's gang to terrorise those unfortunate kids tainted by magic. The headmaster would stop it tomorrow if Runcie denounced his parents. He couldn't do that, but he couldn't fight the bullies either. Runcie dumbly endured their torments, hating himself for not being able to stand up to them. His spirit, his dreams of magic, and all he held dear about Millie and Ansie, were being crushed.

Fulk caught him by the arm. The Blob blocked his escape to the right while Pethick, weasel teeth bared, lurked off to Runcie's left. Fulk's grubby nails dug into Runcie's skin. 'I'm talking to you, Spoon. Didn't the evil witch teach you any manners?'

They always picked on Millie. His father would never have endured it and Runcie couldn't either. 'Mum's not a witch!' he cried, trying to pull free, but Fulk's grip was like being handcuffed to a goalpost.

'Why won't you fight, Spoon?'

Runcie just shook his head.

'Spoon's a slow learner, guys. We'd better teach him his lesson again.' Fulk swung Runcie around and the other thugs converged on him, except for Shylock, who preferred to watch. 'What do we hate?' Fulk chanted.

'Magic!' cried The Blob, swinging a fist the size of a cabbage. It caught Runcie in the ribs and he doubled over, holding his free arm over his face. 'Magic is a lie,' The Blob sneered. 'Your father was a rotten liar who got what he deserved.'

'That's not true,' Runcie wheezed.

'Liar, liar, liar,' chanted the onlookers.

Fulk motioned them to silence. 'What do we hate?' he repeated.

'Magic,' snarled Stinky Morton, darting at Runcie.

But then, before he could strike, a high voice cut through the buzz of the spectators. 'Stop that!'

Everyone froze, though it was only a kid's voice, so Fulk didn't let go of Runcie's arm. Runcie stood up, trying to see who it was. No one had dared interfere before.

'Just walk away and I'll pretend you never spoke,' said Fulk over the heads of the other kids, then motioned to Stinky to get on with it.

'Let him go, right now!'

The crowd parted. The speaker was the new girl, Mariamhie Orpiment. Mariam was half a head taller than Runcie, with an olive complexion, a long proud nose, ever so slightly arched, and the most astonishing hair. Glossy black with a bluish sheen, it was so curly that it spread out to cover her entire back.

Mariam had appeared suddenly two weeks ago and the school was abuzz with rumours about her. One said that she'd attacked the headmistress at her previous school and put her in hospital, another that she'd blown up half the school with illegal chemicals. A third rumour held that she'd killed the school bully in a duel, though no one believed it, for it had been spread by Stinky Morton, the biggest liar at Grindgrim.

One thing was clear, though – she was a rich, posh kid who'd done something really bad and had been sent to Grindgrim, the worst school in the country, as a punishment. Mariam was in Runcie's year though he'd never dared speak to her. She was way too cool to notice him. She wore all the latest gear and, despite the rule against mobile phones, carried the most stunning one Runcie had ever seen. It was turquoise and ivory, the buttons were arranged like rotating wheels, and colours rainbowed across it when it was in use. It rang constantly in recess and Mariam spent most of the time talking animatedly on it. He desperately wanted one the same, not that he had any friends to call.

She came down the path as if she owned the school, brushing past creepy Shylock Homes as if he wasn't there. The throng held its breath but he let her go by and, amazingly, so did vicious Ross Pethick. Walking right up to Fulk, who towered over her, Mariam said fiercely, 'Let him go. He's just a kid.'

So was she, but she was braver than Runcie would ever be. He couldn't even imagine taking Fulk on.

'We're allowed to teach *tainted* kids a lesson,' said Fulk, moving a half step backwards, 'so butt out.'

'Your father's a car thief and your mum fakes credit cards,' said Mariam. 'Maybe I should teach *you* a lesson.'

Pethick choked, and chills ran up and down Runcie's spine. No one spoke to Fulk that way. Mariam was *dead*.

Fulk's hand gave a convulsive jerk, crushing Runcie's arm, then he went very cold. 'If I just say the word, my gang will take you down.'

Mariam turned around, arrogantly staring down Pethick,

The Blob, Shylock and Stinky in turn, before facing Fulk again. 'Go on, scabface. Take me down.'

Runcie had never seen such reckless courage. Could the rumours about her be true?

Fulk flushed, tried to meet her gaze, then his eyes slid sideways. 'I'd watch out if I were you,' he blustered. 'You haven't got any friends here.'

Mariam gave a scornful laugh, though it had a bitter edge to it. 'Who needs friends like yours? Let him go.' Fulk's fingers lost their grip and Runcie pulled free. 'Go on, you,' she said.

It took Runcie a moment to realise that she was talking to him. He trudged along the path, feeling the gang's eyes boring into his back, and sweating. How Fulk would make him pay next time.

'We don't think you're tough at all, Mariam,' Fulk hissed from a safe distance. 'We think you made up those rumours about yourself.'

Runcie looked back. Mariam froze in mid-stride, swallowed, and was in control again. 'Oh, Fulk,' she drawled, 'I'm glad you think so.'

Fulk exchanged an evil grin with Shylock, who turned those sick eyes on her, unblinking. 'We'll find you out.'

She tossed her hair and turned away. When she caught up to Runcie, she said loftily, 'You look like a frightened rabbit.'

'Thanks!' muttered Runcie, then felt ungrateful. But it was bad enough that he'd been rescued by a girl, without her insulting him afterwards.

'You've got to stick up for yourself. If you take it, they'll keep dishing it out. Hold your head up and never look back.' She undermined her words by flicking a glance over her shoulder. 'It's the only way to deal with them.' Mariam looked down her long nose at him, as if realising what an odd, shabby kid he was, then strode away.

Runcie started after her, but stopped. Was it embarrassing to be seen with him? He supposed it must be when you were the coolest girl in the school. So why *had* she come to his defence? Was she just showing off? Runcie didn't think so. From the look in her eye, she'd acted on a reckless impulse and now regretted it.

He didn't understand her. In Mariam's first week the boys had gone in awe of her, and even the good girls wanted to be her friend, but she'd insulted or ignored them all. Now the whole school shunned her and she pretended not to care.

Still, she'd stood up for him where no one else ever had. Runcie squared his shoulders, gave a jaunty smile and strode inside. It was the first good thing that had happened since his mother went to prison ten months ago, the day after his eleventh birthday. Whatever tomorrow held, he'd never forget that Mariam had defied all Grindgrim, for him.

CHAPTER 3

The Intruder

The Nightingales went to bed early because sleeping saved electricity. Normally Runcie stayed up late, reading or using his computer. It was the one time he had all to himself.

He turned the computer on, then jumped. The brass-ringed eye was staring at him again. Restarting got rid of it, though the hard disc spun up with an unnerving wail and the screen filled with mist creatures wringing spectral hands and crying 'Woe, woe!' He hastily turned it off, for there was too much to think about. Why was Ansie's book so dangerous anyway? It wasn't a spell book – it just said that magic was in people's genes, so everyone should be able to learn it. No one but Runcie's brilliant father could ever have come up with such an idea, and proved it.

A lump formed in his throat, because Runcie didn't think he'd ever uncover the truth about his father's work. He just wasn't like Ansie, and that was the problem.

Besides, what if Millie was right, and Ansie's work *was* a load of rubbish? She was a scientist who had brought Runcie up to think things through. She didn't believe in the supernatural and he had begun to doubt magic too. But if it didn't exist, his father was either a liar or an irresponsible idiot who'd wrecked his family, and Runcie couldn't accept either alternative. In any case, why would magic be banned if it didn't exist? It didn't make sense. He felt so confused.

He usually avoided thinking about the other big question because, after nearly two years, it still hurt too much, but tonight it wouldn't go away. Why *had* his father died? Not even the police had been able to explain it. Runcie was determined to find out. He didn't know where to begin, though it must have had something to do with magic. If only he hadn't made that promise to Millie.

He gave up and began to practise spinning his cricket ball, another passion he'd shared with his father, but it spun out of his hand and thumped against the floorboards. Afraid he'd disturbed the Nightingales, he turned the light out and got into bed, watching the frost patterns creeping across his window in the moonlight, and agonising . . .

Runcie roused slowly. His hair was lifting up off his head with a crackling sound, and the rats were scurrying back and forth in the roof, squeaking. A hot puff of air blew across his face, which was even odder, since the window was closed and it was freezing outside.

He opened his eyes. The moon had passed over the roof and the attic was in shadow, so why was there a light in his room? For one horrible moment Runcie thought Fulk's gang had got in, but Mrs Nightingale double-checked the deadlocks before she went to bed. It wasn't the Nightingales, either. Mr Nightingale couldn't climb the ladder and Mrs Nightingale never came upstairs at night, being afraid of the things that lurked in the dark.

The glow from the computer screen lit up the far wall, though he'd definitely turned it off earlier. Runcie was too tired to shut it down but, as he was about to turn over, he saw movement in the shadows by his bookcase. There *was* someone in his room, and he barely managed to stifle a squeak of terror. The figure was so tall that it had to bow its head under the low roof, but its shape was blurry – was it wrapped in a sheet? No, a cloak and hood, of all things.

The hood turned his way, trying to make him out in the shadows. Runcie closed his eyes to slits and concentrated on breathing slowly, as if asleep. The figure stooped, staring at him. A man, surely. Runcie couldn't make out his face, though something reminded him of that eye in his computer screen. So the authorities *were* spying on him. But why would they be interested in a kid? He'd never had anything to do with magic, and there was nothing illegal among his few shabby possessions.

As the man turned towards the computer, his cloak fell open, revealing a cream shirt with frills down the front, tight knee-length maroon pants closed with a brass-buttoned side flap, green stockings and black shoes with enormous silver buckles. He looked as if he were going to an eighteenth century costume party, which made no sense at all.

The light from the screen touched his face. His hair was long and black, his mouth as red as the lining of his cloak, and a monocle glinted in his left eye. His teeth were white and pointed, and a pair of wire-thin moustaches extended out six inches on either side, narrowing to needle points at the ends. Runcie had never seen such a strange fellow.

The man held up a light like a bunch of glowing grapes and took down Runcie's books one by one, examining each before putting it back, humming under his breath all the while, *mmmm-unnggg, mmmm-unnggg.* Setting down the light, he drew a long dirk and, with a wicked slash, slit open the cover of Runcie's maths book. Runcie almost cried out.

The intruder glanced sharply at him, moustaches quivering. Runcie held his breath until the man turned to the rat-gnawed cardboard boxes where Runcie kept his clothes. Finally he went to the computer, fingering the keys as if he didn't know how it worked. But every grown-up used computers, so unless he came from the past, through a time machine or something . . . No, that was stupid.

The intruder brought out a crystal ball mounted on a semi-circular brass ring, like a small world globe. Setting it spinning with a flick of his finger, he squinted through it at the screen. After moving the spinning globe back and forth several times, he muttered angrily and thrust the device into his cloak. Taking a roll of parchment from a pocket, he straightened it. It was the size of a sheet from a small writing pad, though thicker, and a muddy brown colour. Runcie knew what parchment was because his mother had studied old ones, before she'd been sent to prison. He could see writing on it in silvery letters, though he wasn't close enough to read them.

The man held the parchment out at arms-length, then abruptly bent double, crying out in pain. Standing up with an effort, he began to read in a deep, rumbling voice, as if reciting poetry through a tuba. *Tharr immi muliarope jar, visstess moer planxi.*

The letters on the parchment slowly changed to red, glowing gold, and Runcie had to stifle a gasp. It had to be magic! Real magic that he had only ever dreamed about. The intruder must be looking for something of Ansie's – a copy of his book perhaps. He might have known Ansie; might even have been his friend!

Runcie's heart was thundering. Dare he ask? The man looked dangerous, but there might never be another chance. He opened his mouth but no words came out. He felt too afraid, and hated himself for it.

The man read the golden characters again, this time emphasising the last word, and suddenly coloured lights flashed across Runcie's inner eye. Glancing around the room, the intruder noticed the trapdoor and bent to lift it. After briefly shining his light into the darkness below, he put it away and stepped onto the ladder.

The characters brightened, the parchment began to smoulder at the sides and the man faded until Runcie could see right through him. That was *definitely* magic, and so exciting that it overrode Runcie's fears. If he didn't speak now, the man would be gone and he'd never find out why he had come. Runcie jerked upright and gasped, 'What are you doing?'

The man spun around, staring at Runcie in horror. His mouth hardened and he threw himself up the ladder, whipping out the crystal sphere and thrusting it at Runcie. A green cone of light focussed on his forehead and he felt the most piercing pain, as if a match had been lit behind his eyes. He threw up his hands to block the beam.

The intruder bared those sharp teeth and was moving in when he stepped on Runcie's cricket ball. His feet shot from under him, he went over backwards and cracked his head on the edge of the trapdoor hole, the impact jarring the parchment out of his hand. He flailed at it, knocked it out of reach and fell through the trapdoor, crying out the words a third time as he went *thump-thump* down the ladder.

The smouldering parchment burst into flame and Runcie rolled off the bed to smack it out with his pillow. Mrs Nightingale shouted something about it being the middle of the night. Hearing no sound from the room below, he crept down far enough to pull the light cord for the sitting room, expecting to see the intruder lying on the floor, but he wasn't there.

How could he have escaped so quickly? It didn't seem possible. In fact, now Runcie thought about it, he'd heard the man hit the ladder but not the floor, though such a fall should have shaken the rickety old building. There were no footmarks on the dusty floor save the ones he'd made earlier that day. No smudges where a big man could have lain. He'd simply vanished.

Runcie went up, pulled the light cord and closed the trap-door, then dragged his bookcase over it in case the intruder came back. Retrieving the parchment, he brushed away the charred edges. The letters – if they were letters, for they looked more like the strange characters on the ancient manuscripts that Runcie's mother had studied at work – were silver once more.

So, magic *did* still exist. He'd just seen it with his own eyes. Ansie wasn't a fraud! It was the second good thing that had happened to him. For a few brief moments, caught up in the wonder of it all, he was able to put the attack out of mind.

Runcie felt the faint stirring of an unfamiliar emotion – hope. Could he use the parchment? Opening the sound program on his computer, he recorded the intruder's words as he remembered them. No, more emphasis on the last word. He said them again and again, holding the parchment. Nothing happened, though he hadn't expected it would. The parchment probably couldn't be rewoken straight away, if at all. He played the recording back. It sounded right, except that the man's voice had been much deeper. He traced the markings too, in case they faded, daydreaming about the magic.

A dog barked outside and reality intervened. If anyone caught him, he was done for. Get rid of it, right away. He lit a candle and was holding the parchment to it when his hand jerked back. Its magic was powerful enough to make a man disappear – magic he had only ever dreamed about. How could he destroy it?

Runcie sat on the floor, hugging his knees and staring mood-ily at the candle flame. He wanted the magic desperately, for he felt sure it was a link to what had happened to Ansie. What would his father do here? Ansie hadn't been frightened of any-thing, so he'd definitely have used the parchment, but Runcie was afraid to try again.

He guessed that the intruder came from a secret society of magicians, a magical Resistance, perhaps. If they'd been friends of Ansie's, surely they'd help. But then, remembering the fury in the intruder's eyes, Runcie decided that he must be a rival who wanted to steal Ansie's discovery. How dare he?

Runcie imagined the parchment carrying him to a place where he could discover the truth about his father. If only he dared. Why, why had he made that promise?

Going to the window, he stared out into the darkness. Was holding to his promise the right thing to do, or did he just lack the courage to break it in a good cause? Ansie wouldn't have hesitated. He'd have gone after the intruder and made up for breaking his word afterwards. It was another way Runcie couldn't live up to his father. Feeling that familiar despair rising, he crushed it. Not this time.

What if he just kept the parchment to look at? That wasn't having anything to do with magic, was it? Millie had meant learning about magic, or trying to use it, surely? Runcie knew he was treading on dangerous moral ground but couldn't see any way out of it. The parchment was an opportunity that would never come again.

The candle flame guttered in a sudden draught, then went out. It was a sign. He put it away before he was tempted to relight it. He was going to keep the parchment, but just to look at. That wasn't breaking his promise, just bending it a bit in a good cause. He would *never* try to use it.

He rolled it up with the tracing and put both in his jacket pocket. Besides, bad things could happen when a magical object was destroyed, and he didn't want to risk that. And what if the intruder came back for the parchment and found Runcie had destroyed it? No, he'd definitely done the right thing.

So why did he feel so guilty?

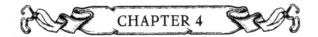

CHAPTER 4

The Punishment Yard

Runcie arrived at school the next morning knowing he was in for it, and feeling more helpless than ever. As he came through the gate he could see Fulk, The Blob and the other bully boys plotting behind the charred remains of the science block, out of sight of the solitary nice teacher hiding on playground duty near the side gate, where no one ever went.

He locked the chain around his bike, took a deep breath and checked the playground. There was no sign of Mariam, thankfully. Though Runcie appreciated what she'd done yesterday, he hoped she wouldn't try it again. He didn't like to rely on other people. It was better if he just took his beating, because Fulk's bully boys had the whole school behind them and they would crush Mariam as they had everyone else. For all her insufferable air of superiority, he couldn't bear to see her brought low.

The bully boys moved towards him and Runcie's stomach cramped. Mariam would confront them as if she didn't care, but he wasn't brave enough. His knees would hardly hold him up. He was supporting himself on the bike racks when tall, red-haired Dulcie Cato, the queen bee of the girly gang, swept by with her six followers and they took up positions around the school gate.

'Here she comes,' said Dulcie loudly. 'Ready?'

What were they up to? Runcie heard footsteps outside the gate and felt sure it was Mariam coming. Go back! he prayed.

The girly gang burst into loud jeering laughter, all together as though they'd rehearsed it. Runcie could feel the heat rising up his face. He checked on Fulk's gang and gulped. Stinky Morton was spit-polishing his battered knuckles, Shylock giving him that mad, wild-eyed stare.

Then Mariam came through the gate, her amazing hair streaming out in the wind. Her olive skin had gone a greeny grey and her eyes were shiny. She'd heard. For a second it looked as if she was going to cry. They'd love that – it would be the end of her.

Mariam set her jaw, swept past the girly gang with her head in the air and stood next to Runcie, her arms folded across her chest.

'I'd sooner take the beating,' he said quietly. 'I don't want you to get involved.'

'But I am involved and I can't back down now.'

It was like being on a train careering towards a precipice. Something awful was going to happen and he could do nothing about it. 'No matter what?'

'If I do, they'll have us both for breakfast.'

They would anyway, sooner or later. No one could beat them.

An evil smile spread across Fulk's scabbed face. 'I'd stay out of this if I were you, Mariam.'

'But you aren't me,' said Mariam. 'You're ugly, stupid and smelly, like your loser friends. Go on, Jones.'

Runcie wanted to unlock his bike, race home and never come back, but he didn't move. How could he abandon her after she'd stood up for him?

'I'm not *that* stupid,' said Fulk, grinning at his mates. 'I know where you live.'

Her jaw tightened but she passed it off. 'We're in the phone book, for those who can read.'

'You're home alone,' said The Blob. 'Your parents are abroad.'

'I'm used to taking care of myself,' Mariam said with a hint of bitterness.

'You'd better be.' Fulk pulled a long pair of scissors out of his pocket and went snip-snip in her face. She flushed. He swaggered off, and the rest of his cronies followed, making snipping motions with their fingers.

Runcie felt worse than if they'd beaten him up again. He was used to it, after all. It was better than getting *her* into trouble.

'Er,' he said, feeling as though he owed her. 'Mariam . . .'

'I'm not looking for a friend, Runcible,' she said, staring after them. She combed her fingers through her hair and turned away, shoulders slumped. The mocking laughter of the girly gang followed her to the school door.

Runcie spent all night sweating about the intruder coming back, but nothing happened. Mariam wasn't at school next day, and Fulk's gang didn't come near him, which was just as worrying. Runcie generally spent lunchtime in the school library – for the bully boys wouldn't be seen dead there – and he loved daydreaming among the books. But today it was closed because the librarian had suffered another attack of nerves, so he had to survive the dangers of the playground. He was creeping through the warren of passageways between the school outbuildings, keeping out of sight, when he noticed a furtive movement down an alley to his left.

Fulk's gang were going into a walled yard, the punishment yard during Grindgrim's centuries as a prison. Rumour had it that spies and traitors had been executed there, and it was a dismal place, always cold and dank, with unpleasant, spreading stains and a smell Runcie didn't want to think about. He'd never been inside, though once, peering through the slit in the gate, he was sure he'd heard a ghostly cry.

Along the wall to the left stood a rotting wooden platform with a swinging trapdoor. Some kids said that it had been a scaffold for hanging villains, others that it had held a chopping block and the severed heads had been dropped through the trapdoor afterwards, though no one really knew. There were corroded iron flogging rings around the walls, and hundreds of little pockmarks in the stonework that Stinky Morton claimed were from a firing squad, though everyone knew what a liar he was.

The bully boys had stopped in the middle and were urging each other on with punches and taunts. Fulk pointed towards the scaffold but no one moved. After another round of jeering and arm-punching, Ross Pethick sauntered across, climbed the platform and stood spread-legged over the gaping trapdoor, putting his hands around his throat and making choking noises. He grinned at the rest of the bully boys, though it looked rather forced.

'Come on, you snivelling cowards!'

The rest of the gang joined him, milling about uneasily. They were definitely up to something, and Runcie was sure it involved Mariam. He had to find out what they were planning, though the punishment yard was a terrible, haunted place and he was afraid to go in. However, if he were really careful he might be able to hear what they were saying from the guard box, a ramshackle construction of weathered boards no bigger than the outside toilet at the Nightingales. He crept through the gate and slid in behind the guard box.

Unfortunately, Runcie couldn't hear a thing. He needed to be closer, though the only cover between him and the scaffold was an ancient well with a low stone rim. A sheet of iron had been bolted over it to stop kids falling in. If he could get that far he should be able to hear, though the first twenty yards were out in the open, and if they discovered him, he'd be crucified.

The bully boys were crouched over something on the far side of the scaffold, sniggering. Runcie's palms were sweating.

He bent double and began to creep towards the well, knowing it was the stupidest thing he'd ever done.

'Oooooh!' came a mournful cry from behind the scaffold. Runcie flattened himself on the flagstones.

Pethick gasped and his hobnailed boots thumped across the platform. Fulk caught him by the ear. 'Quiet! It's just The Blob, playing the fool as usual. Cut it out, Jud.'

The Blob climbed onto the platform, which creaked under his enormous weight. He put his melon head through the trapdoor and made groaning noises. Fulk kicked him in the backside. The Blob straightened up abruptly, hitting his head, and everyone laughed.

Runcie scuttled the last few paces and peered around the curve of the well. The bully boys were sitting in a circle.

'That's that, then,' Fulk said. 'Tonight, eleven o'clock. All right, everyone?'

There was a chorus of yeses, yairs and grunts, then they all stood up. As Runcie ducked back, his heart gave a skip. He hadn't thought they'd finish so quickly. They couldn't miss him as they came past and, he realised in horror, he still had the parchment in his pocket. If they discovered that, he'd be sent to reform school and Millie would lose any chance of an early release. Why, *why* hadn't he got rid of it?

The Blob thumped down from the platform. In desperation, Runcie did the only thing he could think of. He put his hands around his mouth and directed a deep moan into the gap between the iron cover and the rim of the well.

A long, rumbling groan echoed back up. The bully boys stopped, grit squeaking underfoot.

'What was that?' quavered Shylock.

'I don't know,' whispered The Blob, and it did Runcie's heart good to hear how afraid they were.

'Go and see,' said Pethick shakily.

'You go,' said The Blob.

Runcie held his breath. If just one of them dared, he was dead.

After a long silence, Fulk said, unsteadily, 'Come on.'

He headed towards the gate, giving the well a wide berth, and the rest of the gang followed. Runcie crept around the other side, under cover, and was out of sight when Fulk stopped at the gate to look back.

But then, something happened that had never occurred at Grindgrim before. Dulcie Cato appeared outside the gate, her girly gang gathered behind her, and began speaking rapidly to Fulk. Fulk laughed and Dulcie did too. The two gangs rarely spoke save to hurl insults at each other, but now they were in it together. Mariam was history.

Runcie fingered the rolled parchment in his pocket and knew, with a numb, frozen terror, that he had to do something.

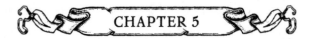

CHAPTER 5

The Gate

Runcie lay in bed, agonising. The alarm clock said ten thirty-five p.m. He'd called Mariam on the way home from school but there had been no answer. He should have gone out to the phone box after dinner and rung her again. It was too late now – the Nightingales were too mean to have a phone and he didn't have a key to the deadlocks. And all the windows had bars, except his, which was two floors up. There was nothing he could do.

Ten forty-five. It was no good. Mariam had twice saved him when she could have turned her back; he had to help her. Runcie scrambled into his clothes and put on his jacket. The frosty glass looked like white ferns in the moonlight. It was hard to get the window open, and when he forced it the rotten timber crumbled, and a pane of glass fell out and smashed on the floor. Runcie caught his breath. The Nightingales must have heard the noise. He'd have to peel turnips until his fingers bled, to pay for the damage.

A dog howled in the next yard, and in the distance he heard a police siren. A chilly wind licked in through the window. Runcie looked down at the steep, silvery roof slates, shining in the moon-light. They would be icy by now.

Ten fifty-two. He was going to be too late, so what was the point? It was all too hard. He had almost convinced himself to give up when he thought of Mariam coolly defying Fulk that first time. If she could overcome her terrors, he could too. He knotted his sheets together, tied one end to the bedstead and tossed the other out the attic window. It only went down to the guttering – not nearly far enough. He pulled it up and tied on his two threadbare blankets, then an old pair of jeans, and threw it out again.

Ten fifty-seven. Runcie put a leg over the sill and slid down onto the roof. His feet went from under him, he landed hard on his knees and began to slide, faster and faster. The sheet was burning through his fingers. He was going to fall off!

As his hands hit the first knot, his feet went over the edge, jammed in the guttering and he stopped abruptly, stretched out on the roof with icy water seeping through his worn shoes. Runcie didn't dare think about the climb or he wouldn't have been able to go on. He wriggled over the edge, the guttering tearing skin off his knuckles, and ended up hanging in mid-air from the next knot.

It was a long way down to the front verandah roof and he would have to pass in front of the Nightingales' bedroom window. If they were awake, and surely they must be after all the noise he'd made, they'd see him in the moonlight. Better be quick, then. If he made it onto the roof he could climb down its iron post.

It must be well after eleven by now. He slid to the next knot, swinging wildly, and his right foot smashed through one of the panes of the Nightingales' bedroom window. The light went on and before Runcie could move, the window was thrown up and a long, bony arm snaked out between the bars. He let out a yelp and slipped, but when his clenched hands hit the final knot, the jeans pulled free. He landed on the verandah roof with an almighty thump.

'You little villain,' cried Mrs Nightingale. 'You'll pay –'

Runcie went over the edge of the verandah, hanging from the guttering, which began to pull out of its brackets. He let go and dropped into Mrs Nightingale's prized daphne bush, crushing it flat in an explosion of perfume. Picking himself up, he bolted for the front gate and out into the street, and didn't stop until he'd turned the corner.

He stopped for a moment to catch his breath, sucked his bleeding knuckles, then trotted on. It was about ten blocks to Mariam's house – which was in the better part of town – though because of the problem with the power stations, only a few street lamps were on. He was approaching one now. Yellow smog wreathed around its pole like an enormous question mark. The street was empty and the tall terrace houses on either side frowned down at him. Most of their lights were out.

The power lines made a humming sound that set his teeth on edge and the street lamp began to flicker, accompanied by bursts of static. The underground cables were humming too, a low, throbbing note. What was going on?

A cat wailed, not far away, and Runcie shivered. He'd never been out by himself this late. The streets weren't safe at night and he didn't know if it was better to stay in the light or hug the shadows where he couldn't be seen.

At the next street lamp he noticed thin strands of green light wavering upwards, then the lamp dimmed as if the power were being sucked out of it. Runcie swallowed and was about to move on when colours streaked across his inner eye. His hair stood up, his skin prickled, then, with an echoing *tchunnk*, every light went out. He restrained the desperate urge to flee. It was just a power failure.

Another cat shrieked, closer. He glanced over his shoulder and the moon seemed to mock his attempts to find courage. It was about to fall behind the row of houses and the thought of darkness was terrible.

Wisps of luminous vapour rose from a cracked manhole cover, reeking like smouldering rat hair, and it looked as though something ghostly was struggling to take shape there, too. It must be really late now. Whatever the bully boys were up to, they'd probably done it already. A spasm twisted Runcie's stomach and he began to run, but his footsteps echoed off the terrace houses as if someone were chasing him. He glanced over his shoulder. Was that shadow moving? He raced across the intersection and pelted down the next street, and the one after that, running until he had such a pain in his side that he could run no more.

Nearly there. As he turned the corner into Mariam's street,

Vulture Avenue, the lights came on. The houses were bigger here and set well back from the pavement. Most had driveways, and hedges that concealed their front gardens. A street lamp glowed at the far end of the block, though through the fog it had a sickly yellow gleam.

Runcie stopped at Mariam's driveway. Apart from a dim light in an upstairs room, her house was in darkness. He slipped into the shadows next to the hedge, but couldn't hear anything except brakes squealing in the next street. He felt so desperately scared that it was tempting to scuttle home and take his punishment, even if it meant bottling the noxious, skin-stripping grog all night.

Suddenly Mariam cried out from behind the house. Without thinking, he scrambled over the gate and began to pick his way up the drive, through the pools of light and shadow from the slanting moon. Gravel crunched underfoot and he froze.

'What was that?' It sounded like Shylock Homes, the thug Runcie least wanted to meet on a dark night.

'Go and see,' said Fulk's voice. 'Well, Mariam? Tell us what you really did at your posh school, and we'll let you go.'

Runcie didn't catch her reply. He crept into the deep shadows against the wall of the house, heart thudding.

Shylock crunched down the drive to the front gate, looked over, then began to crunch back. 'Is anyone there?' he said in his shuddery voice.

Runcie didn't dare to breathe. Shylock was only a few steps away, standing in the moonlight, head darting about like a cobra in a basket. He slouched along the drive towards the backyard. Runcie followed, sweating in the cold night.

'Nothin' there,' Shylock said.

'I didn't think there was,' sneered Fulk. 'Speak up, Mariam.'

'Go to hell!' Runcie heard the sound of a slap.

'You little cow,' cried Fulk. 'You're really getting it now.'

This time Mariam's cry was muffled. Runcie had no idea what to do, and couldn't believe he'd come all this way without either a weapon or a plan. He bent and picked up a couple of handfuls of gravel. Among it was a larger stone, about the size of an egg, which he slipped into his pocket.

He peered around the corner. An outside light illuminated a group of boys and girls gathered near the rear deck, two of them holding Mariam by the arms. Her hair made a shining river of black over her shoulders and she looked terrified. Runcie slipped into the shadows under a small, spreading tree, where he could get a better shot.

'Got the scissors, Dulcie?' snapped Fulk.

She whipped out a pair the size of garden shears and brandished them in his face. He sprang backwards. 'And the razor, Jane?'

Pretty Jane Tresidder held up a cutthroat razor in one shaking hand. Good; at least she didn't want to be here.

'What about the creosote to paint her head?' said Dulcie.

'I've got it,' said Shylock with a creepy laugh.

'Let's do it,' said Fulk. 'Lorty, hold her arms. Get ready with the scissors, Dulcie. Jane, you'll shave her head. Take care, mind,' he chuckled. 'Wouldn't want to cut her ear off. At least, not all of it. Shylock, give her a good coat of creosote. It's poison, Mariam. You're going to be bald and ugly for the rest of your life. I can't wait to see you in the playground tomorrow.'

Mariam let out a shriek and lunged at him. She didn't break free but Fulk sidestepped smartly. 'Hold her down!' he shouted. 'Dulcie, what are you waiting for?'

'Don't tell *me* what to do,' snapped Dulcie.

Fulk drew himself up to his full imposing height. Dulcie didn't back down. Seeing his chance, Runcie hurled a handful of gravel at the group. They spun around. Unfortunately, Lorty didn't let go of Mariam.

'What was that?' hissed Fulk, eyes searching the darkness. He clouted Shylock over the ear. 'You stupid fool! I'll bet it's that rotten little sneak, Runcie runt. Get him!'

Fulk and the others fanned out and headed towards the end of the drive. Almost overcome by terror, Runcie clenched the stone in his fist. Only huge, dull Lorty remained, holding Mariam. His broad, dome-shaped forehead shone in the moonlight and Runcie, in desperation, hurled the stone at it.

'Mariam, run!' he screamed.

The stone glanced off Lorty's thick noggin without doing any appreciable damage, though he let out a cry and clapped one hand to the spot. Mariam kicked him in the shins, tore free and bolted towards Runcie. Since her back had been to the light, she could see him in the shadows.

She fleeted by the bullies, who were looking further up the drive, caught Runcie's hand and hissed, 'Come on.'

They fled towards the back hedge, but there was still a good way to go when two big lads stepped out of the shadows – The Blob and Pethick, his vicious eyes shining in the moonlight.

Mariam let out a muffled gasp and her hand tightened on Runcie's. Fulk gave a nasty chuckle. 'Got them!'

Runcie looked over his shoulder. The bully boys and girly gang had spread out so there was no way past. They began advancing slowly, taking their time, enjoying every moment of their triumph. Dulcie was doing an Edward Scissorhands impression, Shylock swinging the tin of creosote around his head.

'I'm sorry,' Runcie said bitterly. 'I've only made things worse.'

Mariam squeezed his hand. 'Thanks anyway.'

Runcie felt in his pocket in case he'd missed a pebble. He hadn't, but his fingers closed around the soft coil of parchment and, without thinking, he pulled it out and opened it in the moonlight. The strange characters began to glow silver. He scanned them and the events of the other night exploded in his mind.

'Tharr immi muliarope jar, visstess moer planxi,' he said under his breath.

'What are you doing?' whispered Mariam.

Runcie knew it couldn't work for him, but he had no options left. He spoke the words a little more loudly, concentrating on saying them exactly as the intruder had.

The characters on the parchment lit up with a golden glow and it began to smoulder at the edges, burning his hand. He dropped it and it fluttered to the ground, lighting up the grass around their feet.

'He's trying to do magic, the little sod,' cried Fulk, bursting with vindicated glee. 'Get him! He'll go to prison like his witchy mother, and we'll share the reward.'

They moved in slowly now, afraid of the magic. Mariam looked desperately at Runcie. He hesitated for an agonising moment, his thoughts running so fast that everyone else seemed frozen in time. This was it – the choice from which there was no going back. He'd promised Millie, but if he and Mariam were caught they were both finished, and Millie too. Fulk would hand in the parchment, undeniable proof of magic. Yet if they vanished and turned up somewhere else, it was just the bullies' word against theirs. And maybe, just maybe, the parchment could show him the truth he was searching for. Yes! He would do it, for everyone's sake.

Without letting go of Mariam's hand, Runcie snatched the parchment off the grass and roared its words again, in the deepest voice he could manage.

'Don't, Runcible!' cried Mariam, trying to pull free.

He hung on grimly and shouted the last words. Dulcie sprang forwards and was almost within snipping distance when the parchment caught fire, the letters glowing white hot. The house, the backyard, their attackers and the rest of the world vanished.

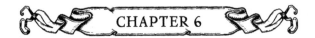

CHAPTER 6

The Wild Sea

'What have you *done*?' Mariam yelled in Runcie's ear.

'I don't know!' He couldn't see anything, couldn't hear anything, couldn't even *feel* anything but Mariam's cold hand in his. Those coloured sparks had appeared in his inner eye again, his stomach was being pulled in three directions at once and he felt sure he was going to be sick. They seemed to be slowly spinning around in mid-air, but *where*? He raised the parchment until he could see the flames, which had frozen as if someone had pressed the pause button. They were cold now, and barely lit up his fingers.

'Do something!' She yanked on his hand.

Do what? He felt like the sorcerer's apprentice, only dumber. He'd used magic without knowing *anything* about it. 'I don't know what to do.'

Mariam began panting. 'Then why did you use the spell?'

'I didn't think –' He could see her staring eyes now, but not the rest of her face. 'Are you all right?' He couldn't work her out. The other day she'd taken on the whole school, yet now she was going to pieces.

She gave a strangled gasp. 'I can't . . . can't breathe . . .'

She was having a panic attack and Runcie began to feel really frightened. The characters were fading and would soon be gone. Wait – maybe he was supposed to imagine where he wanted to end up.

He could visualise Mariam's backyard clearly, complete with bullies searching the darkness. He tried to imagine somewhere safe – the street a few blocks away – but instead saw those icy mountains from his computer screen. He wasn't going there either; they could be anywhere. He blinked and a pretty village appeared, with thatched cottages, green hills and a rustic sign-post like a pointing hand. It looked like something out of a fairytale. Should he try for it? How could he decide?

'Runcible!' Mariam choked, then her eyes rolled up into her head.

His stomach had a football-sized lump of terror in it and his head hurt. If he didn't act they might be stuck here forever. But if he did the wrong thing they could die, horribly. He couldn't decide.

The letters on the parchment were practically gone. He had to do *something*. What would Ansie do? Something clever, of course, but Runcie had no idea what. The only places he could picture were the village and Mariam's backyard. He chose the village, focussed on a brass ring on the door of the nearest cottage and gabbled out the words just as his mental scene changed to roaring darkness. Runcie clung to the image of the big brass ring for all he was worth.

In a flurry of coloured specks, the world dropped from under him and he landed on something hard and wet, with Mariam thumping onto his back. His stomach heaved and vomit burned the back of his throat. He smelt the salt tang of the sea, though it was a richer, spicier scent than he remembered.

Mariam threw herself off and began to shake him furiously. *'Where are we?'*

There was a roaring in his ears and he was drenched by flying spray. Runcie opened his eyes and let out a gasp. He was lying on a black, wave-washed rock and there were nothing but huge breakers in every direction.

He stood up slowly. The rock platform was about fifty yards across, and every bit of it was wet. Weird red and yellow sea-weeds protruded from cracks here and there, like nothing he had ever seen before. Something like an inside-out crab nipped at his ankle then scuttled into a hole, though it had a lot more legs than it should have had.

Runcie bent down, rubbing his bleeding ankle. It was night-time, yet much brighter than the night he'd just left. He turned around. Hanging high in the sky was an enormous moon, at least twice the size of the moon he knew, and it was a baleful, glowing red with black and purple blotches. The hair stood up on the back of his neck as he realised what he'd done. Wherever the parchment had taken them, it was nowhere on Earth.

'Get us out of here!' shrieked Mariam, slapping at her thigh. A dark, slug-like creature dropped off and slithered under a rock, squeaking.

The parchment crumbled to ash and blew away. Runcie tried to speak the words again but they had vanished from his mind. 'I can't . . .'

'You cretin!' Mariam went red in the face and her eyes flashed sparks. 'I wish I'd never met you.'

'I –' began Runcie.

'Did you know I was on a good behaviour bond at Grindgrim?'

'No,' he said faintly, dreading what she was going to say.

'I'm going to be blamed for doing illegal magic.' Her voice rose. 'They'll send me to Ruersham this time.'

'What's Ruersham?' he whispered.

'The National Correctional Institute for Wayward Girls, and it's worse than your mother's prison.' She stumbled away, hands over her face.

Runcie stared after her, sick with guilt. Magic was dangerous as well as illegal, and that's why Millie had made him promise. He should have destroyed the parchment right away. Breaking his word had been a really stupid thing to do, but choosing to come *here* was a thousand times dumber. He couldn't do anything right. He was glad Ansie would never know what a fool he was.

He tried to console himself with the thought that he must have a talent for magic. It didn't help. He'd repaid Mariam in the worst possible way. He wanted to crawl into a hole and die.

Mariam was pounding around the rock platform, practically running. Runcie sat on a wet rock, having no idea what to say to her. He'd never had much to do with girls – especially not rich, self-confident ones.

'Are you all right now?' he said tentatively, when she finally stopped.

'You mean the panic attack? Just one of my many phobias.' Her glare shrivelled him. 'Having my head shaved would be a lot better than this.'

'I'm sorry.'

Mariam went to the edge and stared out to sea. The waves seemed to be getting higher. She shouted something that he couldn't make out over the noise of the surf.

'What?' he yelled. She didn't answer, so he went across. Walking felt strange here – sort of bouncy – and he didn't feel as though he weighed as much. He looked over the edge. In between waves it was about fifteen feet down to the water, but the biggest breakers were foaming around his shoes. 'I'm sorry. When we get back I'll say –'

'We're not going to get back, you little creep! When the tide comes in, the waves will wash us away.'

'I'm sorry.' He couldn't think of anything else to say. Feeling very small and afraid, Runcie reached out to her, but Mariam strode away, her black hair flying.

Then she came storming back. 'I thought you were clever!' she hissed. 'I thought you were different. Why do you think magic is banned?'

'I – I –'

'Well?' She stood over him, fists clenched on her hips.

Runcie didn't know where to begin. His eyes were watering in the fierce gusts and he turned away, afraid she would think he was crying.

'You couldn't have made things worse if you were my enemy. Where did you get that scroll anyway?'

Runcie tried to explain about the intruder but she stalked off again, pulling out her mobile phone. It was the magnificent one he so coveted, and when she turned it on, lights rainbowed across the keys. She put the phone to her ear. 'Nothing,' she said bitterly and, seeing Runcie's eyes on it, tossed it into the nearest rock pool like a piece of junk. The water fizzed and the phone went bang.

As the pieces settled to the bottom, Runcie could have wept. Even if it didn't work here, he would have loved to have it. He'd never owned anything good. Or new, for that matter.

He trudged across the platform. The black rock was criss-crossed with water-filled cracks and gutters. Odd creatures crept under ledges as he went by, only to dart out, clacking serrated pincers, once his back was turned. Clusters of toadstool-shaped seaweeds sprouted from every gutter, their reds and yellows luminous in the gloom. They looked poisonous. To make matters worse, the sky opposite the huge moon was a livid purple. He prayed the storm wouldn't come this way. Runcie looked around to see what Mariam was doing, but she wasn't in sight. A cold fist of panic closed around his heart.

'Mariam?' His voice was snatched away by the wind. 'Mariam!'

He began to walk towards the taller rocks in the centre, where he'd last seen her.

She was crouched down, staring at something. He approached tentatively, expecting another tongue-lashing.

'That's curious,' said Mariam.

Among the tumbled rocks and encrusting seaweed he made out an edge of smooth stone. His eye followed it. It was a rectangular wall with an empty space inside, about four yards by two. He could see weathered characters chiselled around the sides, though they were unreadable. Peering in, he saw stone about six feet down.

'It looks like a monument,' said Mariam. She shivered and sat down on the other side, where it was sheltered from the wind. 'Have a seat, Runcible.'

'Runcie,' he said quietly.

'What?'

'Everyone calls me Runcie.' He slumped on the damp rock.

Mariam sighed, then eyed the gigantic moon. 'That looks ominous. Where are we, Runcie?'

'I don't know,' he said miserably. 'I don't think we're even in the solar system.'

'I'm sure we're not. The animals here are weird. I wish –' She broke off, then said quietly, 'Where did you get that parchment, anyway?'

He explained about the intruder.

'What was he doing in your room?'

'Looking for something.'

She gave him a keen glance. 'Your mother's in prison for magic, isn't she?'

'No, just for having a copy of Dad's book.'

'But *you* don't have one?' said Mariam.

'Of course not. Mum's really anti-magic. She made me promise to have nothing to do with it . . .' Runcie flushed. 'Wait – I've just realised something. I'd assumed the intruder had known Dad.'

'But if he came from another world – this one . . .' Mariam stared into his eyes. 'I've got an unpleasant feeling that we're mixed up in something really big. *And bad.*' After a long pause she went on, 'How did your father die?'

Runcie didn't want to think about that. 'There was a fire,' he said haltingly. 'Ansie . . . Dad . . .' He paused to gather his thoughts. 'Dad had a place out in the country. We lived there before the divorce. The house was hundreds of years old and falling to pieces, but it had an orchard, a lake with an island in the middle, and a patch of ancient forest. I loved it there. The island had a half-ruined watchtower. Dad called it his folly and he used to swim across to it every morning, even in winter, to work. It made Mum really angry.'

'What did he do?' said Mariam.

Runcie took a deep breath. 'Nothing. I mean, Dad didn't have a job. He inherited the house and a bit of money, but it ran out when I was little. He spent his whole life doing research and writing his book. About *magic*!' He glanced sideways at Mariam, afraid she'd get angry again.

'The kids at Grindgrim were always talking about your parents.'

'Mum and Dad had the most furious arguments about his work. Mum was always so serious and responsible, but Dad wouldn't give it up. She left him the day after my seventh birthday, and it was my fault.' Even now Runcie couldn't bear to think about that day.

'How could it be your fault?'

'I was playing with Dad's hourglass when Mum came in and they had an argument. I hated their fights. Dad had told me stories about a magic hourglass that could be used to escape from your troubles, so I turned it upside down and spoke the words of the spell used in his story, "Turn once, turn twice and troubles *away*."'

'Mum hadn't realised I was there. She did her nut, accused Dad of involving me in illegal magic, and left him, just like that. If I hadn't done it, they'd still be together. And that's not all.' Runcie stared at the enormous moon, blinking away tears. 'Dad died the day after my tenth birthday – the worst day of my life. His folly caught fire and everything was destroyed. All they found was his wedding ring, melted into a lump.'

'It must have been a fierce fire, to melt gold,' said Mariam.

'The police couldn't work out what had happened, because the folly didn't have electricity, or even a stove.'

'Perhaps it was just a terrible accident.'

'I suppose so,' he said reluctantly. 'Anyway, Mum went all weird after that. I wasn't allowed to mention Dad's name.'

'She must have been very angry.'

'She still loved him, and she blamed him for getting himself killed, which was pretty stupid. But then, the day after my *eleventh* birthday, Mum was arrested. Despite all her ranting and raving, she'd kept a copy of Dad's book! I feel so guilty.'

'Why?' Mariam said.

'She divorced him because of me. If they'd stayed together she would have kept Dad out of trouble, he'd still be alive and none of this would have happened.'

'You think too much,' said Mariam abruptly.

Runcie didn't know what to say, but then a roaring and a thundering behind them brought him to his feet. A huge wave was foaming across the rock, and the purple storm was closer than before.

He bit his lip. 'I'm really sorry, Mariam.'

She sighed again. 'I'm sorry I yelled at you. It must have taken a lot of courage, going out to take on the bullies all by yourself.'

'I wish I hadn't, now. Sorry – I didn't mean that I don't care –'

She smiled. 'You did your best, Runcie, and I'm grateful.'

'But I –'

'A big wave's coming. Up here!'

As Runcie scrambled onto the rectangular wall he saw a thick brass ring, as big around as a soup bowl, anchored to the end wall. 'I saw that in my mind's eye when we were between your place and here.'

'I dare say that's why the spell carried us *here,* then.'

Again that twinge of guilt. As the wave foamed by, Mariam reached down and touched the ring, but jerked away as if it had burned her. 'What's the matter?' said Runcie.

'It felt . . . oh!' She shuddered. 'Like a graveyard. No, a tomb. I'll bet that's what this was.'

Red-gold lightning jagged down from the clouds, stabbing at the water like a pitchfork. He counted the seconds until he heard the thunder. Fifteen; so it was only three miles away. When he looked down, Mariam was scrunched up, head resting on her knees.

He perched beside her. She sniffled and tried to pretend it was nothing. 'What is it, Mariam?'

'You're lucky to have parents who cared about you.'

Runcie rocked back on his heels. 'How can you say that?'

'Because it's true. I don't think my parents will even notice I'm gone,' Mariam said bitterly.

He recalled her saying that they were abroad. 'Where are they?'

'I can't remember,' she said, deliberately offhand. 'Hong Kong, or Delhi, or Rio. They travel all the time.'

'What for?' said Runcie. 'We never went anywhere. We had no money.' The last of it had gone on those mysterious trips of his father's that had made Millie so angry.

'Mum and Dad have . . . *had* pots of money,' she said. 'They import things and sell them for a huge profit.'

'If they're so rich,' said Runcie, 'how come they sent you to Grindgrim?'

She hesitated for some time before answering. 'To punish me. You've probably heard I was expelled from the best school in the country.'

'No – what did you do?' Until last night, Runcie had always been well behaved. He couldn't imagine doing anything that bad.

She waved a hand in the gloom. 'I'm too ashamed to tell you. I – I did it partly to annoy Mum and Dad. They never take any notice of me except to tell me to work harder. Nothing I do is ever good enough.'

'What did they do?' said Runcie, wondering what she was keeping back.

'After I was expelled, they didn't say anything all the way home. It was awful. I couldn't sleep all night. The next morning they drove me to Grindgrim and left me at the gates. That was the worst day of *my* life. I was terrified.'

'You didn't show it,' said Runcie. 'I remember you coming into class on your first day as if you owned the school.'

'It was all an act. You can't go from the best school in the land to the worst without everyone ganging up on you. If I wasn't tougher than everyone else, the bullies would have had me for breakfast.'

'Well, you certainly convinced me,' said Runcie.

Thunder reverberated back and forth as if they were inside a gigantic squash court. The storm was a tower of purple-black cloud, lit from within by lightning. The seas were sweeping right across the platform now, and every wave was bigger than

57

the one before. Mariam was right. They'd soon be washed into the sea to drown and no one would ever know what had happened to them.

'Mariam?' said Runcie urgently.

'What?' She didn't look up.

A wall of foam was roaring towards them, touched with purple flecks from the light of the moon.

'Grab the ring.' He jumped inside the tomb, just as the wave came over the side like a waterfall.

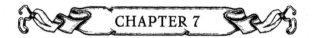

CHAPTER 7

The Arrogant Transportal

Runcie clung desperately to the ring as the flood poured over his head. Mariam was being whirled around, eyes closed, then the wave had passed and they were gasping and spluttering in chest-deep water.

She scrabbled up the wall and perched on top, wide-eyed. 'Something terrible happened here. I felt *death* – lots of it.'

'I didn't feel a thing,' said Runcie.

'You wouldn't,' she said dismissively.

She could be so annoying. 'What's that supposed to mean?'

'My grandmother was fey and I think I am too.' She shuddered. 'I *feel* things.'

As he climbed out, wondering about her, he noticed another curious thing. The water felt *wetter* than sea water – it slipped through his fingers like silk. He tasted a handful but spat it out at once. It wasn't as salty as seawater, but it was shudderingly bitter.

'I'm scared, Mariam.'

'Me too.'

A sudden gust whirled about them. The next wave crashed against the tomb wall but didn't reach the top. Lightning flashed above them like an umbrella of molten gold. Thunder shook the rock.

Then something very strange happened. A perfect circle formed in the middle of one of the lightning branches, coiled around on itself, broke free and drifted across the face of the storm cloud but, as it moved, everything behind it was twisted like a distorting lens. It wandered across the sky and faded out.

'What do you think *that* was?' he whispered.

'I don't know.'

The rock platform was covered in water now, and the next big wave was likely to wash them away. To make matters worse, the moon's ghastly light had turned the stormy skyscape into a madman's nightmare. Another umbrella flash of lightning created a new distorting lens, but this time a ruddy beam of light shone through it. It touched on the sea a stone's throw from them, forming a waterspout that lifted, spinning rapidly, about thirty feet in the air before it was torn apart by the wind and hurled in all directions. A few drops spattered on Runcie's cheek, and they were oddly warm.

The beam carved a line along the water towards them, like a searchlight. Runcie felt a tightness in his chest but, before he could move, Mariam threw herself at him, toppling them both into the tomb. He panicked and began to thrash but she pulled him under. As the beam lit up the water above their heads, he heard an odd humming sound.

Mariam caught hold of a crack in the stone. Runcie, running out of air, gestured to his mouth. She mimed, *careful*.

He drifted up into the shadowed corner and took a deep breath. Mariam bobbed up beside him. 'What did you do that for?' he whispered.

'I had a feeling it was looking for us. A bad feeling.'

'But . . .' His eyes searched her face. 'We can't stay here; we'll drown.'

'I know.' Her jaw was clenched. 'But being seen by that felt *worse*.'

Runcie didn't know what to make of her feelings. He'd been brought up to think things through, but then, thinking too much had brought them here. The ruddy glow went out and when he looked up, the lens was gone. They scrambled out, and only then did it hit him. 'Did you hear that funny humming sound, *mmmm-unnggg*?'

'Yes. What of it?'

'The intruder in my room was humming, just like that. What if it's him?'

'He wants his parchment,' Mariam said soberly, 'and it's been destroyed.' Her eyes met Runcie's. 'Better hope he's not the vengeful type.'

Runcie could see the rage in the intruder's eyes as he'd lunged that night. Vengeful wasn't the half of it. Why, why hadn't he kept his promise?

'Runcie?' Mariam said anxiously. At the look on his face, she said, 'I'll see if I can find some kind of weapon.'

The wind was howling now, whipping her wet hair around her face. As she moved, the sky was lit up by a blinding flash, followed by a shattering blast of thunder. Runcie had just gotten his sight back when a shrill voice pierced his ears.

He turned and gaped. Hovering above the waves ten yards offshore was a battered, bus-sized contraption – he couldn't think of any other word for it – shaped like a long snail's shell. The top of its opening formed an arch that had once been coated with shining gold, though most had peeled off to reveal corroded metal underneath. The floor was flat for the first five or six yards then coiled up at the rear. The inside was lined with rough white tiles and its curving walls resembled a very old, rust-streaked toilet bowl.

A short, plump woman, about fifty years old, stood just inside the archway. Her long grey hair was tangled, her clothes untidy and not very clean, and she wore a pointy-toed shoe on her left foot, though a ragged slipper hung off her right. Her puffy-sleeved blouse was a kaleidoscope of colour in whirling patterns. Knee-length, wide-legged trousers, a lurid lime green, made her pallid legs look like pastry.

The woman yelled something, though Runcie couldn't make out a word of it.

'I don't understand,' yelled Mariam.

The woman looked down for a moment, then shouted, 'Come to the transportal!'

Runcie sighed. The stories he loved often had magical portals in them, though they were generally like a fixed arch or gate. None moved, nor had any been as unglamorous as this one.

'We can't walk on water,' snapped Mariam.

The woman made twisting motions with her hands, whereupon the transportal dropped broken tiles on her head and shoulders. She slammed the side of her fist into the wall, crying out a word in another tongue. The transportal dropped sharply, hitting the sea with a mighty splash. She worked her hands again and it lurched into the air, streaming water which carried away her slipper. A silver fish flapped on the tiles.

The woman tried to edge it back into the water with her toe but the gasping fish sank its teeth in. Runcie smiled as she capered about, trying to kick it off. Finally she bent down, tore the fish off and tossed it into a basket behind her. All the while, the archway was jerking up and down as if trying to throw her out.

'What a nutter!' Mariam muffled a giggle. 'She's not the intruder, surely?'

'No . . .' Runcie looked at Mariam questioningly.

'I don't have a bad feeling about *her*.'

Blood was pouring from the woman's toe, staining the tiles and the wet floor. She carved symbols in the air with her hands and with a tortured wail the transportal vanished, reappeared twenty feet to one side and lurched towards them.

Another set of waves was driving in, higher than before. Mariam stood up on the wall, swaying in the keen wind. Runcie joined her.

'Come, come!' The woman beckoned with her left hand while the right continued its motions, like a conductor to an orchestra. The bobbing archway came to a stop a couple of yards away but two feet higher than the wall.

'Ready?' said Mariam, standing on tiptoe.

Runcie gulped. It was a difficult jump from a standing start, and he'd never been much good at athletics. 'I suppose so.'

'On the count. One, two, *three*.' Mariam sprang and landed sprawled on the rough tiles, her head and body inside, her legs dangling down. She heaved her right leg up over the edge and pulled herself inside.

Runcie didn't jump. He knew he wouldn't make it. He teetered on the edge, staring at the transportal.

'Jump!' the woman roared.

Too late. As he sprang, a wave struck him behind the knees, driving him down. His left hand caught the curved lower edge of the transportal but he couldn't get a grip. He fell on his back into the water, which began to carry him away.

Runcie caught sight of Mariam's horrified face as his head was pulled under. He was whirled about in the black water, tumbled over and driven headfirst at the rocks, but as he threw out his hands to protect himself, an excruciating pain lashed across his back and wrapped around him twice. And then he was jerked into the air by a shimmering whip, reeled in hand over hand by the woman in the transportal. Runcie swung backwards and forwards, cracked his chin on the floor and was dumped on the tiles.

'Stupid boy!' she muttered. With a snap of her fingers, the whip came free and rolled up. She dropped it into an iron-bound chest behind her.

Mariam pulled Runcie in from the edge as, with a gut-wrenching lurch and a flash of colours across his inner eye, the transportal vanished. Reappearing fifty yards out to sea, it shot up into the sky. The wind cut right through his wet clothes and his teeth began to chatter. His whipped skin burned, while the tip of his chin throbbed cruelly.

'Who are you?' said Mariam, more forcefully than Runcie would have.

The woman glanced briefly at her as the transportal plunged through a cloud. Droplets of moisture condensed on her hair and eyelashes. 'I'm Parsifoe, the Magistrorum of Thorasdil Tower, and you're a blasted nuisance.'

'What's Thorasdil?' Runcie mumbled. His teeth felt loose.

'My home and my college!' she snapped, as if that were obvious.

'Was that you looking for us, earlier?' said Mariam.

Parsifoe frowned. 'What do you mean, *earlier*? I came after you the instant I picked up the echoes from your foolish, foolish gate.' Black eyes impaled Runcie like a worm on a hook. 'I'll be making a complaint against your master for this wicked folly.'

Runcie and Mariam exchanged puzzled looks.

Parsifoe turned back to Mariam, saying sternly, 'Explain yourself, child.'

'A circle passed across the sky,' said Mariam, 'twisting everything behind it. And then a yellow beam came out of it –'

'A dimensional lens?' cried Parsifoe. 'Why didn't you say so before? Get up there. Run!' She pointed to the rear, where the transportal coiled up on itself.

'What's the big problem?' said Mariam, with that arrogant air she'd used at school to quell the bullies.

Runcie backed away, embarrassed.

'Go, *go*!' shouted Parsifoe, flapping her hands. The whip stood up of its own accord, its tip questing about in the air, then the transportal shot upwards, scattering fragments of tile everywhere.

Runcie, alarmed, began to squeeze up into the narrowing tunnel, but it smelled as if a rat had died up there a long time ago, so he scrambled down again and sat on a conveniently placed knob, like the top of a mushroom.

He *felt* a grunt of outrage. 'Did you feel that?' he whispered to Mariam.

She was giving him a most peculiar look. 'I thought it was you, fooling around.'

'I'm too sore to fool –' he began. The knob sagged under him like a bedspring, then he went spinning through the air, to slam backside-first into the wall.

'Vile brat!' said a voice like a distant, mournful foghorn. 'It's time you were taught your manners.'

Runcie slid down the wall. 'What was *that*?' He rubbed his bruised bottom.

The coiled end of the tunnel shrank down on his legs and squeezed hard. Mariam's eyes grew until they took up half her face, then she sprang up, beating at the wall with her fists. 'Stop it, stop it. Help!'

Taking Runcie by the arms she tried to pull him out, but he was caught fast and the cracked tiles were pressing agonisingly into his ankle. He sucked in his breath, trying not to scream.

The transportal rolled onto its side, was flung upright, then Parsifoe came hurrying up, walking spread-legged like a sailor. She struck the side wall three times with the butt of her whip. The tunnel gave Runcie an extra-hard squeeze, making him cry out, before shrinking away with a muffled giggle.

'Never do that again, Ulalliall,' Parsifoe said crossly.

'Will if we want to,' the transportal muttered. At least, Runcie assumed it was the transportal speaking, though he found that rather hard to come to terms with. And judging by the look on Mariam's face, she'd had another of her bad feelings about it.

Parsifoe glared at Runcie as if he were to blame. 'Haven't you learned your lesson?'

'Nasty little ruffian,' said the transportal with an aggrieved sniff. 'How dare he put his horrid bottom on us, as if we were a common stool?'

'All I did was sit down on that knob,' Runcie said defensively.

'Knob!' foghorned the transportal. 'We've never been so insulted. You'll rue the day you called our xylotic nifflicator a knob, you little twerp.'

The end of the tunnel began to close over again and Runcie tried to hop out of the way. Parsifoe slapped the wall, then dragged him down by the ear. 'Sit on the floor!' she hissed. 'Don't cause any more trouble.' She stamped back to the entrance.

Runcie sat there, mortified at being hauled by the ear like a naughty boy when he hadn't done anything. Mariam was grinning, though she quickly hid it.

'You weren't to know the stupid piece of junk was alive,' she said defiantly.

Evidently the transportal hadn't heard, for the coiled end of the tunnel was heaving as it sniggered. 'Showed the little beggar, we did. No respect, the brats of today. In our great days they wouldn't have dared to speak in our presence. How we've fallen . . .'

A sound, suspiciously like a sob, issued from a crack in the wall but broke off, and the transportal stopped in mid-air with a jerk that toppled Parsifoe backwards into the open chest. Her plump legs waved in the air like a beetle's when turned onto its back.

Runcie vainly tried to stifle a snort of laughter. Parsifoe pulled herself out and banged down the lid, giving him a black look. She began to speak softly to the floor.

'What's she saying?' said Runcie.

'I can't hear,' said Mariam.

They edged down. Parsifoe had her hand on the side wall.

'Come on, old friend,' she cajoled. 'I'll make sure the lout gets a good flogging.'

Runcie blanched.

'You're so stupid you can't see what's in front of you,' sneered the transportal.

'What are you talking about?' said Parsifoe irritably.

'The brats.'

'What about them?'

'If you don't know, we're not going to tell you.'

'I don't have time for your little games,' said Parsifoe. 'Can we go now?'

The transportal remained in mid-air, vibrating. A cloud drifted through the opening, fogging Parsifoe out for a second. Runcie rubbed his wet arms but it didn't warm them.

'Please, Ulalliall,' said Parsifoe. 'We've been through a lot together. Don't let me down now.'

'Our name isn't *Ula*lliall, its Ula*lliall*,' the transportal said, rather like a goose honking. 'You'd remember that if you were really our friend. We've told you a dozen times.'

'Ula*lliall*, old friend –'

'We're not your friend. We don't even like you. And we haven't *been through* a lot together. You've *put* us through a lot, against our will. You're the worst keeper we've had since the Mad Mountebank, nine hundred years ago.'

'Ula*lliall*,' said Parsifoe, even more nicely, though it seemed rather a strain, 'come on. That's no way to treat your master.'

'How dare you call yourself our master!' bellowed the transportal. 'There's no contract between us and you have no right –'

'Enough!' snarled Parsifoe. 'You're mine and you must obey my command. To Pysmie's Pyramid and be quick about it.'

'We shall not,' said the transportal. 'Your claim on us is illegitimate. You never –'

Parsifoe flushed an unpleasant greeny colour, glanced in the direction of the children then lowered her voice. 'The game was fair and I won you –'

'You used a Cheat-Spell!' said the transportal. 'You might have fooled Ser Mummery but you can't fool us. We've had a hundred keepers smarter than you.'

Parsifoe's cheeks went white, then red. 'I'll use Words of Command.'

'You wouldn't dare,' the transportal said smugly.

Flicking up the lid of the chest with her toe, Parsifoe drew out a battered, grubby book, flicked the pages and rapped, 'Complete Complaisance, Contrary Conveyance!'

'All right,' muttered the transportal. 'We're going. There's no need to get your *gigantic* bloomers in a tangle.'

The transportal passed through cloud, mist then rain. Runcie tried to get a glimpse of this astonishing new world. 'I can't see a thing,' he muttered to Mariam. 'You'd think, after coming all this way, we'd at least get to see what the stupid place looks like –'

The transportal shook furiously, *jumped* then burst into sunshine above a land of steep green hills dotted with white boulders. Orange beasts like stumpy striped buffalo grazed on the lush grass.

'Wow!' said Runcie, moving down so he could see better. On the distant slopes he counted a dozen braided waterfalls, and to his left a patch of woodland displayed all the colours of an autumn forest, though they glowed so brilliantly that the foliage seemed to be lit from within. The transportal drifted over a hedge sagging with black berries, so low that he could hear the bloated bees buzzing and smell the luscious ripeness of the fruit. Runcie's stomach rumbled. Further down by a foaming brook stood a pretty village whose cottages were shaped like thatched eggs, with white walls, roofs like spun gold and round windows that resembled portholes.

'What a lovely place,' said Mariam. 'I hope this is where she's taking us.'

A group of half naked children ran out from behind one of the cottages, yelling and laughing as they batted a large spiny ball, the shape of a sea urchin, about in the air. No, they weren't touching the swooping, darting object, but directing it hither and yon with hand gestures and finger snaps – with pure magic. The children looked up at the transportal, waved cheerily then went on with their game.

Runcie was entranced. 'Me too.'

'What are you doing, transportal?' snapped Parsifoe, shattering his daydream.

'We're showing the brats the grandeur and the glory of Iltior.'

'They see it every day of their lives. To Pysmie's Pyramid!'

Ulalliall snorted, and in an instant the enchanting scene was gone. With a flabby pop they reappeared above a sapphire sea scattered with rainforest-covered islands circled by foam-tipped reefs where red-haired people fished, suspended from tethered balloons. It was so humid that pinpricks of sweat burst out on Runcie's back. A twin-tailed black whale carved a shining furrow across the still water, then burst forth to soar a quarter of a mile on webbed fins before thundering down again. The air smelt like cinnamon.

'This place isn't so bad, either,' Mariam said dreamily.

Parsifoe growled at Ulalliall. *Bang!* Now the transportal was hovering above an endless wetland dotted with waterlilies the size of truck tyres and doughnut-shaped patches of silvery reeds. A startled flock of pink-legged geese flapped into the air, honking. A woman's voice screeched at them, then a missile smashed a tile above Runcie's head. He ducked hastily. Six people, clothed in fluttering ribbons of green weed, burst from the reeds and raced across the water towards the transportal. They weren't *walking* on water, Runcie realised, but sliding on foot floats like broad skis, winding the cranks of crossbows as they came.

Ulalliall let out a squawk and vanished again. 'Disobedient transportal!' Parsifoe raged into the sudden dark. 'I'll teach you.'

She was groping for her spell book when they blasted out of *between* with a *boom-boom-boom* like cannon fire, into the market square of a great city. Runcie glimpsed a magnificent mansion to his left, adorned with thousands of blue pennants. To the right stood a mustard-yellow palace, all twisted columns and shining domes, and in the distance he saw a myriad of silver-and jade-topped towers. Ulalliall shot across the square at knee height, sending stallholders leaping out of the way, vegetable barrows tumbling, and leaving dozens of stalls collapsing in their wake.

'Not Pellissidan!' gasped Parsifoe. 'Get out of here, Ulalliall, *quick*!'

Ulalliall was sniggering so hard that the whole transportal quivered. 'Oops!' it lied, nonchalantly curving around the six-sided square.

Mariam was peering out. 'They're after us.' Dozens of irate stallholders were running towards them, cursing and brandishing fists and sticks.

'Jump, Ulalliall!' Parsifoe moaned, but Ulalliall turned left towards the steps of the mansion and stopped.

'Runcie?' Mariam clutched at his shoulder.

Go, Ulalliall, he thought numbly, but it didn't move. The front doors of the mansion were flung open and a handsome, black-haired young man ran out, crying, 'Ulalliall, I knew you'd come back.'

After him stormed a fat, red-faced man who could have been his father, then a throng of robed men and women, some carrying scrolls tied with red ribbons, others bearing clubs or nightsticks. A pair of moustachioed dandies held aloft crystalline rapiers that fumed like dry ice. The young man raised a hand and his retainers halted. The stallholders froze, muttering among themselves.

'Ulalliall,' Parsifoe said, 'why are you doing this to me?'

'I will not be treated like a servant by a fourth-rate magician!'

'Wizard Parsifoe,' the young man began courteously, in a rather high voice, 'thank you for bringing my transportal back. Should Ulalliall still be in good fettle, I won't insist on the full penalty –'

'Be damned!' cried his father. 'Notaries, serve the warrant. Bailiffs, guards, make ready to seize the cheating harridan.'

'*I* made the wager, father,' said the young man. 'It's between me and the wizard.'

'Only a fool wagers with Cheat-Spell wizards,' snapped the father.

'The game was fair, Ser Mummery,' Parsifoe said weakly. 'I won –' Ulalliall's mocking laugh drowned her out.

A gaggle of men and women now came pounding across from the left. 'Hold that transportal!' shouted their leader, who wore knee britches and a cockaded hat. 'My debt takes precedence.'

'Only after mine,' piped a small, hawk-nosed woman dressed in rainbow robes and a saffron turban. 'My goods were delivered two years before –'

'Where is that knave Helfigor?' said a third merchant, brandishing a gnarled club. 'I demand restitution on his body.'

'Relinquish my transportal, Parsifoe,' pleaded the young man. 'Please . . .'

'Stay back!' gritted Parsifoe, cracking her magical whip. 'Ulalliall –'

The young man sprang backwards, whereupon his father thrust him out of the way and roared, 'Rush her!'

The dandies darted forwards, fuming rapiers to the fore. The bailiffs raised their nightsticks, the merchants advanced from the left while to the right a group of youths and stallholders were heaving up the cobblestones. Runcie felt sure he and Mariam were going to be stoned to death or spend the rest of their lives in some stinking dungeon, and to rub it in the wretched transportal was laughing so hard that it rattled.

But Parsifoe spun the shining whip in a circle and a translucent barrier, like a wet soap bubble, sprang up around them, crackling menacingly on the outside. Their attackers froze then moved hastily backwards.

'Heaven knows I've been patient in this matter,' the father said, staring at Runcie and Mariam meaningfully, 'but it's run out. I don't have the power to curb a wizard, but I have friends who do. The Cybale will be most interested in your passengers, Parsifoe.'

'What?' said Parsifoe, looking puzzled.

'I'm going to sell the debt to your enemy,' he said coldly. 'You're finished!'

'Ulalliall,' hissed Parsifoe. 'Your reputation means everything to you. Would you like the world to know how you *really* escaped the ruin of Anthrimorie?'

'All right!' snarled Ulalliall, 'but you'll be sorry!' There came a blinding flash, a tearing sound like sheet metal being ripped, and they shot into nowhere.

'It was all a terrible misunderstanding,' Parsifoe said distractedly. 'My title is . . . secure.'

Runcie backed towards the rear and Mariam followed. 'What was that all about?' he asked.

'She cheated the young man out of the transportal, obviously, and she doesn't pay her debts. And we're in her hands.' She closed her eyes and slumped against the wall.

Runcie sat down, carefully this time. What was Parsifoe going to do to them?

For a moment the swollen moon shone in through the entrance, but the transportal took a great skip and everything went dark. Eventually the moonlight reappeared and he saw a towering rock in a wild sea. It was nothing like the rock they'd landed on before; nothing like Earth, either. This was an immensely tall, narrow peak rising out of the waves for thousands of feet, with sheer, unclimbable sides of dark green stone.

Ulalliall seemed to be heading for it, though every so often all would turn black, as if they'd slipped out of the normal world. Shortly Runcie made out a bleak tower on top of the peak, built from the same green stone. The tower was dark apart from a glimmer in the topmost room.

They were nearly there when the transportal faltered, then stopped in mid-air again. Parsifoe cast a suspicious glance over her shoulder at the children and began to move her hands more furiously than ever. The transportal jerked closer but stopped again. Parsifoe, now exhausted, turned

76

her face to the sky and raised her clenched fists. She flicked the pages of her book and read three words in a foreign language.

Again Runcie saw that flash of colours which he now associated with strong magic. With a rending scream, the transportal shot across the sky, stopping next to a semi-circular stone-walled balcony. The light was coming from a round doorway.

'Helfigor?' she roarcd. 'Where the blazes are you?'

Only the howling wind answered. Parsifoe ran one hand through her wild hair. 'Stick-at-nothing Helfigor,' she said sourly. 'Ruins my beautiful transportal, then disappears without so much as a by-your-leave.'

'Who's Helfigor?' asked Runcie, heart sinking even further.

'A magician. This is Pysmie's Pyramid, his tower. Go inside and bolt the door.'

Runcie came down tentatively, not liking the look of the place. The tower was battered and crumbling, its stone covered in a sickly green growth that reminded him of Mrs Nightingale's teeth. It was pouring with rain and the light from inside had an unnerving flicker and a baleful orange tinge.

The entrance to the transportal, littered with pieces of tile, was jerking up and down a couple of yards away from the balcony wall and, despite Parsifoe's furious hand movements, Ulalliall would not go any closer.

'Out!' shouted Parsifoe. '*Now!*'

Runcie came down, looking anxiously at the jump. If he missed this time, he'd be splattered on the rocks thousands of feet below. Through the doorway he saw a magician's junkyard. The benches were piled with rat-gnawed books; tattered scrolls; a squashed model of a red sun with five planets, the second of which had a large red and purple moon; and several telescopes, in pieces. Across the room, a small fire burned in a stone fireplace. A hanging cauldron gave off a stream of bile-coloured smoke. He caught a whiff and gagged. It smelt like burnt cabbage.

'Some college,' he said to Mariam.

'This isn't Thorasdil,' Parsifoe snapped. 'I can't get there today. Jump over.'

Runcie didn't move. He was too afraid.

'Oh, for goodness sake!' cried Parsifoe, clouting him over the ear. 'Hasn't your master even taught you obedience?' Picking him up by the collar and the seat of the pants, she heaved him sprawling onto the balcony.

He lay there, listening to the decrepit transportal sniggering and wishing he had a sledgehammer. Parsifoe turned to Mariam, who was standing in the archway, gnawing her thumbnail.

'Keep your grotty hands off me, you thieving old cow!' cried Mariam.

Parsifoe shook with fury. 'I've never heard such insolence.' She advanced on Mariam, who had gone pale and seemed to be regretting the outburst.

'I'm going!' Mariam sprang across the gap.

Parsifoe stared after her, plump hands clenched, then turned away, her back bowed.

Runcie, now faint with hunger, said in a small voice, 'I don't suppose you've got anything to eat?'

Parsifoe spun back. 'After such a display of ill manners and base ingratitude, you expect me to take food from my prentices' mouths for you? It'll do you good to go hungry.' The transportal zigzagged down in the rain and disappeared.

Runcie glared at Mariam. 'Thanks! That was just what we needed right now.'

She glared back, then stalked off and stared over the wall into the rain. Runcie got up, pulled his wet jacket around him and squelched into the untidiest room he'd ever been in. It was eight-sided, like the top of the tower, with slit windows filled in with small diamond-shaped panes of yellow glass. Tables stood on three sides, benches against two others, while the other sides were taken up by two bookcases and the round door. Everything was dusty, cobwebbed and covered in platters half-full of mouldy food scraps, homunculi in bell jars, tongues, lungs and spleens bottled in sickly fluids, and all manner of other unpleasant things.

As he entered, the planets on the squashed model rattled, then squealed along their wires until they were jiggling on the same side, as if watching him. Runcie backed away. Next to one of the bookcases was a small, solid door. He tried it but it didn't budge. They were prisoners.

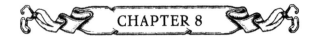

CHAPTER 8

The Golden Stair

Runcie tried to warm himself at the fire but the flames gave out hardly any heat and, besides, they were twisting like a villain rubbing his hands in glee. The wood burned with an unpleasant raspy crackle, while the green fumes from the cauldron hung in the air like knife slashes. He'd thought of magic as a great adventure, but this had none of the thrill of the adventures he'd read about in his warm, secure bed. It was uncomfortable, unpleasant and really grim.

'I'm sorry,' Mariam said, with an effort. 'I'm a bad-tempered cow. I was trying really hard, but I just snapped. Who does she think she is, treating you that way?'

'She expected us to be more grateful. I'm starting to think we should have stayed on the rock platform. Who do you reckon Parsifoe and Helfigor are?'

'Third-rate scoundrels.'

He leaned against the wall, wearily. The model planets rattled as they followed his movement. 'I wonder where this world can be?'

'Probably on the other side of the galaxy,' Mariam said gloomily. 'We'll never get home now.'

The minutes crept by interminably. 'What time do you think it is, back home?' he asked.

'Morning, I suppose.'

No wonder he was so tired. Runcie had just closed his eyes when a whispering whoosh sounded from outside, like a Rolls Royce gliding into a stack of pillows, and a golden glow spread through the door.

'What was that?' said Mariam listlessly.

'It must be Parsifoe coming back.' She didn't seem quite so bad now.

'It didn't sound like her transportal.'

They went to the door together. The glow brightened and Runcie had to shield his eyes. And then he dropped his arms in astonishment.

Beside the balcony wall floated a magnificent white and gold staircase framed by pairs of marble columns and roofed over with beaten gold. The stone was so white that it dazzled the eye. The golden glow came from the upper end of the stair, so he couldn't see what was at the top. A whiff of perfume, like winter violets, reminded him of a favourite patch of his father's wild garden.

'It's another transportal,' Mariam said.

A woman appeared in the glow and began to descend the steps. She was tall, slender and beautiful, her pale-as-milk skin set off by a mass of brilliantly red hair hanging in ringlets to her shoulders. Her pearl-white blouse had wide sleeves and an embroidered front, and she wore loose green trousers over emerald boots.

She stopped on the lowest step, green eyes twinkling, and she had the kindest, warmest smile. 'Hello.' She reached down. 'My name is Thandimanilon, but you can call me Thandie if you like.'

Runcie, enchanted, shook her hand. 'I'm Runcible Jones. Everyone calls me Runcie.'

She turned to Mariam, studying her from head to toe. 'Who are you?' Thandimanilon said, the smile fading.

Mariam didn't answer and Runcie felt embarrassed. He hoped she wasn't going to be rude to Thandimanilon as well.

'Mariamhie,' she said abruptly.

'Very well.' Thandimanilon looked thoughtful. 'You can come too.' She smiled at Runcie and it warmed his heart. 'Step inside.' She swept her arm up the staircase.

Runcie began to climb up onto the wall.

'Runcie,' said Mariam out of the corner of her mouth, 'we don't know anything about her.'

'We know plenty about Parsifoe,' said Runcie, feeling his swollen ear. 'She's cranky, dishonest, her transportal is falling to pieces and she's going to have me flogged.'

'You're right to be wary, children,' said Thandimanilon. 'There are many evil sorcerers on Iltior, and if you fell into their hands . . .' She gave an elegant shudder.

'Is Parsifoe one of them?' said Runcie. She hadn't seemed *that* bad.

'Oh, I wouldn't called her *evil*.' Thandimanilon tilted her lovely face to one side, considering. 'Paltry Parsifoe's hardly bad at all, *most of the time*. Just mean and crotchety and, well, I'm not one to tell tales but . . . just look at this place.' She peered down her elegant nose at the tower.

'She said it was Helfigor's,' said Mariam. 'Who's he?'

Thandimanilon wrinkled her nose. 'He might have become a great magician. Within the *second* rank, of course – he could never have reached the first.' Her beautiful features began to twist into a sneer, but she cut it off midway. 'Helfigor's shiftless; always chasing one chimera or another, neglecting his respon-sibilities. What Parsifoe sees in him I'll never know. Still, the way she's let herself go I don't suppose she gets many offers.'

'She saved us from drowning,' said Runcie, uneasy despite his own low opinion of Parsifoe.

'Only because she wants something from you. But how could *she* take you back to your master? I can tell you made a gate by accident. A magical ring, wasn't it?'

'No, a parchment,' said Runcie, without thinking.

'A *parchment*? Really?'

Mariam was mouthing at him but Runcie couldn't work out what she was trying to say. 'I read it aloud and we were carried through a gate to a rock in the sea.'

'Which rock?' said Thandimanilon.

'It had a long stone tomb with a brass ring, though when Mariam touched it –' He broke off. Mariam was shaking her head furiously.

'Go on,' said Thandimanilon.

'Mariam felt that something bad had happened there.'

'Indeed!' said Thandimanilon, studying Mariam keenly. 'There was a terrible gate accident at Tangsted Way Station, centuries ago and, despite the magic of the place, it's not been used since.' She turned to Runcie. 'What words did you speak?'

'I can't remember,' said Runcie. 'After the parchment burned, I forgot them.'

'Gate spells are powerful magic. It could have killed you both. Or dropped you in a place where I wouldn't leave my worst enemy.'

Runcie hadn't imagined the spell going wrong. He'd been even more foolish than he'd thought. 'It did leave us . . . *somewhere*, but we got out of it.'

Thandimanilon looked troubled. 'What do you mean, Runcie?'

He explained how they'd first ended up in that black nothingness.

Thandimanilon clutched his hand in hers, squeezing it tightly with her eyes closed. 'You were in the most deadly peril, *between*. You could have ended up in – no, let's not talk about *that*. Against all odds you survived. But how, Runcie?'

Runcie was touched. He couldn't remember when a grown-up had last been kind to him. He explained what had happened.

'And by some marvel you got out of there? How did you remember the words?'

'I'd practised them before. I traced the symbols on the parchment, too.'

'What a careful lad you are,' said Thandimanilon. 'Do you still have the tracing?'

Runcie felt in his pocket, hoping it hadn't been washed away.

'Runcie!' hissed Mariam.

He took no notice. If she could rely on her feelings, so could he, and he trusted Thandimanilon. The roll of tracing paper was sopping but his marks were still legible.

Thandimanilon's eyes were gleaming. 'I'll take that.' She scanned the paper. 'Ahh! Why did you copy the symbols, Runcie?'

'To remember them. It was exciting,' Runcie admitted. 'Magic is banned on Earth, you see.'

Thandimanilon's head lifted sharply. 'Earth?' She looked deep in his eyes as if trying to work something out, then smiled. It was a calculating smile, and for the first time he felt uneasy. 'So!' She let out a great gust of breath. 'I thought you were run-away sorcerer's prentices, but you're not, are you?'

'No,' he whispered, hoping he hadn't got it wrong yet again.

'You're from Earth, the world we call Nightland, where magic is practically unknown. And you came here *entirely* by accident.'

'Yes,' quavered Runcie.

'Do you often do illegal things? Are you a ne'er-do-well, Runcie? A bad kid?'

He couldn't bear for her to think ill of him. 'No, of course not. It's just . . . I've always dreamed about magic. I can't explain it.'

Thandimanilon gave him a stern, headmistressish look. 'You've taken the first step on the downhill path, Runcie. Beware! Now, you do want to go home, don't you?'

'Of course –' It was visiting day at Millie's prison next Sunday week, so he had to get back soon, though he'd be peeling turnips until his fingers were worn to stumps to make up for all the trouble he'd caused the Nightingales. And despite all its dangers, Iltior was a wonderful, magical dream . . . 'Can you send us home?' he asked, half hoping that it would take ages. He did want to go home, but he wanted to see more magic first.

'I expect so.' She glanced at the tracing paper. 'Though it won't be easy. Come up; you must be freezing.' She held out her hand.

This time he didn't hesitate. Taking her warm hand, he climbed up and stepped onto the white marble. Mariam remained where she was.

'Are you coming, Mariamhie?' said Thandimanilon imperiously.

Runcie couldn't blame her. Why was Mariam hanging back? She was blinking her dark eyes as if trying to tell him something, but he was too exhausted to work it out. 'Come on, Mariam.'

'I don't think we should, not without thanking Parsifoe. She rescued us, after all.'

'But *why* did she rescue you?' said Thandimanilon. 'It wasn't for your benefit.'

'Why else would she do it?' said Mariam.

'On Iltior, children have special *uses* in magic, and some magicians don't observe the Code as scrupulously as they should. Of course . . .'

'What?' Mariam snapped.

Thandimanilon pursed her lips. 'Parsifoe is such a minor magician, I'm surprised she managed to bring you here at all.' Thandimanilon darted a sideways glance at Mariam. 'And two lost Nightland children so far from home, with no one to look after them . . . for a wizard of low moral character it must be very tempting. I'll say no more. Stay if you wish. On Iltior we allow children to make their own choices, for good or for *ill*.'

Thandimanilon turned away with such indifference that Runcie felt a spasm of panic. It sounded as though Parsifoe was really awful. 'Come on, Mariam. If we stay here I'm going to be flogged.'

Mariam came across the balcony, dragging her feet, and began to climb onto the wall. Thandimanilon didn't reach down to help her. Mariam stepped across onto the lowest step of the stairs and stopped, looking up.

Thandimanilon clapped her hands, said, 'Miluviand if you please, Niddimaun,' and, with a luxurious sigh, her transportal began to drift away.

The door inside the upper room of the tower crashed open and a gasping Parsifoe burst out. 'Stop! Bring them back, Thandimanilon.'

Thandimanilon's transportal froze in mid-air and she drew herself up to her full imperious height. 'How dare you order *me* about, Paltry Parsifoe?'

Parsifoe stumbled to the wall, covered in sweat. 'Children, go with her and you'll spend the rest of your lives regretting it. Thandimanilon is thoroughly wicked and only wants to use you in her despicable magic.'

Runcie cried out, but Thandimanilon turned to him with that carefree smile. 'Go or stay, Runcie. It's your choice. Not for a minute would I compel you against your wish. And nor would I flog you,' she said quietly.

He fingered his sore ear, looked from beautiful, enchanting Thandimanilon to dumpy, red-faced Parsifoe, and back again. Parsifoe's shabby snail transportal came creeping around the side of the tower, to hover next to the balcony wall.

'Would you trust your lives to *that*?' said Thandimanilon.

'Ulalliall was perfectly good before I lent her to Helfigor,' Parsifoe said defensively.

Runcie hadn't realised that Ulalliall was a she, though it fitted, somehow.

Thandimanilon curled her elegant lip. 'What can you expect, keeping such company? Well, children? Transportals often go wrong. You could die in that contraption.'

'Master,' cried Ulalliall, 'will you let her insult us –?'

'Oh, it's master now you want something from me,' Parsifoe snarled. 'Too late, Ulalliall. You *are* a contraption, and a wretched one at your best.'

Ulalliall gave an aggrieved sniff.

'Well, children?' Thandimanilon said imperiously.

'I'll stay with you,' said Runcie.

'Stout lad. What about you, Mariamhie? Be quick – transportals are exhausting to use. I can't hold Niddimaun here forever.'

After a long hesitation, Mariam said crossly, 'I'll go with Runcie.'

'There you have it,' Thandimanilon said to Parsifoe. 'Freely have they made their choice. Go up, children.'

Runcie and Mariam went up the steps to a landing covered in gold leaf and sat down on velvet cushions.

Suddenly Ulalliall began to heave. 'You've mocked us once too often, you old bag. We know their precious secret and we're not going to tell you.'

'What?' cried Parsifoe, alarmed.

Ulalliall's derisory laughter echoed up the stairs. 'Not even Hapless Helfigor could forgive you this blunder.'

'Speak!' cried Parsifoe, jumping aboard Ulalliall and fumbling for the spell book. 'Or you'll regret it.'

'Iltior has been meddling in their affairs for thousands of years,' Ulalliall said, 'and now it's come back to haunt you.'

Thandimanilon spun around, staring at Ulalliall.

'Runcie,' Mariam hissed in his ear, 'I'm getting a very bad feeling.'

Runcie needed no urging. He scrambled to his feet just as Parsifoe found the page. 'Will you speak, Ulalliall, or must I –?'

'They're from Nightland, you fool,' Ulalliall sneered. 'They're the ones spoken of by the seer, Trounce, long ago – *the*

Nightland children who will change Iltior forever. And you've given them away.'

Parsifoe stared wildly at Thandimanilon, who looked equally shocked. 'Ahh!' said Thandimanilon, seeming to calculate opportunities and weigh risks. 'And they're mine.'

'You knew all along, Ulalliall,' Parsifoe gritted, '*and you didn't tell me?*'

'We're 3,062 years old,' Ulalliall said loftily. 'We know everything.'

'Thandimanilon,' Parsifoe said urgently, 'for two thousand years we've fought to preserve beautiful Iltior just the way it is. If this foretelling comes to pass –'

'Iltior is under threat,' Thandimanilon said coldly, 'precisely because the clans won't allow change. It's time the rubbish of centuries was swept away, and we Cybale are going to do it.'

'The children must be sent home.'

Thandimanilon snorted. 'Dimensional gates are First Order magic, way beyond your meagre powers. Even *I* would find it difficult to make one.'

'Mariam?' Runcie whispered, 'What are they talking about? How can *we* change things?' Suddenly he didn't want to stay here at all.

Mariam looked just as scared. 'I don't know.'

Parsifoe's hand flashed up and her whip erupted into a series of coruscating coils that shot towards Thandimanilon. The air sang; then Runcie caught a pungent whiff of ozone. Mariam caught his wrist and they bolted down the stairs.

Thandimanilon put up her open hands, facing Parsifoe, said 'Reflector, Repulse!' and the air in front of her formed a curving mirror that bounced the coils back at Parsifoe.

She ducked, they shot over her head, burned a hole in the side of Ulalliall's arch and flopped to the floor. Ulalliall let out a squeal of outrage.

Before the children reached the bottom of the stairs, Thandimanilon double-clapped her hands. Coloured spots rotated in front of Runcie's eyes and the transportal shot upwards. 'I now hold your debt to Ser Mummery, Parsifoe,' Thandimanilon shouted down, 'but I'll deal with you another time.'

Within seconds the top of the greenstone tower was no more than a dot, which winked out as they slipped into black nothingness. Runcie shivered in the wind and pressed up against Mariam for warmth, but she moved away fretfully. He supposed she blamed him.

Thandimanilon came up and crouched in front of him. 'Is something the matter, Runcie?'

'I'm cold and frightened. And so very hungry,' he said faintly.

She took his hand, and once more he felt that she really did care; that he'd made the right choice. 'You poor boy. Didn't Parsifoe feed you?'

'She said it would do us good to go hungry.'

'Incredible!' Thandimanilon ran down, returned with a large golden box and flipped up the lid, revealing thousands of small coloured objects, all flickering from one shape and colour to another. Scooping out a handful, she poured them into Runcie's lap, then gave Mariam another, slightly less generous handful.

Runcie took a yellow one, shaped like a bow tie, and it flickered red then blue in his hand. He put it in his mouth, rather gingerly. It shot up, bounced off the roof of his mouth then spun around on his tongue before dissolving in an explosion of tangy sweetness more intense than anything he'd ever tasted. It was more than just a sweet, though. It partially filled the hollow inside. He chose another, which melted like chilli chocolate, warming him all the way down. A third was like a cheese and pickled onion sandwich and settled beautifully into his stomach.

Thandimanilon shovelled another double handful into his lap. 'Everyone expects children to act like serious little grown-ups. But I say, let children be children, and spoil them while you can, for all too quickly they must face the cruel and unforgiving world.'

The transportal moved through nothingness for a long time before reappearing smoothly in the real world though, frustratingly, still in darkness. Runcie noticed a continuous flashing in the distance which, as they approached, became an arc of storms curving around a mountaintop. The transportal slowed. He saw a steep mountainside covered in forest and something shining like ice, far off. To the left, rivers of orange lava flowed down the flanks of a volcano.

'Are you angry with me, Mariam?' he said quietly.

'I was, but now I'm confused too. One minute she seems like the perfect, kindly aunt, the next like a black sorcerer.'

'But you don't have a bad feeling about her, like you did about the lens earlier?'

'No. Well, not like earlier.'

'What do you think Ulalliall meant by *meddling in Earth's affairs*?'

She didn't answer.

The transportal dropped suddenly and the volcano disappeared behind a ridge rising up to a flat-topped peak on which he saw a fairytale castle with dozens of spires, minarets and dome-topped towers. All were impossibly narrow and tall, and all so bright and beautiful that he caught his breath.

Unfortunately the transportal whirled by and on towards a light in the distance, a solitary tower set on a saddle between two rocky, horn-like peaks. It was this tower which the storms surrounded, and lightning showed it to be built from blood-red stone, except for the window edges, which were black as slitted eyes. Runcie hoped they weren't going there.

They were. At the top, hundreds of feet high, a circular roof of red metal, like an upside-down saucer, was supported on slender black columns and topped with a series of gigantic brass globes. The central ones were held up by three panthers carved from dark stone, and more globes were mounted on fittings projecting from the sides of the tower. Some even had staircases or observation decks, while the upper globes were linked by woven metal cables as thick through as Runcie was tall. Lightning struck continually at the globes, making them glow, while currents arced between them with a crackling roar.

As the transportal curved towards the tower, the thunder became deafening. They drifted towards two of the larger globes on one side, stalled for several heartbeats then, the moment after the globes were struck by twin bolts of lightning, darted between them into a cylindrical cavern beneath the roof. It was the size of an aircraft hanger and had another globe suspended in its centre. The transportal passed beneath the globe, fell into blackness, doors slammed above them and Runcie dropped a short distance to the floor. The transportal had vanished.

It was so quiet here that he could hear Mariam's heavy breathing. 'Where has she gone?' she said in a low voice.

As his eyes began to adjust, Runcie saw that they were in the middle of a chamber the size of the Nightingales' house. He could make out pieces of furniture further away and an object hanging from the ceiling. A chandelier, he thought. He caught the faintest mouth-watering waft of bread baking in a distant kitchen.

'I suppose she's gone to put the transportal away,' he said thickly.

Mariam didn't reply.

'Wasn't she the most beautiful woman you ever saw?' he went on. 'I've never seen hair that red before.'

Mariam spun around. 'Runcie,' she said, choking, 'her hair was as black as mine.'

'What are you talking about . . . ?'

'Her hair was as black as a panther's and she had skin the colour of honey.'

'It was red,' said Runcie desperately, chills running up and down his arms. 'And her skin was white as milk.'

'What was she wearing?' cried Mariam.

'A white blouse and old-fashioned baggy green trousers.'

'I saw a long gown of red silk embroidered with silver and golden threads.' She caught him by the shoulders. 'You know what this means?'

He gulped. 'What?'

'It was an illusion. She was showing you what you would most want to see, to make you believe her. And because I listened to you – fool, fool! – we're in her power.' She wavered across to the far side of the room and stood there with her forehead resting on the wall.

Runcie swallowed. He'd never trust his feelings again. 'So who is she?' he said in a tiny voice.

'Better to ask what she wants us for. And what we're going to do to Iltior.'

CHAPTER 9

The Brass-Topped Tower

We've set something terrible in motion, Runcie thought. No, *I have.* 'Mariam?'

'Yes?' she snapped.

'What do you think Ulalliall meant?'

'When she called us "*The Nightland children who will change Iltior forever?*" I don't know. But Thandimanilon saw a great opportunity.'

'Parsifoe thought we were a terrible threat. I hope we're not going to start a war or something.'

'We've got to think of a plan, Runcie, though without knowing anything about this world . . .'

'But we can decide what we want,' Runcie said boldly, even though he didn't feel bold. He was scared out of his wits, and Mariam sometimes made him feel like a little boy, but if she could act confident when she was quaking inside, it might work for him too. 'First, we don't want to be separated.' He looked at her anxiously, afraid she might feel better off without him.

'We stick together no matter what. I'm glad you're here, Runcie. I don't feel so alone. Second, we're not going to change anything.'

'And third, we want to get home as soon as possible.'

'And take our medicine,' Mariam said dismally.

'If we think up a really good story, perhaps we won't get into too much trouble.'

'Perhaps,' she said doubtfully, then brightened. 'Well, at least it's a plan.'

Runcie felt better too, though he knew it wasn't going to be that easy.

A faint light appeared, outlining a doorway, and a hulking figure was silhouetted against it: massive, squat and headless. Mariam gasped. Runcie turned to run but there was nowhere to run to.

The chandelier began to glow and the figure became a man, as muscular as a gorilla, whose leather jerkin strained across his mighty chest. He did have a head, but it was twisted sideways and bowed on his thick neck, which didn't make him any less frightening.

'Who are you?' Mariam said, tilting her chin up, but her voice cracked.

'Hfar Slessar Heunch, at your service,' the man rumbled, shuffling forward and turning his head sideways, the better to look at them. A long, strong-boned face was etched with deep pain lines. The light caught his eyes, which bulged as if he had to strain to see. He turned his head one way and then the other, in painful jerks, but his eyes did not leave them. 'Welcome to Miluviand.'

'W-what do you want?' said Runcie.

'To take you to dinner,' said Heunch, reaching out hands the size of wicketkeepers' gloves.

Runcie's knees were knocking. Mariam was backing away.

'Take my hands!' Heunch rapped.

He had a deep, raspy voice, like a stone door grinding across a gritty floor, which Runcie found impossible to resist. He extended his small hand.

It was swallowed up in Heunch's paw, the skin of which was as deeply cracked as an elephant's foot. Mariam shook her head, turned and bolted. She didn't get far. Heunch clicked his fingers with a sound like a bone snapping, and Mariam ran on the spot for a second, then began to back towards him, reluctance in her every movement.

Heunch kept his hand out, rock-steady, for the full minute it took her to reach him. She turned and, with a shudder, allowed him to take her hand. Heunch rotated on one foot, swung Runcie and Mariam around to face the door and marched them across, not lifting his feet as he moved. *Rasp-rasp, rasp-rasp*. With every step he took a sharp little breath, as if in pain.

They went down many sets of magnificent stairs made of a lustrous red stone that shone as if waxed. The rails were carved with all manner of beasts, familiar as well as strange. The risers showed hunting, fishing and whaling scenes in gruesome detail, and more often than not the hunters were being eaten by their prey. *All too quickly they must face the cruel and unforgiving world,* Thandimanilon had said.

Finally Heunch turned towards a pair of doors tall enough for a double-decker bus to pass through. They opened before him to reveal a high-ceilinged dining hall whose walls were covered in tapestries and paintings on wooden panels. A single table, set with about a hundred places, extended down the centre of the room, but there was no food on it.

Letting them go, Heunch made a gesture towards the stacked fireplace to his left, as if throwing a handful of sand at it. The wood burst into flame. 'Stand by the fire,' he rasped. 'Dry yourselves.'

Runcie did so, rubbing his squashed hand. Mariam, shuddering, wiped her hand up and down her pants. They stood with their backs to the fire as he shuffled out.

'Are you all right?' said Runcie, not understanding how she could be so brave one minute and so timid the next.

'Ugh! He's so creepy, it sends shivers up my spine.'

'But you stood up to the whole school, and even to Thandimanilon.'

'This is different. I don't like things I don't understand.'

'Like when we were *between* and you had the panic attack?'

'Mind your own business!'

And those slithering creatures on the rock. And now Heunch. Mariam wasn't as tough as she'd made out and he liked her all the more for it.

Their clothes began to steam. Runcie turned to face the flames, which were whirling and dancing in the most marvellous colours and patterns, more beautiful than anything he'd seen back home. What was it about Iltior? Everything seemed richer and more interesting here. Even the water was *wetter*.

Despite their situation, his spirits lifted, and he looked around. A tapestry map on the wall showed a continent surrounded by islands. Runcie went closer. The continent was extremely mountainous and had an ice-covered plateau in the centre – was that the ice he'd seen on the way? The coast was cut by many long, narrow bays, while lines of islands arced off on all sides into an endless ocean, which made him feel lost and helpless again.

He went back to the fire. 'What's she going to do to us?'

'I don't know. I'm starting to think we were better off with Parsifoe.'

'Then why didn't you stay?'

'Someone has to look after you. You really are a duffer, Runcie.'

Mariam didn't say it crossly this time, and he didn't mind her saying so. Despite everything, he felt that they might become friends, and he hadn't had a real friend since the divorce.

Despite the blazing fire, the room was cold, so they didn't move until their clothes had stopped steaming. By then Runcie had begun to see the holes in their so-called plan. How could two kids hope to outsmart a world of such clever and cunning adults?

Mariam went to the window, pressing her nose to a tiny pane. 'It's still dark.'

He stood beside her, staring out, and suddenly it all became too much. 'How are we ever going to get home again?' he said miserably.

'We may not be going home.'

And all because of his broken promise. He imagined a grief-stricken Millie living out what remained of her life in a stinking cell. He'd lied to himself, as well as to her, when he'd justified keeping the parchment. To say nothing of using it.

He sniffled, but Mariam was looking at him so he wiped his eyes and pretended it hadn't happened. 'We've got to,' he said quietly, but with an unshakeable resolve, and the decision was made. He *had* to find the way home. He *had* to make up for what he'd done and put things right, and he was going to. No matter what it took.

Suddenly the stacked fireplace at the far end of the room blazed up, a leather armchair rotated silently and Thandi-manilon sat facing them, though try as he might, Runcie could not see through her illusion.

'You like maps, don't you, Runcie? I expect you want to know all about Iltior.' She looked paler now. Her skin was almost transparent.

'I'd like to know *something*,' muttered Runcie.

'Ours is a small world, and mostly ocean. There are two continents: the one you saw on the map, called Finnitan, and another on the other side of the world, though we don't go there.'

'Why not?' said Mariam.

'It's hard to get to, even in a transportal. And dangerous.'

'Does Iltior have a government?' Runcie wondered.

Her lip curled. 'Iltior doesn't believe in government,' she said sarcastically. 'Each county has been ruled by its clan since ancient times, and presently the clans are grouped into twenty-seven squabbling factions. We also have councils, not that they ever do anything.'

'What about the magicians?' he asked eagerly.

'We First Order sorcerers, magicians and wizards number sixty-four.' Thandimanilon's eyes met Runcie's. 'I dare say there are hundreds of lesser magicians, not that anyone counts such rabble.'

'Do all wizards have their own towers, or do they serve –?'

'Wizards don't serve!' she snapped. 'We maintain, shape and improve the magical realm. Some magicians are allied to the factions, of course. I am Cybale, which ruled all Iltior in ancient times, *and will again*.' She considered Runcie. 'Yes, magicians dwell in towers. The clans have their citadels, the merchants their boroughs and the people their hamlets. Thus is Iltior ordered. Come, sit down, children.' She indicated the rug beside the fire with a sweep of her hand. 'I imagine you're still hungry?'

'I'm starving,' he said. The magical lollies had gone with the transportal.

She moved her fingers in her lap and a silver tray popped into the air between Runcie and Mariam. Mouth-watering smells arose from underneath an embroidered cloth. Runcie swallowed.

'Take the tray,' said Thandimanilon, and once they'd placed it on the floor between them she said, 'Eat!' As Runcie reached for the cloth, she lifted the velvet cover off a broad pedestal beside her to reveal a diorama – a quintet of musicians performing in front of a tavern audience. He stood up, staring. The players looked like tiny people frozen in mid-performance.

Thandimanilon touched the base of the diorama and the musicians sprang to life. The fiddler's bow went back and forth, the flute player's fingers flickered up and down, and the dark-haired singer's throat moved as she sang. Runcie didn't understand the words but the song was in a haunting, melancholy key that brought tears to his eyes. At the end the players bowed, cheers rang out and every woman, man and child in the audience raised their tankards, then froze in position.

'Wow!' said Runcie. 'If I could do such magic –'

'That wasn't magic,' said Thandimanilon through pursed lips. 'It's an automaton; a model driven entirely by clockwork, and it's an art that all your *science* could not duplicate.' Having made her point about the superiority of Iltior, she settled back in the chair and her eyes fluttered closed. She was exhausted. Using the transportal must have worn her out. It was useful to know.

Mariam folded the cloth neatly beside the tray, which held a host of little dishes, each with a painted china lid, as well as plates, knives, forks, drinking bowls and a jug of something thick, pink and foaming.

Runcie lifted the lid of the first dish, which contained a thinly sliced grilled meat, like crispy bacon. He hadn't eaten bacon since he'd ended up at the Nightingales, so he took half. It tasted much better than bacon. It was so unbearably delicious that he could only eat a tiny piece at a time, savouring every morsel.

Mariam was picking at shreds of something yellow, like sugared lemon peel, lifting them up and letting them fall as if fearing they were poisoned. Runcie glanced surreptitiously at Thandimanilon, who now held a silver goblet in her hands and was staring at the steam rising from it. But it was more than just steam – little sprites were whirling about a bright speck in it, like dancers around a campfire. Another marvel!

After much to-ing and fro-ing, Mariam gingerly put one of the yellow shreds in her mouth, chewed, and such a look of bliss crossed her face that Runcie snorted with laughter. She didn't notice – Mariam was transported.

'Everything on Iltior is brighter and more beautiful,' he said.

'For most people,' said Thandimanilon, without taking her eyes off the dancing sprites, 'life is short, often brutal and generally tragic. But we know how to make the most of it.'

Runcie took a segment of red candied fruit from another dish and it tasted even more glorious than the first dish. It was the best food in the world. He wished she'd play the automaton again, but wasn't game to ask.

After he'd eaten himself to a standstill, he looked up to see Thandimanilon's eyes on him. 'Is this . . . ?' he began.

'Yes, Runcie?' she said absently.

'Is this food an illusion, like the different way you look to Mariam?'

Thandimanilon shot upright. 'To suggest that your host would feed you illusory food – nay, even to *think* it – is a mortal insult,' she said furiously. 'Duels have been fought, and men have died, for less.'

Why couldn't he think before opening his mouth? 'I'm sorry,' he stammered. 'I didn't know.'

'No one – not even the biggest scoundrel on Iltior – would commit such a breach of guest-right.' She slumped back in her chair. 'Since you aren't of this world, I'll forgive you this once,' she said with an exhausted wave. 'But be warned, Runcie! Few Iltiorians are as soft-hearted as I am. Most would make you pay *cruelly* for such an insult.' She turned to Mariam. 'So you see me with black hair and honey skin, do you?'

She knew everything they'd said. Runcie filed that away as well, not that it helped.

Mariam swallowed a candied fruit, thrust out her jaw and said with the arrogance she used to cover her fears, 'Of course.'

Thandimanilon was studying her with real interest now. 'How *very* curious. That was my true likeness long ago, but I became what I am ten years past, and it's no illusion. Do you often see the unseeable?'

'How would I know?' snapped Mariam.

Runcie couldn't work out why she was so rude to adults when it could only hurt her.

Thandimanilon jumped up, swept across and looked deep into Mariam's eyes for a full minute. Mariam glared back. Thandimanilon's face fell, then she trudged back to her chair. 'So seldom does *that* talent come to anything,' she said, and turned back to her sprites.

'I have some questions for you,' said Thandimanilon when Mariam had finished eating. 'You're the first children ever to cross from Nightland – Earth – to Iltior, so I must know how you came by the parchment.'

Runcie explained about the intruder.

'A man came to your home, *all the way from Iltior?*' said Thandimanilon in astonishment. She waved her hand through the steam and the sprites popped out of existence. 'What did he look like?'

Runcie began to describe him – the cloak, the eyes and the teeth. But when he mentioned the long, needle-pointed moustaches she shot up in her chair again, her eyes glowing like the core of a nuclear reactor. 'Go on!'

'He was humming as he searched the room, *mmmm-unnggg*,' Runcie added.

'Was he?' said Thandimanilon, and sat back, thinking, for a long time. 'Such great magic,' she said softly. 'Why would he risk it without me?'

'Do you know him?' asked Runcie.

She looked up, her noble brow wrinkled, but didn't answer the question. 'Even ordinary gates within Iltior are hard to make, Runcie, and they often go astray. But to direct a *dimensional* gate across the abyss between Iltior and your distant world requires one of the greatest spells of all. It's dangerous magic which costs an adept much of his power, and it takes long to recover from . . .' Her voice faded away, then returned as a whisper. 'You can see how that small trip in my transportal has exhausted me, and transportals are far easier to use than dimensional gates. Only a handful of magicians could make a gate to your world, and the pain is so great that they could not do it twice in the one year.'

'So that's why he didn't come back for the parchment,' said Runcie.

'He couldn't. Losing it must have hurt him cruelly, poor foolish man.' Thandimanilon rubbed her eyes. 'Why was he spying on *you*, Runcie?'

'I – I don't know,' said Runcie. He didn't want to mention his mother or father. 'I don't know anything about magic . . .'

'Come, lad,' she said sternly. 'You carried yourself and Mariam here through a gate, safely. True, you merely activated an existing spell, but without a talent for magic you couldn't possibly have done so.'

'Magic is a crime on Earth,' said Runcie. 'My mother was –' He broke off, and a flush began to make its way up his throat.

'Go on,' said Thandimanilon softly. 'What are you hiding, Runcie?'

'Dad was writing a book about magic!' Runcie cried, and then it all poured out of him. 'Mum left him because of it, and now he's dead and she's in prison. My family has been destroyed because of magic and I wouldn't do it even if I could.'

'But you *did* do it,' she said. 'And knowingly, so don't tell me any more lies. What did your father write about?'

'I don't know,' Runcie lied.

'What was his book called?'

'*Theurgic Structures*, whatever that means,' muttered Runcie.

'You're a clever, thoughtful boy,' said Thandimanilon. 'I'm sure you know what it means.'

It was impossible to deceive her. 'Dad reckoned that the ability to do magic was coded into our genes –'

'Genes?' she said, puzzled.

'What we inherit from our ancestors. Dad said anyone should be able to do magic, but we'd turned to science long ago and forgotten how.'

'*Anyone from Nightland can do it* . . .' Thandimanilon went even paler.

What's she so worried about? Runcie mimed to Mariam. She shrugged.

'It's your evil world!' Thandimanilon burst out. 'Resonances from Nightland are corrupting our children, filling the weak-minded with vile ideas, even changing our speech to yours. And we won't have it!' She glared at him.

It wasn't right, the way she kept criticising Earth; he didn't like it at all. Though after the way his family had been treated, Runcie couldn't find it in his heart to defend his world either.

'What do you mean by resonances?' said Mariam.

'Corrupt influences seeping from your world, a world that doesn't even know we exist.'

She dipped three fingers in her goblet and flicked them at the fire. The flames roared scarlet, then died down to reveal a scene in the coals, a group of brightly dressed Iltiorian children magically batting one of those spiny balls about. All but one child.

A boy of Runcie's age sat under a tree, slack-jawed, eyes staring and dribble running down his chin. His empty hands were held out in front of him, his thumbs moving in rapid, repetitive patterns that Runcie knew all too well.

'We've lost many of our best and most brilliant to that madness,' said Thandimanilon. 'No one knows what the boy is seeing, but we know the evil comes from your world, via *resonance*, and seldom can we bring them out of it.'

Runcie gave Mariam an uneasy glance. It was as clear as anything that the boy was playing an imagined computer game, and it looked so *wrong*.

'Resonance takes many forms,' Thandimanilon went on, and he saw in the flames, in turn, an old Iltiorian woman absurdly cavorting as if at a karaoke night, a robed wizard acting out a TV pizza ad then, chillingly, a group of little children goose-stepping like Nazi soldiers. 'But the most insidious resonances can't be seen, Runcie. The ideas that shiver into the lives of ordinary people, making them hate beautiful Iltior and yearn for what must never be – a world made of concrete and an empty, treadmill life.'

'I – I'm really sorry,' said Runcie.

Thandimanilon's glare softened and he took the opportunity to ask, 'Ulalliall said Iltior had been meddling in our affairs for thousands of years. What did she mean?'

'Our ancestors foresaw the damage Nightland science would do long ago, and went to your world to stop it. If only they had.'

'What did they do?'

'I can't talk about it, but be warned: it's time for desperate measures and we won't baulk at them. Enough of that. What happened to your father's book, Runcie?'

Runcie didn't want to answer, but he did. 'It was destroyed in the fire that killed Dad –' Just what had his father been up to? If his book bothered the greatest magicians of Iltior, it must have been important. But was it good or bad?

'Really?' said Thandimanilon. 'And your mother is in prison. Why, exactly?' She tilted her beautiful face to one side, inspecting him like a bird eyeing a juicy snail.

'She had a copy of his book.'

'Ahhh!' sighed Thandimanilon. 'And perhaps the intruder thought *you* had a copy. Tell me, Runcie, what's happening in your world?'

'I don't understand what you mean,' said Runcie.

'I meant anything strange or unusual.'

'There's a problem with power stations and stuff, but that's been going on for ages.'

'What's a power station?' said Thandimanilon.

Runcie couldn't even begin to explain.

'Do you understand about power?' said Mariam.

Thandimanilon frowned at her. 'Of course. We adepts draw on a kind of power, the force we call *quintessence*, to do magic every day of our lives.'

'Well, we have computers to write with, fridges to keep our food cold and stoves to cook on. We have all sorts of other appliances to make our lives easier, and they all need power. We make it by burning fuel in power stations, and lately they've been going wrong. It's all very worrying.'

'I see.' Thandimanilon was smiling now. Why was she so pleased to hear it? 'Go to bed. You'll have to do the tests in the morning.'

'What tests?' said Runcie and Mariam together, but Thandimanilon waved them away with an exhausted flourish.

CHAPTER 10

Tested for Magic

Heunch took them down another set of stairs, thence through an archway shaped like a cloverleaf into a chilly dormitory whose walls were painted with scenes of forests, mountains and flower-filled meadows. The vaulted ceiling was so perfect a semblance of Iltior's starry sky that Runcie expected to see the red moon rise from the far corner. The dormitory contained two rows of six-poster cabinet beds, each with a canopy and sliding wooden side panels that could be closed in winter, though all were open now. There were twenty-six beds, most occupied by sleeping girls.

Mariam jerked her hand out of Heunch's, wiping it furiously. He turned his black eyes on her and she backed away.

Heunch pointed to the first empty bed, four along on the right. 'You will sleep here,' he rasped. 'You can wash in there.' He jerked his head at an archway to his left. 'Make haste. When I return, I will extinguish the lights. Runcible, come with me.'

Runcie was dismayed. There was so much to talk to Mariam about; so much he didn't understand and, unfathomable though she was, he'd be lost without her. Already their plan was coming apart and he didn't see how it could possibly work anyway.

Mariam's mouth opened and closed; she didn't want to be separated either. Heunch led Runcie across a hall into another dormitory half-full of sleeping boys. The walls displayed the same landscapes, though the season was winter. Snow lay thickly on the ground, the mountains were bleak crags hung with green icicles, and a storm was brewing in the distance. It was even colder than the girls' dormitory. The icicles could have been growing out of the walls.

Heunch pointed to an empty bed, then to the washing room. The bed made a rude noise. Heunch muttered something, whereupon the bedsprings emitted a raspberry-like groan. He thumped the bedhead with his fist. 'Enough!'

He blew into Runcie's eyes, and Runcie was overcome by such sleepiness that he almost nodded off where he stood. As Heunch turned to the door a bed slat flicked out, striking him hard between the shoulder blades with the sound of wood on wood. He went out without seeming to notice.

Runcie plodded into the washing room, poured icy water into a bowl and washed his face and hands. Not seeing a towel he dried himself on his shirt, staggered back into the dormitory and threw off his clothes. Aah, it was so cold.

On the far wall, the storm seemed closer than before. The lights began to dim; the painted landscapes too, though the storm clouds still glowed with every lightning flash. He scrambled into bed before it grew completely dark, slid between the sheets and

113

struck a barrier. Some practical joker had short-sheeted the bed. He scrunched up, toes curled against the cold, fuming with exhausted rage. Then, to his alarm, the bed began to heave in creaking mirth. It was *aware*, like Ulalliall. Runcie kicked out irritably and his foot tore through the threadbare sheet.

A hiss erupted from beneath the bed. 'You little swine,' it whispered in a voice like sheets slithering across rope. 'You'll be sorry.'

Heunch lurched out of the darkness, thumped the bedhead so hard that the slats rattled and roared, 'Enough, I said.'

The bed made no more sound. Runcie sat up, watching the storm uneasily and feeling panicky about what was going to happen tomorrow. *It's time for desperate measures*, Thandimanilon had said. What did she mean by that?

But he had learned one useful thing. Thandimanilon knew the intruder well, and *he* obviously knew something important about Ansie and his book, so it must be possible to discover what that was. Runcie's spirits rose. His quest was on track at last.

But what were he and Mariam going to set in motion here? They'd stumbled into something dark and deadly, though he was too tired to think about it. The ominous clouds faded, a silent bolt of lightning arched down to the tallest mountain peak, and he collapsed into sleep.

'Aah!' Runcie jerked bolt upright, drenched in sweat. He couldn't recall the nightmare but his skin felt as though something with lots of furry legs had crawled across it. A boy muttered irritably from further down the row. Shadows moved on the painted walls, as if a host of troops in shiny, beetle-shell armour were creeping up on him, then he saw the glint of oiled knives.

Runcie tried to slip out of bed but couldn't move. He made a mewling sound in his throat. The bed was shaking in silent, malicious mirth. And then something came gliding in through the cloverleaf entrance and headed straight for him.

'No,' he gasped. 'Please don't hurt me.'

The figure banished the shadows on the wall with a wave of its hand. With another gesture it stilled the bed – Runcie distinctly felt the life drain out of it. The figure settled beside him with a weary sigh.

'Go back to sleep, Runcie,' said Thandimanilon. 'You can come to no harm in my realm.' She put her arm around him, holding him and stroking his damp brow.

He lay back and, after some minutes, the skin-crawling disappeared. He felt perfectly safe now. His eyes closed, she drew the covers up around his chin and stood by until he was drifting off again.

When Runcie finally roused, the dormitory was empty and vivid red sunlight was slanting into the room. He went to the window and squinted up at the glowing orb, which was far bigger than the sun he was used to and a molten, brilliant crimson.

He washed his face and hands, put on his salt-crusted clothes and went to the door of the girls' dormitory. It was empty and all the beds had been made. He turned back and made his own,

115

rather gingerly, then wandered along the hall, wondering where he might get breakfast.

'Good morrow, Runcie,' said Thandimanilon, dressed all in yellow today, apart from a jet black sash looped around her waist. 'Come this way.'

She led him up several stairs then out through a door in the wall, and Runcie's head reeled; for an instant he'd thought there was nothing under him. Thandimanilon caught his arm and the vertigo eased. They were on an arching glass bridge curving across a broad well that plunged hundreds of feet down the centre of the tower.

Lights began to glow above them. Suspended in the centre of the shaft was a large chamber whose brass walls were etched through to reveal scenes of magic and mayhem in inlaid ebony. They went in and Thandimanilon closed the door. The chamber had six sides – no, seven. The red flagstones were covered in the centre by an indigo carpet as soft as velvet, and a statue of a white panther stood by the fire. Mariam was sitting on a stool nearby and her eyes lit up as Runcie came in.

Thandimanilon went to the fireplace and warmed her hands. On the mantelpiece beside her, Runcie's eye was caught by a three-masted sailing ship in a bottle, on a stormy sea. But it wasn't a model – the sails were cracking in the wind and real waves broke over the bow. He moved closer, fascinated, then jumped. The ship was worked by a ghostly crew, and they were all glaring at him.

'You don't like my ghost galleon?' said Thandimanilon.

'How did they get in the bottle?'

'That ship, and its crew, did my great-grandfather a monstrous injury a century ago, such that he vowed eternal revenge. He imprisoned them in the bottle and set them to sail an endless sea until the sun grows cold. The last of the crew died seventy years ago, but their ghosts sail on, trapped forever.' She stared at Runcie. 'You won't ever do me an injury, will you?'

'Of course not,' he said, feeling faint.

'Then you have nothing to fear. Oh, they're perfectly safe, Runcie. Those ghosts are tethered and, despite their black hatred of me, they can't escape.' She turned away. 'This is my testing room. No one can cheat in here – my protection spell renders it impervious to all outside influences.'

She held his gaze for a moment, then raised her hand and the walls darkened to the colour of the carpet. The only light came from coals glowing in the fireplace, a pair of dim glow-flasks high on the walls, and the green eyes of the statue.

'I'm going to test you now,' said Thandimanilon.

'What for?' said Runcie anxiously. He'd forgotten about that.

'To see what kinds of magical talents you have, and how strong they are. Magic is our Art, Runcie, but unlike your *science*, it doesn't tear the world apart. Sit in the amber chair, please.' She pointed.

In the miserable times after his parents had split up, daydreaming about magic had been his only escape, though one tinged by guilt. Yet here, magic was what people expected. He could hardly wait to find out what his talents were.

117

'What are you going to do then?' he said, holding his breath.

'Teach you how to do magic, of course. It's a crime to have such great abilities and not know how to use them.'

Such a thrill coursed through Runcie that for a moment he couldn't breathe.

'I thought you were going to send us home,' said Mariam imperiously.

Runcie ignored her. He wasn't going to let anyone spoil this moment. *Ah, but what about your promise?* Magic is allowed on Iltior, he told himself. *That doesn't make it safe though, does it? Or right.* But it's not up to me. Thandimanilon is making me do it. His conscience retired, temporarily vanquished.

'You have to repay me first,' said Thandimanilon.

'What do you mean?' cried Mariam, her self-possession vanishing.

'You asked me to send you back.'

'I did not!'

'Runcie said, "Can you send us back?"'

'I meant *are you able to?*' said Runcie, not sure what to think.

'It's too late to change your mind now,' said Thandimanilon crossly. 'The cost has been incurred. Surely you didn't think I'd send you back for nothing?'

Her astonishment seemed genuine. 'But on our world no one –' Runcie began.

'You're on Iltior now, children. If you ask for something you have to pay for it.'

'We don't have any money . . .' began Mariam.

'Now you insult me!' Thandimanilon sprang up, tossing back her flaming curls. 'To offer mere *gold* for such a service – I never heard the like.'

'How are we supposed to pay?' Runcie said.

'Like for like, of course. You must repay a wizard's service with service.'

Mariam collapsed like a punctured balloon. 'For how long?' she said despairingly.

Was it like a fairy contract, where he'd condemned them to a lifetime of slavery without realising? And was *this* going to change Iltior forever?

Thandimanilon shrugged. 'That depends on how well you serve. It may not be long at all. But enough – to the chair, Runcie.'

It was made from carved pieces of amber that began to glow like molten gold as soon as he sat down. The amber was pleasantly warm and had a silky feel against his skin. It seemed to be softening and shaping itself around him.

Thandimanilon pulled the cover off a tall device in the corner, rather like a gigantic old brass microscope. She tugged gently and it floated across the room at ankle height, to settle behind Runcie's chair. He sighed; magic was everywhere.

The 'scope was about fifteen feet high, with a brass barrel covered in knobs and cogs. Mounted below the bottom lens were three discs, the diameter of tractor tyres, in which were set many coloured panes. To Runcie's left, the statue's eyes were fixed on him.

'Put your hands in the gauntlets, Runcie,' said Thandimanilon from behind him.

A pair of amber gloves sat on the armrests. He slid his fingers in. They felt luxurious.

'Heunch!' rapped Thandimanilon.

A pile of straw in the corner rustled, then Heunch stood up and made his painful way over, drawing on a pair of fur mittens. Taking up an amber skullcap, he rubbed it vigorously then set it on Runcie's head. Static electricity drew his hair up.

Heunch rubbed Runcie's gauntlets just as vigorously, followed by the arms of the chair, the sides, back and headrest, then stepped away with another crackle. Runcie felt the tickle of sparks jumping in his hair.

Thandimanilon adjusted the 'scope until its tall brass barrel sat directly above Runcie's head. 'Ladder, Heunch.'

Heunch carried across a wooden ladder, stood it up, and it stayed up, *by itself.*

'Close your eyes, Runcie, and don't think. Just remember when you used the parchment to open the gate.' Thandimanilon climbed the ladder one-handed.

Mariam was sitting bolt upright, fists clenched in her lap. Runcie closed his eyes, wondering how someone so brave could be so scared of magic. Too bad; he was glad he had the talent and she did not. At this moment he felt very close to his father, which helped to overcome the guilt.

'Ready, Heunch?' came Thandimanilon's voice from high above.

Runcie imagined her peering down through the barrel of the 'scope. *Click-whirr*. He opened one eye. Heunch was rotating the topmost disc so that first one, then another of the coloured panes passed beneath the bottom lens.

'Eyes closed!' snapped Thandimanilon. 'Don't *think*.'

Runcie closed his eyes but couldn't stop thinking. *Click-whirr, click-whirr*. Patterns and colours drifted through his mind: now a spray of light like a Roman candle stuck in a wall, now wavering rainbows like oil on a pond. His fingers tingled in the gloves; there was more static in his hair. Perhaps he would become a great magician here. His father would have been so proud . . .

'Are you sure that's the right one?' said Thandimanilon crossly.

'Yes, Dark Lady,' said Heunch.

'Do it again.'

Heunch rubbed the amber, then lurched behind Runcie and began rotating the discs. *Click-whirr, click-whirr*. Runcie drifted back into those lovely daydreams.

'It's showing nothing!' Thandimanilon was glaring at Runcie as though it was his fault. She reached down to stroke the head of the white panther, which stood beside her now, its mouth opened wide in a fearsome yawn. It wasn't a statue at all. Runcie gulped.

'But Dark Lady –' said Heunch.

'Are you sure the thaumoscope is working?'

'The alignments are the same as before; the auras are perfect.'

'Who was the last child tested?' asked Thandimanilon.

'The one you snatched –' Thandimanilon cleared her throat pointedly and Heunch amended, 'Tigris, Dark Lady.'

'Bring her in at once.'

'At once, Dark Lady,' said Heunch, bowing with that odd, sideways jerk of the head, though more deeply than before, as if he were making a point. Heunch, Runcie thought, bitterly resented being treated as a servant. The amber skullcap was lifted from Runcie's head with a staticky crackle, the 'scope pushed back, and Heunch shuffled from the room.

'Get out of the chair, Runcible,' said Thandimanilon, and stalked out.

Runcie pulled his hands from the gauntlets. She'd never called him Runcible before. What was the matter?

He climbed off the chair and sat on the stool beside Mariam. 'I'm feeling –'

'Don't talk to me!' Mariam said between her teeth.

His head snapped around. 'What's the matter now?'

'As if you don't know,' she said, 'sitting up there grinning like an ape and batting your eyelashes at her. Cooperating!'

Runcie had no idea why she was upset. 'I wouldn't know how to bat my eyelashes.'

'Magic got us into this trouble, and yet you're loving every minute of it. You're such a *child*, Runcie.'

On the mantelpiece, the ghost galleon crashed through a mighty wave. A thin wail reached Runcie's ears, then flying spray blotted out all but the tops of the masts. He tore his eyes away.

Heunch came back, followed by a slender, barefoot, black-eyed girl, smaller than Mariam, whose dark hair was scrunched up on either side of her head like twin balls of steel wool. She wore a loose blouse and culottes, both made of grey silk that rippled as she walked. Though slim as a reed, she had the hard muscles and conscious grace of an acrobat. She gave Runcie and Mariam a sad, faraway smile as she passed.

'Take the chair, Tigris,' said Heunch with a leering sideways glance at Runcie.

Tigris looked over at Runcie and Mariam, and said, 'Hel-lo,' in a tinkling voice.

'Hi,' said Runcie. Mariam nodded stiffly.

Tigris sat on the chair and slid her hands into the gauntlets. Thandimanilon burst through the door, climbed to the top of the vertical ladder and gestured to Heunch. He put on the fur mittens and rubbed the amber skullcap, but as he put it on Tigris's head there was a tremendous crackle and her hair stood out in all directions.

Heunch shuffled to the 'scope, drew it across and began to turn the discs. With another crackle, a mauve aura formed around Tigris then drifted towards the ceiling like steam, maintaining her shape all the way.

'Ah!' said Thandimanilon.

Heunch rotated the discs to one position after another. In some positions the aura disappeared, while in others it grew so strong that Tigris vanished behind it. Finally Thandimanilon said, 'It's working perfectly. You may go, Tigris.'

The girl, with another sad, faraway smile, went out. Runcie could hardly breathe. He didn't want to think about what it meant.

Thandimanilon stalked across and stood glaring down at Runcie. 'Back in the chair, Runcible!'

Runcie scrambled onto the amber chair and slipped his hands into the gauntlets. They felt cold and clammy now. Heunch rubbed the skullcap and put it on Runcie's head. The crackle was faint. He glanced sideways at Thandimanilon. His heart was beating so hard that it was a wonder it didn't burst out through his ribs.

As the discs turned, Thandimanilon made a clicking sound with her tongue. And then Runcie heard faint, mocking laughter, coming from the chair itself.

'Get down, Runcible!' said Thandimanilon sharply.

Ha ha ha! said the chair. *Serves you right, you presumptuous little villain. How dare you sit on* me *and pretend to have talent.*

The skullcap was lifted off; the amber jerked away from the back of his neck. Runcie's heart wasn't pounding now. It hardly seemed to be beating at all. He crept over to sit beside Mariam, who avoided his eye.

Thandimanilon swept across to stare at them, tapping one elegantly shod foot. 'The boy has no talent at all.'

'Not a skerrick, Dark Lady,' said Heunch. 'The 'scope never lies.'

'Then how did he trigger the parchment?'

Heunch didn't reply. Runcie felt all his hopes and dreams

come crashing down. He wanted to scream, *No, I did it, I did it.* He stared at the floor.

'He can't have.' Thandimanilon scrutinised Mariam, glanced at Runcie dismissively, then turned back to Mariam. 'Can *she* be the one?'

Again Heunch said nothing.

'You, Mariam,' said Thandimanilon. 'Go to the amber chair.'

Runcie looked pleadingly at her, as if to say, *Tell them it was me,* but Mariam was staring straight ahead, her jaw clenched. Without a word, she went to the chair, climbed onto it and sat there stiffly.

She's really pleased, Runcie thought. She wanted me to fail. What a rotten little sneak she is. Though even as he had that thought, he knew it wasn't right.

'Put your hands in the gauntlets,' said Thandimanilon.

Mariam looked as if she were trying to stare through the wall. The knot in her jaw was bigger than before, and her chin was trembling.

'Gauntlets!' snapped Thandimanilon.

Mariam slowly slipped her hands into the amber gauntlets, which took on a darker glow. Heunch rubbed the skullcap, raised it high, then began to lower it onto Mariam's head. There was no static as it went down, no sparks as it settled on her curly hair, which shone blue-black in the light. Heunch exchanged another of those twisted glances with Thandimanilon, who pursed her lips.

He began to rub the chair with his mittens. Shortly Thandimanilon beckoned him to the 'scope and climbed the ladder. She looked down through the eyepiece as Heunch rotated the top disc to one position after another.

Nothing happened. Runcie realised that he was holding his breath. He let it out slowly as Heunch began to rotate the second disc. Again nothing.

'Do you want me to go on, Dark Lady?' he said.

After a long hesitation, she said, 'To the very end.'

Heunch kept on, but no aura appeared. Runcie's heart began to beat again. Of course it hadn't been Mariam. They'd do his tests again and discover just how powerful his talent was. They must!

Heunch was rotating the last disc quickly now, *Whirr-click, whirr-click.* Nearly done. Runcie was about to come to his feet when, on the third last position, the amber chair emitted a faint gleam, though he didn't see the least trace of aura around Mariam. Heunch kept going, *whirr-click, whirr-click,* then stopped.

'Go back,' said Thandimanilon.

'Dark Lady?' he said, puzzled.

'To the third-last position, fool.'

Again that resentful look, but Heunch *whirr-clicked* back. And then the whole chair began to glow, the amber skullcap too, until they became like liquid, flowing gold. Mariam screwed up her eyes, though not in time to prevent a tear leaking out.

'Ahhh!' sighed Heunch.

'Indeed,' said Thandimanilon. 'It was her after all, and such an *unusual* talent – a Re-sighter. That's why she can see my previous semblance. She's the one we've been searching for all this time, Heunch. And if she can find . . . *the place*, we Cybale will rise again, stronger than ever. Do we know the Re-sighting spell?'

'It's long forgotten, Dark Lady.'

She clapped her hands crossly. 'We'll have to recreate it, and that could take ages. Mariam?' she said kindly.

Mariam's olive skin had gone a sickly shade of green. What did Thandimanilon mean? Why was Mariam the one they'd been searching for? What place was she going to find for them, and what would happen if the Cybale did rise again? Runcie could hardly breathe – already their arrival was changing Iltior and he didn't think it was for the good.

'Yes?' whispered Mariam hoarsely.

'You can get down now.'

Heunch took away the skullcap. Thandimanilon climbed down the ladder as Mariam trudged back to Runcie, staring at the floor. She did not meet his eyes. She was still trembling.

'What about the boy?' said Heunch.

Thandimanilon glided across, gnawing her lip. How beautiful she was. She did seem to care, and he remembered how she'd comforted him in the night. 'He's no use to us,' she said after a long pause. 'What are we to do?'

Heunch didn't reply, for she was speaking to herself. 'I'm sorry, Runcie,' she went on, 'but pretending to be something you're not is never a good idea. What do we call that, Heunch?'

'Fraud,' said Heunch. 'Attempting to gain a benefit by false pretences.' He looked almost as sorrowful as she did.

'But –' cried Runcie. 'But I didn't, truly –'

'Runcie, Runcie.' She shook her red ringlets into a cloud around her face, lifted him to his feet and hugged him, and he felt that wonderful warm, protected feeling again. 'I'm sorry. I like you, I really do.' Impulsively, she pulled the engraved silver bracelet from her left wrist and fastened it around his. 'Take this for your trouble. I've had it for many years and it's precious to me but . . . just take it.'

The bracelet, scribed with intricate patterns that moved and flowed before his eyes, was utterly lovely. Runcie slid it up and down his wrist, took it off and put it on again. He'd never owned anything beautiful before.

'It's too much,' he said, having no idea what was going on, but thinking that Ansie would be so disappointed in him. 'I didn't do anything.'

'Better to err on the side of generosity than meanness.' She turned to Heunch.

'Yes, Dark Lady?' said Heunch.

'Throw him out,' said Thandimanilon.

CHAPTER 11

Sleeping in the Muck

Runcie, frozen by horror, sat there holding the bracelet while Heunch put away the ladder and hauled the 'scope back to the corner, where he covered it with its dust cloth. And then he turned to Runcie.

'Come with me, lad.'

'But you were going to send me home.' Runcie looked around for help. Mariam, still staring at the floor, didn't seem to have noticed.

'You cheated and you can't pay,' said Heunch.

Runcie tore off the bracelet. 'Take this, please.'

Thandimanilon's face went purple. The white panther growled and Heunch crushed the bracelet against Runcie's wrist. 'You dare offer my master's gift *in payment of a debt*! That's a mortal insult, boy.'

Mariam roused at the commotion. 'What are you doing?' she said shrilly.

'Runcible has no talent,' said Thandimanilon. 'He can't stay here.'

'Then I'm going with him.' Mariam stood up so abruptly that her stool crashed against the wall.

'You have to repay me first.'

'You can go to hell.' Snatching up the stool, Mariam ran at Heunch.

Thandimanilon snapped her fingers and in an instant Mariam had drooped like melting wax. Only her eyes moved, and Runcie saw something terrible there as Heunch led him away. Runcie struggled but there was magic as well as strength in Heunch's grip and Runcie couldn't fight either.

Heunch took him to an outside landing, from which an iron staircase curved down into mist-streaked nothingness. The next few minutes were just a blur of steep, mossy steps and wind-whipped mist. And then Runcie saw his end. The ground was not in sight – the stair simply stopped in mid-flight. Thandimanilon must have ordered Heunch to throw him off.

'No!' Runcie gasped, trying to pull away, and his sweaty wrist slipped free. He pushed Heunch hard in the chest, his feet flew from under him and he went down with a thud that shook the stairs. Runcie ran for his life.

He was halfway up to the next landing when Heunch roared, 'Putty Patellas, Puny Pipsqueak!' and Runcie fell, bouncing on his backside down every step. He tried to get up but his knee-caps had gone as squishy as plasticine.

Lifting him up, Heunch proceeded to the last tread and there, to Runcie's utter, gut-crawling horror, swung him back and forth, once and twice. This was it. He was going to die. He closed his eyes as Heunch swung him a third time, then tossed him hard.

But Heunch turned at the last minute and Runcie shot towards the tower. His eyes came open, a slimy hole appeared before him, like a funnel passing down inside the stone wall, and he flew into it. There was nothing to catch onto; the stone was too slippery. He dropped headfirst through a clot of goo as thick and clinging as the contents of a giant's nostril, then slid into a twisting hole coated with the same repulsive ooze. It had just enough drag to stop him breaking the sound barrier as he fell.

He hurtled through a soapy bubble, which burst in cold trickles down his cheeks. On the other side there was a smell like rotten eggs. Runcie plunged through a second bubble, was whirled around until his brains were spinning in his head, then shot out the lower end of the hole and landed face down in something soft and stinky. Air escaped from the hole in a series of farts, as if the very tower was mocking his failure. And maybe it was.

Runcie stung all over, though at least his kneecaps had set again. He spat out something with the slippery texture of onion peel and wiped muck off his face. He was lying on a mound as big as a house; an enormous compost heap with stone walls on either side. It was gloomy down here and green vapours drifted up to join the mists wreathing through the trunks of giant trees. He couldn't see their tops.

His feet sank through decaying vegetables as he got up, squelched down to solid ground and looked back. The lower

part of the tower was solid stone with not a door or window anywhere. He couldn't even see the hole he'd fallen from.

Runcie didn't understand. Thandimanilon had been so
kind, comforting him in the night and giving him the beautiful
bracelet. He looked down, expecting it to have disappeared
like a fairy gift, but it was as solid as ever. Throwing him out
made no sense, unless it was another test. Yes, it had to be. She
expected him to find the way back in by himself.

Well, he'd always been good at tests. Feeling better, he began
to pick his way around the tower, though that proved harder
than expected. There were drifts of snow in the hollows, and in
places nothing lay below the walls but sheer cliffs of icy rock. It
took him hours to scramble all the way around, and by the time
he'd reached the compost heap again he'd found neither door
nor window, path nor footprint.

If it *was* a test, he'd failed it, and he was all alone in a deadly
world he knew nothing about. What was he to do? He tried to
recall what he'd seen as the transportal approached – just
mountains, forest, a volcano and ice in the distance. Apart from
the fairytale castle there hadn't been a light anywhere. Unfortunately, Runcie didn't know in which direction the castle lay,
though he suspected it was a long way off.

At the edge of the forest he found a trickle running out of a
split rock. After washing his face and hands, he had a drink.
The water was so cold that it hurt his teeth, but as refreshing as
lemonade.

He circled the tower again, through the forest this time,

looking for a path, road or any kind of building. By the time he'd returned to his starting point it was late afternoon and cold, but he had found nothing. The forest looked as though it had been here forever, and his footprints the first sign that any human had ever trod through it. Runcie sat down with his back to one of the trees, pulled his jacket around him and stared miserably at the compost heap. There was a depression near the left-hand wall, as if wild pigs had rooted there.

It would be dark soon, and all kinds of dangerous creatures must hunt on this mountaintop at night. Runcie couldn't defend himself against anything bigger than a dog, so he'd better find somewhere to hide. He headed into the forest but the trees had towering trunks without a handhold in the first thirty or forty feet. His stomach rumbled. It felt like a week since he'd last eaten. He pressed on, looking back all the time. He dared not lose sight of the tower, for Mariam was the only friend he had.

He couldn't work her out. She'd made out that she was afraid of magic, and all the time she could do it brilliantly. Why couldn't *I* be the talented one, he thought with a trace of resentment.

No, that was mean. Mariam had looked really scared. And why wouldn't she be? Thandimanilon was going to force her to use magic, to help the Cybale rise again, whoever they were.

He missed Mariam, too. She'd know what to do here, and he couldn't bear being so alone. He sat down on a cold rock and groaned. Iltior seemed as much against him as his own world.

'Whissi yar?' said an amused voice.

Runcie spun around. 'Who's there?' He couldn't keep the fear out of his voice.

With a snort of derision, a boy appeared, a year or two older than Runcie. He was clad in brown, cast-off clothing – a loose blouse, a man's big sleeveless jerkin that came down to mid-thigh, and baggy trousers torn off at the knees. They were three sizes too large and held in place by a tarry length of rope. His bare feet were filthy, as were his face, hands and neck, but he wore his rags with pride.

'Hello?' Runcie said tentatively.

'Who are you?' the boy said in a nasal accent. His tangled brown hair, which was clotted with burrs and bits of yellow straw, had a white lock at the left temple. His eyes were a darker brown, his nose blobby and his mouth wide but twisted.

'Runcible Jones,' said Runcie, wrapping his arms around himself in a feeble attempt to keep warm. 'But everyone calls me Runcie.'

'What are you doing here?'

'Thandimanilon threw me out of her tower. She tested me for magic and I failed.'

'Failed?' said the boy, incredulously. 'At what?'

'Everything,' said Runcie. 'I don't have any ability.'

The boy looked him up and down, lip curling, as if such a thing wasn't possible.

'You can't do magic at all?'

'None whatsoever,' Runcie said miserably. The only talent

he had, if you could call it one, was seeing lights and colours when strong magic was used nearby. But what use was that – he couldn't do a thing with it. Losing his dream of magic was almost as bad as being marooned here.

The boy snapped his fingers and blue fire appeared from his fingertips, lighting up the space between them. 'Even my baby sister can make cold fire. No wonder the Dark Lady threw you out.' He came closer. 'You're useless.' He laughed. *'Completely* useless.'

'What's your name?' said Runcie, to change the subject.

'Jac Sleeth,' said the grinning boy, who had a rich, earthy smell.

'Do I call you Jac?' Runcie said politely.

'Certainly not! We're not friends. You call me Sleeth.'

'Er, okay. What are you doing here, Sleeth?' Using his last name sounded wrong.

'I live here.'

'In the tower?'

'No, *here.*' Sleeth pointed towards the compost heap.

'But that's disgusting,' said Runcie. It explained the state of the boy's clothing, and his smell.

'Where are *you* going to sleep tonight?' said Sleeth. 'Leopards hunt in these mountains, and panthers hunt the leopards. And tiger cats –'

'I get the picture,' snapped Runcie. 'I don't know where I'm going to sleep, but it certainly won't be on top of a compost heap.'

'Not on top,' Sleeth sneered. '*Inside* it, of course, where it's warm and safe.'

He sauntered away, not looking back. It was nearly dark now, and the mist was looping and coiling between the trees as if it had a purpose in mind, and not a good one. This whole world was more *alive.*

A ragged howl floated down the ridge. It wasn't the call of a wolf, but something more savage and relentless. Runcie turned around, stamping his feet and blowing on his hands, but neither made any difference to the cold that was steadily creeping over him. There was nothing for it but the compost heap, if Sleeth would let him in.

As Runcie set off, the howl came again, closer, and it was answered by a higher call. Looking over his shoulder as he walked, he tripped and slid down a bank into a drift of snow. He got up, rubbing it out of his eyes, and continued, but fell into deeper snow. Icy particles slid inside his socks and every snowflake made its own freezing pattern on his skin. He tramped back but couldn't find the bank. Now Runcie felt like an idiot. He turned the other way, but there was no bank in front of him either.

A screech echoed down the slope, rebounding eerily off the unseen wall of the tower, then another cry, even closer. He panicked and ran, knowing it was the worst thing he could do but unable to stop himself. Again came the answering, high-pitched cry – they weren't far away. Pounding through the dark, he crashed into a tree and was knocked off his feet.

Hot blood dripped from his earlobe onto his neck, and his chest and right hip throbbed. Runcie didn't go on, for this was as good a place as any to make his last stand. His groping hand came down on a fallen branch, so he huddled in the angle of the tree's roots, holding the flimsy weapon out and knowing he was going to die. Would the beasts kill him first, or eat him alive?

'What *are* you doing?' Sleeth's voice was a mixture of sarcasm and incredulity.

'I ran into the tree,' said Runcie. 'I was lost.'

'But you could hit the tower with a stone from here.'

Runcie didn't say anything. He felt too stupid.

'Oh, come on,' sighed Sleeth. 'Follow me.'

'I can't see you,' said Runcie.

Sleeth conjured blue ghost-light from his fingertips. 'I forgot you don't have any magic,' he said with that twisted grin.

He hadn't forgotten at all. Sleeth just wanted to rub it in.

'How are you going to get inside?' Runcie said as they approached the heap.

Sleeth went down on his hands and knees, scooping away the rotting scraps and mouldy bones to reveal a piece of timber. He dragged it out of the way, pointed his glowing hand, and Runcie saw a winding tunnel barely wider than his shoulders. The vast weight of compost was held up by boards and flimsy props, dangerously angled. Something howled in the forest but he didn't move. If he knocked a prop out, tons of rotting compost would fall in and suffocate him.

'Can't you keep them away with magic?' he said with a shudder.

'Big cats have their own magic and even if it's your mindsake you have to be careful. *Listen!*' Sleeth wasn't joking this time. 'Did you hear that?'

The howl had sounded really close. Runcie went down on his belly and wriggled inside. His knee dragged through a puddle of green seepage and the stink went with him. He eased past the first prop, then the second, holding his breath. It was warm here. Ahead the tunnel took a sharp turn to the left. He crawled around the corner into darkness, and everything he touched felt slimy.

His hand struck a prop and something splatted on the back of his neck. Runcie scraped it off, turned side-on and eased around the prop. One shoulder bumped it, then his knee, delivering another disgusting splat, but the prop held.

Rays of light streaked around the corner as Sleeth followed. Ahead, the tunnel opened out to the area of a dining table, and high enough that he could sit up with his head bent. Half-rotten timbers curved above him to form a vault supported by a line of spindly props.

He found a place to sit, out of the line of drips coming between the timbers. It was really warm here, so he took off his jacket and put it on the cleanest patch of floor. It didn't smell so bad now – the compost had a humid, earthy aroma.

'It must have taken you ages to make this,' said Runcie.

Sleeth just shrugged.

'Er, Sleeth?' Runcie said after a long silence.

Sleeth was sitting with his legs crossed, making a complicated series of movements with a stubby wand rudely carved from yellow bone. Runcie got the impression that he was practising another kind of magic, though nothing came of it. Sleeth scowled and began again.

'Sleeth?' Runcie repeated.

'What is it?' the boy snapped.

'I don't suppose you've got anything to eat? I'm starving.'

Sleeth pulled a filthy length of sausage out of a baggy wallet hanging from his belt. It was like a long squishy salami, though a horrible yellow-green colour. He twisted off a quarter and tossed it at Runcie.

He caught it, raised it halfway to his mouth and gagged. He'd never smelt anything so revolting; the fumes were making his eyes water. 'Are you sure it's not off?' Runcie gasped.

Sleeth bit off a small segment and chewed it with gusto. 'It's made that way. It smells bad but tastes beautiful. I got it from the Dark Lady's pantry.'

Runcie's head jerked up. 'How did you get inside?'

Sleeth looked shifty. 'She, er, took me in, a long time ago.'

'Really?' said Runcie disbelievingly. 'What for?'

Sleeth gave an odd twitch of the left shoulder, as if to say, 'Mind your own business.' He took another bite, chewing with his mouth agape.

'It was to test you for magic, wasn't it?' Runcie guessed. Again that twitch. 'And she threw you out. You don't have any magic either.'

Sleeth snorted and flicked his glowing fingers in Runcie's face.

'Or not enough,' said Runcie.

'I've got plenty of magic,' Sleeth snarled. 'I'm the best prentice in the world.'

'Yeah, right,' said Runcie. 'That's why you're living in this stinking hole.'

'I am the best. *I am!*' Sleeth turned away.

Runcie stared at the boy's dirty neck. 'Why did she throw you out?'

'She called me a thief and a liar,' said Sleeth quietly. 'Good night!' He thrust the rest of the sausage back in his wallet, rolled over and pillowed his head on his arms. The light from his fingertips went out and it became as black as pitch.

Runcie lifted the sausage to his nose but, in the dark, its smell was even worse. He put it in his pocket and curled up on the floor, pillowing his head on his coat. He felt exhausted but his mind was churning. One minute Thandimanilon had been kind and caring, the next she'd thrown him out like a piece of rubbish. Why? And what might Sleeth, a self-confessed liar and thief, do in the middle of the night?

There was no answer, so he went back to the useless plan. Even if he got away, where could he go and whom could he trust? He could ask Sleeth, but could he believe anything Sleeth told him? Runcie agonised about that until growling sounds outside gave him something else to worry about. When he drifted off to sleep hours later, his dreams were even more troubled.

He woke several times to see Sleeth sitting up, fingers lit by pale fire, practising his magic with what seemed like increasing desperation. He didn't look proud now. His shoulders were slumped, his mouth downcast, and the pale lock of hair drooped like a white flag.

'What's the matter with you, boy?' Sleeth said in a high, cracked voice, not his own. 'Are you lazy, or don't you care?'

After some minutes an image appeared in the air, a white-haired man lying in bed, face racked with pain. A woman sat beside him, weeping as she spooned potion into his mouth. Sleeth choked, wiped away tears of frustration and worked his fingers ever more furiously.

Runcie must have moved, for Sleeth's head whipped around and the finger-light went out. Runcie was too exhausted to wonder about it.

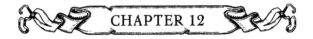

CHAPTER 12

Rat Cunning

When Runcie roused, Sleeth had gone and the space was lit by daylight. Feeling weak from hunger, he settled against the wall and inspected his sausage. It looked like something a camel might have thrown up. How could Sleeth eat such a thing? Because he was a low, filthy brute. And how long before I'm just as low? Runcie thought ruefully.

After wiping the dirt off, he smelled his fingers. The stench didn't seem quite so horrible now, so he held his nose and brought the sausage up to his mouth. Urk! It was too revolting. But he was *so* hungry. I'll just try a teeny bit, he thought. Even if it has gone off, that much can't do any harm. He bit off a small piece. The smell went up his nose, his stomach heaved, but then the taste flooded his mouth and it was the most delicious thing he'd ever eaten, even better than Thandimanilon's wonderful dinner. He took another small bite. This time the smell didn't seem nearly as bad and the flavour was even better.

He was just finishing the last piece when Sleeth wriggled in, carrying a gourd of water which he passed to Runcie. He offered another segment of sausage, though now Runcie was no longer hungry it smelled revolting again. Sleeth closed the door, leaned back against the wall and began to weave cold fire with his fingertips.

Runcie's interest in magic rekindled. Even if he couldn't do it, he was going to take every opportunity to find out about it, starting now. He watched the boy's thick, dirty fingers dance, weaving light into a scene set between the trunks of giant trees. There was snow on the ground, which he made with just a flicker of his index finger. Several angled movements created a pile of sticks in a stone hearth; a snap of finger and thumb set them ablaze. A boy appeared, approaching the fire warily. He looked disturbingly like Runcie; no, a caricature of him, his honey-coloured hair wilder and yellower, his nose longer, his chin more pointed.

The boy settled down by the fire. Runcie was staring at his image in wonder when a pair of eyes appeared in the forest, reflecting the firelight redly. He caught his breath, but the boy, his mouth as round as an O, screamed silently, ran into the forest and crashed into a tree. Sleeth chuckled; the image disappeared.

He was being mocked. 'How did you do that?' said Runcie, entranced and annoyed in equal measure.

'It's just finger-magic. I can do it in my sleep. What's your mindsake?'

That word again. 'What do you mean?' said Runcie.

'Your *mindsake*,' said Sleeth, as if reminding someone

extremely stupid of what was blindingly obvious. 'Even people who can't do *any* magic have a mindsake.'

'I don't know what you're talking about.'

Sleeth pursed his lips and made a squeaking click, then sat back with the superior smile Runcie found so hard to take. How could this filthy urchin feel superior to him? But of course, he was just as filthy. And he couldn't do magic.

A movement caught the light in a gap between the timbers on the far wall, then a long snout poked out, with a set of black whiskers. The head turned this way and that, a pair of dark eyes catching the residual light clinging to Sleeth's fingers. A large rat sprang onto the floor and scurried across to Sleeth's lap, where it began to sniff around.

Sleeth scratched it behind the ears, reached into his wallet and brought out a generous piece of sausage. The rat took it delicately, nodded to the boy then walked away, giving Runcie a measured stare before it disappeared through the boards, its long brown tail waving.

'Is that your pet?' said Runcie.

Sleeth launched himself through the air, knocked Runcie down into a noxious pool of seepage and snarled, 'How dare you! It's my *mindsake*.' He banged Runcie's head into the floor a couple of times, then let him go and went back to his former position. The cold fire wove up from his fingertips again. Sleeth looked perfectly calm, save that his dirty face was red.

Runcie got up. Clearly, a mindsake was *not* a pet. 'I'm sorry,' he said, rubbing the back of his head. 'I don't have a mindsake, whatever it is. No one does, where I come from.' Runcie added, in a wistful voice, 'It looked like you were friends.'

'It's not a friend either,' said Sleeth. 'Well, a mindsake *can* be, but for me it's a companion, a guide and an advisor wherever I go.'

'Do you take – does it go with you, then?'

Sleeth just shook his head, as if astonished that anyone could be so ignorant. 'It's a *mindsake*,' he repeated. 'Your mindsake is summoned for you on the first midwinter day after your fifth birthday. At least, that's how it usually happens . . .'

'Is that how you got yours?' said Runcie.

Sleeth was staring dreamily into space. 'I was only three when I first saw mine,' he said softly. 'But I wanted it so desperately, after . . .' He clenched his jaw.

'Yes?' said Runcie.

'I summoned it on my fifth birthday, all by myself. Not many people can say that.'

'So a mindsake isn't a particular animal but a *kind* of animal.'

'Of course. My mindsake is the rat. But not just any old rat – it's the long-tailed bush rat. Barn rats or tree rats or city rats won't answer my call – there's no bond between us.'

'And wherever you are, you can call your mindsake and it will come?'

'The nearest one will, if it's not doing something more important.'

'You mean it doesn't *have* to come?'

'Of course not,' Sleeth said scathingly. 'It's not a compulsion; it's a bond of fellowship. Companions and friends know what they can ask of each other. Not like you and me. Assuming we *were* friends, I mean.'

'I'm glad we sorted that out,' Runcie said sarcastically.

'Mindsakes help each other, where they can. It's like comradeship and support and comfort all rolled into one.' He looked steadily at Runcie. 'You must be so lonely.'

'Since I've never had a mindsake, I don't miss it.' But how wonderful it would be to have such a companion. The Nightingales wouldn't let him have a pet and he'd often felt abandoned. 'Can you talk to your mindsake?'

'Only great magicians can do that. But one day . . .' A dreamy expression crossed Sleeth's face.

'Do great magicians have a powerful animal for their mindsake?'

'Some do, but you can never tell what mindsake is going to be summoned for you, or even if it'll *fit*. Thandimanilon's is the white panther, and it's perfect for her. Old Gryffyth the Wise had a giant sloth, but he couldn't get it to come down out of its tree.' Sleeth looked through Runcie, his thoughts far away. 'It never did anything for him, but some mindsakes are like that.'

'What's Parsifoe's?' Runcie was still worrying that he'd made the wrong choice.

Sleeth shrugged. 'Cockroach? Slug? Earthworm?'

'Don't you like her?'

'She's not a very good wizard,' he said as if nothing else mattered.

'But is she a bad person, like Thandimanilon?'

'Not particularly.'

It didn't help. Runcie looked up as the rat, or another just like it, poked its snout out between the boards and twitched its whiskers. 'How do you call it?' Runcie said.

'With mindsake magic,' said Sleeth. '*You* couldn't understand.'

Runcie turned away abruptly. None of the things he was good at, like reading and computers and exams, were any use on Iltior. Not like Mariam! He wondered if Thandimanilon had begun Mariam's training already, and what place she was supposed to find that was so important. He was really worried about her now.

'Is Thandimanilon a kind of schoolteacher in magic?'

Sleeth scowled. 'She's the Dark Lady of the Cybale, and she's really *wicked*.' He said it with immense zest. 'But very beautiful.'

'I suppose it's okay to be evil if you're beautiful,' Runcie sneered.

'The Dark Lady isn't *evil*,' cried Sleeth, shocked. 'She's *wicked*, I said.'

'What's the difference?'

'Evil is doing bad things to hurt other people. Wicked is – well, it just *is*. Wicked people love what they're doing so much that they get carried away.'

'It's funny,' said Runcie. 'Thandimanilon lied to me, tricked me and threw me out, yet I don't hate her for it. She gave me this bracelet . . .' He turned it on his wrist.

'You can't help liking wicked people, despite what they do,' said Sleeth, giving the bracelet a covetous glance. 'Anyway, it *is* all right to be wicked if you're beautiful.'

'So on Iltior I should only trust ugly people?'

'You're so thick! Ugly people really *are* evil,' said Sleeth. 'Well, a lot of them are.' He peered at Runcie in the dim light. 'In your case, ugliness just means stupidity.'

Runcie had to restrain himself from hitting Sleeth. 'I'm *not* stupid. Anyway, you're the one who's living at the bottom of a stinking compost heap.'

'True,' said Sleeth, frowning. 'But one day, after I've done my duty, I'll be even more powerful and wicked than the Dark Lady.' He grinned at the prospect.

A chill settled over Runcie and he couldn't shake it off.

'And in the meantime,' Sleeth went on, 'I'm free and I've got a wallet full of Gorbal's Premium Sausage from her private pantry. What more could anyone want?' He twisted a length of sausage in two and handed the smaller half to Runcie. 'Friends?'

Sleeth changed like a chameleon, but Runcie desperately needed a friend who knew what was going on. He bit off a chunk of sausage, breathing out, and revelled in the glorious taste until every skerrick was gone.

Then he began to fret about Mariam again. Thandimanilon

was planning to use her for something bad, he knew it. 'Sleeth?' he said.

'Yes?'

Sleeth was chewing with his mouth open and his gob looked like a cement mixer full of ground-up food and strings of saliva. His fingers were moving in his lap. Did he never stop practising? 'You didn't tell me why Thandimanilon is training kids in magic.'

'Who knows? The Cybale are always plotting against someone.' Sleeth licked his dirty fingers.

'Who are the Cybale anyway?'

'They enslaved the whole world in ancient times, and they want to take it over again, but they can't.'

'Why not?'

'They lost their best magic ages ago, and don't have the power.'

'And Thandimanilon is the boss of the Cybale?' asked Runcie.

'Along with her sorcerer friend, Lars Sparj.'

'Is he wicked too?'

'No, he's just cold, angry and cruel. Keep well away from him, Runcie.'

'Don't worry. I will,' said Runcie. Then another thought occurred to him. 'Why does Thandimanilon want all those prentices, anyway? What good would kids be against adults?'

Sleeth rolled his eyes. 'You have to learn magic as a child or you can never be fluent at it. Once you're grown-up, it's too late.'

'Surely you're not saying that grown-ups can't use magic?' said Runcie. 'Thandimanilon –'

'Of course they can use it, much better and stronger than kids can. But grown-ups can't *learn* new kinds of magic very well. You have to start when you're little. After Father was –' Sleeth broke off, blinking. 'Mother spoke magic to me every day, before I was even born.'

'I don't suppose her prentices are in any danger, though,' said Runcie after a pause.

'Of course they are,' Sleeth said scornfully. 'They might all be killed, and Thandimanilon too.'

'Killed?' squeaked Runcie. 'But she's got my friend, Mariam.'

'Ooh!' grinned Sleeth. 'How'd an ugly little rat like you get a *girlfriend?*'

'She's not my girlfriend,' said Runcie, flushing and feeling annoyed about it. 'Mariam saved me from being beaten up by a gang of bullies. Twice.'

'Why didn't you say so?' said Sleeth. 'That's different, even if she is a girl.'

'I just did – oh, never mind. I've got to get her out of there.' The first stage of his new plan, rescuing Mariam, still seemed impossible. Runcie suppressed the thought that she might come to enjoy learning magic in Miluviand. If it were him . . .

'There's no way to get inside,' said Sleeth, and momentarily Runcie saw the despair of last night, though Sleeth quickly put on his normal face. 'I've already looked.'

'Then how did you get the sausage?' Runcie was sure he'd caught Sleeth in a lie.

'I stole it just before the Dark Lady threw me out.' Sleeth tore off another chunk of Gorbal's Premium Sausage and chewed it with open-mouthed gusto.

'We've got to find a way in,' said Runcie.

'I don't have to do anything –' Sleeth broke off, looking thoughtful. After working his fingers furiously for a while, he gave Runcie a sly glance from under his lashes. 'Why should I help you?'

'You said we were friends,' said Runcie.

'So I did.' Sleeth wiped a sausagy dribble off his chin, leaving a clean streak through the grime. 'And it would be an adventure, breaking into the Dark Lady's tower.' He gave Runcie another cunning glance. 'But of course, she'll torture us *cruelly* if she catches us. Anyway, I can't get inside.'

Runcie gulped, but he had to get Mariam out. 'There must be a way, surely?'

'Oh, there's a secret way all right, but it's too well protected.'

Runcie's gaze wandered across the sagging boards. Something moved behind one of the gaps and he had an idea. 'I'll bet a clever bush rat would be able to find a way in.'

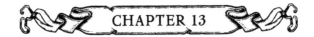

Memory Bubbles

'You'll have to pay,' said Sleeth.

'In what – cheese?' Runcie thought he was being funny.

The next second he was on his back and Sleeth was banging his head on the floor again. 'What did I say?' cried Runcie.

Sleeth banged his head a few more times to reinforce the point, whatever it was, then went back to his finger-magic, glaring at Runcie whenever he thought of it.

'I thought we were friends,' said Runcie after he'd recovered.

'You don't joke about people's mindsakes.'

'I'm sorry. I can't pay you anyway. I haven't got any money.'

Sleeth's gaze shifted to the bracelet. 'I'll have that.'

'But it's all I have,' Runcie said plaintively.

He rotated the bracelet on his wrist. It was the only precious thing he'd ever owned. Sleeth's eyes were glued to it, and they were hungry, desperate eyes, but Runcie couldn't bear to give it up. 'Can we check on Mariam first?'

'All right,' said Sleeth, 'but you've got to pay for that, anyway.' He held out his dirty hand.

*

That afternoon, the rat slipped out of Sleeth's pocket and stood on his right knee, its long tail outstretched. Sleeth began to groom it with a rudely carved wooden comb, running it carefully down the rat's back and examining the teeth after each stroke. With a careful finger, he eased something onto a bowl-shaped leaf and combed the rat again. What *was* he doing?

After some minutes, Sleeth scratched his mindsake behind the ears and gave it a red nut. The rat stood up on its back legs, holding the nut in its front paws. With a ratty nod it turned away, walking on its back legs until it was past Runcie. Turning its long head, it gave him a proud stare before scuttling into its hole.

Sleeth held the leaf close to his eye, picking out a number of motes which, after a glance at Runcie, he palmed and surreptitiously transferred to his pocket. He arranged the rest in a line.

'What are you doing?' said Runcie.

'Organising my memory bubbles, *of course.*'

'What are memory bubbles?'

'Do I have to explain everything? They capture moments of time.'

'How did they get there?'

'I put them in my mindsake's fur and it found a ratty way into Thandimanilon's tower, where it rubbed the bubbles off.'

'How does that help?'

'The bubbles slowly set,' Sleeth said in exasperation, 'and when they do, a picture of the place freezes into them.'

'Really?' Runcie moved closer, staring at the bubbles, but could see only coloured patterns, like an oil slick. 'I can't see any pictures.'

'You have to blow them up first,' Sleeth said as though Runcie were an idiot.

Runcie sighed. On Iltior, he *was* an idiot.

Sleeth picked a tiny straw from behind his ear and poked the first bubble. Runcie edged closer. The bubble slipped out of the way, and again on the second attempt, though the next time the straw slid through it. Sleeth put his lips to the other end and blew the tiniest of breaths.

Runcie watched, fascinated, as the bubble expanded and the coloured lines unfolded to become a picture that he recognised at once. It was the girls dormitory, though all he could see were the legs of the six-poster beds stretching into the distance.

Sleeth puffed until the bubble burst. 'Sometimes you don't see much.'

'Perhaps if your mindsake was a spider –' Runcie didn't finish, afraid that Sleeth would be insulted and attack him again.

Sleeth shuddered. 'The Night Stalkers have spiders for their mindsakes. They're the mark of evil.'

Runcie's skin prickled. 'Who are the Night Stalkers?'

Sleeth opened his mouth, then snapped it shut. 'I can't tell *you* that.' He licked the end of the straw and poked it into the next bubble. It showed part of the testing room, including the amber chair, but the room was empty.

'Can anyone make memory bubbles?'

'Certainly not. The spell is known only to sorcerers.'

'Are there different kinds of magic, then?'

'Of course,' said Sleeth. 'Dozens of kinds, and a guild for each. You have to be in a guild to learn its most important secrets.'

'But you said your baby sister could make cold fire.' Runcie was finding it hard to get a grip on what magic was.

'Everyone can do that, but real magic has to be taught.'

'Are you in the sorcerer's guild?' said Runcie.

'No, I'm only a prentice. I would have been admitted when my training was finished . . .'

'So you're not a sorcerer at all?'

Sleeth laughed hollowly. 'Kids can't be any kind of magician. But I can do more magic than any prentice my age.'

Runcie found that hard to believe. And yet, Sleeth *did* seem to know an awful lot about magic. 'If we find a way in, what's to stop Thandimanilon catching us?'

'She goes to bed at ten in the evening and doesn't get up until after sunrise.'

'Ten o'clock!' exclaimed Runcie.

'She's frail,' said Sleeth. 'And everyone loves her all the more for it. She works her wicked magic even though she can't stand up afterwards.'

'What about Heunch?'

'He sleeps on the rack.'

'Really?' said Runcie. It was so fascinatingly medieval.

'Heunch was once a great lord, until an enemy cast a terrible spell on him that not even Thandimanilon could remove.

At least, she removed it three times but it kept coming back. Heunch had to indenture himself to her in repayment.'

'He seemed angry about something.'

'He can't bear to be a servant, but he's loyal enough. He stretches himself on the rack every night to ease the pain. It takes him ages to loosen the chains and shackles, and unwind the rack afterwards. He's too proud to ask for help, so he can't harm us.'

Sleeth blew up the next bubble to the size of an orange. 'Spit in your hand.'

'What?'

'Do you want the memory bubble or not?'

Runcie spat in his palm, rubbed it around with a fingertip and held out his hand. Sleeth deposited the bubble on the wet patch, withdrawing the straw with a swift flick. Runcie brought the bubble up to his face, then caught his breath.

The colours swirled and shifted, and he felt the shivery feeling of magic in his hand. If only he could do it. He turned the bubble and Thandimanilon was reflected there, but far more lifelike than a photo – he half expected her to walk onto his palm. She stood, tall and beautiful, with an elegant wizard's baton in her left hand, leaning forward as if speaking to someone. Runcie had to turn his hand to see who it was.

Mariam was looking at something shining through the bubble – a series of words that hung in the air to Thandimanilon's left, where he couldn't read them. Thandimanilon was touching the first word, which glowed pink.

'What's she doing?' said Runcie.

Sleeth didn't answer. He was studying another bubble, half concealed in his hand. Runcie caught a glimpse of a long dark tunnel and something fish-belly white, with grotesquely bulging eyes, at the end of it. Sleeth looked up, realised Runcie was watching him and popped the bubble between finger and thumb.

Runcie repeated the question.

'She's teaching your friend about the Four Basic Laws of Magic,' said Sleeth.

'What are they?' Runcie said breathlessly, as if he were about to learn the greatest secret of all. It woke his old daydreams of magic, the great adventure.

Sleeth gave him a pitying look. 'The First Law says that *Magic is wilful.* It wants to go wrong. The Second Law – *Same cause, different effect* – is also called the *Law of Chaos.* The Third Law states that *Nothing comes from nothing.* There's a cost to everything and it must be paid.'

'What about the fourth law?'

'It's the hardest, and the worst. The Fourth Law of Magic goes, *Action causes reaction.* It's called the *Law of Consequences.* Even the best-directed magic has consequences and after-effects, and produces *waste.*'

'Waste?' How could magic produce waste? 'What kind of waste?'

Sleeth shuddered. 'Bad waste. If you ever meet one of the Waste Waders, the phantoms that feed on it, you'll know it. It's ill luck to talk about them.' He turned back to Runcie's bubble. 'Your friend is quite pretty, considering. What's her name?'

'Mariam.'

'She looks worried. Is that what you wanted to know?'

Runcie nodded.

'Better get some sleep. We'll go in a couple of hours.'

Runcie couldn't get to sleep, but he pretended to so he could watch Sleeth, who was definitely up to something.

He blew up the bubbles he'd hidden in his pocket, studied them carefully, then popped them. Runcie caught tantalising glimpses of magnificent halls, heaped treasure chests and finally a grim, bloodstained dungeon cluttered with instruments of torture. He closed his eyes, his heart pounding. If Thandimanilon caught him sneaking into her tower he might end up in that dungeon, or on Heunch's rack. Suddenly, it didn't seem like an adventure at all.

Sleeth had gone back to his finger-magic. 'Stupid boy,' he said in the cracked voice he'd used the previous night. 'Is that the best you can do?' After much straining, the image of the pain-racked, white-haired man in the bed appeared. Sleeth groaned.

'Is that your father?' Runcie said softly.

The image vanished and it became pitch dark. 'Mind your own damn business!'

It reminded Runcie of just how much *he* had lost. He sniffled.

'What's the matter with you?' said Sleeth.

'At least you still *have* a father.'

'He might as well be dead!' Sleeth said bitterly, but after several deep breaths he went on softly, 'I'm sorry, Runcie.' For the first time, his voice sounded kind. 'What happened to your father?'

Runcie told Sleeth the story of his life. It was easier in the dark.

Sleeth said nothing for ages afterwards, then lit one finger and met Runcie's eyes. 'Who did it?'

'Wh – what do you mean?'

'Isn't it obvious? Your father died mysteriously and your mother went to the dungeons for having his book. Now an intruder has searched your room for it, so why do you think your father's death was an accident? *Someone got rid of him.*' Sleeth's finger went out.

Runcie was too shocked to speak. Why would anyone want to harm his father? He sat in the darkness for ages, mind awhirl. This changed everything. If Ansie *had* been killed, someone on Iltior knew why, and who'd done it. The thought was too painful to follow through, for Ansie hadn't been able to save himself from the fire. Runcie had a mental flash of his father's agony in the burning folly: his hair shrivelling up, skin blackening, eyes . . . he had to block out the horror.

Mariam was right – he thought too much. But there was so much to think about. Millie would know about his magical disappearance by now, and that he'd broken his promise. Every hour would increase her torment, so he had to follow the plan

159

and get home as quickly as possible. Besides, every moment spent here increased the risk that he and Mariam would change Iltior forever. What if they were going to start a war or something? The thought was too dreadful.

But their coming to Iltior might have set things in motion already, in all sorts of ways. How would he know? Even if he tried to avoid changing things, he'd never know whether that was the right thing to do or not.

Besides, nothing was as important as finding what he'd been searching for since his father died – the truth about Ansie's work. He could only do that here on Iltior. At least he'd be able to set Millie's mind at rest when he did get home. And clear Ansie's name. He had to, no matter what.

Then up bobbed the thought Runcie had been avoiding all this time. What if Ansie had been up to no good, and that's why he'd been killed? Maybe he was a criminal who deserved everything he'd got. And if that was true, surely it would be better to leave things as they were. Could he bear to find out? Or tell his mother the nasty truth?

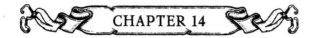

CHAPTER 14

The Ravelled Map

Runcie was standing well inside a narrow cave, a cleft really, which ran into a cliff some distance below Miluviand, and he was feeling more bewildered than ever. Sleeth had gone all distant as soon as they'd set out, as if he had something else on his mind. Moreover, Runcie had no idea what he was going to do once he got inside the tower, assuming he survived the traps along the way.

He sniffed his fingers. The rock smelt like bat poo. 'What do I do now?' There was no answer. Some *friend*, he thought. 'Sleeth?'

'What?' came Sleeth's voice from the entrance.

Something cold and heavy settled to the pit of Runcie's stomach – Sleeth wasn't coming and Runcie couldn't do it alone. He wasn't strong or brave; he was just a small scared boy, lost in a terrifying world. 'How do I find the way?'

Sleeth sighed ostentatiously. 'Isn't it obvious?'

Runcie felt an urge to punch him in the mouth. 'I can't see in the dark.'

161

Sleeth's bare feet slapped on the rock and his fingers glowed. 'Give me your hand.'

Runcie put out his hand, tentatively. Sleeth flicked his fingers back and forth across Runcie's palm and a series of yellow marks slowly came into focus.

'Aah!' Runcie shook his hand furiously. 'It's burning. What have you done?'

'Sorry,' Sleeth grinned slyly. 'I forgot the last part of the spell.' He rubbed his thumb across Runcie's palm, snapped his fingers and the pain faded to a dull ache.

Down near Runcie's wrist, a brighter line wavered back and forth, but in the middle of his palm it blurred into squiggles. Runcie gave Sleeth a look of deep suspicion. 'What's this supposed to be?'

'It's a Ravelled Map, of course. You start off here at the bright line, and as you go the map unravels so you can tell where you are, then ravels up behind. You can fit a whole map on the palm of your hand.'

'Will it still be there when I'm coming out?' Assuming he *was* coming out again.

'It's good for about half a day.'

'Is there any way to hide it if I'm caught?'

'Put your hand in your pocket,' said Sleeth unhelpfully. He pointed up the cleft. 'That way.'

'So I just walk up the cleft –' said Runcie, feeling really afraid.

Sleeth's hand went dark and Runcie heard him walking out

again. He didn't like the idea of Sleeth being behind him, in the dark. He was sure the boy was using him for something.

Well, standing here wasn't getting Mariam free. He held out his hand. The Ravelled Map shed just enough light to show dark rock on all sides. The cleft was a little wider than his shoulders in the middle, but narrowed at the bottom. He went on, though it was hard going – his shoes kept jamming and pulling off.

After scrabbling along for about ten minutes, banging his knees and elbows, the crevice ended in bare rock. The Ravelled Map, now tingling like a nettle sting, showed a yellow scribble near his wrist, the path he'd already taken, while the way ahead looked like a coiled spring.

The walls were solid rock though, studying the map more carefully, Runcie noticed that the coiled path took a right angle and ran up towards his thumb. Was he supposed to climb to the top of the cleft? It didn't look easy, but by bracing his back against one wall, and pressing his feet against the other, he managed to inch his way up to the roof, about ten feet above. The rough stone dug into his backbone and his knees felt wobbly.

Unfortunately the roof rock proved just as solid. Sleeth had tricked him and robbed him. As Runcie turned to go down, something soft and clingy touched him on the ear. He tried to brush it off but his hand caught in a stringy strand of cobweb. He gave it a yank and a muffled click sounded above his head.

The Ravelled Map shone on something pale, up in a crack, like a little roll of paper. Perhaps it's a scroll, he thought, with an Opening Spell! As he reached for it, however, it began to look unnervingly like a finger bone. He retreated rapidly. What if it were a trap?

Crabbing down to the floor, Runcie felt around until he found a thin little bone, probably from the wing of a bat. He climbed up and carefully poked the finger bone. Dust went up his nose; Runcie sneezed and nearly fell. His eyes were watering, his nose running. He wiped his eyes on his sleeve and then, having nothing else, his nose. Millie would have been disgusted.

Runcie was reaching up again when the oddest barking sound echoed in his ears. No, not barking, but distant, echoing laughter. *Arrhh har har, aaa-aaarrhh har har, a-a-a-aaarrhh har har!*

It went on for ages before breaking off in mid *har*. Runcie rubbed chilly sweat off his brow. It definitely wasn't Sleeth – no boy's throat could have shaped such age-old, gravelly sounds. What if Thandimanilon's whole tower was *awake*, like Parsifoe's transportal? Had he been discovered, or betrayed? Runcie closed his eyes, overcome by shivery dread. He wanted to scream and run but there was nowhere to run to. No, he wanted Millie to take him in her arms and tell him it had just been a nightmare. And most of all, Runcie wanted his father to give him one of those lopsided grins that meant he was in charge and Runcie could come to no harm.

But none of those things were going to happen. He had to save himself. He wiped his oozing nose on his other sleeve and screwed up what little courage he had left. He *would* find the way into the tower and get Mariam out, no matter what it took.

Runcie gingerly probed the crevice, half expecting to be caught by one of the ingenious traps that had been so thrillingly scary when he'd read about them in the comfort of his bed, long ago. He didn't discover anything else, so he took hold of the finger bone and tried to pull it free.

With a sound like someone cracking a set of knuckles, a skeletal hand fell down in front of his face, swaying on its arm bones. Runcie scrabbled away as best he could while ten feet up the crevice, and pressed up against the end of the cleft, breathing heavily.

The arm slowly stilled. It must have been very old, for the bones were yellow, and it was much longer than his; definitely a man's arm. Was it the last remains of someone who had been trapped and died trying to get in? *Or out?*

He went back, biting down on his fears. Could the arm be a door-pull? With a shudder, he gave the hand a sharp tug. A hole snapped open above him and the rest of the skeleton fell through, hanging upside down by its toe bones. It swayed back and forth, the jaw clacking up and down in a macabre laugh.

Runcie gasped. Catching hold of the other side of the hole, he pulled himself up into the darkness, the skeleton's ribs and heels scratching his back as he went. He was in a small circular space like the bottom of a dry well. The wall next to him was covered in a fur of mould. He reached out to touch it but drew back sharply, for it was full of tiny barbs that caught in his skin.

Further inspection revealed a steep, crumbling stair built into the curve of the wall, also covered in the furry mould. The barbs plucked at the soles of his shoes as if trying to trip him up. Runcie began to make his awkward way up, but had only gone a few steps when a puff of wind stirred his hair. It was followed by a low, throbbing note, and in the darkness below, bones chattered as if the skeleton was dragging itself up through the hole. Runcie fled, up and up.

The stairs seemed to have been curving around the well forever, though the Ravelled Map showed that he was only halfway up the coiled path. His legs hurt and he had a stitch in his side. Each gasped breath echoed hollowly in the shaft, making it impossible to hear if he were being pursued. He didn't dare stop to listen.

He kept going, staggering like a zombie, his exhausted gasps echoing round the tower. Or was it Sleeth? Runcie stopped and turned. 'Sleeth?'

'Sleeth . . . lleeeth . . . eeeeeth,' went the echoes, growing deeper and more drawn out each time. There was no answer.

Having stopped, his leg muscles felt too weak to go on. But he must. Surely it couldn't be far to go now? The dim light shed by the Ravelled Map showed only the next four steps. He plodded on, looking no further than the next step, when *whack*! A blow to the top of the head flattened him.

When the pain had died down to a dull throb, Runcie rolled over and looked around. He hadn't been attacked; he'd cracked his head on the roof at the top of the stairs. The stone was different here – bluish white and highly polished. Runcie could see fossils in it; segmented creatures with rollers instead of feet and eyes like cut rubies. Fossils had been his favourite thing in science, and he was studying these ones in the glow from the map when he noticed one pair of eyes blinking. He lowered his hand, the better to see, but the blinking stopped.

No; the map was blinking – at least, the unravelled section – and a single pair of eyes reflected its light. He touched them, but nothing happened. Runcie touched the blinking map to the eyes, first the left and then the right.

The roof separated into segments, as if a pie had been sliced into a dozen pieces, and they flicked up to create a round opening. Dust sifted down like flour into a mixing bowl. Runcie climbed onto a floor ankle deep in dust, sneezed twice, and was looking around when a hollow voice said, 'Who's there?'

Runcie's hair stood up, for it was not the kind of voice that could have come from a human throat. He didn't answer. He wasn't game. He closed his fist, extinguishing its light, slunk back against the wall and tried to look like stone.

'Who – is – there?' cried the hollow voice, angrily.

Runcie felt his way back towards the hole but the stone points had closed so tightly that he couldn't feel the joins.

'Speak now or die horribly!'

CHAPTER 15

The Ghastly Chamber

Runcie almost climbed out of his skin. 'Runcie,' he said softly.

'*What?*' roared the voice.

'My name is Runcible Jones, but everyone calls me Runcie.'

'Everyone? So you know *people*, do you?'

Runcie didn't know how to answer. It seemed such a stupid question.

'You know people?' roared the voice.

'Yes,' Runcie squeaked. 'Of course –'

'There's no *of course* about it. I don't know any people. Do you, Nibber?'

'Not a one,' said another voice, more screechy than hollow. 'The last person down here died seven hundred years ago, and he wasn't much of a fellow anyway.'

'To be perfectly correct, Nibber old chum,' said a third voice, as high-pitched as fingernails squealing down a blackboard, 'there *was* the chap whose bones we use for the door pull. He tried to get in just the other day.'

'That was three centuries ago last month,' said the hollow voice scornfully. 'Your memory is going, Gaspard.'

'I remember his death agonies after we caught him, Unggah,' squealed Gaspard. 'And I remember how long he screamed. It would have sent shivers up my backbone, when I had one.'

'W–who are you?' said Runcie, slugs crawling down *his* spine. 'Are you *ghosts*?'

He could have identified each of them from their scornful laughter. The hollow, shivery *Ha ha ha* of Unggah, the screechy *Arrrhhh harr har* of Nibber and the squealing chuckle of Gaspard.

'We eat ghosts for breakfast, Runcible,' said Gaspard. 'We've chewed through hundreds of them, in all.'

'At least we used to,' added Unggah, 'until we devoured the last ghost of Miluviand eighty-eight years ago. What a sad little wisp she was – her soul was hardly worth the effort.'

'And now I wish we hadn't,' screeched Nibber. 'At least they had something different to say. Not like you misery guts, telling the same stories over and over again.'

'Guts!' chuckled Gaspard, as though Nibber had said something really witty. 'Very droll, old chap.'

'I remember when *I* had guts,' said Unggah mournfully. 'I remember when they were full too – and not just with some squeaking little ghost that wasn't even an appetiser. I'd give my right arm to be sitting down to dinner.'

'Give my right arm,' chortled Gaspard. 'You're in fine form today, Unggah.'

'No, he's not,' said Nibber sourly. 'We've had this conversation three hundred and thirty-six times in the past thousand years –'

'We've had *every* conversation three hundred and thirty-six times,' said Unggah. 'And I dare say we'll have them a good few hundred times more before we're finally unbound from this dismal crypt.'

There was a brief silence. 'If you're not ghosts,' said Runcie in a small and very polite voice, 'what *are* you? If you don't mind my asking.'

After another round of hair-raising laughter, Unggah said, 'You won't get around us that easily. We've heard every plea there is, and pretending you've got nice manners won't make any difference.'

'Make any difference to what?' Runcie was trying hard to keep the squeak out of his own voice.

'To the manner of your ultimate demise,' said Nibber. 'Flesh and blood boys don't last long, unfortunately, but your ghost should be good for twenty or thirty years of entertainment. If we're really lucky, we might even get a new conversation out of it.'

'Death is so dreary, Runcible, and so blessed long,' said Unggah. 'We'll do anything for a bit of novelty.'

Runcie felt an overwhelming urge to scream and run, which he tried desperately to restrain. If he wasn't careful he was going to die here. But I've got to get through, he thought. For Dad's sake. And Mum's. And Mariam's. These creatures seemed to want to talk, so what if he humoured them? He wasn't sure

170

how to go about it, though. He'd always been the quiet type who only thought of the clever reply when it was too late.

'How about keeping me alive?' said Runcie. 'If you're used to killing people, that'd be a novelty in itself.'

That set them off on another round of laughter. 'Ah, Runcible,' said Nibber. 'What a jolly lad you are. The problem is, there's so much more conversation in death agonies.'

'And why should you have life when we've lost ours?' said Gaspard. 'That wouldn't be fair.'

'It seems perfectly fair to me,' said Runcie, quaking but knowing he had to keep his wits about him.

Suddenly Nibber burst out of the wall right in front of Runcie. He was sure it was Nibber. He was a little, rotund fellow wearing a red velvet top hat, pinstriped tails and dark green spats, and carrying a gold-topped cane. A brace of cutlasses were thrust through a belt scalloped like a string of intestines. Nibber had a huge conker of a nose and a grim smile. One of his front teeth was solid gold, which looked very peculiar, since the rest of him was a shimmering, transparent greeny-brown colour, like a rotten patch on the skin of a pear. The gold tooth seemed to be floating in mid-air. The other peculiarity about Nibber was a bullet hole in the middle of his ghostly forehead.

'I thought you said you weren't a ghost?' said Runcie.

'He's sharp, this lad,' said Unggah, a bow-legged rider with a red-feathered arrow through his black heart. He wore a big, floppy yellow hat, and his wooden pegleg had green drooling tongues painted on it.

'Too sharp for his own good,' screeched Gaspard, his swollen bald head flying out of the wall as if it had been headed into goal. 'He'll come to a sticky end.' Nothing followed the head but a stump of neck, sliced through at an angle and crusted with rusty stains that looked as though they'd been nibbled by cockroaches.

'Excuse me,' said Runcie, knowing that he had to be as entertaining as possible, though he had no idea how to entertain a trio of vicious spectres. 'If you aren't ghosts, what are you?'

'Have you ever come across the word *ghastly*, boy?' said Nibber, taking off his top hat and frowning at what he saw inside, before putting it smartly back on over the bullet hole. 'Well, we're *ghasts*, and we're like all the most horrid ghosts in the world rolled up together.'

'Horrid?' said Runcie, attempting a joke. 'Is that worse than *evil*, or only as bad as *wicked*?'

'Ooh!' sneered Nibber. 'An educated boy. Interested in semantics, are we?'

'I might be,' said Runcie stoutly, 'if I knew what it was.'

'You won't need to know, where you're going,' said Unggah. 'Let's kill him now and set his spirit free for endless torment.'

The three ghasts drifted towards Runcie. He set his back to the wall and raised his fists, not that they would do any good against such intangible creatures.

'You're not real,' said Runcie. 'You can't touch me.'

The ghasts stopped a couple of paces in front of him. Nibber was bobbing up and down on his toes, Unggah tapping his pegleg on the floor, while Gaspard's bloated head was rotating as if impaled on a spear, inflating its eyeballs like party balloons.

'I thought you were a clever lad?' sneered Nibber. Quick as a flash, his gold-topped cane lashed out and smacked Runcie across the knuckles.

'Ow!' cried Runcie, shaking his hand. 'You cheated. You hit me with your cane.'

'Where did you go to school, boy?' said Unggah, twanging the arrow through his black heart. He swung his real foot to kick Runcie in the shins.

'Aah! That really hurt.' Runcie took a mighty kick at the pegleg, trying to knock Unggah's feet from under him. His foot went through the spectral leg and he ended up flat on his back with the ghasts standing over him, laughing their heads off, though not in Gaspard's case, of course.

'That's the other difference between ghasts and ghosts,' said Nibber. 'We can hurt you but, in our own domain, you can't even touch us. You're completely helpless, boy.'

His only hope was to entertain them so they'd want to keep him alive. Unfortunately, Runcie's only acting experience, in the school play, had been such a humiliation that he hadn't been invited back. At the time he'd been glad Ansie was too busy to come. Now his life depended on acting brilliantly. He had to offer them a story that, in a thousand years, they'd never heard before.

'It's going to be awfully boring once you've killed me,' he said, doing his best to conceal his stark, staring terror. 'What if no one else *ever* breaks in? Imagine what it'll be like once you've heard each other's stories five hundred times; or a *thousand*. After a thousand times, Mr Nibber, you'll be bored before your friends even open their mouths. And just imagine what it will be like after two thou–'

'You're making it worse for yourself,' said Gaspard, darting and bobbing at him, yellow teeth snapping.

'I'm giving you something new to talk about,' Runcie improvised desperately.

'More of the same, more of the same,' groaned Nibber. 'They all think they're so blessed interesting, but when their heads are on the block –'

'Heads on the block!' snorted Gaspard. 'Priceless, priceless.'

'– they all trot out the same old boring rubbish,' Nibber continued.

'Ah,' said Runcie, trying to put forth an air of mystery, 'but I *am* different.'

'They say that as well,' said Nibber mournfully. 'I don't know what humanity is coming to – there's not an original thought among them.'

'Give the lad a go,' said Unggah, doing a twirl on his pegleg that left glowing wisps of ghast-matter trailing behind him. When he stopped they snapped back into him like rubber bands. 'You never know, there just *might* be something different about the boy . . .'

'Give him *the look*, Gaspard,' said Unggah. 'Then we'll see if his courage is made of different stuff.'

'Splendid notion,' agreed Nibber. 'The look, the *look*.'

This was it – another test, and he'd better pass it or he was dead. Runcie braced himself as Gaspard's swollen head bobbed towards him, jaw clacking grimly.

The head came up so close that their noses touched, and it took all Runcie's courage not to scream and run. Gaspard's flesh barely existed, but Runcie could still feel it. The nose was deathly cold, clammy, and wobbled like a slimy jelly. And he could smell Gaspard's dead breath – well, not breath, since there was nothing below the severed neck, but certainly something old and disgusting. The smell that remained after everything human had rotted away.

'The look!' cried Unggah and Nibber together, holding back explosions of laughter.

Gaspard gave a silent chuckle that caused his severed throat to stretch and contract. He eased back a fraction, then his slimy eyes slid out of their sockets and began to bob up and down as if on springs, though their dull pupils remained fixed on Runcie the whole time.

Runcie's skin crawled, for he felt sure something was watching him from *inside* the greenish eye sockets. He bit his tongue to stop himself from screaming; that would be the end of him. He just stared into the ghastly cavities, shuddering from head to toe.

The minutes dragged out until it seemed like an hour. The other ghosts weren't laughing now, though he did sense that something had changed. He couldn't tell what.

'Bah!' Gaspard's eyeballs slurped into their holes. 'So he's

got a bit more backbone than the others. Let's do him anyway –
I'm hungry for the live part of a soul.'

'No.' Nibber tapped forwards, peering at Runcie from one
side, then the other. 'There *is* something different about the
boy. Tell us about yourself, lad.'

They won't be happy when they find out, thought Runcie.
Or maybe they will. 'I can't do magic.'

'Can't do magic?' sneered Unggah. 'What are you – some
kind of a freak?"

'Hold on,' said Nibber, drawing closer. Taking off his velvet
top hat, he put it upside down on the floor and sat in it, his little
legs sticking up oddly. Something unpleasant gleamed in the
depths of the bullet hole. He withdrew a silver snuffbox from a
fob pocket, opened it, pinched up some grey snuff and sniffed
deeply. He sneezed so violently that writhing green slugs shot
out his nostrils. 'That's better. Go on, boy.'

Runcie was hard pressed not to throw up. 'Er,' he said,
trying to think of something really interesting, 'I failed Thandimanilon's tests and she threw me out.'

'You're not the first,' said Unggah, disappointed. 'That's not
very interesting.'

'But I failed *completely*,' said Runcie. 'I don't have any magic
at all. I suppose it's because I'm from Earth –'

'You're what?' screeched Gaspard. He pursed his lips as
though sucking through a straw and the eyeballs withdrew into
his head. 'A Nightlander?'

The ghasts gathered around, those with hands poking and

176

prodding him. Gaspard's gelatinous nose gave a long, quivering sniff. 'Certainly *smells* different.'

'Do you know about Earth?' said Runcie.

'Of course. The Night Watchers have been keeping an eye on it for thousands of years, with dimensional lenses.'

'Why?' said Runcie, thinking that the eye on his computer must have been a Night Watcher. Were they different to the Night Stalkers Sleeth had refused to talk about?

'Nightland and Iltior are linked, of course,' Nibber said, 'and Nightland's bad influences seep through to Iltior.'

'You Nightlanders outnumber us a hundred to one,' added Unggah. 'The two worlds are out of balance and the resonances are getting worse.'

'Oh!' said Runcie. 'Then what do Night *Stalkers* do?'

'They take the fraught way to Nightland, to stamp out magic wherever they find it.'

Ulallial and Thandimanilon had both talked about Iltior interfering in Earth's history, but this only raised more questions. 'Why?'

'To stop your world from seeing ours.'

Ahhh! thought Runcie. He wanted to know why that mattered, but the ghasts looked impatient and he still hadn't asked his most important question. 'Have you ever come across Ansible Jones?'

'No!' snapped Unggah, fiercely twanging his arrow.

'Do you know anything about *The Nightland children who will change Iltior forever*?'

The ghasts, shocked, went into a huddle from which all Runcie made out were the ominous words, 'Has the time of the ghasts come at last?'

'Quick, boy,' rapped Gaspard. 'What's your story?'

Runcie began his tale, starting with the eye in the screen, the bullies at Grindgrim Academy, and the intruder. He must have told it convincingly, for the ghasts said not a word until he was up to the part about Parsifoe's decrepit transportal, and the fish sinking its teeth into her toe, where they burst into shivery laughter.

'That's priceless,' said Nibber. 'Poor old Parsifoe's always good for a laugh.'

'Who'd have thought she'd still be in business?' said Gaspard.

'Who'd have thought Ulalliall the Great would put up with her?' said Unggah.

Runcie went on with the tale, but when he reached the point about going with Thandimanilon, Gaspard's eyeballs rotated until they looked back inside his head, as if he couldn't believe what he was seeing.

'You left Parsifoe to go with *Thandimanilon*?' The eyeballs swivelled out again, covered in glistening ectoplasm. One looked left at Nibber, the other right to Unggah. It was most disconcerting.

'What are you?' said Nibber. 'A fool, an idiot or a *complete moron*?'

'Thandimanilon seemed nice,' Runcie stammered. 'Parsifoe was going to flog me.'

'Not as much as you deserve.'

'But Thandimanilon was so kind . . .' Runcie said dreamily, even now feeling himself under her spell.

'Ah, she's a wicked one,' Gaspard said admiringly. 'If I were young again –'

He broke off as the other ghasts fell about, laughing until their bones rattled. A gangrene-coloured flush mounted his face and he snapped his jaw closed.

'Go on with the tale, Runcible,' said Nibber, his grin displaying a transparent mouthful of yellow, angled teeth surrounding the gold one. 'It's a good yarn, *so far*.'

The ghasts loved the part about Runcie's humiliation in the amber chair, and Heunch throwing him out into the compost heap. 'What did you do then, Runcible?' said Gaspard. 'How did you find the way in?'

Without thinking, Runcie glanced at his left hand, which he'd kept tightly closed to hide the Ravelled Map. Seeing a faint gleam there, he clenched his hand more tightly.

All three ghasts looked down. 'What have you got in your hand?' said Nibber grimly.

'Nothing,' said Runcie, which of course was the truth.

'He's practising deceit on us,' said Unggah incredulously.

'Then he needs a lot more practice. Open your hand, boy!' Nibber clacked towards him, scowling.

Runcie, now thoroughly frightened, unfolded his hand and the Ravelled Map shone out in the darkness.

'Aha!' cried Gaspard. 'Liar! You said you couldn't do magic.'

'A Ravelled Map is strong magic,' said Unggah. 'Where did you come by it, boy?'

'It was given to me,' Runcie said weakly.

'Magic is never *given*,' said Nibber. 'Not for nothing.'

'I didn't know that,' said Runcie. 'I'm sorry. I –'

'I'm beginning to smell something really *nasssssty*,' said Gaspard. A jelly-like tear quivering on his left eyelid drooped down to form a luminous green strand in front of his upper lip. A black tongue oozed out and licked it up.

'So am I,' said Nibber, poking a skeletal finger into the bullet hole in his forehead and twisting it back and forth. Runcie could see the finger bones go halfway through his skull, which was an even more horrible sight than Gaspard's eyes. 'And I've a sneaking suspicion . . .' He withdrew his finger, which had something dangling from it like a ghostly boogie.

Unggah took off his pegleg and prodded Runcie in the chest with it. 'Out with it, boy. Who gave you the map?'

'It was just a boy I met,' said Runcie, not wanting to tell tales.

'No one would give away such precious magic without wanting something in return, Runcible,' said Unggah. 'Who was it? Speak or *die*!'

'It was a boy called Sleeth,' Runcie said hastily. 'But I'm sure he didn't mean –'

'Sleeeeeeeth!' sighed Gaspard. 'Nasty, naaaassssty.'

'We know Sleeth,' said Nibber.

'We hate Sleeth,' said Unggah. 'Why did he give you the Ravelled Map, boy?'

'So I could get into Thandimanilon's tower and rescue Mariam,' said Runcie.

The ghasts screeched with laughter. 'Best story yet, Runcible,' said Nibber. 'You've turned out to be an entertaining chap after all. But seriously –'

'I *was* being serious,' Runcie said quietly. 'Mariam is my best friend and she's in trouble, and I'm going to do everything I can to get her out.'

The ghasts seemed to be weighing Runcie up. 'You'll die horribly,' said Gaspard. 'Or wish you had.'

Runcie swallowed. 'What else can I do?'

'Why, the blessed lad means it,' said Nibber, rubbing furiously at his bullet hole. 'I've never heard the like.'

'He *is* different,' said Unggah. 'The boy is almost . . . *noble.*' He said it with an air of astonishment.

'But still a fool,' grated Nibber, 'who's been used by a scoundrel.'

'Thandimanilon –' Runcie began.

'Not Thandimanilon,' said Gaspard, his eyes shining. 'She's wicked and we love her for it.'

'Aye,' said Nibber, 'but if we catch her we'll eat her soul just the same. What a prize that would be,' he said dreamily. ''Course, we never will catch her. She's too cunning to come anywhere near our crypt, and we can't get past her ghast barrier. Ah, but if we could, we might break our ghast-bonds forever . . .'

'Thandimanilon is noble too, in her wicked way,' explained Unggah. 'But Sleeth, he's a villain. A dire, out-and-out scoundrel. After last time I swore –'

'Have you met Sleeth?' said Runcie.

'Met him?' cried Nibber. 'We nearly *et* him a fortnight ago,

181

but the villain tricked us, then taunted us from a safe distance. He knows too much magic for his own good.'

'Aha!' cried Gaspard. 'I know what the little devil is up to.'

'What?' said Unggah and Nibber together.

'Look at the map. You'll see.'

Three heads and two ghastly bodies bent over the Ravelled Map. Nibber's bony finger, to the tip of which still clung the white, quivering object that Runcie didn't want to think about, touched the ravelled section. It sprang into a series of lines that ran back and forth like a maze.

'I told you so,' crowed Gaspard.

'The rotten little sneak,' said Nibber.

'What?' cried Runcie. 'What's Sleeth done?'

'He's betrayed you,' said Gaspard. 'He fed you to us, Runcible. The arrogance. The conceit. The dire –'

'The map leads into our crypt,' interrupted Nibber, 'but it doesn't lead out again.'

'But . . .' said Runcie, staring at the yellow markings. 'Sleeth told me it was the secret way into Thandimanilon's tower.'

'He threw you to us as a decoy,' said Unggah, 'hoping to sneak past while we were tormenting and devouring you.'

'I smell a plot, *against us*,' said Nibber.

The ghasts conferred again, then broke up, grinning evilly. 'If he's not very careful he'll tear open the ghast-barrier,' crowed Unggah. 'And then, if we can get past Thandimanilon, we're free to rouse all the ghasts on Iltior.'

'Let's get after the dog,' cried Gaspard.

'I'm a little faint,' said Nibber with a meaningful leer. 'What say we snap up Runcible first, as an appetiser?'

Runcie couldn't take any more. He was going to crack, and then they'd have him. He ground his fingernails into his palms. He had to hold on just a little bit longer. For Mariam's sake. And his father's.

'If you do, you might miss Sleeth,' he said desperately.

'It won't take a moment,' said Unggah.

'We can bolt you down in the very twinkling of an eye,' said Nibber. His eyes weren't twinkling though.

'But then you won't have time to savour me,' said Runcie. 'Surely, for your first life and soul in what, eighty-eight years, you'd want to take your time?'

'That's true,' said Gaspard. 'I've bolted souls before and regretted it bitterly.'

'Besides,' said Runcie with a flash of inspiration, 'you're now in my debt and you haven't paid me.'

'How so?' said Gaspard, his eyes boggling in and out.

The gesture wasn't scary now. Runcie was beginning to find it almost tiresome. 'I'm the first kid ever to come to Iltior from another world, so my story is a unique gift. *And* I told you the truth. I don't think you've heard much truth lately.'

'Only in our victims' death agonies,' said Nibber, 'which isn't the same thing.'

'There you are,' said Runcie. 'Show me the secret path to Thandimanilon's tower and we'll call it quits.' He folded his arms and stared at the three ghasts, astonished at his boldness.

'Well!' exclaimed Gaspard. 'What a feisty little chap you turned out to be.'

'Downright presumptuous,' said Unggah. He tilted his head to one side and his floppy hat fell off, revealing two words chiselled into the back of his skull like an epitaph on a gravestone – *Unggah sucks.*

Gaspard chortled and Nibber mocked. Unggah hastily crammed the hat back on his head, scowling. He clenched his bony fists, swallowed, then with an effort regained his composure. 'The lad has a point. It would make a good ending to his story. And since we're doomed to hear it at least five hundred times –'

'I don't know,' said Nibber, frowning.

'We don't have time to debate the matter,' said Unggah. 'Sleeth is getting away.'

'Besides,' added Gaspard, 'this lad hasn't got any wickedness in him, so there wouldn't be a lot of fun in it.'

'Aye, you're right there,' said Nibber. 'The wickeder they are the more they squeal, and that's the best bit. They just can't believe it's happening to them.'

'No sense of irony,' agreed Unggah. 'And we relish irony.'

'Save where it concerns ourselves,' amended Gaspard.

'All right, give the lad his freedom.' Unggah put out his ghastly hand. 'No hard feelings, Runcible. You know how it is, being dead for a thousand years. You'll do anything for a bit of excitement.'

'I can . . . imagine,' said Runcie, shaking the hand. It was freezing cold and horribly clammy and, worse, his hand went into Unggah's almost to the bones, which gave him the most peculiar shuddery feeling.

He shook Nibber's hand, which felt even more disgusting, then stopped. The head of Gaspard was staring at him, eyes popping, and then it came right up to him, as if to touch noses. Runcie forced himself not to back away. Gaspard touched his nose to Runcie's, slid out his black tongue against Runcie's chin, and retreated with another hollow *Ha ha ha*. The ghasts drifted up to the ceiling and began to disappear through it.

'Hey!' cried Runcie. 'What about the Ravelled Map?'

'Blast!' said Nibber. 'He spotted the trick.'

They drifted back down. 'Hold out your hand,' said Nibber.

Runcie did so and Nibber pressed a finger bone hard into his palm, which burned like a shard of poisoned ice. The Ravelled Map vanished and was replaced by another, in red this time.

'And this is a true map that will take me straight to Thandimanilon's tower?' said Runcie. 'There's no trick in it?'

Crack. It sounded like a piece of rock falling down a step, somewhere above them.

'There he goes!' cried Gaspard, and shot up through the stone.

The other ghasts followed, leaving the crypt completely dark apart from the faint red glow from Runcie's hand. He turned around, worked out his direction from the unravelled part of the map and set off, not at all sure that the ghasts hadn't tricked him.

As usual, he started to think, *What would Dad do?* only to realise that it no longer mattered. He'd survived death by a whisker, solely by his own perseverance. Many others, kids and adults, might have been devoured – perhaps even his father – but Runcie had endured, and he'd learned a lot from it. It didn't matter that he was neither big nor strong, brave nor quick-witted. He had courage of a different sort, perhaps the most important of all – the determination to fight on no matter what the odds. To endure, and never give up while there was still the smallest chance.

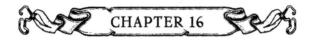

CHAPTER 16

The Testing Room

As he walked, Runcie tried to make sense of all he'd discovered so far. Parsifoe wanted him and Mariam sent home before they changed Iltior forever. Thandimanilon was furious about influences, *resonances*, from Earth corrupting Iltior, but excited about Mariam's Re-sighter talent, which she planned to use in some wicked Cybale plot. And the Night Stalkers' job was to stamp out magic on Earth because, strange as it seemed, it threatened Iltior somehow. His heart missed a beat. Were they involved in Ansie's death? And was the intruder a Night Stalker? Thandimanilon definitely knew him.

To make matters worse, Runcie still didn't know what Sleeth was up to, and the ghasts were hoping to use him to break free. It was all very alarming, and he didn't see what he could do about any of it. He really needed to talk to Mariam. She'd know what to do. And she was the only person he could bear to discuss Sleeth's revelation with.

He had been climbing for hours without getting far on the new Ravelled Map, and had gone through a series of low-ceilinged dungeons where rusty chains hung from the walls, and instruments of torture stood in racks next to horribly hacked and stained chopping blocks. He saw bones aplenty, though thankfully they didn't move or speak as he crept by. Their ghostly souls had been devoured long ago.

As he crawled through a hole into a mill with enormous, corroded gears, Runcie saw, from the corner of his eye, something pale flit back into the stone. How long had this sad little ghost been hiding from the ghasts? Hundreds of years, surely, for it was just the barest wisp. Runcie, pitying it for its miserable existence, said softly, 'I won't hurt you.'

It squeaked and pressed further into the wall, and he went on. When his legs were so weary that he couldn't face the thought of another step, and the light from the Ravelled Map had practically faded to nothing, he ran into a stone wall. Only the last tiny bit of the map was unravelled now, so where was he?

Unless the ghasts had tricked him he must be well up into Thandimanilon's tower. He examined the stone, but couldn't find anything that felt like a lock, button or lever. Sitting on the top step, he leaned back against the wall. He was so tired that he could have slept standing on his head, but he had to work out what to do next.

If he got through, he'd go to the girl's' dormitory, wake Mariam and they'd flee the way he'd come in. Runcie hoped he could remember it, and that the ghasts wouldn't feel free to consume them both. And after they got out? He couldn't think that far ahead, but it all seemed so very hard.

Runcie sighed, leaned back against the stone and closed his eyes. Then they snapped open, for the wall had definitely moved. Jumping up, he pushed hard and a rectangular slab of wall swung out and up, knocking him down three steps before coming to the horizontal and slowly swinging down again. Scrambling up the steps, he dived through and landed on carpet. The room was dark, though he could make out painted panels on the walls and a long window through which the stars shone faintly.

He reached the cloverleaf door of the girls dormitory without seeing anyone. There were no lights on inside, and all he could make out were the shapes of the beds. Mariam's had been the fourth on the right. Feeling a trifle embarrassed, he walked down between the rows of sleeping girls, counting.

'Mariam?' he said softly at the fourth bed. 'It's me, Runcie.'

The girl muttered something and Runcie backed away as she sat up, light streaming from her fingers. He saw short blonde hair and a pale face before she cried out, loudly enough to wake everyone in the room. Runcie slipped behind the end of the bed, but more girls were sitting up, spraying light everywhere and making enough noise to rouse the whole tower.

'Mariam?' he hissed.

The racket broke off. A small girl began to cry at the end of the row.

'Runcie?' came Mariam's voice from the bed opposite.

He ran to the head of her bed. There were tears in her eyes, which astonished him. 'I thought I'd never see you again,' she said.

'So did I. I know a way out, Mariam. If you want to go . . .'

Mariam was out of bed in a flash. 'Of course I want to go, you numbskull.'

'Get dressed, quick.'

'Turn your back.'

Runcie did so, feeling uncomfortable before all these staring girls, and shortly Mariam said, 'I'm ready. What about you, Tigris?'

After a long hesitation, a girl spoke dismally from the next bed. 'You can't change anything, Mariam. The mighty are too mighty.'

The name, Tigris, was familiar – the slender, sad girl Thandimanilon had called in to test the 'scope. 'We'd better go,' said Runcie. 'Thandimanilon could have heard the noise.'

Before they reached the entrance, all the lights came on. Runcie stopped so suddenly that Mariam ran into him.

'I did hear.' Thandimanilon was wearing a clinging gown of shimmering grey-green silk, against which her red hair stood out as bright as a lantern. Her slender feet were bare, and she was supporting herself on the wall as if she could barely stand up.

'Runcible!' she said frostily. 'How did you get in?'

'I came through the crypt of the ghasts,' he said, struggling to keep the tremor out of his voice. No – after surviving them, he wasn't going to let Thandimanilon cow him. Even so, he could feel her spell working on him.

Thandimanilon went even paler. 'You got through their

crypt, *alive*!' She reached out to him, but drew back. 'It's hardly possible. Explain.'

'It was terrible. They attacked me but I couldn't even touch them –'

'Not in *their* domain,' said Thandimanilon. 'Their magic has grown strong over the centuries, and every soul they devour strengthens it further. One day the ghasts may rise again …' She trailed off uncomfortably.

If only Runcie had told her about Sleeth cracking the ghast-barrier, what followed would have been very different, but he was still angry about being thrown out and so said nothing.

'They were about to kill me,' he went on, 'when I realised my only chance. They were so desperately bored with their lives . . . er, their unending deaths, that if I could entertain them with a tale they'd never heard before, I might just survive.'

'You took on the ghasts?' cried Thandimanilon. 'How?'

Runcie began to tell the story, but stopped at the point where Gaspard had given him *the look*, for every girl in the room had her mouth open. It was a wonderful moment.

Mariam was quite overcome. 'You risked a horrible death to save me?' she said in an odd voice.

'Yes, of course,' he muttered, embarrassed. He finished the tale, though without mentioning Sleeth either. Despite his treachery, Runcie felt guilty about dobbing him in to the ghasts.

'What a ploy,' Thandimanilon said admiringly. 'Ah, Runcie, how you've grown in the few days since we parted. If you just had a trace of magic, I could do so much with you. But alas –'

'I'm going,' said Runcie boldly.

'Not with my most promising prentice.' Then Thandi-manilon scowled at Mariam, 'nor my most troublesome one.'

Runcie grinned at Mariam, pleased to hear it. She grinned back.

Thandimanilon had just drawn her wizard's baton when there came a crash from upstairs, followed by a youthful cry of pain. 'Stay here, children.' Gathering up her gown, she ran unsteadily for the stairs.

'That'll be Sleeth,' Runcie muttered, wishing he could get his hands on the villain.

'Jac?' said Tigris. 'Here?'

'Who's Jac?' said Mariam.

'Jac Sleeth,' said Tigris. 'He was my first friend after Thandi-manilon brought me to Miluviand. He looked after me.'

'Really?' said Runcie. 'He claimed he was a prentice here but Thandimanilon threw him out.'

'He was,' Tigris said quietly. 'That was a terrible day. And it wasn't his fault, either.' She glared at a group of girls whisper-ing in the far corner.

So he hadn't lied about that, at least. 'He sort of helped me after Thandimanilon threw me out,' said Runcie. 'Coming? It's this way.'

'Aren't you going to help *him*?' Mariam said, following.

'He also sent me to the crypt of the ghasts,' Runcie said savagely.

Tigris hadn't moved. 'Come with us,' said Mariam.

'I can't,' said Tigris. 'The debt isn't paid.'

'What debt?' asked Runcie, exchanging glances with Mariam, who shrugged. Before Tigris could answer, an echoing scream made Runcie's hair stand up.

'What was *that*?' said Mariam.

'It didn't sound like Sleeth,' Runcie said slowly.

'It sounded like the Dark Lady,' whispered Tigris. 'But she's a First Order wizard. Nothing could harm her.'

'Unless . . .' said Runcie with a shiver.

'What is it?' said Mariam.

'Her barrier spell keeps the ghasts out, but if Sleeth has torn it open and they followed him in . . . They really want Thandimanilon's soul, Mariam.'

'I'm sure she can handle a few mouldy old ghasts,' said Mariam.

'She's been ill,' said Tigris. Then, reluctantly, 'and as her prentice it's my duty to aid her.'

'Not mine,' said Mariam. 'Runcie?'

Runcie rocked back and forth, staring at the floor. He didn't want to go anywhere near the ghasts. What could he do anyway? Nothing, and he certainly didn't owe Thandimanilon a thing. And yet . . .

'Oh, come on!' said Mariam. 'You're not thinking about going up there? She threw you out, Runcie.'

'But she was kind to me, too,' said Runcie, still under Thandimanilon's spell.

'We'll never get another chance to escape.'

He knew it. If he stayed to help, Mariam would be held, he'd be thrown out again, and he might lose all chance of discovering the truth about his father. But . . . 'I can't let them kill and devour her. I just can't. You go, Mariam. I'll tell you where –'

There came another, fainter scream. 'Oh, for goodness sakes,' snapped Mariam. '*All right!*'

Tigris fleeted off and Mariam raced after her. Runcie was exhausted and had no chance of catching them. By the time he reached the door into the central well of the tower, all was silent. He trudged across the glass arch, through the open door, and stopped dead. Mariam and Tigris were just inside, perfectly still.

There was wreckage everywhere. The light flasks had burst and the huge 'scope had been toppled onto the amber chair, smashing it into gleaming fragments. Wisps of coloured aura drifted up, coiling and twisting around each other as if in anguish at the ruin of such great and ancient devices.

Sleeth, his eyes the size of teacups, was clinging desperately to the top of the ladder, which was standing up by itself again, swaying wildly back and forth while Gaspard snapped at his face. Sleeth had a bite mark on his cheek and another on his arm, and his mouth was stretched into a wide, keening moan. Serves you right, Runcie thought.

'I didn't mean it, Dark Lady,' Sleeth wept. 'I was trying to trap the ghasts so they'd never trouble you again. I thought I had them.'

On the floor behind him Runcie made out the tattered remnants of a dimly shining net, like a large lobster trap, though magic was fizzing from the holes torn in it.

'I wanted to prove myself so you'd take me back.' Sleeth lurched wildly as Gaspard went at him again. 'I must become a sorcerer, Dark Lady – everything depends on it.'

He threw himself backwards so hard that the feet of the ladder skidded, tilting until it was almost horizontal, and tried to snatch his bone wand from the floor, but missed. The ladder whipped up so quickly that Gaspard's head was sent spinning across the room, to bounce off the wall. The head shook itself, chuckled grimly and went at Sleeth again, snapping its teeth like castanets. Runcie could tell that Gaspard was playing with Sleeth, drawing out the attack so the memories would last longer.

'Dark Lady!' Tigris ran towards her, but stopped halfway with a cry of dismay.

Thandimanilon lay in the far corner, surrounded by strands of woven white light, kicking feebly. Her magnificent white panther, her mindsake, lay beside her, its four legs rigid.

'Lars?' she cried, delirious with grief. 'Lars, Snowmane is *dead*.'

Nibber had hold of a strand of light and was unravelling it like silk from a cocoon, then gruesomely pulling it through the hole in his forehead and out his left ear, where it emerged in brittle black lengths like knitting needles. Unggah, wearing the white panther-shaped aura over his shoulders like a fur stole, passed his skeletal hands down each needle until it glowed red at the tip, then hurled it at Thandimanilon.

Most bounced off her light cocoon, evidently a magical barrier, though it was thinning as Nibber unravelled the strands. As Runcie watched, a needle shot between them into her shoulder, leaving a red blotch with a white spot in the centre; one of many.

Thandimanilon arched up in a silent scream which was awful to watch. The ghasts grew more solid, as if feeding on her pain. Gaspard emitted a gleeful chuckle before turning back to Sleeth. He tried to climb down the ladder but was forced to spring back up.

'You were supposed to fall into my trap,' squealed Sleeth.

'You're a crafty lad, Sleeth,' said Nibber, 'but not half as crafty as you think.'

'You've got to climb out of your coffin early to catch a ghast,' said Unggah.

'Please let me go,' wept Sleeth. 'Thandimanilon's soul is worth a hundred of mine.'

'Why, so it is,' said Gaspard, chin wagging cheerfully, 'and we'll get centuries of pleasure out of devouring it – to say nothing of the power to break our ghast-chains forever. But you're such a sneaking little weasel we can't resist having you too. The time of the ghasts is at hand, Jac Sleeth, and all thanks to you.'

'But, please . . .'

'*Arrrhhh harr har,*' gasped Nibber, wiping shiny slobber off his chin. 'Keep begging. You're a treat, Sleeth my lad.'

'The irony,' said Unggah. 'It's killing us, Sleeth.'

'Killing us,' chortled Gaspard. 'I've heard that joke a thousand times and it still makes me laugh my head off.'

Gaspard's oozing eye remained fixed on Sleeth the whole time, and the other ghasts were being just as careful. Nibber was still unravelling Thandimanilon's cocoon and Unggah hurling the black needles at her. They weren't taking any notice of the children.

'They're too powerful,' said Runcie, so tired that he couldn't think straight. It felt as if he hadn't slept in a week. 'There's nothing we can do.'

'I know what we *should* do,' said Mariam quietly. 'Run for our very lives, back the way you got in, and hope to get away while they finish each other off.' She glanced at Tigris. 'After all, it's not as if *we* owe Thandimanilon anything.'

Tigris didn't move, and neither did Runcie or Mariam. Thandimanilon's light cocoon was nearly unravelled and most of the needles were getting through. The white patches were spreading up her throat. Even her flaming hair was losing its colour.

'Lars?' Thandimanilon writhed under the impact of three needles at once.

'How do you stop ghasts anyway?' Mariam said to Tigris.

'I don't know.'

'They can move through walls,' said Runcie, 'but they're a lot more solid than ghosts. You can't touch them but they can hurt you.'

'Wait,' said Mariam. 'Thandimanilon said they couldn't be touched *in their domain*. But they're not in their domain now. And all the lights are broken. Maybe they don't like light.'

'Or heat,' said Runcie, 'since they live in such a dank crypt. They haven't gone anywhere near the fire.'

'How much light can you make, Tigris?' Mariam said quietly.

'Lots.' Tigris took a whippy ebony prentice's wand from a long pocket. 'I'm good at that sort of thing.'

'Get one of those 'scope lenses. When I say the word, make all the light you can and shine it through the lens onto one of the ghasts. It might do some good. Runcie, gather handfuls of amber and chuck it in the fire. When it catches alight, we'll attack the other ghasts with it.'

'What if it doesn't work?' said Runcie.

'We run for our lives,' Mariam said.

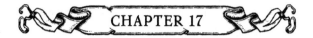

CHAPTER 17

Twice-Dead

'Ready?' Mariam snapped.

Runcie swallowed. 'I guess so.'

'All right. Let's do it.'

They moved into the centre of the room. Gaspard's head had its teeth deep in Sleeth's shoulder and the boy's blows were having no effect. Even Thandimanilon's hair was white now. Only three windings of her cocoon remained.

Runcie picked up as many chunks of amber as he could carry, choosing the biggest so that they would burn longest and brightest. He glanced at the ghasts but they weren't taking any notice. Mariam was also loaded with the gleaming lumps. But as they headed for the fire, he felt that disembodied voice again.

Don't destroy me, children, it quavered. *Four hundred years I've served. Nine hundred children sat in me to be tested, and many became the greatest magicians on Iltior.*

Even though it had mocked him for having no magic, Runcie was moved by its plea, and he hesitated. Mariam was staring at him. 'You heard too?'

He nodded. 'What are we to do? Thandimanilon is dying.'

Mortal people die. That's their fate. But great artefacts can live forever.

Mariam jerked her head at the fire. Runcie leaned forward and, as the chair's voice grew shrill in his head, regretfully allowed the amber to fall onto the coals. Mariam fed hers in, piece by piece.

Hate! Death! Ruin to all your clan! raged the voice. Runcie tried to block it out.

The amber didn't ignite immediately, though once it caught, it burned with a red-gold sputtering flame and an overpowering smell of incense. Showers of sparks fountained off each piece. They were beautiful, though nowhere near as beautiful as the amber chair had been.

Hate, hate, hate . . . The chair's voice faded away.

'Let's do them,' said Mariam, setting her jaw. 'Grab a big piece in the fire tongs.' She picked up the ash scoop.

Over at the ladder, Gaspard's head was taunting Sleeth with *the look*. Runcie picked out the largest piece of amber. Mariam caught Tigris's eye, nodded and scooped up three or four spitting chunks.

'Now!' she said.

Tigris whipped her wand back and forth above her head and light burst forth, so bright that Runcie dropped his amber. He groped for it before it set fire to the carpet. Mariam was running towards Thandimanilon with the ash scoop, sparks trailing in the air behind her. Unggah dropped the white panther's aura, which hung limply in the air, and the two ghasts rose to meet her. In the other direction, Gaspard's head was wheeling through the air towards Tigris, eyeballs lashing around it like a pair of moons orbiting a planet. Her light didn't seem to be affecting him. Runcie began to run, then stopped.

Sleeth was sliding down the ladder. He hit the floor, turned Thandimanilon's way then cried in anguish. 'Dead! Dead! Dead!' His frame convulsed and he wailed, 'I've failed you, Father. I wasn't strong enough.'

'What's he on about?' Runcie called to Mariam.

'I have no idea. *Come on.*'

'No!' Sleeth whispered, his face twisted as if by an invisible grip. Then a look of the most desperate determination came over him. 'The Dark Lady is dead – it doesn't matter to her. But there's still one chance, Father, if I dare seize it.' He agonised for a moment. 'I must!' He snatched his prentice's wand and ran for the door.

Mariam was brandishing her scoop at Unggah. Runcie ran towards Nibber, holding the tongs low in the hope that the ghast wouldn't realise what he was up to. Unfortunately, Nibber seemed to have worked that out already. Dropping his handful of black needles, he flew at Runcie, arms outstretched. Before Runcie could raise the tongs, Nibber's hands clamped around his neck and began to squeeze.

It was the most hideous feeling, a stinging cold that fastened itself around his windpipe, for the ghast's flesh, only half there, slid right though Runcie's skin. Nibber had a pungent reek of the grave, but worst of all, worse than the crusted hole in his forehead, was the look in his eyes. Runcie could read Nibber's desperate longing to consume his life and soul.

As they hit the floor, the tongs jarred out of Runcie's hand. He forced two fingers under the ghast's left hand and prised, praying that Mariam had been right. 'Yes!' He caught hold this time, strained, the ghast's tenuous sinews gave and he forced it away. Nibber grabbed him by the shirt, lunging for his throat with slimy black lips, but Runcie was ready. Drawing his knees up to his chest, he put his feet against the ghast's ribcage and thrust with all his strength.

Nibber went flying through the air to land on his back ten yards away, and one arm broke off at the elbow. Runcie was reaching for the tongs when a stray beam from Tigris's lens dazzled him. By the time he could see again, Nibber had collected the hand and forearm, dived and landed on Runcie's back, driving him into the floor. The amber shot sparks on his cheek. Runcie jerked away then the ghast threw its good arm around his throat and pulled his head back so hard that he saw stars.

Runcie rolled onto his back – the ghast was practically weightless – and something crunched. He staggered to his feet with Nibber on his back, ankle bones locked around his waist, the loose arm whacking him down the right side like a jockey flogging a racehorse.

Runcie could feel his throat being crushed and the dead lips sucking at the back of his skull. Mariam came pounding towards him with Unggah thumping away behind, his pegleg knocking on the floor. Her attack had also failed. Runcie was going down for the last time when she caught his arm and whirled him around. As Nibber shot past, Mariam brought her fist up out of nowhere and punched the ghast through his blobby nose, right into his skull. Nibber's head went back and he let out a thin, wailing cry, as if she'd actually hurt his long-dead nerves.

His grip relaxed just long enough for Runcie to slip free. He fell to his knees, gasping for air as the ghasts went for Mariam. Nibber caught her by the hair and held her while Unggah raised the pegleg above his head to deliver a deadly blow.

Runcie's eye fell on the fire tongs and without thinking he scooped them up, lurched forwards and rammed the red-hot, sputtering piece of amber right into the bullet hole in Nibber's forehead.

Nibber gave a hideous shriek, his arm and legs flew out to form a star and the loose forearm went skidding across the floor. His skull lit up like a Halloween pumpkin, sparks shot out his ears, then with a steamy hiss he collapsed into a heap of bones and bubbling ectoplasm. The white panther's aura bounded across, batted at the bones, snarled and sprang towards Thandimanilon.

Gaspard came zooming around the walls, shot between the rungs of the ladder and cannoned off the barrel of the toppled 'scope. His eyeballs had been sucked right back inside his head. He hovered above the remains of Nibber, jaw clacking incoherently.

'You killed him,' wailed Unggah, letting his pegleg fall to

the floor. 'Twice-dead he is, and that's the end of him. What are we going to do without him?'

'He bored me beyond the grave in his first death,' shrilled Gaspard. 'Yet now he's gone, I don't think I can bear the loss.'

'You won't have to,' said Mariam in a fury, racing to the fire and filling the ash scoop with spitting amber. 'If you're not gone –'

Gaspard's jaw set hard. 'Nibber will be avenged!' He dropped like a stone through the floor, eyeballs glaring up at them afterwards.

Mariam brandished the sparking scoop at Unggah, who shook his fist at her and dived straight through the carpet, leaving his pegleg and floppy yellow hat behind. A skeletal hand reached up and wrenched the pegleg down.

Mariam stood by the yellow hat, panting, then kicked it all the way to the fire and let the amber slide onto the coals. 'Well done, Runcie.' She shook his hand. 'That was a brilliant idea.'

Runcie smiled weakly. 'What did I do?'

'You've discovered how to kill a ghost,' said Tigris. 'Attack it the way it died the first time.'

Runcie felt his bruised throat, remembering Gaspard's ominous words, *The time of the ghosts is at hand.* 'Have they really gone?'

Wisps of light still licked at Tigris's fingers. 'Yes, but gone *where*? And how did they get so strong?'

'By consuming souls for a thousand years, I suppose.'

Runcie checked the room, only now noticing the ghost

galleon lying upside down in the corner, surrounded by broken glass and a puddle of seawater. The ghosts were gone, of course, their tethers broken. He shivered and headed for Thandimanilon. Before he reached her, the crouching aura of the white panther was sucked back inside it, and its eyes opened. Runcie froze as it sprang up and stood guard.

'Lars?' whispered Thandimanilon. 'Lars, quickly. The vile boy . . .' She tried to raise her head but couldn't get it off the floor. The white panther began to lick her face, and each lick took away a small patch of the icy white, though it mewled in pain as it did so.

'Who's Lars?' Mariam asked.

'Count Lars Sparj, her man-friend; a Cybale sorcerer of fearful power,' Tigris said. 'And bad tempered too.'

'Was she calling Sleeth the "vile boy", or me?' said Runcie.

Mariam spun around. 'Sleeth, of course. I notice the stinker didn't stay to help.'

Tears were running down Tigris's cheeks. 'Please,' she said softly. 'He was my friend.' Mariam and Runcie exchanged sceptical glances. 'He was the most brilliant prentice Thandimanilon had ever seen,' Tigris went on. 'And the hardest worker. He'd prop his eyes open with twigs so he could keep working.'

'Yet she threw him out,' said Mariam. 'Why?'

'That's his business,' Tigris said stiffly.

'We'd better get moving . . .' Runcie was thinking about his father, and how Sleeth's question had changed everything, but there wasn't time to explain it. 'Where can we go?'

'Tigris could think of only one wizard who might help,' said Mariam.

'Who's that?' From the sick look on Mariam's face, he could guess.

'Parsifoe. Tigris says she's not as bad as she seems.'

Runcie rubbed his ear and thought about being flogged. 'But not very reliable. Is Thorasdil near here?'

'It's way over the sea, but I might be able to call her for you with the message harp,' said Tigris.

'How would we pay Parsifoe?' said Runcie.

'She was desperate to send us back,' said Mariam. 'And avoid whatever changes we're supposed to cause, so maybe she won't want paying . . .'

Thandimanilon groaned. 'Come on,' said Runcie. 'Before Heunch turns up.'

'Or Lars Sparj,' said Tigris. 'He'll blame you.'

'Is there any other way out?' said Runcie. 'I wouldn't dare go through the ghasts' crypt now.'

'I don't know,' said Tigris.

Mariam grimaced. 'Then you'd better call Parsifoe. We'll have to follow Sleeth. Where would he go?'

Tigris hesitated. Being Sleeth's friend, she didn't want to say, yet as Thandimanilon's prentice she had her duty. 'For Thandimanilon's treasure chest,' she said reluctantly. 'This way.' She headed for the door.

'What's the matter with her?' said Runcie quietly.

'She hates it here,' said Mariam, 'but she can't leave.'

'So I gather, but why not?'

'She won't say. She seems embarrassed about it.' Mariam caught his eye. 'Thanks for coming back, Runcie. You must have been terrified down there.'

'A dozen times I thought the ghosts were going to kill – no, *devour* me. And I was afraid that you'd come to enjoy learning magic, and then I'd be all alone –'

'Runcie, you really are the thickest boy I've ever met, and after a fortnight at Grindgrim that's saying something.' Mariam put an arm across his shoulders, though she didn't keep it there long. 'I'm terrified of doing magic.' She turned away, her face set.

'Why is that?' he said.

'Let's just concentrate on getting out of here,' she said crossly.

Runcie puzzled at her words as they climbed two sets of stairs. Had she done magic before? Surely not, or Fulk's gang would have known.

Tigris was waiting outside a pair of ebony doors, each carved with the figure of a graceful panther pursuing its prey. The right door was open.

'Jac's been here,' she said. A tiny harp hung from her hand, and hopefully she'd called Parsifoe with it. 'Careful.'

'I'm not scared of sneaky little thugs like Sleeth,' Mariam muttered, though she eased her way along the door and looked carefully before going in.

Runcie peered over her shoulder. A lantern glowed to the right of a gigantic ten-poster bed. He edged in, Tigris following reluctantly. The bed was heaped with gorgeous, silky animal furs and Runcie reached out to stroke the nearest, but an eye opened in its head and five long claws extended. He yelped and sprang to safety.

'It's alive!'

'They all are,' said Tigris. 'The animals' spirits are kept when their fur is taken.'

'Why?' said Mariam.

'Wouldn't you rather sleep under a live fur?'

'Certainly not!' Mariam shuddered at the thought.

A chest on the far side of the bed stood open, piled high with gold, platinum and a dragon's hoard of jewels. 'He hasn't taken her treasure,' said Runcie. 'I wonder why?'

'What could be more valuable than gold and jewels?' asked Mariam.

The blood drained from Tigris's face. 'Only Thandimanilon's spell book,' she whispered. 'But Jac wouldn't take that.'

'Why not?'

'A wizard's spell book is priceless. Losing it would ruin her.'

'Couldn't she copy out another one?'

'A spell book is a wizard's heart and soul, so soaked with her magic and how she's used it that it takes on a life of its own. Such things can never be copied. And if it fell into the hands of an enemy . . .' Tigris looked around wildly. 'Jac is good, deep down,' she said as if trying to convince herself. 'He wouldn't do such a thing.'

'He let the ghasts in,' muttered Runcie.

Tigris gave him a tragic look. 'I'm sure he didn't mean to. Anyway, Thandimanilon's spell book would be protected with her strongest magic. Jac couldn't possibly break it.'

'Then why are you so worried?' said Mariam. Tigris didn't answer. A door stood ajar on the far side of the bedchamber. Mariam crept across. 'Shh! We can't be far behind him.'

'Nor Thandimanilon far behind us,' muttered Runcie, glad Mariam had taken over. He was too tired to think straight. 'And when she catches us here –'

It began with the faintest quiver underfoot, as if something heavy had been dropped nearby. Runcie hardly noticed it until red lightning forked across his inner eye. His head whirled and he fell against Mariam.

'Runcie!' She tried to hold up his dead weight. 'What's the matter?'

His eyes fluttered but the dizziness went as quickly as it had come. 'Someone's using strong magic. It – it often gets me that way.' He found his feet, though he had to cling to her arm for a moment. 'I'm all right.'

Tigris's eyes opened like windows into her head as the floor shook violently. They were thrown against the wall and the floor jerked the other way as a phantom whirlwind passed through the tower, twisting everything in its path, then it went completely dark, apart from drawn-out streaks of whirling light. Runcie clapped his hands over his ears but the noise was still unbearable. Cracks snaked across the ceiling.

The noise cut off as suddenly as it had begun. The shaking stopped and the light flickered on. 'What's happening?' Mariam cried.

Tigris drew in an almighty breath, as if about to scream, and her eyes crossed.

Mariam slapped her across the face. '*What is it?*'

Tigris raised a hand to her cheek; her eyes uncrossed. 'Jac's gone mad. He's used wild magic – the Anti-Clockwise Cyclonic Unbinder – to break her protection spell.'

'Great!' said Mariam, 'and we're going to be blamed for it.'

'We've got to catch him before he gets the book,' said Runcie.

They crept down a hall. 'He's in the room at the end,' said Mariam. 'How do we do this?'

'Take him by surprise,' said Runcie.

They edged past a narrow iron stair to the door. 'Ready?' whispered Mariam.

Runcie gulped. It wasn't much of a plan. Sleeth was powerful and desperate, the worst combination of all. 'Yes.'

She kicked the door wide and they ran in. Sleeth's head jerked up. He was standing next to a shattered glass cube, about a yard across, lifting out a heavy leather- and brass-bound book. Magic foaming from the glass made the air shimmer like lemonade.

Runcie threw himself at Sleeth, who swatted him over the side of the head, knocking him into a bookcase. Books cascaded down on him. Mariam swung wildly at Sleeth, who kicked her in the stomach. She fell to her knees, gasping.

'Jac,' pleaded Tigris from the door. 'Haven't you done enough?'

'Stay back.' He pointed his wand at her. 'I've got no choice.' Snapping the book shut, he thrust by her and they heard him thumping up the iron steps.

Mariam got up, clutching her stomach, and gave Tigris a black look. 'I'm sorry,' said Tigris. 'He was my friend . . . I've never been in a fight anyway.'

'I've been in dozens and lost every one of them,' Runcie said ruefully. 'Let's get after him.'

They went carefully up the stairs, though it sounded as if Sleeth had run all the way to the top. The stairs emerged in the cavernous space, as big as an aircraft hanger, under the saucer-shaped roof. It was dark, though between the black columns Runcie saw the bloody moon low in the sky. The gigantic brass globe suspended above them was touched by red reflections.

'Where is he?' whispered Mariam, stopping at the top of the stair.

Something struck one of the brass globes outside, which reverberated like a gong. Shortly, Runcie heard Thandi-manilon's desperate cry, 'Heunch, they've got *my book*.'

Thud, thuddy-thud, thuddy-thud. It could only be Heunch, lurching up the iron stairs.

Now Runcie felt the oddest sensation, like a shockwave racing out in all directions. *'Lars!'* Thandimanilon's call for help shivered with her despair. 'Lars, wherever you are, come quickly before all is lost.'

Runcie ran towards the suspended globe, just as Thandi-manilon's transportal materialised on a platform near the entrance, first the white columns, then the white risers of the stairs and finally the golden treads and roof. In front of it stood Sleeth, holding the book awkwardly in his right hand while he tried to read it by the light of his left.

'Who calls forth Niddimaun the Old?' said a throbbing voice, like the lowest note of a town hall organ. It came with a rush of wind that ruffled Sleeth's hair.

'Transportal,' said Sleeth, 'I command thee . . .' His voice cracked and he trailed off.

'Impertinent boy!' It blasted forth like a hurricane, knocking Sleeth off his feet. 'No one *commands* Niddimaun the Old. Niddimaun saw twenty-three Cybale masters grow old and die. Niddimaun crossed the known world a thousand times, and even the unknown. Niddimaun was there at the fall of Anthri-morie itself, when the empire was buried under fifty slarbs of ash.'

The transportal began to fade. Sleeth fell to his knees and frantically turned the pages, tearing them in his haste to find the right spell as Heunch's *thud, thuddy-thud, thuddy-thud* grew louder every second.

'Come on,' hissed Runcie. Mariam was behind him. He couldn't see Tigris but Runcie didn't think she was going to help.

No one moved. Mariam had her hand up to her ear. Now Runcie heard it too – *swish-swish, swish-swish* – from the direction of the main stair. Thandimanilon was coming. And in the distance, over the icefield, a spark of light curved towards them.

'Lars Sparj,' he said with sinking heart. They were going to be caught; *blamed.*

'We've got to stop Sleeth,' said Mariam.

'I know,' Tigris said miserably, though she didn't move.

Runcie and Mariam ran for the transportal, which was a good fifty yards away.

Sleeth found the page and was reciting a Spell of Command. 'Mechanism, Materialise!'

The transportal reappeared. 'Niddimaun the Old will not be commanded.'

Sleeth sprang up the steps. 'Transportal, go west!'

'Niddimaun the Old will not –'

Sleeth, now red in the face, turned the page and screamed, '*Occident, Ornery Object!*'

The transportal shuddered violently, faded then solidified as they reached it. Runcie staggered up the steps, Mariam beside him, and they threw themselves at Sleeth.

He sprang backwards, completed the spell and snapped the book shut with a triumphant flourish. 'Too late!' he jeered, swirling his wand above his head. The transportal lifted sharply.

At the last second, Tigris came vaulting up the steps, turned a perfect somersault, landed like a cat behind Sleeth and snatched the wand. Runcie grabbed his arms. Sleeth tried to tear free but Mariam wrenched away the book, whereupon the transportal stopped in mid-air, five feet above the platform and at the very edge of the tower.

'Take it down,' panted Mariam.

Runcie held Sleeth's arms until he stopped struggling. Sleeth, face twisted in agony, mutely shook his head. 'I thought you were my friend,' he said bitterly to Tigris.

Tears were streaming down her face. 'I *was*, Jac.'

'Niddimaun the Old –'

'Shut up, transportal,' Sleeth screamed, spit flying from his mouth. With a furious movement he pulled free, whirled and advanced on Tigris.

She pointed the wand at his heart. 'Don't, Jac.'

'Go on. Kill me. You might as well.'

'Jac, please.' The wand wavered, then he sprang and tore it out of her hand, just as Heunch came thudding across. He leapt, threw his arms around one of the white columns and struggled to haul his twisted body up onto the steps.

'I'm sorry, Tigris. I must fulfil my quest.' Sleeth thumped Heunch's thick fingers with the brass-bound book and he fell off.

'No matter who you hurt?'

Sleeth couldn't meet her eye. 'No matter who.'

Tigris collapsed, weeping as if her heart was broken. Sleeth raised his wand and the transportal lifted.

Thandimanilon staggered across, shouting hoarsely. 'Stop, Niddimaun.' The transportal stopped abruptly and she gasped,

'I never thought *you* would betray me, Tigris. Surely you realise the consequences?'

'I wasn't – I never –' began Tigris.

Thandimanilon cut her off with a furious gesture and turned to Runcie and Mariam. 'For saving my life I would have sent you home, children, but you've made your choice and you're going to pay for it.'

'But we haven't done anything,' said Runcie.

Thandimanilon swayed, then clung to the lowest step. 'The wheels of Iltior are turning at last, Runcible Jones, and you began it. *You* decided to use the parchment. *You* chose me over Parsifoe. *You* brought Mariam to me – the precious Re-sighter who will find our lost city at last. *You* made it possible for Sleeth to break into my tower. *You* slew Nibber, allowing Sleeth to get away.

'You've given the Cybale our chance, Runcie. Lars!' she called to that racing spark in the sky. 'I see the way.' Shakily drawing her baton, she began to speak a counter-spell.

Heunch tried to heave himself onto the steps as, with a whistle that grew to a shriek, another transportal skipped across the fluffy clouds like a stone across water and shot towards them. Approaching, it had the look of a yawning cavern; no, the open mouth of a black shark, complete with teeth. And standing between them, legs spread for balance, black hair and scarlet-lined cloak streaming out in the wind of his passage, was a man whose appearance shrieked of menace – Count Lars Sparj. His mouth was red, his teeth white and pointed, and a pair of wire-thin black moustaches extended out for six inches on either side. The monocle gave him the look of a one-eyed predator.

Lars Sparj was the intruder! Runcie couldn't move; could hardly breathe. It was his worst nightmare come true. But then Thandimanilon, halfway through her counter-spell, suddenly collapsed. Sleeth spoke a command and Niddimaun shot up vertically, tearing Heunch's hands free.

'Jac, no!' Tigris tried to throw herself out but it was too late. The transportal jumped *between*.

She lay on the golden steps and wailed in despair.

CHAPTER 18

Gatewrecked

Runcie desperately wanted to talk to Mariam about Lars Sparj, and whether he could have been involved in Ansie's death. It seemed probable, since only the most powerful magicians could make a dimensional gate to Earth, but Runcie didn't get the chance. The transportal exploded out of *between* and began spinning inside a cloud, and though Sleeth shouted one command after another, none had any effect. He'd lost control.

'Take me back, Jac,' wept Tigris.

'Niddimaun will not –' began the transportal.

'Stop fighting me,' cried Sleeth, 'or I'll cast Baloch's Atrophising Bedazzler on you.'

The transportal gave a violent backwards lurch, trying to throw Sleeth out. He stabbed the air with his wand, crying weakly, 'Instrument, become Inanimate!'

A yellow flash made the cloud sparkle like diamonds in snow, whereupon the transportal dropped sharply and kept falling. Sleeth, after a dreadful pause, tore open the spell book and gabbled, 'Apparatus, Animate!' Nothing happened. 'Consciousness,

Contraption!' he said desperately. They continued to fall, and finally he gasped, 'Flawless Flight!' With an alarming metallic groan the transportal reappeared facing the other way, jerking upwards so hard that Runcie's stomach twisted into a double knot.

Tigris came to her knees. 'He's going to kill us all!'

'Up the stairs,' said Mariam.

Runcie didn't see how that would help, but followed the girls up as the transportal faded, only to reappear a section at a time. The blood drained from Sleeth's dirty face and he sat down hard.

'What's the matter with him?' Mariam whispered, wrapping her arms around herself against the chill. Wisps of cold mist drifted by.

'Transportal magic is exhausting, even for First Order magicians,' said Tigris dismally.

Sleeth slumped sideways, his head thudding against the marble step. 'Useless boy!' he said in that cracked voice. 'Can't you do anything right?'

'What's going to happen now?' said Mariam.

'I can recite the warnings, if you really want to know,' Tigris said.

Mariam and Runcie exchanged glances. 'Go on,' said Mariam grimly.

'Transportals can go wrong in *four* main ways,' said Tigris. 'By a failure of *control*, if the person using the transportal doesn't understand the spell, or hasn't mastered it.'

'Or both, in Sleeth's case,' said Runcie.

'A failure of *direction*, if the user doesn't know where they are, or can't properly imagine where they're going.'

'Or both,' said Runcie gloomily. Mariam shot him an irritated glance.

'A failure of *quintessence*, if the user can't draw enough to maintain the transportal in flight,' Tigris said. 'All these ways can lead to it going to a bad place or, worse, no place at all.'

'Thandimanilon warned us about that,' said Runcie.

'The fourth is a failure of *strength*,' said Tigris. 'If the user isn't strong enough to endure the effects of the spell on mind and body.'

Sleeth's left hand was feebly trying to open the book, but failing. 'I don't want to know any more,' said Mariam. 'Thanks all the same.'

'What happens if he loses all control?' said Runcie.

'He's bedazed the transportal, so it can't save us.' Tigris looked down.

Through the base of the cloud, Runcie made out a series of rocky peaks partly covered in snow, an awfully long way below.

'We'd better help the wretch,' said Mariam. 'Come on.'

As they approached Sleeth, Runcie picked up the boy's distinctly composty odour. Runcie supposed *he* must smell the same, though Mariam had been decent enough to not mention it. 'Sleeth?' Sleeth's eyelids fluttered. 'The spell is failing and we're all going to die.' Runcie shook him by the shoulder, the one Gaspard's head had sunk its ghastly teeth into, and Sleeth winced.

'Do that again,' said Mariam. 'The pain might rouse him.'

Runcie punched Sleeth on the shoulder. It felt shamefully good.

Sleeth's eyes opened; he batted Runcie out of the way and sat up. 'What are you staring at?' He turned the pages of the spell book, listlessly. The dirt stood out like bruises on his white face.

The step wobbled beneath Runcie's knees. He poked the marble and his finger went in half the length of a fingernail before the step became solid. 'The transportal's failing!'

'It's not failing,' said Tigris. 'It's just not all *here*.' She leaned over Sleeth's shoulder, wrinkling her nose, and pointed to the bottom of the page. 'There!'

Something shot across the sky with that high-pitched whistle they'd heard earlier from Lars Sparj's transportal. Runcie's heartbeat leapt.

'Jac!' Tigris stabbed her finger at the second-last line. 'Read it, quick!'

Runcie's knees were sinking into the marble now, and the whistle rose in pitch like an approaching train. Underlining the symbols with a filthy fingernail, Sleeth closed his eyes and spoke the spell.

The transportal vanished silently, hung in darkness for a long time while he groaned beside Runcie, then reappeared in a cloudless sky. Runcie saw a lake beneath them, and hills covered in forest. They were much closer to the treetops than before. It was dawn here, for a sliver of red sun was visible at the horizon.

'Jac, you've got to take me back,' begged Tigris. 'Please.'

'Oh Tigris,' he said nastily, 'You betrayed Thandimanilon by helping Mariam to escape, and now you've fled and betrayed her doubly. How will you ever make up for it?'

She fell to her knees, clutching at his arm. 'Jac –'

He dropped the book, grabbed for it but missed and the transportal fell out of the sky. Sleeth thrust Tigris out of the way and tried every spell he could choke out but, apart from a brief, hovering hiccup when they were just above the treetops, none helped. The transportal resumed its relentless plummet.

'All–is–lost,' came Niddimaun's fractured lament.

The base of the transportal hit a yard-thick branch and the paired marble columns broke away. The children slid towards the steps, looking out onto the long fall below, but before they could be emptied out like rubbish from a bin, the transportal toppled backwards and jammed in a fork of the tree, a good hundred feet up.

A crack opened across the fifth step. The spell book fell through, bounced off the trunk and Runcie lost sight of it. The golden roof crinkled like a sheet of aluminium foil, the bottom steps tore away, then the transportal's complicated, crystal-laden heart and core fell out, hurtled to the ground, hit a boulder and smashed into a thousand pieces. Wave after wave of Niddimaun's feelings passed through Runcie – disbelief that this could be happening; a dawning realisation; the pit of the stomach plunge; refusal to accept its fate; the brittle agony of being smashed to pieces; bitter regret at all that was

221

being lost; and finally a fragile, wispy sadness as the life, memory and wisdom of two thousand years were undone and faded to nothing.

Tigris's mouth was wide open but she couldn't utter a word. Runcie had to steady himself; Niddimaun's undoing had hurt him too and he was all aquiver .

'This is all your fault!' Sleeth screeched. He swung wildly at Runcie, but missed and fell down again.

'Because I should have been devoured in the ghasts' crypt?' said Runcie pointedly.

'I didn't mean you to be,' Sleeth said shakily, 'but now I wish they *had* got you. You've ruined everything.'

After checking that his wand was secure, Sleeth made his way down to the fork and kept going, clinging to the trunk's rough bark with fingers and toes. Runcie's stomach lurched. The ground was such a long way below.

Mariam had gone green. 'I've never climbed a tree in my life.'

'It's not as hard as it looks,' said Tigris, moving down as if the branch were a garden path.

Runcie followed carefully. The climb to the fork wasn't difficult, though it was scary, but the fork was so wide he could comfortably stand next to Tigris. Mariam was inching backwards down the branch and her eyes were huge and white-rimmed. Her left foot went over the edge and she jerked it back, moaning. She slid her right foot onto a dead branch, which broke. Mariam cried out and hung on desperately.

'Are you all right?' said Runcie.

'No, I'm damn well not!' Mariam probed with her left foot, sketching circles in the air without connecting to anything, then tried to go back up. Runcie made an anxious move towards her.

'Let me,' Tigris said quietly. 'I wanted to be an acrobat, once.'

After many anxious moments, she got Mariam to the fork. 'Climbing down is a little tricky,' said Tigris, 'but you can do it. The bark has deep cracks, so if you slip your feet and fingers in, like this,' she showed them how, 'you can get a good grip.'

Sleeth, now halfway to the ground, looked the size of a possum. Runcie headed down and found it wasn't quite as bad as it seemed, though his fingers were soon aching and his knees had such a tremor he was afraid they would give out on him. He went down the last few feet in a rush and seated himself on the gnarled, bulbous base of the tree. Mariam looked as though she was going to be sick, though with Tigris showing her where to put each hand and foot she finally reached Runcie, who was dangling his feet over the edge, unable to watch.

From there they jumped down onto soft, leaf-covered ground. It would have been a lovely place for a picnic, except that the area was littered with splinters and shards of the trans-portal's core. The flower-scented air was warm and the great trunks stretched in all directions as far as they could see. Twenty or thirty yards down the gentle slope, a rivulet chattered across a bed of round yellow stones.

223

'It makes a nice change from Sleeth,' Runcie said, sniffing the air.

'Have you smelt yourself lately?' Mariam said with a shaky grin. 'Sorry about up there, Runcie. I – I'm not good with heights, confined spaces and stuff.'

'At one point I thought I was going to wet myself,' Runcie said generously.

'Yeah, right!' Mariam rolled her eyes. 'Thanks anyway.'

Tigris circled the tree but Sleeth was long gone, with the spell book.

'Well,' said Runcie. 'At least we're free.'

'Splendid!' said Mariam. 'We haven't any food or money, and we've no idea where we are or where we can possibly go. We've done something that's going to change Iltior forever, for *evil*, and Lars Sparj is hunting us ruthlessly, but we're free. Hooray!'

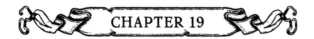

CHAPTER 19

The Cutthroats

Tigris stared at Mariam, not understanding her sarcasm. 'It's *not* good. The transportal's dying magics will draw other magicians here.'

She hastily led them away down a winding animal trail. To their left an outcrop of blue rock was dotted with coin-sized patches of red lichen, while its round top had a circular covering of leaves like a Frenchman's cap. She hopped across the stream, using the largest pebbles as stepping stones.

'Why?' said Mariam.

'Evil magicians will come for the magic left in it, like vultures to a corpse.'

'How does magic work anyway?' Runcie asked. He'd been wondering about that for ages.

'I couldn't possibly explain it to *you*,' said Tigris. Then she coloured. 'Because you don't have any magic, I meant. Sorry.'

It hurt, but he tried to ignore it. 'Well, when you draw on, er, *quintessence* to use a spell, where does it come from? And how do you get it?'

'It's just there. You find it with the Art of Seeing. It takes ages to learn to *see* properly. It's . . . hard to explain.'

'Surely *quintessence* has to come from somewhere?'

'No one cares,' said Tigris, who clearly didn't find it odd. 'There's plenty of it.'

After several hours they passed out of forest onto a series of steep ridges and valleys, set together like the teeth of a saw. The valley bottoms were covered in a tangle of brambles and spiky bushes, the slopes in shoulder-high bracken, while the ridge tops were bare apart from jagged rocks and occasional ruined watchtowers. This country must have been forest once, for several times they passed through stands of fire-blackened trunks pointing mournfully to the sky.

'Did you call Parsifoe?' Mariam asked Tigris.

'Yes, before Jac's Unbinder Spell. But she'll never find us here.'

'Can't you call her again?'

Tigris bit her lip. 'I didn't bring the harp. I – I wasn't coming with you, remember?'

"She's probably been arrested by now and her transportal seized,' Mariam said gloomily. 'Then she brightened. 'With any luck, Ulalliall will get a flogging.'

'If only,' said Runcie.

'What's this place called?' he asked later on, as they slogged up a steep ridge. The sun was high, his cheeks glowed from sunburn and his stomach felt like an empty bag.

He flopped onto a cabbage-shaped rock that rose above the bracken, giving them a good view over the valley they'd just crossed. An overhang left the rock in pleasantly cool shadow. Mariam lay on her back beside him, eyes closed.

'I don't know where we are,' said Tigris, standing by the rock gnawing her fingernails until they bled. 'I come from the Northern Isles, a thousand miles from Finnitan.'

'Why did Thandimanilon abduct you?' said Mariam abruptly.

Tigris coloured. 'It isn't done to pry into people's private affairs.'

'We have to know, Tigris,' Mariam said with the rich-girl arrogance that Runcie found so hard to take.

'She holds our debt,' said Tigris, going crimson and hanging her head. 'Debt so huge we can never repay it.'

'Can't your parents go bankrupt?' said Mariam.

'What is *bankrupt*?' asked Tigris warily.

'They just say they can't pay their debts, get a tiny punishment, and a few years later all their debts are wiped away.'

Tigris's head shot up and her eyes grew wide in horror. 'That would be the most shocking dishonour. Besides, it's a *clan* debt, hundreds of years old.'

'Then surely it's nearly paid?' Runcie couldn't comprehend such a thing.

Tigris shook her head. 'It grows larger every year.' She put her hands over her face, then began to weep in choking sobs.

'What's the matter?' Mariam said awkwardly.

'Now I've gone, Thandimanilon will take my little sister,

227

Fliss, to satisfy the debt. She's only six, and not strong like me.' She rose abruptly and walked away out of sight.

'Are you thinking what I'm thinking?' Mariam said when Tigris was out of earshot.

'I'm too tired to think about anything.'

'I'm wondering if we can trust Tigris when things get bad. You saw how she hung back in the tower, until the very end.'

'Are you worried that when Lars finds us, Tigris won't try hard to escape?'

'Worse,' said Mariam. 'Thandimanilon *really* needs me, Runcie, and if Tigris is forced to choose she'll give me up to save her sister. How could she do otherwise?'

Shortly Tigris came back, avoiding their eyes. Runcie studied her covertly. He liked the slender, sad girl and wanted to trust her, but the worm of doubt had been raised. It made him feel really uncomfortable.

'I hate to complain . . .' he said as they set off.

'Do I sense a whinge coming on?' Mariam stopped, one hand on the big rock.

'What did you have for dinner last night?' Runcie said sharply.

Mariam didn't pick up the message. 'Oh, it was a feast!' She smiled at the memory.

'What, better than the dinner we had the first night?'

'That was nothing.' Mariam had gone dreamy-eyed at the memories. 'We started off with a creamy dessert at least ten times as good as chocolate –'

If she hadn't been a girl, Runcie would have thumped her. 'I had nothing for dinner!' he said, salivating. 'Or lunch, though I went close to *being* lunch for the ghasts. And do you know what I ate for breakfast?'

'Sorry,' said Mariam insincerely. 'What?'

'A piece of sausage the colour of gangrene, covered in dirt and rat hairs. And the smell . . . the smell . . .' Runcie choked. Even that thought was making him salivate.

'What did it smell like?' Mariam said innocently.

'It's too disgusting to say.'

Mariam burst out laughing, but broke off at once. 'I am sorry, Runcie. That must have been terrible.'

'I was so hungry that I did eat some. It wasn't *so* bad, once I got over the smell.' Runcie felt the fib was justified, in the circumstances.

'It's a wonder you didn't get food poisoning,' said Mariam, her lip quivering, somewhere between admiration and disgust.

'Sleeth said he'd stolen it from Thandimanilon's private pantry,' said Runcie. 'But I don't believe the wretch. Er, sorry, Tigris.'

'After Thandimanilon threw Jac out,' said Tigris stiffly, 'she discovered that he'd taken her entire supply of Gorbal's Premium Sausage. It's one of the greatest delicacies in the world – a single sausage is worth a wizard's ransom.'

'Really?' said Mariam, giving Runcie a jaundiced look. 'And that's what you've been living on, is it?'

'Didn't have much,' Runcie mumbled.

'You lying toad. How much, exactly?'

'Might have been a length, in all.' He held his hands out a couple of inches apart. Mariam sniffed and, reluctantly, he spread his hands to a foot.

Tigris clapped her hand over her open mouth. 'You ate a whole length of Gorbal's Premium Sausage? Thandimanilon will have you whipped until you bleed.'

'And to think I was feeling sorry for you,' cried Mariam, pretending rage. 'You greedy little sneak. You might have saved a bit for me.'

Tigris, who couldn't tell whether they were serious or joking, walked away again.

'Ex-*cuse* me!' he said coldly. 'I'd just been thrown out to die while all you could think about was the magic you were going to learn.'

She went still. 'That's not funny, Runcie. I was terrified.'

'I'm sorry.' He'd trespassed on a topic she didn't want to discuss. 'Let's talk about something else.'

'Did you really sleep in a compost heap?'

'Yes.'

'It's no wonder you smell so funny,' said Mariam, wrinkling her nose and smirking. 'Still, you are a *boy*!'

'I wish *you* were,' said Runcie. 'I'd rub your nose in a cowpat. And after I gave away Thandimanilon's bracelet for you, too.'

'What?' cried Mariam.

'Nothing.' Runcie wished he hadn't mentioned it.

She seized his wrist, then stared into his eyes. 'Tell!'

He explained, reluctantly.

'You gave away that beautiful bracelet, just for *me*?'

'I was worried,' he muttered.

'Oh, Runcie.' She gave him a hug. 'I take back all the horrible things I've thought about you.'

'*What* horrible things?'

'Nothing,' she said hastily.

'Well,' said Runcie after a long pause, 'In spite of *that*, I'm glad we're back together. Do you know, Mariam, you're the best friend I've ever had.'

'Really?' She beamed from ear to ear.

'I've never been friends with a girl before.'

'I've hardly been friends with anyone,' said Mariam. 'I put people off.'

'I thought you had millions of friends,' said Runcie. 'When you came to Grindgrim you were talking on your mobile all the time.'

Mariam went pink. 'Actually, I wasn't talking to anyone.'

'But it never stopped ringing.'

'Er –'

'What?'

Now her face was flaming up to the roots of her hair. 'I'd never tell anyone else this in a million years, and if you breathe a word about it, you're *dead*.'

'Oh?' said Runcie, thinking, Wow!

'I programmed it to keep ringing, and pretended to have

those wonderful conversations, so the kids would think I was really popular. I'm pathetic, aren't I?'

'I'm sure I would have done the same if I'd had a mobile,' Runcie said loyally. 'I so wanted one like yours, I nearly cried when you chucked it into the water.'

'I was just showing off.' She ducked her head. 'Sorry.'

Runcie hastily changed the subject. 'Mariam, I can't go home.'

'Why ever not?' She was staring at him as if he'd gone mad.

He told her what Sleeth had told him about his father's death. 'I'm really sorry. I've just got to find out what happened to Dad . . .'

'Well, of course you do. And I'll help you any way I can –'

Just then Tigris reappeared. 'I – I found something to eat,' she said tentatively, afraid to intrude. She emptied handfuls of leafless twigs from her pockets.

The twigs were swollen at the tips like green olives. 'What are they?' Runcie hoped they weren't something gruesome, like ghast-maggots or compost slugs.

'Ecretair pods,' said Tigris. 'You twist them off like this and eat them whole.' Seeing Runcie's doubtful look, she popped one in her mouth.

He twisted off a pod. Yellow sap oozed from the torn end and he licked it, gingerly. It had an acid taste that wasn't unpleasant. He bit into the pod, which was as crunchy as a freshly picked pea, and both sweet and tart.

'Tastes OK,' he said, trying another. He'd begun to twist off

232

the rest of the pods when a distant, metallic *clack* echoed across the valley.

'Don't move!' Tigris squeezed his arm.

'Is it Lars?' said Mariam, creeping across.

Tigris shrugged. 'It was definitely a signal. From the ridge top.' She slid into the bracken, pulling Runcie down after her. 'We've got to get out of sight.'

'Where?' Mariam was stuffing the ecretair pods into her pocket.

A drawn-out call drifted down the wind. 'Keep below the bracken,' Tigris hissed.

She moved so quickly on hands and knees that Runcie couldn't keep up with her. 'Do you get the impression she's done this before?' he said to Mariam, shortly.

She nodded, lacking the breath to answer. They'd gone a few hundred yards when Tigris hissed from somewhere ahead, 'Stop!'

Runcie and Mariam froze. They heard nothing for a few heartbeats, then the *clack* sounded again.

'Come on,' called Tigris.

They crawled down the slope and through a damp patch where the bracken was tall enough for them to stand up beneath the fronds. Runcie smelt a bog further down. They zig-zagged on, thought twice more Tigris called on them to freeze as the signals sounded.

Around midday, they emerged onto a dry slope covered in chest-high prickly heath with little pink flowers. It was harder to move unseen here. They crawled beneath the heath along the face of a ridge covered in sharp black stones, until their hands and knees were bleeding and they'd been pricked all over. After an hour the ridge tapered into a broad valley scattered with copses of trees. A river meandered along the centre and a white, chalky road ran beside it.

They'd just taken shelter beneath a jutting shelf of rock when three horsemen came pounding down the road from the right, puffs of white chalk rising from their mounts' feet. At the point where the road curved left towards the children, the riders pulled their lathered horses to a stop. Two more riders cantered out of a grove of trees and the groups conferred, with much arm-waving and rising up in their stirrups to look over the valley, before turning up into the heath in the general direction of the children.

Tigris let out a little gasp. 'Do you *know* them?' said Mariam.

Tigris ground her fists into the dirt. 'It's Thormic Weasand.'

Runcie parted the leaves to look out. The riders were close enough that he could see their faces. The leader was a small, gaunt man with hollow cheeks, strands of long brown hair like woven coconut fibres and a necklace that could have been made from human teeth. Objects like shrunken human heads were plaited into his horse's mane.

'And his cutthroats,' Tigris whispered. 'My parents sent me away, because of the debt, but Thormic hunted me down and sold me to Thandimanilon. Keep still.'

'Their horses can probably smell us,' said Mariam.

'The wind's blowing our way.' Tigris cautiously scanned the sky, which was empty apart from a solitary white bird-of-prey wheeling above the ridge behind them.

'I don't suppose that bird is your mindsake?' Runcie said hopefully.

Tigris looked wistful. 'Mine is the yellow swamp frog, but I haven't seen one since I was taken.'

The riders disappeared into a dip in the slope and Tigris set off in a bent-over scuttle. Mariam went next, with Runcie close on her heels, though it was hard to keep up. He was so tired. He skirted a bush and there was no one in front of him. Runcie looked around frantically. He could hear the horses' harness jingling.

An arm emerged from the bush and jerked him under. Tigris was crouched against the stems so the foliage covered her completely. He could just see Mariam's shoulder.

'Shhh,' said Tigris. 'You're panting.'

Runcie did his best. Tigris arranged the overhanging foliage to cover him and sat back. The leading horse was so close that he could hear every footfall. A man's harsh voice called out in a language he didn't know. A woman answered shrilly, to their right.

He felt an urge to spring up and cry, 'I'm here. Just get it over with.' Was Thormic using a spell on him? Runcie concentrated on his breathing. I won't give in, he told himself. I survived the ghasts and I can beat these thugs too.

The horse stamped its feet and snorted. Had it smelt them?

Another horse whinnied, further away. The woman called out. The man answered, a single terse syllable, 'Kah!'

Tigris drew in a sharp breath. Her fingers were spread as if to ward something off. *Crash-thump.* The man was whacking the bushes with a long stick. Tigris started; her hand began to shake. This was it.

The thumping continued, a few bushes away, before the woman called out and the horse moved. Had she found their tracks? The horse went by, so close that Runcie could see its hooves and hear their echoing clomp on the hard ground. They were as big as the hooves of a draught horse, but deep red, and each was surrounded by a fringe of hair like a grass skirt, coated with white chalk from the road.

The urge to cry out was almost irresistible. Runcie could feel his mouth being forced open. He fought it with every ounce of his strength, stopped his mouth with one hand, then the other, but even that wasn't enough. Tigris put her hand on his arm and the pressure eased before building again. No, never give in. *Never give in.*

The horse stopped and shifted its weight, then moved forwards again. No one breathed until it could no longer be heard.

'I thought Thormic had us then,' said Tigris in a low voice.

'I almost exploded,' said Runcie. 'Were you warding him off?'

'I didn't dare. If I'd used kid's magic he would have found us instantly.'

'How can you be so calm?' said Mariam. 'I thought I was going to vomit.'

'So did I.' Rising to her knees, Tigris parted the foliage and looked out. 'Sooner or later they'll pick up our tracks. We'd better get going.'

They followed, too exhausted to speak, around the end of the ridge and across the next valley. Beyond the ridge after that they saw a snow-capped range, two or three days' walk away. Hours later they were back in forest, a strip of tall trees that followed the course of a different stream. Runcie guessed that it was around five p.m., though the days seemed to be longer on Iltior.

'Where are you taking us?' said Mariam, looking at Tigris in a new light.

'I don't know this country. We've got to find a safe camp for the night,' said Tigris. 'Not here – it's the first place they'll look.'

Shortly they entered a clearing where a grassy bank ran down to a gravel shoal. 'I'll see what I can find to eat.' Tigris headed along the bank. 'Keep a sharp lookout.'

Mariam washed her face and hands, had a drink and sat in a patch of shade. Runcie sat beside her. 'She just saved our lives. Do you still think she's going to betray us?'

'It wasn't a real test, Runcie. There was no way Tigris was going to give herself or us up to Thormic. But had it been Thandimanilon, I'm not so sure.'

'I want to trust her,' said Runcie.

'So do I. When I was in trouble at Miluviand, she looked after me.'

'She always looks so sad.'

Mariam lay down and closed her eyes.

'Don't go to sleep, Mariam. I need to talk to you.'

'What about?'

'Lars Sparj. He was the intruder.'

'What?' she said sleepily.

'He's the man who dropped the parchment in my room.'

Her eyes sprang open. 'Aha! And you think he's a Night Stalker.'

'He's got to be. And if he is,' said Runcie, 'he could be the man who killed Dad.'

'We'll have to find out.' She closed her eyes again.

Runcie sat there, trying to control the waves of hate flowing through him. No, he thought, I want justice. I don't *know* that Lars killed him.

'Mariam,' he said shortly. 'What did you mean, "When I was in trouble?"'

Mariam didn't answer. She was fast asleep.

'Do you call that keeping watch?'

Runcie woke with a start and shot up, looking around frantically. Mariam rolled over, rubbing her eyes.

'You were snoring so loudly I could hear you over the ridge,' said Tigris.

'I don't snore,' said Mariam. Runcie laughed mockingly and she punched him in the shoulder. 'I do *not* snore.'

'I could have dropped this down your throat without touching the sides,' said Tigris, almost smiling. 'It's all right. Thormic has gone south.'

She was holding something up by the feelers, like a large prawn or crayfish, though it had more than ten legs.

'What's that?' he said.

'Lirron. They're delicious. I got half a dozen. Come on. We've been here too long.'

Tigris was so thoughtful that Runcie felt even worse for doubting her. They walked for hours through the dark and, when they had been climbing for a good while, crossed a slope dotted with clumps of pale tussocky grass that sawed at their ankles, and jagged edges of slate, jutting out of the ground at an angle, which cracked into their shins and knees. The moon was covered by filmy cloud and it was difficult to see where to put their feet.

Several times they heard the swish of night birds, and once the hoot of an owl. It was hard not to feel hunted. The crest of the ridge was so clustered with sharp rocks that it was difficult to pick their way across it. Beyond the crest, outlined against the sky, was a higher and more jagged ridge. Tigris immediately set off for it.

They went down a little dip which was boggy at the bottom. Frogs croaked as they skirted the wet area and Tigris stopped for a moment, staring into the gloom. Runcie hoped she'd find her mindsake – he'd love to see something take the sadness from her face. The marsh fell silent, she shook her head and pressed on faster than before.

They laboured up a steep slope covered with saw grass. The top of the ridge proved to be a series of tall, angular rock outcrops. Tigris headed for the nearest, which soon loomed high above their heads. It must have been close to midnight. Runcie's feet hurt, his legs ached and his empty belly was tormenting him. He concentrated on putting one foot in front of another, and enduring.

The rock outcrop was made of dozens of thick layers angling up from the ridgetop like a gigantic deck of cards. The softer layers had weathered away to form a series of down-sloping caves. Tigris climbed up to one of the widest and slid inside. Runcie saw the tiniest glow of reflected finger-light.

'Come down,' she said. 'This is the best camp we're going to find.' At the bottom the cave opened out and its floor was covered in springy moss. 'I think we can have a tiny fire. Enough to cook dinner, at any rate.'

They collected handfuls of kindling. Tigris lit it with a finger, wrapped the crayfish in moss and put them in to cook. They crouched over the fire so it couldn't be seen by a night bird.

A pair of eyes glowed in a crevice. 'Was that a rat?' said Runcie. 'A bush rat?'

'Yes,' said Tigris. 'But it doesn't mean Jac is nearby.'

'Of course not,' said Mariam sourly.

The ten minutes the crayfish took to cook were the longest of Runcie's life, for the smell brought tears to his eyes. Finally Tigris announced that dinner was ready. She peeled the moss away. Runcie picked up a cray and began to tear off the shell. He burned his fingers but was too ravenous to care.

He was about to bite into the sweet-smelling flesh when a man's voice, echoing and chilly, spoke from the darkness above them.

'Did you really think you were safe here?'

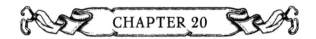

The Broken Staff

Runcie gasped and dropped his crayfish. Tigris threw herself backwards into the deepest crevice. Mariam remained where she was, shoulders slumped.

Runcie couldn't see anything save a figure blotting out the stars. 'Who are you?' he said, trying to keep the tremor out of his voice.

'Someone you don't want to get on the wrong side of,' said the man roughly. 'What a trio of fools you are! I could smell your smoke from the bottom of the hill. Come out!'

'What are we going to do?' Runcie whispered.

'If we go up at the same time,' Mariam said hopelessly, 'we can make a run for it. One of us might get away.'

'You won't,' said the man, who must have had very keen hearing. 'Come up one by one. Bring your dinner – I haven't eaten all day.' He snorted.

The thought of this black-hearted scoundrel eating his hard-earned food was too much to bear. Runcie had had enough of being bullied, hunted, beaten and mocked, and never being able to do anything about it. This time he was going to do something he'd never dreamed of doing before – attack a grown-up.

Bending low, he gathered his crayfish and passed them to Mariam. 'Get ready to run,' he muttered, shaking with fear and fury.

'Runcie?' she said, alarmed.

'Just go up!'

Mariam started, then began to climb the slope. Tigris emerged from her cranny and went after her. When they were nearly there, Runcie followed. The moon came out. The man was standing on the outjutting lip of the cave, about six feet above ground level, a knobbly stick in his left hand.

'Go along that way and down,' he said, pointing with his stick.

Mariam turned to the left. Tigris followed. Runcie took a deep breath, then launched himself at the man's middle, carrying him backwards off the ledge. They soared through the air together and the man landed on his back with Runcie on top of him. The stick jarred out of his hand, rolling down the hill.

'Run!' Runcie yelled, diving for the stick.

As his fingers closed on the wood, he realised that it was no ordinary stick. It was silky smooth, very heavy, and his skin tingled at its touch. But then – horror of horrors – the stick jerked as if unpleasantly roused from slumber. It was a wizard's staff and if the wizard got it back his evil powers would be many times greater. No time to think. Runcie swung the stick above his head.

What . . . The voice sounded in his head, dull and slurred from sleep. *Who are you? Put me down.* It grew stronger by the second. *Master, master!*

'No!' The wizard hurled himself at Runcie.

The staff grew heavier; the tingle became an electric shock running up to his elbow. Runcie brought the staff down with all his force onto a rock. *Aah, ahh, no!* A length of wood split off the side and went thrumming through the air. The rock shook violently and, with a crack like a gunshot, split in two. Runcie was thrown backwards, his arm wrenched to the shoulder and his palm stinging as though he'd held onto an exploding firecracker. He sensed a shockwave racing out in all directions. The cries in his mind were pure anguish until, suddenly, the staff's presence was gone.

Rolling over, he stood up shakily. The split in the rock was emitting puffs of yellow steam and the wizard lay doubled up in agony. Runcie sprang, thinking that if he landed hard on the staff he might snap it in two, rendering the wizard helpless long enough for them to get away.

He was in mid-air when the wizard choked out, 'You little fool, you could kill us both.'

Runcie managed to jerk his feet out of the way but landed awkwardly and toppled onto his back. He was just getting up when the wizard crab-lurched across, holding his stomach with his left arm, and caught Runcie by the chin.

'Sit!' he snarled, steel-hard fingers digging into Runcie's jaw. 'Don't even blink or, by the powers, you'll spend the last seconds of your miserable life regretting it.'

Runcie slumped to the ground. There was such power in the wizard's moon-touched gaze, and such strength in his fingers, that he knew he was beaten.

'You imbecile! You've told every sorcerous villain within twenty leagues where we are. And if you've hurt my staff, you'll wish I'd fed you to Thormic.'

The wizard took a staggering step backwards, then whirled. Runcie couldn't see Tigris but Mariam was standing ten feet away, her chest heaving, holding a rock in her hands.

The wizard was watching her just as warily. 'Put it down, girl.'

She let the rock fall. He bent and picked up the staff, dropped it as if it had given him a shock, then retrieved it with a rag-covered hand.

'Tawcryffe?' he said softly, holding the knobbly end up. 'Come back. I need you badly.' He put it to his ear, nodded then took the rag away. 'Tawcryffe, the stupid boy didn't know what he was doing. We've suffered worse injuries together, you and I. I'll have you whole again before you know it.' The wizard laid his bristly cheek against his staff. 'Tawcryffe?'

Runcie caught his eye. The wizard looked as if his best friend had just died. Giving Runcie the blackest of glares, he turned away, pointing the staff at Mariam. She came across, reluctance in her every movement.

'Why didn't you run?' muttered Runcie.

'Where to, Runcie?' Mariam didn't look pleased with him. 'Why didn't you tell me what you were going to do? We've got to work *together*.'

She settled beside him, staring up at the wizard. Mariam was right. It was another of his failings. He'd had to rely on himself for so long he'd forgotten how to trust others.

A grim smile flickered on the wizard's whiskery lips. 'At least the girl has sense, even if the lout lacks the brains of a squashed gnat.' The wizard turned, extended his staff towards a bony outcrop further down the slope and said kindly, 'Come out, child.'

After a momentary hesitation, Tigris slipped around the side of the rock into the bright moonlight and began to make her way up the hill, to sit beside Mariam.

'Eat your dinner,' the wizard said. 'You're going to need it before tonight is over.'

No one moved. 'Come on!' He prodded Runcie in the chest with the splintered tip of the staff. Runcie sensed no presence in it now, and began to feel the faintest stirring of unease. Had he done the wrong thing? The worst thing possible?

Mariam slipped two crayfish into his lap. He identified the peeled one by feel and bit off a piece. It was already cold and he was so afraid that he didn't even taste it, though his belly felt better for having something inside. Mechanically, he began to peel the other crayfish.

The wizard lowered the tip of his staff, caressing the knobbly end with his fingers and murmuring to it. After some effort he created a faint, sputtering light at the tip. He waved it back and forth across the ground like a blind man's cane, said 'Ah!' and bent to pick up the wedge of wood, about the length of a ruler, that had split off the side. The light went out. He bent over, holding the staff between his knees, and fitted the wedge back in place, running his fingers up and down. Taking some line from his pocket, he bound the wedge on, and intoned, 'Splinterbind, Tawcryffe.'

'What's he doing?' whispered Runcie.

'He's trying to bond the two pieces together,' said Tigris.

'Like glue?'

'Like the way broken bones grow together. But I don't think it's working.'

'Is that bad?' Runcie said uneasily.

Tigris didn't answer, though she was breathing heavily. Raising the staff high, the wizard traced an archway in the air. Nothing happened. He looked anxiously over his shoulder down the slope. Runcie couldn't see anything there. The wizard traced the arch again, this time embellishing it with coiled patterns down either side. The tracings glowed ever so faintly before fading away.

'Aaarrgh!' The wizard squeezed his palms against the sides of his head.

'Is he trying to make a gate?' Runcie whispered.

Tigris said, 'I think so, though it's not going right either.'

'Luckily for us.'

'I wouldn't bet on it,' Mariam muttered.

The wizard, now clutching his forehead with his free hand, traced the archway a third time, making his marks in the air slowly and deliberately. They barely glowed this time, and only for a few moments, before little eddies whirled them away.

The wizard fell to his knees, breathing heavily. Shaking his head between his hands, he groaned, 'Tawcryffe, old mate, if you don't come back, we're done for.'

'Should we run for it . . .?' Runcie whispered to Mariam.

The wizard raised his head and red moonlight glinted in one eye. 'Don't move. Don't even speak –' He forced himself to his feet, staring down the slope.

Runcie had heard it too, a rhythmic thudding like the beating of a mighty pair of wings. His stomach churned. 'What's that?'

'Whatever it is, I'll make sure it gets you first!' hissed the wizard. 'Girls, go ahead. Keep low.' He pointed across the ridge. 'You, idiot boy, stay right beside me. Any more foolishness and I'll give you such a clout over the head that it'll fly off your shoulders.' He cocked his head, though this time Runcie didn't hear anything. 'Get moving.'

Tigris began to pick her way between the jutting rocks. Mariam followed close behind, then the wizard, swinging the damaged staff from side to side as he strode. Runcie had to trot to keep up with him.

He glanced up at the grim visage. The wizard had a tangle of silvery hair that stuck out in all directions like a mad scientist's though, when he'd bent over, moonlight had reflected off a round bald patch in the middle. His nose was a vast, potato-shaped blob. A dark, bristling moustache emphasised the fierce curve of his mouth and his chin jutted like a knob hacked out of granite. He wore a gold ornament in his left ear. Runcie didn't dare ask where they were going.

*

They climbed one ridge after another until Runcie could barely keep his eyes open. The only sleep he'd had in the past two days had been that brief snatch by the river. Lacking the strength to raise his head, he just plodded along on blistered feet, no longer caring what happened as long as the journey came to an end, and bitterly regretting his rash attack. If he hadn't broken the wizard's staff, the gate would have worked and they'd be a thousand miles from whatever was hunting them. If it scared the wizard, it terrified Runcie.

At the top of a cone-shaped hill they passed through a maze of crumbled stone walls, the ruins of a castle or fortress. The wizard stopped by a tilted slab of white stone covered in weathered markings and stood looking down, head bowed, murmuring what sounded like a sad ballad. The short grass here was spotted with little flowers that gleamed like drops of blood in the red moonlight. The trodden flowers released a smell like jasmine, only sweeter. It reminded Runcie of Millie, in the time before she'd gone to gaol.

With a shivery flutter, something flitted out of the darkness to land on the wizard's shoulder. Moonlight touched the large eyes of a small black bat. It squeaked in his ear, then was gone. Runcie wasn't game to ask him about it. The wizard drew a wineskin from under his coat, drained it, let out a weary sigh and turned away. Runcie felt utterly melancholy.

'Where's Tigris?' the wizard said suddenly.

'She was behind me a minute ago,' said Mariam.

The wizard slipped off, cursing. 'I hope she's all right,' said Runcie. 'She's not taking it very well.'

Mariam didn't answer and shortly the wizard reappeared with Tigris. 'Went the wrong way,' he muttered. 'You'd think we were on a picnic.'

Twice more that night they heard the thudding of gigantic wings. Each time the wizard pleaded with his staff, before whispering a series of strange words. He seemed to be attempting magic to hide them, though, judging by his increasingly florid oaths, it wasn't working very well.

'Ought to be able to *conceal* us completely,' he said, 'even without my staff. What's the matter with me tonight?' He glared at Runcie as if he'd been undermining the spell, then stalked off.

They followed uneasily. 'He can't be much of a wizard,' Mariam said scornfully.

Perhaps an hour later, the wizard stopped, his head whipped around and he stared back the way they'd come. 'We're being followed.'

'By that flying thing?' asked Runcie.

'By something on the ground. Sit down; be quiet.' The wizard walked off.

Runcie collapsed onto a rotting log, arms dangling like a rag doll.

'You look as if you dropped dead and kept walking,' said Mariam with a sour chuckle.

'So tired . . .'

'Serves you right. If it hadn't been for you –'

'Thanks for reminding me. I thought you were my friend.'

'I'm pointing your faults out so you can learn from them.'

'Remind me to do the same for you one day!' Runcie snapped.

He rubbed his eyes and looked around. It was just starting to get light and some time back they'd passed out of the ridge country onto a plain covered in yellow, shoulder-high grass and scattered with trees whose foliage looked like clusters of umbrellas. The air smelled of freshly mown hay mixed with cow manure. They'd been following a path winding through the grass which, ahead, was flattened along the edge of a stream whose bank had been churned to mud by a herd of animals. Runcie didn't even think of trying to escape. He didn't have the energy.

'What does he want us for?' he said to Tigris.

'I expect he wants to sell Mariam, because of her special talent. Iltior is full of bandits and wicked wizards, Runcie. I wish –' She broke off, gnawing at her lower lip.

As Runcie glanced at Mariam, he felt a sudden pang. It seemed so unfair that she, who didn't want anything to do with magic, should have such a talent while he should have none.

Mariam said quietly, as if she'd read his mind, 'You should be glad you *don't* have any magic. Shh, here he comes.'

Runcie felt even worse now. The wizard was carrying a pair of freshly skinned hares in one hand. The other held his staff and a small branch hung with fruit like bumpy orange bananas. In the light of the rising sun his eyes were a deep brown. He wore baggy red trousers, soiled about the cuffs, a threadbare yellow shirt with sweat stains under the arms, a rudely embroidered blue waistcoat and a long grey coat, unbuttoned down the front so it flapped as he walked.

'Wash your faces and drink your fill while you have the chance,' he said. 'Don't do anything silly, will you?' He shook the knobbly end of his staff under Runcie's nose. There were blue jewels embedded in it, connected by silver lines.

'No,' Runcie said hoarsely.

He hadn't realised how thirsty he was. He followed the girls to a spot upstream of the boggy patch, where the water was clear. Going down on his belly, he scooped up handfuls of the silky Iltiorian water, then rubbed it over his face. He drank as much as he could hold, but the cold made his belly ache afterwards. Runcie rolled onto his back, looking up at the sky, which was brightening by the second.

'Come on,' said the wizard. 'There are eyes in the sky, and not just my own.'

Runcie scrambled up, straining for the sound of wings but thankfully not hearing them, and they followed the wizard back into the long grass. Shortly he stopped, broke off several handfuls of stems and began to weave them into a canopy shaped like a round tent. Clouds of saffron yellow pollen drifted in the air. Runcie sneezed.

The wizard scowled, tied the sides to the surrounding stalks with knots made from grass and, when two-thirds of the wall was done, said, 'Go inside. Don't touch the wall – it could undermine my *concealment*.'

They went in, sitting on the dry ground while he wove the rest of the shelter around them. There must have been magic in it, for the moment it was completed the light faded out. The shelter looked as though it had been woven from thousands of stalks, rather than a few dozen.

The wizard came in and inspected the wall. 'It might just do. Get some rest. We've got hard days ahead of us *now*.'

Runcie's face grew hot. Tigris and Mariam avoided his eyes. Unable to bear the silence, he lay on his side, pillowed his head on his hands and tried to sleep.

The wizard drew a small set of silver pipes from inside his coat and blew a blast that tickled Runcie all over, though it made no sound.

'What are you doing?' said Runcie after several more blasts.

'Calling for help, but there's no reply. Since Tawcryffe won't come back, I can't call far enough.'

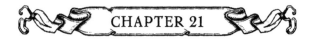

CHAPTER 21

Sleeth's Quest

Someone was shaking him. Runcie roused to the mouth-watering smell of roasting meat. The wizard was sitting cross-legged beside a small fire, over which the hares, threaded on a green branch, were roasted to perfection. The knobbly fruits were cooking in the coals, and the smoke was being drawn into a whittled pipe suspended from a grass stalk at the top of the shelter. A bubble of tar oozed from the other end of the pipe. More magic! It still gave Runcie a thrill.

'Breakfast,' said the wizard, smacking his lips. He eased one hare off the spit, broke it in half with his fingers and tossed the rear half to Runcie.

Runcie caught it but dropped it in his lap, for it was too hot to hold. 'Aah!' he cried, clawing it out onto the dirt.

The wizard managed a wintry smile. Runcie avoided his eye, brushing the dirt off and trying not to drool. He waved his half in the air to cool it and nibbled at a leg. It was unbearably delicious. The wizard began on his own portion.

'Should I wake the others?' said Runcie.

'Let them sleep. It'll give us the chance to have a nice little chat.' Runcie blanched. 'After you've eaten,' the wizard said blandly. 'I wouldn't want to spoil your breakfast.'

Somehow the rest of the hare didn't taste quite so good.

'Well, Runcible,' said the wizard when Runcie had reduced his portion to bones and was licking his fingers, 'where do we go from here, you and I?'

'I – I don't know. What are you going to do to us? Mr Wizard,' he added hastily. Manners seemed more important in this world than back on Earth.

'Mr Wizard!' The wizard chuckled grimly. 'Won't Parsifoe laugh when she hears.'

'Do – do you know Parsifoe?' said Runcie.

The wizard scowled. 'Indeed. Better than anyone.' He stroked his tangled moustaches. 'We've known each other a very long time.'

'What are you –?' Runcie quavered.

'I'm not going to *do* anything to you,' said the wizard, 'apart from putting you over my knee and whaling the living daylights out of you.' He gave Runcie a ferocious glare.

Runcie blanched, but he had to know their fate. 'Then what do you want us for?'

'I don't want you at all, *boy*. You're a confounded nuisance. If you think I've nothing better to do than go chasing halfway across Iltior to rescue you from your own stupidity –'

'Rescue us?' said Runcie. 'We thought you were abducting us.'

The wizard looked thunderstruck. 'Why the devil would I want to abduct you? What possible use are you?'

'I – None, of course – that is –' Light suddenly dawned. 'Are you Helfigor? Parsifoe's boyfriend?'

The ribcage of the hare's carcass snapped in the wizard's right hand. 'Boyfriend – you've got a hide!'

'I'm sorry,' said Runcie hastily. 'It's just . . . I got the impression . . .'

'Parsifoe and I are *colleagues*,' said the wizard. 'And old friends. How dare you liken me to some loutish, lovesick mooncalf? I never heard such impudence.'

'I didn't mean anything by it. It's just . . . but you *are* Helfigor the Wizard?'

'Of course I'm Helfigor. Who else would I be?'

Runcie breathed a sigh. The ghasts had made it clear that Parsifoe was far preferable to Thandimanilon. Surely Helfigor couldn't be that bad either, though the early impressions weren't promising. 'Did Parsifoe send you after us? That was kind of her, after we . . .'

'Foolishly rejected her generous offer of shelter, to run off with wicked Thandimanilon? She did not. You made your choice and Parsifoe couldn't possibly take on two First Order wizards to get you back.'

'But you came because Tigris called Parsifoe.'

'She heard a call for help, but couldn't tell who it came from.'

'Then why did you come after us?'

'You stole Thandimanilon's transportal and wrecked it, a crime so horrendous that ten lives of slavery, mixed in with five of torture, would not suffice to assuage it.'

'But –' cried Runcie.

Helfigor held up a callused hand. 'I was all for letting you suffer. There's no child alive that isn't the better for a regular thrashing, but Parsifoe, soft-hearted as ever, prevailed upon my good nature.'

Runcie didn't believe that anyone could be so heartless, until he noticed the faintest smile beneath the bristling moustache. Could Helfigor be having a joke at his expense?

'It wasn't us! Sleeth stole the transportal. We were trying to stop him, but –'

'Sleeth?' said Helfigor. 'Jac Sleeth, Thandimanilon's prentice?'

'She threw him out a few weeks ago,' said Runcie. 'For dishonesty.'

'I doubt that,' said Helfigor. 'All prentices borrow the occasional thing from their masters – why I even indulged in the odd bit of petty larceny myself when I was a callow lad.' He coloured ever so slightly. 'Well, *I* thought it was petty, but there's no accounting –' Helfigor looked away, then continued. 'The contract of prenticeship can't be broken for so small a crime. For wicked Thandimanilon to cast out such a brilliant student, Sleeth's villainy must have rivalled her own.'

Runcie surreptitiously studied the wizard. Helfigor seemed a bit of a villain too. 'Who is Sleeth, anyway? I mean, where did he come from?'

The deep eyes met Runcie's; considered. Helfigor sighed. 'It's a tragic story. He's the most dazzling prentice of his generation, no question . . .'

'But pure evil,' said Runcie.

'It's not as simple as that,' Helfigor said. Then, after a long pause, 'You might as well know the full story. His father, Croome Sleeth, was cursed by an enemy long ago.'

'Why?' said Runcie.

'Ancient rivalries which I won't go into. Clan Sleeth are allied to the declining Wulffen faction, while his enemy is associated with the rising Cybale.' Helfigor grimaced, then went on, 'But it came to a head when a magical duel thirty years ago, between Croome's great-uncle and another young sorcerer, Lord Shambles, went wrong, hurting Shambles grievously. When he finally recovered, full of festering hate, he set out to kill, in different agonising ways, every adult male in Clan Sleeth. Over the last thirty years he's done just that, save one – Sleeth's father. Croome still clings to life by a thread.'

'What did Shambles do?'

'He put a wasting spell on Croome, sixteen years ago, and he's been dying ever since. It's a diabolical curse, for the pain never stops but the spell won't let him die.'

Runcie recalled Sleeth's finger-images of that white-haired, pain-racked man in the bed. 'Can't another magician break the spell?'

'Croome and Nyris, Sleeth's mother, did everything in their power to remove the curse, but it was too well set. No outsider dares intervene in a clan-feud, so in the end there was *no other way* . . .'

'Than what?' asked Runcie when Helfigor did not go on.

'That's why they had Sleeth,' the wizard said cryptically.

'I don't understand.'

'Only a wizard of the First Order could break the wasting curse, but none survived in Clan Sleeth. So Nyris conceived Croome's child for that purpose – to become a First Order wizard and save his father. The child was Jac Sleeth.'

'That's horrible,' said Runcie.

'Even before Sleeth was born, Nyris began to shape him into the wizard he had to become. She worked magic on him in the womb, day and night and, from the moment of his birth, surrounded Sleeth with spells and mage-lore. There was nothing else in his childhood.

'Nyris was obsessed with her husband, and even prepared to sacrifice their child to give Croome a chance of survival. She drove it into Sleeth, before he could walk, that he had to be the best. He had to save his father, *whatever it took*. There was no right or wrong, just success or failure, and failure was unthinkable.'

'So that's why he's always nagging himself,' said Runcie. 'It's his mother's voice.'

'We wizards often speculate about what Sleeth might become. There hasn't been a prentice like him in five hundred years.' Helfigor stared into the coals.

After a long pause, Runcie said, 'What do you mean, sir?'

'I won't burden you with our worries, lad.' Another pause, then he went on, 'I'm told Sleeth never questioned the reason for his existence, for he loves his dying father. Yet a deep-set bitterness gnaws at him – that he's only valued for what he can do for Croome. Perhaps that's why Thandimanilon had to be rid of him.'

'Is Sleeth truly evil, then?'

'Not yet, Runcible, just badly twisted. But one day – well, that will depend on the choices he makes. Each wrong act makes the next one easier, until a man becomes so warped he can't tell the difference between right and wrong. Then you might well call him evil.'

'How come he ended up with Thandimanilon?'

'That's the second great wrong done to him –'

Something landed on the side of the shelter with a scritching noise. Helfigor eased the stems apart, slipped his arm through and withdrew it. A jet black bat was clinging to his wrist, standing upright on spindly legs. Helfigor bent his arm; the bat hopped, straight-legged, onto his shoulder and put its muzzle to his ear. But then it turned its head and, as if to conceal its mouth from Runcie, lifted its bent wing to cover the lower half of its face. The stretched skin looked like black vinyl.

A brief, high-pitched squeaking ensued. Helfigor nodded gravely and for a second his eyes grew as large and round as the bat's. It stepped back onto his wrist, he put his arm through the stems and the bat was gone.

Helfigor looked worn. Drawing a large silver flask from his coat, he drew the bung and took a hearty swig. 'That's better. And before you ask, the bat is my mindsake, and I don't know where we'd be without it. Intelligent animals, bats. Observant, too.'

Runcie shivered. He wouldn't want one for a mindsake. 'You were saying?'

'What?' The wizard shook himself and continued. 'Sleeth had to be taught by a wizard of the First Order, but Nyris didn't have the gold to pay for it. The family treasures had been exhausted long ago, so there was no choice. She had to do it.'

'Do what?' said Runcie, exasperated.

'She *sold* Sleeth to Thandimanilon.'

'Sold him! Why?' Runcie couldn't imagine Millie doing such a thing, even to save his father. That thought raised other, unhappy ones.

'In exchange for his wizardly training and a chest full of potions for Croome. But being sold came as a shattering blow to Sleeth. He felt even more worthless.'

'And the other prentices gave him the worst time for it,' said Tigris. She sat up, rubbing her eyes and yawning.

'What for?' said Runcie.

'Because Jac was poor and shabby, and didn't know anything except magic. But most of all because he'd been sold by his own mother. The other children came from rich, powerful families who could afford to pay whatever Thandimanilon asked.'

'Not all of them,' Helfigor said quietly. 'Not you, gentle Tigris.'

A shadow crossed her face. 'A few of us, who had the talent for magic but were from poor families, came to our prentice-ship in other ways.'

'A wicked, wicked deed, to steal a child from her family,' said the wizard.

Tigris's eyes grew misty. She didn't speak for a long time, before whispering, 'But it was a badge of honour too. The other kids thought I was a hero.'

Runcie marvelled at how she could have endured so much, yet remained so good. He'd never heard a harsh word from her. 'You must miss them.'

'I do.' Her eyes brimmed with tears. 'Especially little Fliss. She couldn't understand why I went away.'

'So why did Thandimanilon throw Sleeth out, after she'd paid so much for him?'

'The rich kids taunted him until he couldn't take it any more,' said Tigris. 'They dared him to prove he was better at magic.'

'I hadn't heard that.' Helfigor leaned forward again.

'They knew he couldn't refuse,' said Tigris. 'Magic is all Jac has. They dared him to steal Thandimanilon's Great Orb, which maintains all Miluviand, use it to work his strongest magic then put the orb back, undetected.'

'Did he succeed?'

'He did,' said Tigris with a touch of awe. 'No one knows how he got the deadly orb and survived. Jac was terrified, but he's so brave and noble.' Her eyes shone for a moment, but then she shook her head. 'At least, he *used* to be. He brought it right into the common room and the little prentices thought he was wonderful. But the ones who'd dared him hated Jac all the more.'

'Why?' said Runcie.

'Because a kid who'd been *sold* into prenticeship had proven himself braver and cleverer than them. They betrayed him to Heunch and, when Jac was caught with the orb, Thandimanilon threw him out. Not for the crime, but for being caught.'

'I dare say she said that,' said the wizard, 'but I see a darker reason. Sleeth was too clever and, as a First Order wizard, he'd become a rival and a threat.'

After a long silence, he went on, 'You'd better tell me your story, Runcible. The *full* tale, mind. No lies, and nothing left out.' He glanced at the girls. Mariam was still sleeping soundly. Tigris had her head pillowed on her arms and her eyes were drooping.

Runcie told the full tale, which took a long time. Twice Helfigor slipped out of the shelter to keep watch. By the time Runcie finished, the sun was directly overhead and he could barely keep his eyes open.

'A fine tale,' said Helfigor to himself, lifting the woven side of the shelter again. 'It gives me much to think about. Go to sleep, Runcible. We won't be moving until night.' He took another long swig.

'It's Runcie. Can I ask you something, sir? Have you ever heard anything about my father, Ansible Jones?'

'Only what you just told me. Why?'

'Sleeth reckoned someone must have killed Dad, though all he did was write a book about magic. Why would that matter to anyone on Iltior?'

'Ah, well,' said Helfigor. 'Our two worlds are *linked*, Runcie, and things that happen in one world sometimes affect the other. For thousands of years Iltior and Nightland were in balance, but recently you've transformed your world through the evils of science, and it's upset that balance.'

'Science isn't evil,' said Runcie. 'It's given us good health, long lives, mobile phones, computers . . . lots of stuff that Iltior doesn't have.'

'It's destroyed your forests, your rivers, even your air, and made you slaves to your devices,' Helfigor said fiercely. 'That's why science is banned on Iltior.'

Despite his own mixed feelings about Earth, Runcie was sick of Iltiorians criticising it. He wished he could defend his world, but it was clear that Helfigor wouldn't be swayed by any argument a kid could think up. He changed the subject. 'Er, Thandimanilon said that Iltior had meddled in Earth's affairs, long ago. What for?'

Helfigor took a huge swig and sighed. 'It's one of our greatest shames, but what else could we have done?'

'I don't understand.'

Helfigor swayed, burped, and Runcie caught a potent whiff of brandy. 'I shouldn't tell you, but . . . I suppose, because of your father's death, you're entitled to know. In ancient times, the resonances from your world were so weak that they seemed harmless. But one day about twenty-five centuries ago, our wizards, while studying Nightland through a dimensional lens, made a horrifying discovery.'

'What?' Runcie cried, so loudly that Mariam muttered in her sleep.

'In a rustic, mountainous backwater, an alarming new culture had developed. One whose corrupting resonances might, in time, reach across the void to threaten Iltior.'

'Really?' Runcie imagined a savage warrior race storming out of the east, waving bloody scimitars.

'Their abhorrent beliefs included personal freedom, democracy, free speech, private property, scientific inquiry –'

A light went on, from Runcie's ancient history classes. 'But . . . surely you're not talking about the ancient Greeks?'

'Indeed I am, and Iltior had to stop them.'

'How?'

'Dimensional gates had been created by then, though only the greatest wizards could use them. So our most resourceful magicians were dispatched to your world – the first Night Stalkers – and eventually one survived to gain the ear of the Persian Emperor, Darius. He wanted to crush the turbulent Greeks too, before their ideas polluted the ancient world, but he failed, as did Xerxes after him. Miraculously, the outnumbered Greeks defeated his Persian army, the greatest ever assembled, and soon the Greeks' insidious culture, and their evil *science*, had spread across the known world.'

Runcie looked down at the dirt, wondering if Helfigor was

telling the whole truth. Nibber had said that the Night Stalkers went to Earth to stamp out magic, so why was Helfigor talking about science? Runcie could hardly accuse him of lying, though, so he said nothing.

'Our Night Stalkers did their best to destroy it,' Helfigor went on. 'They burned the seventy-two books of Democritus, the most dangerous scientist of ancient times, and supported his opponent Socrates in every way. Socrates' enemies got him in the end but fortunately his views prevailed for another two thousand years.'

'Burning books is evil,' said Runcie, feeling very disillusioned.

Helfigor looked uncomfortable but covered it with a gulp of brandy. 'Iltior was fighting for its survival. The Night Stalkers destroyed the books of every other scientific thinker they could find. They failed with Archimedes and a few others but, by the time the Romans came along, it seemed enough. *They* weren't interested in science, thankfully, and after the Great Library at Alexandria was finally burned, Iltior felt safe.'

Runcie gave Helfigor a look of deep disgust.

The wizard ignored it and continued, slurring a little. 'But evil will keep bubbling to the surface, no matter how often it's stamped on, and we had to be forever vigilant. Iltior fought every scientific mind for the next thousand years, though the man who defeated us wasn't a scientist at all. The Night Stalkers did their best to bankrupt him – the wicked inventor of printing, Gutenberg. Unfortunately his creditors published his Bible and, if only we'd known it, our cause was lost. Then we made a fatal mistake.'

Scritch, scritch. It was the bat again. This time Helfigor spoke to it outside, and returned looking agitated.

'Is something the matter?' asked Runcie.

'Nothing you need worry about.'

That was, of course, more worrying. When Helfigor did not go on, Runcie said, 'What fatal mistake?'

'Science was developing so rapidly that Iltior couldn't train enough Night Stalkers to fight it. So many had been lost that few wizards dared to go anymore.'

'What did they do?' said Runcie, exasperated.

'The Night Stalkers tried to use the Church, for it feared science almost as much as it hated magic. It worked for a while: the mapmaker Mercator was prosecuted for heresy, the philosopher Bruno burned at the stake and the great Galileo was forced to recant, though that turned out to be the Church's last gasp. When it realised it was losing its place in the world, it turned on our envoys. Iltior lost countless Night Stalkers to the Inquisition's torturers before the Church itself lost power.

'But by then your world had turned its back on magic, which allowed science, unfettered, to get out of control.' Helfigor broke off, wrenched the stems apart and squinted out briefly, before continuing. 'And just as we'd foreseen, science transformed your world, its population exploded and resonances began to undermine ours.'

'I still don't understand why,' said Runcie.

'I'll put it simply. If one person on your world thinks, believes or does something, its resonance is tiny. But when a *million* people do that thing, the resonance hits Iltior like a tidal wave.'

Again Runcie saw the mad boy playing the imaginary computer game, and suddenly he did understand.

'But then it got worse,' Helfigor went on grimly. 'Science began to pull down the world it had created – you Nightlanders now have every material possession you could wish for, but you're more miserable than ever. All the wonder went out of your world when you gave up magic, and science's trinkets could never replace it. People yearn for the supernatural, Runcie, but they don't know where to find it.' He caught Runcie's eye. 'And so we come to your father.'

Runcie sat up abruptly.

'Just recently, magic began to reappear on Nightland,' Helfigor went on, 'and the Night Stalkers couldn't allow that to happen either.'

'Why not? What have they done? And what are they going to do?'

Helfigor tilted the flask, discovered it was empty, and looked shocked at himself. 'I – I've said too much. Don't ask me any more questions, boy!' he growled.

It was finally starting to make sense. The Night Stalkers must be behind the anti-magic laws that had banned Ansie's book and sent Millie to prison. 'Er . . . why didn't Iltior attack Earth's magic in olden times?'

Helfigor clenched one fist, but answered. 'We didn't mind you having magic then, but it's different now. We can't allow your world to have the clear sight of magic while it possesses the overwhelming power of science. This is our very survival, Runcie, and I'm sure that's why your father's book was destroyed . . .'

And why Dad was killed. Runcie didn't speak for a long while. He couldn't bear to think of Ansie dying, all because his life's work had unwittingly threatened another world.

'And the Cybale?' he said at last.

'They're power hungry and they don't like to share it. They don't believe in ordinary people having magic,' he said in outrage. 'Or mindsakes! The Cybale would rule Iltior with a stone fist, as they did long ago.' His eyes met Runcie's. 'But until now they haven't had the means.'

'Until . . .' said Runcie, already knowing what Helfigor was going to say.

'You and Mariam came, to change Iltior forever.'

And if they got Mariam they'd use her talent to find their lost city and its forgotten magic. But the foretelling had said *the children*, so he must be important too. 'So why did Thandi-manilon throw *me* out?'

'I don't know. It doesn't make sense for her to keep one child and not the other . . . unless that's how it was meant to be: Mariam under her control but you the wild card, thrown into the world to see what happens. Already Iltior is changing and it's tilted the balance the Cybale's way.'

'What are they going to do?'

'I don't know,' Helfigor said heavily. 'The wild card has been used, it's worked beyond their dreams and now it's time to shuffle it back in. Lars and Thandimanilon will exert all their power to get you two back, and how can I stop them? Lars isn't a clever man, but he's a powerful sorcerer, and without my staff –'

'I'm really sorry about that,' said Runcie.

Helfigor sighed. 'In your situation, I might have done the same.'

'Did I destroy it? I –'

Helfigor smiled patronisingly. 'Oh no. It takes powerful magic to destroy a wizard's staff. You could break it in half and Tawcryffe's presence would survive, though you might not. But after such an injury, she might not come back for days . . . or years.'

'Can't you order her to come back?'

'Do you order your closest friends about? Unless it's the most desperate emergency, Tawcryffe won't return until she's well again . . . and maybe not then. And unfortunately, Runcie, your enemies have transportals at their disposal . . .'

'While without your staff you can't even make a gate.'

'Alas no. Gates take a mighty toll, Runcie, even on a . . . great wizard such as I.' He coloured.

Runcie's heart sank further, for he wasn't sure Helfigor was good enough to make a gate, even with ten staffs. He returned to his other question. 'Lars was definitely the intruder. Do you think he killed Dad?'

'I don't know. No one wants your world to get magic.'

It was all very frustrating. 'Helfigor?' said Runcie, for something else had occurred to him.

'Yes, lad?'

'If our two worlds are linked, and Earth affects Iltior through resonance . . . how does Iltior affect Earth?' Iltior was darker and more dangerous than he'd thought. Far more dangerous, and Earth knew nothing about it.

'A very important question. Unfortunately I don't know the answer.'

CHAPTER 22

The Beat of Mighty Wings

A shrill cry shivered through Runcie's dreams, jerking him unpleasantly awake.

'What's that?' hissed Mariam.

'I don't know,' came Tigris's worried voice.

Runcie scrambled up. It must have been late in the afternoon, judging by the light. Helfigor wasn't there! Where had he gone? Despite his earlier warning, Tigris had pulled the woven grass apart and was peering through. 'What's the matter?' Runcie said hoarsely.

'Shh!' said Mariam.

The cry came again, from the sky above them, a jagged squeal, rising and falling. He couldn't imagine what kind of creature would make such a sound.

'Do – do you think it's looking for us?' He could barely get the words out.

'I hope not.' Tigris wiped sweat off her brow.

Something shot overhead with a leathery *flap-flappetty-flap*. It was the kind of noise a pterodactyl's wing might have made as it hovered above its prey, back in the age of the dinosaurs. Mariam's eyes were sticking out like boiled eggs.

'It's after us!' said Runcie. 'Come on.'

'Helfigor said to stay here,' said Tigris faintly.

'What if it's got him?' said Runcie. 'If we stay here it'll get us too –' Mariam gave him a look and he broke off, abashed. His rash attack on Helfigor had put them in this situation. From now on he was going to think first, but even so . . .

'He's a wizard,' said Mariam. 'Surely no wild beast could harm him?'

But Thandimanilon had called Helfigor shiftless, second-rate and a man who neglected his responsibilities. Even Parsifoe had said, 'Stick-at-nothing Helfigor, never there when you need him'. And Runcie had damaged Helfigor's staff, robbing him of most of his power. What if he'd run away?

They heard another *flappetty-flap*, a triumphant shriek, then a shivery cry of terror.

'It's got him,' said Runcie.

'No, that sounded like a *kid*,' said Mariam.

'It sounded like Jac!' Tigris jerked up the side wall.

Another of those eerie squeals was followed by a man's voice, yelling.

'*That* sounded like Helfigor,' said Runcie. 'And if he's in trouble . . .' He couldn't help remembering that the wizard had drunk all that brandy.

Tigris stopped, half in and half out, then she was gone. 'Tigris, wait!' Mariam said something shockingly rude under her breath. 'Come on.'

It was almost dark outside, though a blood-coloured moon was rising in the distance, bathing the landscape in its ghastly glow. The air had an acrid smell, like a freshly lit match. Runcie couldn't see anything in the sky, and didn't hear anything either, apart from a faint *chirr-chup, chirr-chup* from somewhere to their right.

Tigris was about twenty steps away, crouched down. The grass rustled ahead of them, as if something were moving quickly through it. In the distance, the horizontal rays of the moon picked out the umbrella-shaped top of a tree swaying as if in a high wind, though the air was perfectly still.

'We stay together,' said Mariam, taking charge again.

She wove through the grass, bent low, Tigris at her heels and Runcie a few steps back, already regretting coming out of the hide. Any kind of beast could be lurking in the tall grass and they'd never know until it was on them.

Tigris stopped, cupped the air with her left hand then squeezed it into her right, five or six times, before sniffing her hand. She did the same in the other directions, explaining, 'A tiny magic. The beast is that way.' She pointed left of the tree.

They'd been creeping through the grass for a few minutes and were by the umbrella tree when Sleeth let out another cry. Something went *thump*, like a stick hitting a soccer ball, and the beast gave a coughing grunt.

Thump-thump. Runcie heard a hoarse, strained chant, followed by a clap. Sparks sizzled from the heads of the grass stems, which bent back towards the shelter.

'That was definitely Helfigor,' whispered Runcie.

Mariam picked up a fallen branch. Runcie armed himself with a stick, though it was so worm-eaten it would hardly have stopped a rabbit. Tigris drew in a sharp breath.

A vast creature, three times the height of the children, rose out of a hollow fifty feet away. It had massive haunches and a long muscular tail, though it walked on its back legs and the front ones were more like arms. It moved forward but its feet made hardly any sound and, even in the depths of his terror, Runcie realised how odd that was. Such an enormous beast should have shaken the ground. Then it turned and moonlight shimmered through it, as if it wasn't completely there.

'What is it?' he whispered.

The creature's broad chest was partly covered by a leather waistcoat with many pockets or pouches. Muscles bulged beneath a covering of overlapping, pearly scales. Its arms were long, the strong fingers ending in black claws, and one hand held a glittering rod, like an extra large magician's wand. A pair of huge leathery wings, partly furled, explained the flapping they'd heard earlier.

The creature turned again, showing its wheelbarrow-sized head in profile. It was boxy, quite unlike the long snout of a dragon or a crocodile, and something round sat on top, though Runcie couldn't make it out. Two intelligent golden eyes were the size of soup bowls and its mouth was decorated with an awful lot of teeth, plus three sets of fangs that protruded like those of a sabre-toothed tiger. Its leathery lips and throat were stained red, as if it had fed recently, and none too daintily. Runcie shivered at the thought.

'It's a wyrm,' whispered Tigris in a mixture of awe and terror. 'A *ghoolwyrm*! But it can't be.' Letting out a despairing moan, she began to back away.

'What's a ghoolwyrm?' said Mariam.

The wyrm darted forward, lunged and stood up again, clutching Sleeth around the waist with its left arm. It lifted him off the ground with an effort as if, despite its size, it wasn't very strong. It was moving sluggishly, too, which gave Runcie a glimmer of hope.

Sleeth was kicking his legs furiously and beating at its mighty arm with his free hand, though his other hand maintained a death grip on Thandimanilon's spell book. 'You've ruined everything,' he said in his mother's cracked voice, then went still.

'Why can't it be a ghoolwyrm?' Mariam said.

'The last wyrms died three thousand years ago,' said Tigris from behind them.

'Then it must be a ghost or a ghast,' Runcie said with a shudder. 'Look – you can see right through it.'

'No, it's a spell-creature,' said Tigris. 'A conjuration.'

Something didn't add up, though Runcie didn't get the chance to think about it, for Helfigor staggered out of the grass to the wyrm's left, making a wild ratchetting sound and brandishing his damaged staff. The wyrm turned those vast eyes on him and a glow appeared around the wizard's head, like the halo around the head of a saint.

'It's strong enough to attack a wizard,' said Mariam. 'I've got a bad feeling about this, Runcie.'

Helfigor gasped, doubled over in pain, then thrust his staff at the wyrm. Runcie bit his lip. If Tawcryffe let Helfigor down now . . .

A blister of yellow light formed at the tip. Helfigor roared, 'Cease to be, Corporeal Conjure-Creature!' The blister grew into a brilliant bubble, whereupon the ghoolwyrm threw one arm across its eyes. Helfigor stepped forward, holding up the dazzling globe. 'Put the boy down, wyrm.'

The wyrm turned to him, one corner of its mouth curled, and then it *spoke*. 'And if I don't?' it said in a ground-shaking voice that sounded curiously amused.

'The link to your master leaves him exposed, wyrm. Release the boy or I'll banish you so violently that Lars Sparj won't be able to lift his staff for a year.'

'He's bluffing,' said Tigris hoarsely. 'Lars Sparj is a First Order sorcerer; Helfigor can't hope to defeat his conjuration.'

The wyrm made a circle with its rod and Helfigor's bubble burst into splinters that winked in the red moonlight like shards of glass. The wyrm threw back its head and drew breath, hard. Leaves and dry grass lifted in the air and drifted towards it.

The night went still. The debris drifted to the ground, more sparks discharging from the tips of the grasses. Helfigor shook his battered staff at the wyrm but nothing happened. He mopped his brow with a shaking hand, then choked out spell after spell. One turned the air green momentarily, another sent grass seeds flying everywhere like chaff, but none affected the wyrm, which was growing ever more solid.

'Helfigor must be trying to stop it materialising any further,' said Mariam in a dead voice. 'But it's weakening him.'

Runcie was so desperately afraid that he could barely stand up. He wanted to run for his life but he knew he couldn't get away.

The wyrm raised its rod and purple bolts sizzled down into it from all directions; the creature settled under a greater weight. The moon was barely visible through it now. Helfigor staggered and fell to one knee. The wyrm turned, its eyes lit upon the three children cowering in the grass and it took a step towards them, its tread now shaking the ground.

Helfigor turned to run, saw the children standing there, and stopped, eyes closed, fists hanging at his sides as if searching inside himself for courage. With a shaky roar, he turned back and hurled himself at the monstrous beast.

Mariam gasped. Runcie could hardly bear to watch. The wyrm blew out a freezing breath and ice swept across the wizard's cheeks like frost forming on a window. Within seconds, Helfigor's face was covered. Icicles grew from his chin and the tip of his nose, his wrists and fingers, and all along his staff. He forced himself on, moving ever more stiffly. Patches of frost cracked off his lips and nostrils, but the spaces were filled in at once. Helfigor creaked to a stop, turned and tried to run, but managed no more than a quiver.

'It's got him,' whispered Runcie. 'It's frozen him up, Mariam.'

The wyrm's long tail whipped around in front of it, circled Helfigor's waist and tightened like a boa constrictor. The wizard's precious staff snapped in two with a sound like a sonic boom.

'Tawcryffe!' Helfigor thrashed in agony and ice flew in all directions.

Runcie felt a distant, fading wail as Tawcryffe's *presence* fled, then frost covered Helfigor completely. The wyrm tossed its head and the circular object – a pair of spectacles with lenses the size of hubcaps – dropped over its eyes. The frames were bolted into the bone on either side of its skull. It bent, studied Helfigor, then flipped the spectacles up and peered at the children.

Mariam's cold hand reached out and caught Runcie's. 'We're done for. What does it want, Tigris?'

Her knees were knocking. 'To take Jac and the spell book back to Lars.'

'And then?' said Runcie.

'It'll come back for you, Mariam. And me, of course, to pay the debt.'

'At least that'll save your little sister,' said Runcie thoughtlessly, for he was thinking, and what happens to me?

Tigris moaned. 'They used to eat us, Runcie. If it touches me, I'll go mad.' She looked half mad with fear now. Her throat was quivering and, without warning, she bolted into the grass.

The wyrm let fall its victims and bounded towards them, not at all sluggish now.

'Run!' said Mariam.

They ran for their lives. The raspy grass heads smacked Runcie in the face and he could feel each thump as the wyrm came after them, its breath hissing and the grass shussing against its leathery calves. Runcie, gripped by a terror greater than anything he'd ever felt, understood just why Tigris had fled. What if it disobeyed its master? Those mighty jaws could bite him in half, and the thought of being crunched up, bones and flesh all together, was far worse than ending up in Lars Sparj's clutches.

Thump. He ran harder. *Thump.* There was a burning pain in his side. *Thump-thump.* Runcie imagined the beast springing into the air, to fall on him from above. He looked back, caught one foot and fell sprawling. Mariam didn't notice.

He clawed at the dirt and rolled over. If he was going to be eaten alive, at least he'd die facing it. The wyrm soared above him and Runcie balled up his fists, but just as he expected it to plummet down at him, its wings cracked and it dived, right where Mariam had been headed.

'Mariam,' he roared. 'Look out!'

He scrambled up, feet skidding on the dry soil as he took off. Runcie had no idea what he was going to do, but he had to do something.

Thump, then *hissss*. Runcie could feel the wyrm's frost-breath swirling all around as he burst through into an oval patch where the grass had been flattened. The wyrm, twenty yards away, had its back to him. It was so big that he didn't come up to its hips, and one sweep of that monstrous tail could smash every bone in his body.

Mariam was standing stock-still against the far wall of grass, her small fists clenched, leaning forward defiantly but all covered in frost. Its ice breath had got her too. Runcie was about to launch himself at the wyrm, to certain death, when he realised that Mariam was beyond help.

The wyrm turned, stooped towards him, then said in that deep, amused voice, 'Runcible Jones, I presume?'

Run, you fool! Runcie's knees gave, he hit the dirt and one hand closed on it. He sprang up, hurled his handful at the yellow eyes and ran for his life, hoping that, if he could draw it away, Mariam might thaw out.

Behind him he heard a leathery crack as the wyrm took off. It flapped overhead, only to plunge down into the grass to his left. Runcie approached carefully this time. Tigris was only half frosted, and the wyrm was darting at her for another blast when Runcie heard distant galloping hooves. It's help! We're saved. But judging by the people they'd met so far, that wasn't likely either.

The wyrm took to the air, staring in the direction of the sounds, then glided down to its first victims. It tucked Sleeth, now just a motionless boy-shape under a thick layer of frost, into one dinosaur-sized armpit and Runcie caught a waft of its body odour, which was overpoweringly strong. Holding Sleeth in place with its upper arm, the wyrm sculpted the air with the glittering rod.

A scalloped oval of air began to shine, like the shimmer in a beetle's eyes. The wyrm ran its splayed claws around the scallops, which solidified to reveal an oval gap between the outside and inside. It slipped one claw into the gap, heaved and, with a creak, a lustrous mother-of-pearl gate opened in the air five feet above the grass.

Runcie couldn't see what lay on the other side, for it was completely dark, though the air billowing out was as cold as a freezer. The wyrm's long tail lifted, wavering through the air with Helfigor's frosty body scattering icicles everywhere. It poked Helfigor through the gate, flicked and withdrew. The wizard was gone.

The wyrm began to clamber into the hole, Sleeth still crushed in its armpit. The gate proved a tight fit and its toe claws scored grooves down the threshold as it forced its way through, its tail extending out behind for a good few seconds.

Runcie ran back to Mariam and tried to rouse her, but he might as well have been shaking a lump of ice. He headed for Tigris, who was thawing, and began clawing the ice off her. Before he'd finished, the wyrm burst from the gate, snatched Mariam and was gone again. Runcie and Tigris stumbled to the gate, which was creeping shut. Tigris pulled herself up and peered through.

'What do you see?' said Runcie, dread closing around his heart like a frosty fist, that he'd never see Mariam again.

'Just moonlight shining on ice. Like a glacier or something.' Her voice sounded like ice being crushed.

'Not Miluviand?'

'No. Perhaps the wyrm's gate can't go that far in one go.'

Runcie wasn't sure if that were better or worse. He picked up the knobbly half of Helfigor's staff, climbed up and poked it through the gate. It felt as if his arm was barely there.

'Careful!' Tigris said sharply, taking the other half staff. 'Gates can go wrong.'

'How wrong?'

'Your arm might stay there when you pull back.'

Runcie whipped it out, then stood there, crippled by self-doubt. He'd made so many blunders, how could he be sure this wasn't another? No, he wasn't going down that road again. He had to risk the gate, for Mariam's sake. He poked around again. 'It feels solid. Come on.'

Tigris shook her head; her teeth were chattering.

'Tigris? What is it?'

She clenched her jaw, repeating, 'They used to *eat* us, Runcie.'

A flight of arrows whistled over their heads, one shattering on the pearly surrounds of the gate. It had a red tip and a yellow striped shaft. 'That's Thormic's,' she said wildly.

Runcie hefted the knobbly half staff, not that it would be any use against either wyrm or cutthroats. 'I'm going after Mariam. Come on.' He climbed up onto the sill of the gate, braced himself, put his feet flat against the gate and tried to hold it open. Tigris didn't move and he was tempted to leave her behind, but they had to rely on each other. 'We've got to stick together, Tigris.'

Tigris took a shuddery breath, then caught hold of the sill and began to heave herself up. The gate was still creeping shut. Runcie's knees buckled. He tried not to think of the gate closing on his leg, or around her middle. 'Hurry!'

More arrows struck the gate and three came right through, except for their feathers. The longest arrow just pricked the end of his nose as Tigris settled on the sill beside him. The gate jerked, nearly closed. Runcie slipped and his left leg fell into the gap. He tried to lift it out but the edge of the gate was pressing into his calf through his trousers.

He cried out as it broke the skin, terrified it was going to take his leg off. Tigris caught it, twisted and jerked it out, and they swayed together on the narrow sill. Runcie caught her eye. 'Ready?'

Pfft, pfft. Two bright red arrows tore through, leaving fuming black slits that spread like charring paper. Thormic's magic was destroying the gate before their eyes.

Before he could move, the gate snapped shut, sweeping them into the darkness.

CHAPTER 23

The Ghoolwyrm's Icy Lair

Runcie, hurtling through pitch darkness as if he'd been fired from a catapult, let out a squeal of fright. 'Tigris?'

No reply. He was accelerating through the air, the wind plucking at his ears. 'Tigris!' he shouted, clinging to the broken staff for all he was worth. He thought he made out a distant cry, though he couldn't tell where it was coming from. It was so cold that tears were freezing on his cheeks and an icicle growing on his upper lip. He wiped it away but his nose kept dripping.

He hit a pool of air so cold that it was like diving into a lake in winter – for a few seconds he couldn't draw breath. After the sickening feeling of passing through a second gate, Runcie smashed through something brittle, showering shards everywhere.

As he went skidding headfirst across a floor as smooth as an icy pond, the dark receded. It *was* ice, on a lake or underground river, and so clear that he glimpsed creatures in the depths scattering from his shadow.

Runcie shot up a ramp and fell, arms flapping, to slam into the ice with his chest and chin. He was on the floor of a cell, like a circular birdcage, whose bars were also made of ice. A barred top clicked into place and locked.

He sat up, rubbing his battered chin. Tigris was crouched, knees drawn up to her chest and arms wrapped around them, on the floor of a similar cage a few feet away. Her half staff lay beside her. They were in a winding tunnel or cavern, about twenty feet wide and nearly as high, whose ice walls were smooth, as if melted by running water. Smaller caverns ran off the main tunnel here and there, which in places was cut across by narrow, jagged crevasses. It looked as though they were inside a glacier, though the ice was green, just as it had been on his computer at the Nightingales. He couldn't see the entrance.

'Tigris?' he said softly. 'Where are we?'

She didn't raise her head and her voice was muffled, despairing. 'In the ghoolwyrm's lair, from where there can be no escape.'

His stomach twisted itself into a knot. 'But . . . I thought Lars Sparj had conjured the wyrm to hunt us down?'

Tigris didn't respond.

'I hope Mariam and Helfigor are all right,' he said.

'And Jac.' A shudder racked her slender figure.

And if he hadn't damaged Helfigor's staff, none of this would have happened. Thankfully, Tigris was too generous to point that out. 'You know all about ghoolwyrms, don't you, Tigris?'

'Everyone knows about wyrms, Runcie. They're where magic *comes* from.'

'How do you mean?'

286

She sat up, glanced at him then, oddly, put her hand over her mouth to stifle a giggle. He hadn't seen her smile before and it quite transformed her.

'What's the matter? I could use a laugh.'

'You've got a moustache of . . . er, frozen snot,' she said, amused and embarrassed.

'My face is so cold it's gone numb,' he said, flushing. He scrubbed his upper lip with his sleeve. 'You were saying?'

The smile disappeared. 'The wyrms owned Iltior for a thousand, thousand years, and they preyed on us. We only survived by hiding in the densest forests and the narrowest caves where they couldn't go.'

The knot in Runcie's stomach tightened. 'Couldn't people fight them?'

'Wyrms were much bigger, plus they had magic and we didn't. *And* they could fly. They beat us every time.'

'So what happened?' Runcie imagined mighty heroes fighting back-to-back against impossible odds and miraculously vanquishing the enemy in the nick of time.

She gave an eerie laugh and his daydream vanished. 'Not what you're thinking. "No army could storm their alpine lairs,"' she quoted, '"no warrior fight his way through their magicked gates." Besides, there were no warriors left, just old men and beardless boys, and not many of either. It looked as though humankind was doomed.'

'I'd really like to hear the tale,' said Runcie, 'if you know it.' Anything to stop him thinking about their fate.

'I learned it when I was little. It goes on for hours but the ending is the best.' Tigris began to speak in a storyteller's voice. 'Finally, when their food was almost gone and all seemed lost, one terrified woman summoned up the courage all others lacked. Jasinthe Noellar was her name, and she became the greatest hero in the world, for she dared what no one else could. In a long-forgotten codex rescued from a burning library, she had discovered a passage into the wyrm's lair and resolved to attempt it, in the hope that there would be a future for her children.

'Jasinthe crept through an ancient labyrinth no other adventurer had survived, solving traps and puzzles both magical and mechanical, then crept like a spider down the terrifying drop of a shaft so narrow no grown man could have fitted through it.

'On she went, through the clinging slime of slug-encrusted tunnels where she bit her fingers to the bone to keep from screaming in disgust, and along other paths so horrible no bard could bear to describe them. Finally she had to wriggle on her belly past two thousand hibernating wyrms whose snoring mimicked a herd of stampeding elephants, into the deepest and most terrifying cavern of all.

'The treasure cave of the Great Mother lay in the vein of pure silver at the heart of the High Peaks of the Uttermost Ghool. There Jasinthe found, there she untethered and there with quaking heart she took up the gold-coated, diamond-studded ancestral egg, which was the source of all the wyrm's magic.'

Runcie let out a sigh. He loved tales of desperate daring and unfathomable magic, especially where they involved small heroes fighting against impossible odds.

'But of course,' Tigris went on, 'great treasures are never left unguarded, nor relinquished that easily. The ancestral egg was protected by the wyrm's most powerful magic and as soon as Jasinthe touched it, it cried out a warning to Shadpath – the Mother of all Wyrms. She lay in the hatching chamber immediately below, breathing magical fire over her clutch of eggs which were, after twenty-seven years of tending, finally ready to hatch. With a trumpeting cry of rage, Shadpath abandoned the eggs to die and thundered up to the treasure cavern, summoning her guards as she went.

'They cornered Jasinthe, but she'd known all along that there was no way out. She had sacrificed herself to save her children, and all the children of the world. Staggering under the weight of the ancestral egg, Jasinthe hurled it into the underground stream whose enchanted waters had bathed it since time began. And then she turned to meet her doom. And meet it she did.' Tigris shuddered.

After a decent interval of contemplation, Runcie said quietly, 'What happened to her?'

'It's too gruesome to say – especially *here*.' Tigris continued her tale. 'But Jasinthe had done what she went there to do. Though Shadpath's magic froze the stream in its bed, and her guards hurled themselves recklessly off the cliffs after the treasure, the egg was already out of sight. The torrent issuing from the cliffs carried it over the Crystal Falls, down and down, until it smashed into a million pieces on the rocks at the bottom of the High Ghool. The wailing wyrms gathered up what they could find, though most of the fragments had been carried away by the waters. But, even worse than losing their precious egg, magic – their wyrm magic that had allowed them to rule Iltior unchallenged for aeons – was free in the world. Soon human beings would have it too.'

'And then people overthrew them?' said Runcie.

'Not for a long time,' Tigris said in her own voice. 'Wyrm magic was very difficult to learn and they fought desperately to get it back. Finally our greatest mage, Ancharium, realised that we could never defeat wyrms wizard to wizard, for their magic must always be stronger. However, he found another way. Only so much magical *quintessence* could be drawn at a time, and the more we used, the less was left for them.'

'So the answer was to give magic to everyone?' Runcie guessed.

'That's right.' Tigris sat up. A little colour had come back to her face; reliving the famous tale had inspired her. 'He ordered that every child be taught magic from birth. The war went on for centuries more, with everyone using magic for small things and great, until, without warning, the wyrms collapsed and died. We could choose to use magic or not, you see, but they were creatures of magic and, starved of it, they couldn't survive. In a few weeks the wyrms were gone, save for their magical bones, which were locked away in lead-lined vaults in Anthrimorie, just in case.'

'And the people of Iltior have had magic ever since?' said Runcie.

She flashed a pallid smile at him. 'Unfortunately the magicians turned on each other, and fought for two terrible centuries until a power-hungry faction, the Cybale, led the magicians into a terrible battle, betrayed them to death and seized all magic. They took the ghoolwyrm as their totem, but the Cybale soon became as cruel as the wyrms, and the people ended up no better than slaves.' Tigris lapsed into silence, discouraged again, and Runcie could think of nothing to say that might cheer her.

So that's why no one wanted the Cybale to rise again, he thought. And our coming to Iltior has given them their chance.

Miserable, freezing hours went by. They couldn't sit down, for the floor was solid ice and the bars too cold to lean on. Runcie tried to break them with the staff but the ice proved as tough as steel. Tigris tried her kid's magic on the lock, though the great spell that bound it didn't even quiver. She slumped to the floor, gnawing her bloody nails.

'Where did transportals come from, Tigris? Ulalliall is over three thousand years old, so she must have been made when wyrms were still around.'

'Yes, the first transportals were crafted near the end of the Wyrm War.'

'So why do they speak, and all that? And why are they so cranky and arrogant?'

'Well,' she said, thinking, 'our history lessons say that back then, wyrm magic was developing *resistance* to us. Even though magicians were using wyrm bones, it was getting harder to draw on magical *quintessence,* and it hurt to use it. I think that's why *presences* like Ulalliall and Tawcryffe were crafted into magical objects – they could draw on *quintessence* over a long time and store it for whenever it was needed. The Wizard Wars were fought over that.

'But *resistance* became ever stronger, and *presences* more and more important and cranky, until the hardest part of a wizard's training was finding a way to work with them. Wizards were always looking for an easier source of magic and, not long after the Cybale fell, one was found. It was called *violent quintessence,* a force so rare, powerful and deadly that most of the wizards who tried to use it died horribly. Thandimanilon's tower, Miluviand, was specially built to tap into *violent quintessence,* but she won't touch it. No one risks it anymore.'

'Why not?'

'They don't need to because, just recently, a strong and safe source was discovered – *steady quintessence* – and now most wizards draw on that. It's changed the way magic is used. Presences like Ulalliall and Tawcryffe aren't nearly as important as they used to be, and they're bitterly angry about it.'

It explained a lot, not that it was any help here. 'What's the wyrm going to do?' said Runcie. 'Eat us?'

'Ghasts and conjure-wyrms don't need to eat.'

But there was blood on its muzzle, Runcie recalled, so it had to be more real than either. He had an idea. 'If Lars conjured up the wyrm from thousands of years ago, maybe it doesn't know how well kids can do magic. What are you good at?'

'There's no point,' she said dismally.

Tigris was prone to despair and if they were to survive he had to help her overcome it, though he'd rarely taken the lead before. On the other hand, he knew all about fighting despair. 'I don't think Jasinthe would ever have said that.'

She reacted as if he'd struck her. 'You don't know what it's like!'

'I know you're really clever and we need your help.'

She turned away, holding her cupped hands out before her, and began to murmur in a foreign tongue. After an effort, something yellow eased into being and Tigris let out a sigh. Runcie stood up on tiptoe. A small, brilliantly yellow frog was crouched in her hands, gazing up at her with such a charming lopsided look that it seemed to be smiling. Tigris bent over, touched her lips to the top of its head and it vanished.

'Wow!' said Runcie, who'd always liked frogs. He'd love to have one for a mindsake. 'That was brilliant. How did you do it?'

'It wasn't my real mindsake; just an *envisioning* of it. I'm not strong enough to hold it for long, but even an envisioned mindsake helps. I feel better now.' A little colour appeared in her cheeks. 'I'm fairly good at fire magic. What about you?'

'I can't do magic,' Runcie said sharply.

'You must be good at *something*.'

Only reading and computers, and making stuff out of bits of junk, none of which were any help here. 'I could try to pick the lock,' he said, not that he had the faintest idea how. It wasn't the kind of thing good kids did.

He climbed to the top of the cage. The ice lock, which was the size and shape of a grapefruit, was so clear that he could see the intricate workings inside. Unfortunately, he didn't have a clue how it operated. He felt in his pockets but found only fluff. 'I don't suppose you've got a hairpin?'

Tigris had conjured a small flame at the base of one of the ice bars. She drew her fingers around the flame, which grew until it surrounded the bar.

He slid down. 'Tigris?'

Without looking up, she unfastened the ball of hair above her left ear and extended her arm through the bars, holding a long hairpin. Runcie could just reach it. She looked silly, with her hair hanging down on one side and balled up on the other, but he didn't know her well enough to make a joke about it.

Up at the lock again, he slid open a cunningly designed key-hole cover and had just begun to probe with the pin when something entered the cavern entrance so quickly that, like a plunger down a plughole, it sent a furious rush of wind before it. Ice crystals were blasted into their faces. Runcie lost his grip and fell; Tigris's small fire was blown out.

The wyrm scrabbled forwards, still holding a frost-covered Sleeth in its armpit. Mariam hung like a rag from its other hand, while Helfigor was held in a coil of its elongated tail. Setting its prey down, the wyrm cast a swift glance at the cages then dropped Mariam and Sleeth. Neither moved, though they seemed to be alive. It didn't appear sluggish now, nor transparent. The wyrm looked like a real live predator, and a hungry one.

Delving in the recesses of a side cave, it hauled out bundles of crumbling sticks, which it formed into a triangular stack, then stood Sleeth and Mariam in the centre with only their heads and chests visible. It curved its long tail around in front of it; a ripple ran from one end to the other and Helfigor was set on his feet.

Shaking the hubcap-sized spectacles down, it said softly, 'It's so long since I've had cooked meat that I can't remember the taste.' Its voice was a deep rumble, like the purring of an enormous cat. The wyrm glanced at the bound children, saying with a sly chuckle, 'though I do recall *live-cooked* brats being tastier.'

Helfigor's throat moved, but no sound came forth until the wyrm drew one claw along the line of the wizard's lips and they parted like a zipper.

'You've had your fun, Lars,' Helfigor croaked, as if his vocal chords hadn't thawed. 'State your ransom and it'll be paid as soon as my allies can gather the gold together.'

'I have all the treasures of the wyrm at my disposal,' sneered the wyrm. 'What care I for your sad cupful of mites?'

Helfigor seemed taken aback. 'Lars?' he said uncertainly.

The wyrm waited, head tilted to the side, watching him with one bowl-sized eye, oddly magnified by the spectacle lens. The other eye was fixed on Mariam and Sleeth. It clashed the black claws of its right hand against those of its left and a yellow spark drifted towards the frozen wizard, settling on the icicle-clad tip of his nose. Colour spread out from the spark, then the ice began to crack off.

Helfigor's face was almost normal again, though his limbs and body remained coated with frost. 'What do you want of me, Lars?'

The wyrm leered at him, displaying at least eighty finger-long teeth. Another wave rippled along its tail, like a whip cracking in slow motion. The tip had a hooked barb, not unlike the sting of a scorpion, which was snapping up and down as if the wyrm had just realised what it was for.

'What do *I* want!' it said, its voice so deep and shivery that Runcie could feel the ice vibrating beneath him. Colours flickered along the triple crests that ran from the top of its head all the way down its backbone, and its toe claws dug into the ice, tearing it up into curls as if it were butter. 'I want to know what humans have done to my world.'

'Wyrms have been extinct these past three thousand years,' said Helfigor. Through sheer will, he forced his right fist above his head and brandished it at the great beast. A weak aura shimmered around his knuckles for a moment, and a few ice crystals were shed from the roof to land in his hair. 'Go back to your master, chimera,' he shouted, 'and go empty-handed. These children are in my care. Not you nor Lars Sparj may touch them.'

The wyrm raised its little finger and Helfigor's aura vanished. Its vast mouth broke into an unmistakeable sneer. 'Lars

Sparj meddled with forces beyond his comprehension. Conjured I may have been, *but not out of nothing.*'

Helfigor swayed. 'What do you mean?' He tried to force himself forwards. His body tilted over and one arm twitched, but his feet wouldn't move.

'Why does Lars want Mariam?' said the wyrm.

Helfigor, thoroughly alarmed, managed to drag the pipes from inside his coat and blew a silent, tickling blast, though it had no more effect than his previous calls.

The wyrm waved its left hand and Helfigor froze below the chin, tilted forwards. The wyrm turned away, whereupon an echoing rumble came from the region of its belly. 'So long it's been,' it said in a whisper. 'So very, very long.'

It took several striding steps, bent down and carved a circle in the ice floor with a claw. Chips of ice squealed up. It stamped inside the circle with one foot and a disc of cut ice rotated upwards. Tossing it out of the way like a Frisbee, the wyrm slid into the water. Its shadow glided this way and that, snapping up fish and other swimming creatures, before disappearing into the depths.

Runcie went back to his furious lock-picking, though to no avail.

'Helfigor!' hissed Tigris.

'Who's there?' he said faintly.

'Tigris and Runcie. It's got us in cages. Can you help?'

The tendons stood out in Helfigor's neck. 'Alas, no.' After a long pause marked out by the distant creaking of the ice, the frost slowly crept up his lips again.

'It's up to us,' said Runcie quietly. 'And I'm *not* going to be eaten.'

'It's no use, Runcie,' she said dismally. 'We can't do anything.'

'I'm not giving up,' said Runcie. '*Never*, while I've a breath left.'

A light slowly grew in Tigris's dark eyes. 'Thanks, Runcie. You give me hope where I've had none.'

'I do?'

She looked embarrassed. 'Let's get to work.' She conjured her little flame around the nearest bar, though it didn't seem to be making an impression on the iron-hard ice.

Runcie was about to resume his hopeless lock-picking when he had an idea, one that no one from Iltior would ever have thought of.

'Tigris, could you melt a little hole in the floor? I need some water.'

'I should be able to, if it's just normal ice . . .' She bent her head, strained and, with a little *pouff*, flames leapt up around her hands like a fire in a wastepaper basket. Kneeling down, she shaped the blaze with her fingers and the surface of the floor began to melt into a hollow. 'How much do you need?'

'A couple of double handfuls . . .'

'What's the matter?' she said as he trailed off, miserably.

'I don't have anything to carry it in. I'm sunk before I begin.'

With a tinkling laugh, Tigris swept the fire into nothingness with the back of her hand and curved the other hand down into the small pool she'd melted in the floor, then out again.

With movements too swift to follow she wove trails of water into a pail made of ice, the size of a child's sand bucket. Dipping her fingers into the water, she arched them back and forth above the pail until a glittering crystalline handle had been created there and fixed at either end with a deft squeeze of finger and thumb. Scooping it full of water, she held it out to him between the bars.

Runcie laughed as he took it. Magic was wonderful. 'Just like that?'

'Just like that. Quick, before the water freezes.' She warmed her blue fingers in her mouth.

He climbed up, careful not to spill a drop, held back the keyhole cover and poured the water in until the lock was full. Letting the cover spring closed, he climbed down and handed her the half full pail. Ice crystals were spreading across the surface.

'I don't understand.' Her eyes searched his face.

'It's a different kind of magic,' he said, staring up at the lock. 'I don't know if it's going to work . . .' Creak, creak, *crack*! He scrambled back up. The lock had split along its seams. Bracing himself, he kicked it hard and it fell apart. Runcie climbed out and sprang across to the top of Tigris's cage. 'Quick, the water!'

She handed it up to him. 'How did you do that?' She was looking at him in an entirely different light.

'It's just primary school science,' he said, deliberately offhand.

Tigris gave a yelp and backed away.

'What's the matter?' He nonchalantly poked his finger through the ice crust and poured water into the lock. He seldom got the chance to feel clever; especially not on Iltior.

'Science is a crime,' she whispered. 'Even for First Order wizards.'

'Really? Why?'

'It would ruin our world as it has yours. You could be sold to the slavers for doing it.'

'We could be eaten any minute! Anyway, it wasn't really science.'

'You broke the lock with it,' she said accusingly.

'Water expands when it freezes. Dad was always putting his beer bottles in the freezer and forgetting about them until they burst.'

Tigris's look held a mixture of alarm and awe. Runcie felt like a fraud; anyone could have done it.

'Runcie! It's coming.' A shadow swooped under the ice, devoured an unsuspecting fish with a snap of its jaws and streaked for the circular hole.

The lock cracked apart. 'Can you make shapes that look like us, in there?'

'I suppose so.' Tigris wove her fingers together and flicked them at his cage, then hers. Vaguely kid-shaped shadows grew inside. They didn't look very convincing.

He scuttled back to his cage and grabbed the half staff. They'd just slipped into a dark crevasse cutting across the far wall of the cavern when the wyrm burst up through the hole.

After casting a fleeting glance at the cages, it unzipped Helfigor's lips again. 'Talk, wizard.'

'What's your name, wyrm?' said Helfigor.

The wyrm flipped the spectacles down, tapped them with its

glittering rod and the coating of ice melted away. 'You may call me Wyrmhilte.'

'Is that your secret name, wyrm-mother?'

Wyrmhilte's leathery lip curled with contempt at such an obvious ploy.

'You don't plan to eat *me*, then?' said Helfigor.

The wyrm turned up her flared nostrils. 'I'm not so hungry that I'd feed on a wizard's rank flesh and splintery bones. Will you talk?'

'No,' said Helfigor.

Picking up a bundle of sticks, Wyrmhilte thrust her rod into the end and flames grew there. She tossed the bundle at one corner of the triangular stack, then laid a knuckle on Sleeth's mouth and the frost melted off him completely.

'I'll tell you everything you need to know,' said Sleeth eagerly.

Wyrmhilte lifted him out with a claw through his jerkin. Runcie watched them walk up the tunnel together. Sleeth was moving like a frozen robot, the spell book clutched in his hand. Mariam's stack of sticks had begun to smoulder.

'Tigris, do you think you could thaw Helfigor?' It was a big ask, pitting her kid's magic against a mighty wyrm's.

Tigris gnawed at her fingernails, which she'd bitten to the quick, leaving her fingertips flecked with blood. 'I *could* have a go with cold fire.'

'Will that thaw him?'

Tigris sucked at her forefinger. 'I don't know. I can't use hot fire, obviously.'

'What if . . .?' Runcie's palms were damp with sweat and he had a sick feeling in the pit of his stomach. 'What if I run and free Mariam, while you sneak around behind Helfigor and try to thaw him?'

'If Wyrmhilte sees you, you're dead.'

He'd been trying not to think about that. 'She's going to eat us, anyway.' He began to creep around the edge of the ice ramp, sick with terror.

The smouldering stack was about ten yards away. Wyrmhilte was still walking away with Sleeth but as Runcie moved, she turned, so he ducked into shelter again. Wyrmhilte and Sleeth came back, stopping by the stack of sticks.

'Eat them if you must,' Sleeth was saying, 'but listen to me first.' Leaning forwards, he said with a cunning leer that looked out of place on his boyish face, 'I can be of great use to you.'

'*Really?*' said Wyrmhilte. 'How?'

'I can free you from Lars Sparj. His Spirit Conjuration spell is in this book.' Sleeth held it up. 'It's Thandimanilon's book of spells.'

'What sort of child are you, to betray your own kind to an enemy?'

'A driven one,' said Sleeth. 'I'm bound to a secret quest that I must fulfil.'

'You won't,' Wyrmhilte said with calculated indifference.

'But,' cried Sleeth, 'you don't understand . . .'

Wyrmhilte began to laugh, a thundering that shook her from her long tail to the triple crests on her head. Her tail coiled and uncoiled; her chest heaved, and pieces of ice broke off the roof to shatter unnoticed on her shoulders.

'What is it?' cried Sleeth in anguish.

'I'm going to eat you too,' said Wyrmhilte. She tilted her head to one side. 'Assuming I can wash the dirt off.'

Sleeth's grubby face had gone white. 'But . . . you're not real. You can't act for yourself. A Spirit Conjuration can't be broken by the spirit that has been conjured.'

The wyrm laughed mockingly. 'Lars Sparj didn't understand what he was dealing with. It takes a mighty spell to re-clothe the spirit of a long-dead creature with living flesh; an even mightier one to give it life, purpose and intellect. The conjuration always takes the easiest path to completion: the closest spirit of its kind or the most recently dead, suited or not. But should there be one *not dead at all*, it will always raise it first.'

'What do you mean?' quavered Sleeth, lips standing out like purple bruises on his bloodless face.

'I wasn't dead, as the rest of my kind are. Before the last wyrms expired from a dearth of magic, the Mother of all Ghoolwyrms laid me, her daughter and heir, and all her goods and treasures, in a crevasse here in the Glarr Ice Cap. Here I froze instantly, and here I lay, lost in icy dreaming. Over the aeons my body learned to endure the dearth that had killed my people, and then Lars's conjuration woke me. And since I have *never* been dead, he can't control me.'

'But,' spluttered Sleeth, 'before, you said you were taking me to Lars.'

'I was weak at first,' said Wyrmhilte. 'More phantom than real; and more *here* in the ice than there. I didn't know what had happened, so I bowed before the sorcerer and did his bidding while my strength came back.'

'So what do you want of *me?*' said Helfigor thickly.

Wyrmhilte's head darted around. 'I want your aid in my quest, wizard.'

'And that is?'

'To restore my kind to their rightful place on Iltior.'

CHAPTER 24

The Re-Sighting

Tigris made a choking sound and her mouth opened wide. She was going to scream, and then Wyrmhilte would have them. Runcie clapped his hand over her mouth and held her tightly, a darker cold creeping over him. If wyrms came back to terrorise Iltior, that would be his fault too.

Helfigor's frosted body gave a convulsive jerk and the ice crazed all over him. 'But you have no *kind*,' he whispered. 'Wyrms have been extinct for three thousand years.'

'Except for me,' said Wyrmhilte, 'and my mother's last clutch of eggs, frozen at the very instant before hatching.'

Helfigor's eyes were staring in horror, his hair stirring like a clump of blind worms. 'And . . . and if I don't?'

'I will cook the children and eat them. Starting with her.' He pointed a black talon at Mariam.

'I won't be held to ransom,' said Helfigor. 'Not at any price.'

'So be it,' said Wyrmhilte. 'Once you've fed my fishes, I'll ask another wizard, and another. It won't take long. Treachery is meat and drink to your kind.'

Tigris was shuddering in Runcie's arms and he couldn't think straight for dread. How could his one small mistake, using the parchment to escape the bullies, have led to such a cascade of world-changing consequences? And was there anything he could do to stop it?

'But first, why does Lars want the Re-sighter?' Drawing her glittering rod, Wyrmhilte shook it until its tip was enveloped by a black spinning globe, encircled by coloured bands like the rings of Saturn. It wobbled, emitting narrow beams of black light and threads of sound that rasped like saw blades.

Wyrmhilte directed the globe to float in mid-air above Mariam's head, then lowered it until it touched her. Mariam immediately began speaking in a distant, stilted voice, as if she were reliving someone else's tale of long ago.

'Molten fire rains from the sky.' Her face grew red, droplets of sweat the size of peas broke out across her forehead and her voice fell to a whisper. 'On the Five Hills, the great brazen sickles sag on their pedestals. Liquid gold runs through the city square, unheeded . . .'

Mariam trailed off, looking around the cavern as if she was seeing some other place. She wiped her sweaty forehead with her arm. The front of her shirt was sodden.

'. . . red-hot cinders are rising over the window ledges. Windows are bursting, roofs collapsing. Every house in the street is aflame.'

'What's she on about?' Runcie whispered.

Mariam fanned her face with her hand, gasping as if the air

were burning her windpipe, and said in a dead voice, 'Alone, abandoned, I wander the tunnels of the city of the dead. Beautiful Anthrimorie, your Citadel of Magic is lost forever. Lava crackles atop fifty slarbs of ash as the city dies roof by roof, window by window, tile by tile. And I can't get out. *I can't get out!'* she shrieked, beating at the bundles of wood as if trying to break down a door.

'Enough,' said the wyrm. The black globe went out with a fizzing pop.

Mariam looked around sheepishly, as if she'd been caught doing something foolish. The flush faded; ice formed on her wet shirt and she sagged against the glowing sticks.

Wyrmhilte was staring at the floor between her feet, deep in thought. Helfigor looked as though he'd been woken by a smack in the mouth with a stinking fish – he knew exactly what Mariam's words meant. And Runcie noticed something else. Tigris had partly succeeded, for the wizard's left arm had thawed to the elbow, as had his left cheek.

A little apart, Sleeth's eyes lit up with an unholy glee. He understood too. He began to edge away.

Now, Helfigor, Runcie prayed. If you've got any strength left, attack before it's too late. He waved. Helfigor looked up and Runcie tossed the knobbly-ended half staff to him.

Helfigor's thawed arm snapped up and caught it. The silvery lines on the staff began to shine, the blue jewels to glow, and then it shook in his hand. 'Tawcryffe,' he said with a catch in his voice, 'you're back! Cracked Cavern Ceiling, *Crumble!'*

The roof above Wyrmhilte caved in, burying her. A table-sized wedge of ice, pointed like a chisel, speared straight through the floor in front of Runcie and a jet of water shot up from the hole. A flying ice chunk scattered the sticks, leaving Mariam swaying dazedly.

'Is Wyrmhilte dead?' said Runcie, putting out a smoking patch on Mariam's coat by pressing a lump of ice against it. She hardly noticed.

'It takes a lot to kill a wyrm,' said Helfigor, the last ice flaking off. 'Come on.'

'Where are we going?' said Tigris.

'To find the gate Wyrmhilte used to bring us here. I may be able to reopen it, with a lot of luck.'

Crack-craaack, crack-craaaaack.

A fissure curved across the floor, beginning at the wedge-shaped hole near Runcie and ending under the mound of ice. Another fissure zigzagged out from its other side.

'Run!' roared Helfigor.

Grabbing Mariam by the wrist, Runcie bolted in the direction of the entrance but, before they had gone a dozen yards, cracks snaked in all directions, part of the floor collapsed under the weight of ice and water hit them in a freezing, knee-high wave. He staggered as the cracked slab beneath him began to tilt and would have slid backwards into the water had Helfigor not jerked him to safety. Far below, the wyrm's shadow tumbled over and over before disappearing in the depths.

'With a broken staff, that hurt me more than I can say.' Helfigor took in the sodden, bedraggled children, shuddering with cold. 'We need fire, quickly.'

Runcie pointed wordlessly at the scattered sticks, which the water had carried up the tunnel, though they were covered in a film of ice.

'I can't set them alight like that,' said Helfigor, leaning on his staff. 'Yet we must have fire.'

Runcie trudged after the scattered bundles, his feet thudding into the floor like frozen blocks of wood. He heaved a bundle above his head, feeling the ice stick to his fingers, then slammed it down. Ice flew everywhere. He sent the bundle skidding across to the wizard, then bashed the ice off another bundle, and a third. Soon the pile of sticks was waist high though, try as he might, Helfigor was too weak to set it alight.

Mariam's teeth were chattering, and Runcie's wet feet felt as though they were freezing inside his boots. 'Have a go, Tigris,' he said, then, remembering that she was prone to despair, 'You're *really* good with fire magic.'

After several attempts, Tigris managed to set the damp, powdery wood alight. Everyone pressed close, holding their hands out to the pale flames. They didn't produce much heat, but it was enough to save them.

Runcie's hands were starting to hurt as they warmed up when Tigris said, 'Where's Jac?'

'Just after Mariam had her vision, he seemed mighty pleased about something,' Runcie said.

'Did he now?' Helfigor said grimly. 'We'd better make sure of him.'

They searched the crevasses and crannies on the far side of the collapse hole, but saw no sign of Sleeth. Helfigor collected the other half of his staff. 'He must have fallen with the wyrm. He's lost to the depths, and I can't help thinking it's for the best.' Tigris stiffened and tears formed in her eyes. 'He was a most unhappy kid,' Helfigor went on kindly, 'set an impossible task. He's at peace now.' He looked around, sniffing the air, then headed towards the entrance.

'Where are we going?' said Runcie.

'Confound it, boy, will you stop pestering me!'

It was dark around the corner. Shortly Runcie, trudging along in silence, caught sight of a fleeting glow in the distance, as if someone had conjured finger-light. 'Helfigor?'

Helfigor looked all in. 'Not now,' he growled.

'It's Sleeth!'

'*What?* Where, boy?'

'There.' Runcie pointed as the glow reappeared.

'What's he playing at?' the wizard mused.

The air rippled. Helfigor went still, his battered nose up as if sniffing out a faint, elusive magic, then he bolted. The children followed as best they could in the dark, stumbling over lumps of ice, but after a minute Runcie heard an ear-popping thud and red lightning flashed in the distance, outlining a small figure with one arm upraised.

'The wretch has opened Wyrmhilte's gate,' panted Runcie.

With a shattering roar the floor burst apart ahead of them and Wyrmhilte erupted into the tunnel, sending plates of ice the size of tabletops spinning in all directions. She bounded twenty feet forwards onto solid floor, shaking herself like a gigantic, scaly hound. Her head shot around; her eyes took in Helfigor and the children, dismissed them and turned the other way, towards the scalloped oval gate. In three bounds, Wyrmhilte landed just a swipe away from Sleeth.

Thandimanilon's book of magic lay open in his hands. 'They – they were going to escape,' he lied. 'I was trying to close your gate before they could get to it.'

With a snap of Wyrmhilte's finger and thumb, the gate closed. She flipped down her ice-covered spectacles and pressed a finger against each lens, melting the ice. The left lens was cracked in two places, making it appear as though she had three left eyes.

'Why should I believe you?' she said with a purring growl. Bloody contusions were swelling across her head and back beneath the pearly scales, while her left shoulder hung oddly. The cave-in had hurt her badly.

'Because I can help you,' said Sleeth.

'Help *me*?' said Wyrmhilte, pretending astonishment. 'How?'

'This book contains the greatest spells of the sorcerers' guild. It can teach you more about *our* magic than you could learn by yourself in a hundred years.'

The wyrm lunged and snatched the book from Sleeth's hand. 'And now I have it.'

Sleeth hid his dismay, saying smoothly, 'It's written in a code that takes long to learn, but I can help you decipher it.'

'And what do you demand in return?'

'I wouldn't dare demand anything from one so great as you,' said Sleeth with breathtaking obsequiousness. 'But since you ask, I want to become a great sorcerer, so as to serve you better.'

'Is that so?' said Wyrmhilte. 'And what of your friends here?'

'They're no friends of mine. They've tried to ruin me, over and again.'

'Then it wouldn't bother you if I ate them?'

'Not . . . not at all.' Sleeth avoided looking in Tigris's direction as he said it.

Tigris let out a muffled cry and clutched at Runcie's shoulder.

'The only way out of here is through the gate, so we'll have to attack,' Helfigor muttered. 'Runcie, you and Mariam take Sleeth. Tigris and I will go for the wyrm. Be ready the moment I say the word.'

'Are you strong enough?' said Mariam.

'I'll have to be, won't I?'

The wizard didn't look it; Runcie expected him to collapse at any moment. But at least Mariam seemed her normal self again.

'Excellent,' said Wyrmhilte to Sleeth, after a considering pause. She held out the book. 'Let's begin right away.'

'Go!' hissed Helfigor. He traced an oval in the air with the staff, whereupon the ice liquefied beneath Wyrmhilte and she fell through. She caught the edge but her injured shoulder popped out of its socket and, with a grunt of pain, she slid under the water.

Runcie raced around the hole and launched himself at his quarry but Sleeth, wearing that sneering smile, bashed him with the heavy spell book. Runcie went skidding across the floor into the side wall, nose first. Sleeth had done it to him again.

Hot blood flooded his mouth and chin. He struggled to his feet in time to see Mariam go for Sleeth, though more cleverly. She feinted a slap across the face but, as Sleeth blocked her, she swung a hooked right foot and neatly cut his feet from under him.

Sleeth landed hard and the spell book went flying, scattering loose pages behind it. The look on his face was wonderful to see: Sleeth couldn't believe that a girl had taken him down, and a Nightlander at that.

Mariam looked down at him, hands on her hips, and couldn't resist a scornful laugh.

'You'll be sorry,' Sleeth spat, then scrabbled after the book.

A breeze tossed the loose pages like autumn leaves. Mariam and Runcie leapt for the book but Sleeth got there first. Snatching it up, and as many of the loose pages as he could reach, he riffled them, held one up in triumph and, as Mariam tried to grab it, shouted, 'Adit, Approach!'

Runcie froze as the words came back at them, louder and more drawn-out until they resembled a drum roll on a gigantic drum. The final boom was like a jet going through the sound barrier, then Wyrmhilte's gate zoomed up to Sleeth and sprang open. Through it, Runcie saw the top section of Thandimanilon's tower, where she and Lars Sparj were running up the steps into his transportal.

'You'd dare go back?' gasped Runcie, wiping his bleeding nose on the back of his hand, 'after all you've done to her?'

Tigris let out a choked cry and Runcie whirled. She was walking towards the gate, to Thandimanilon, with a look of despairing resolve. The moment he'd been dreading had come, and at the worst possible time.

'Tigris!' Runcie caught her by the hand. 'Don't go.'

Sleeth took advantage of the confusion to grab Mariam, spinning her around and cruelly twisting her arm up behind her back. 'For the location of Anthrimorie,' he said, cunning eyes shining, 'Thandimanilon would forgive me a dozen lost transportals. I'll be her master prentice before the day is out.'

'Runcie,' whispered Mariam. 'Help!'

Sleeth backed towards the gate, the book tucked under one arm, dragging Mariam who was struggling furiously but unable to get free. Tigris began tearing at Runcie's hand so he let her go. She darted to the gate, looked through, then back at Sleeth.

'I'll give you a chance, Tigris,' said Sleeth. 'Help me take Mariam back and Thandimanilon may even forgive you.'

Her mouth opened and closed. 'No, Jac,' Tigris said desperately, but didn't move to stop him either.

'Not even to save little Fliss?' said Sleeth, as Mariam tried to kick him, backwards.

Tigris couldn't meet anyone's eyes. She licked her lips, looked down and whispered, 'Oh Mara, help me.'

Mariam caught Runcie's eye and jerked her head sideways. What was she trying to say? The pages of the spell book fluttered and he understood. He nodded. Mariam stamped her heel hard on Sleeth's toes. He cursed and swung her out of the way, but Runcie dived, tore the book out from under Sleeth's arm, rolled across the ice and came to his feet. The hole in the ice was only twenty feet away and he knew he could lob the book straight in.

For once, it was Sleeth who didn't know what to do. He looked from Mariam to the book, and back to Mariam.

'Let her go, you rotten little mongrel,' panted Runcie, 'or it goes down the hole.'

'All right,' said Sleeth. 'Pass it over first.'

'In your dreams,' snapped Runcie.

'How do I know –?' Sleeth began.

'Because *I'm* trustworthy and you're not.'

Sleeth considered that, nodded, then let go of Mariam's arm. She whirled, clouted him hard over the ear then marched to Runcie's side with her head high. Runcie sent the book skidding across the ice. Sleeth gathered it up, jammed the loose pages back in, at which the book cursed him in a thin, reedy voice, then stepped into the gate, grinning like a loon.

'You can't escape, Mariam. For the secret of Anthrimorie, Lars Sparj will hunt you to the furthest corners of the world.'

With a mocking laugh, Sleeth vanished, reappearing a second later on the back of the transportal platform in Miluviand. He called out to Thandimanilon and Lars Sparj just as the black transportal lifted.

Mariam ducked out of sight, white-faced. 'I'm cursed, Runcie. Doomed.'

Tigris was still standing by the gate, stepping forwards and back in an agony of her own. Sleeth shouted at Lars and pointed to the gate. The transportal hovered and Lars Sparj's head whipped around.

Runcie edged along the wall beside Mariam. 'I wouldn't believe anything that little stinker says.'

'Yeah, right.'

Tigris, her sad face tormented, was looking down into her cupped hands as if trying to envision her froggy mindsake again. When it didn't appear, she began to scramble into the gate, just as the transportal turned towards it. With a desperate cry, Wyrmhilte came right out of the water and hurled her glittering rod at the gate. It flared as bright as the sun, a wave of heat washed over them, then the gate was gone and the rod fell to the ice, glittering no more. Wyrmhilte dropped into the water with an almighty splash.

Tigris was bowled over and something fell from her coat, chiming as it slid across the ice. It was the little message harp she'd said she left in Miluviand, and suddenly it all made sense – her unbearable torment, the disappearances on the way, this attempt to escape – and it didn't help that Runcie and Mariam had previously discussed the possibility. Since coming through the wyrm's gate Runcie had thought of Tigris as a comrade and a friend, and it hurt.

'You were calling Thandimanilon the whole time!' he shouted. 'You betrayed us so she could get Mariam back. I can't believe you could do it.'

Tigris didn't deny it. She lay on the floor, hands over her face, wailing in anguish, 'I'm sorry, Fliss. I did everything I could and it was *all wrong*.'

Runcie opened his mouth to scream at her, but Mariam caught his arm and pulled him away. 'We all make mistakes, Runcie, but not everyone gets a second chance.' She stared into his eyes for half a minute, then turned and walked off.

Was she talking about his mistakes, or Tigris's, or her own? Mariam was right, of course, and besides, they still had to fight the wyrm. Runcie looked down at Tigris and, despite the betrayal, his heart went out to her. 'Come on, Tigris. We need you.'

She got up, looking so wretched that he had to do something. He put his arms around her awkwardly. 'It'll be all right. It really will.'

Tigris managed the smallest and most tentative of smiles. 'I hope so, Runcie.'

Helfigor was bent over, gasping. The wyrm lay on its back in the water, looking more dead than alive, and the surrounding ice was speckled with its blood. Helfigor's frost-blistered hand raised the pipes and he blew another of those silent chords, but this one raised goose pimples all over Runcie's arms. He could almost hear the song it came from, and it was a tragic one – a lament for all that had been lost, *or was going to be.*

'We've got to help him,' said Runcie.

As he and Tigris approached, the tip of Wyrmhilte's tail slid out the other side of the pool, felt its way along Helfigor's foot to his calf, up his lower leg, then ever so slowly began to wrap itself around his hips. Helfigor didn't move. Runcie thumped the tail with his club, to no effect. The ice-clotted water lapping against Wyrmhilte's chin was stained the most brilliant, iridescent crimson and there didn't seem to be much life in her eyes, though her tail looked unaffected.

'Helfigor!' Runcie yelled.

The wizard still didn't react. The pipes must have taken the last of his strength. Runcie tried to uncoil Wyrmhilte's tail, avoiding the snapping sting, but it whacked him off his feet. He got up painfully as the tail pulled the wizard to his knees and he dropped the pipes. Whether Wyrmhilte was dying, or just slipping under the water to recover, she was going to take Helfigor with her. And then they would starve in this icy wilderness.

Runcie was heaving uselessly at a loop of tail, lost in these morbid terrors, when he heard an unmistakeable thudding boom that could only be the black transportal materialising at the cavern entrance. Lars Sparj had come for Mariam.

'Give me a hand,' Runcie panted, but Mariam picked up Helfigor's pipes and walked away. 'Mariam,' Runcie said desperately, 'If you give up now, we're lost.'

'She's searching,' Mariam said obscurely. 'But she can't find us.'

'Come back!'

She was walking towards a dark side passage, the useless pipes to her lips. Runcie could have wept with despair. It felt as if his only friend had abandoned him.

Wyrmhilte had rallied again and was inexorably pulling Helfigor in. Grabbing a chunk of ice the size of a football, Runcie heaved it at Wyrmhilte's head. It bounced off her crested skull but she didn't let go. It occurred to Runcie that she could easily have killed him and Tigris, but she hadn't harmed them. She wanted them alive.

'Tigris,' he gasped, 'Use your fire magic.'

'To do what?'

'Boil the water in the hole or something.'

'I'm not strong enough to heat all that water,' she said apathetically.

How could he get her to use her talents? Now Helfigor's legs were dragged in, stirring the crimson water. It looked hopeless, but Runcie couldn't give up. He wouldn't, even if he had to get nasty. 'You betrayed us, Tigris,' he said coldly, 'and you've got to make up for it. So *do something*!' He stumbled forwards, scooped a double handful of water and hurled it at the wyrm's spectacles, where it froze into a pink and white crust. '*Now!*'

As Wyrmhilte flipped the spectacles up, Tigris drew a deep breath and thrust her hands at the wyrm's eyes. Wyrmhilte clapped one hand to her left eye as if something had stung her there, then slapped her hand down. A jet of water shot forth, knocking Tigris flat on her back.

'Again.' Runcie heaved her to her feet. 'You hurt it.'

'It's blocking me. I can't *see* the source, Runcie.'

Helfigor was going under. 'Try again!' Runcie shouted, and as he took hold of the wizard's wrists, in his inner eye he saw a curved, shimmering sheet like the wall of a monstrous balloon. It was magic, he knew, but what could it mean? The patterns became brighter, more dizzying. Tigris gasped and spots appeared before Runcie's eyes, like tiny whirlpools in the wall of the balloon. He tried to see beyond one to something solid, *real.*

Tigris sang out and the vision whirled sickeningly, then vanished, and for a moment Runcie thought he was going to throw up. He'd just lost his grip on Helfigor, who was being dragged under, when a cry of anguish knifed through the air. The wyrm was clutching at her eyes with both hands, steam puffing out between her fingers. Helfigor shot up, grabbed the edge and tried to drag himself out as Wyrmhilte plunged her steaming eyes beneath the water.

'What did you do?' said Runcie, awed.

Tigris gave him an odd look. 'I did what you said, and suddenly the *quintessence* was there, more than I've ever had before. I boiled Wyrmhilte's tears in her eyes.'

They heaved Helfigor out. As Wyrmhilte scrambled from the hole, thunder echoed down the side tunnel and Mariam, who was running their way, was tumbled aside as if by a fist of air. Then Runcie saw the most wonderful sight of all – Parsifoe's battered snail transportal, Ulalliall, materialised in the narrow tunnel, shattering the ice on either wall.

Ulalliall shot over Mariam's head, shedding broken tiles and rusty water, and skidded to a stop on the other side of the hole. Dumpy little Parsifoe leapt off with the shining whip in her hand and cracked it at Wyrmhilte. The whip lashed several times around her tail, then Parsifoe hauled it back as if she were playing a great fish on a line.

The wyrm flew at Parsifoe with her wings clubbing the air and her black claws extended. Parsifoe jerked the whip sideways and threw herself the other way as the wyrm, whose tail had been severed in front of the stinger, crashed to the ice.

Helfigor had the two pieces of the staff under his arm as Tigris helped him to the transportal. 'Get inside,' Parsifoe roared, keeping Wyrmhilte at bay with flicks of the barbed whip.

Mariam came lurching the other way and fell in. As Runcie dragged Helfigor into the transportal he heard a grinding crash followed by a volley of oaths, as if Lars Sparj's transportal had stuck fast. Parsifoe was backing towards the steps, her whip carving silvery flashes through the air as she kept Wyrmhilte at bay. Whenever it struck the ice, it left fuming trails behind.

Then Parsifoe stumbled. The wyrm went for her but, displaying a sprightliness quite out of keeping with her age and figure, she sprang backwards onto the threshold. She cried, 'Elevate, Escape,' the transportal lifted sluggishly then shot backwards, almost throwing them down the wyrm's throat. She snapped, 'Translocate To Thorasdil!' and Ulalliall began to dematerialise, just as Lars Sparj's black transportal battered its way through.

Wyrmhilte cried out, clapped her hands above her head and a thousand tons of ice caved in between her and the black transportal. The tunnel roof was collapsing in a line towards them as Wyrmhilte went backwards through the hole in the ice. The transportal blinked out of existence, reappeared over a black forest, winked out again then fled as though the whole of Iltior were hunting it.

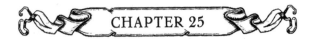

CHAPTER 25

The College of Magic

After an endless, shuddering flight punctuated by many head-spinning jumps *between*, they arrived at Thorasdil, Parsifoe's College of Magic, in darkness. They saw nothing but a skyscraping tower rising from the sea, and Ulalliall was so exhausted by the long journey that they all had to help heave her inside.

'I'll need Ulalliall's core upstairs,' said Parsifoe.

'Really?' Helfigor snorted. 'Whatever for?'

'To strengthen Thorasdil's protection spell . . . and other things.'

Once the door of the ground floor had been bolted, barred and webbed with spells, Parsifoe lifted the floor of the transportal and began to take out the core, which was mounted on a black obsidian slab and covered by a bell-shaped dome of thick, bubble-filled orange glass. Inside Runcie saw seven stubby greenstone columns, three pairs of coiled foghorns and a fiendishly complicated array of crystals, cogs and spirals. There was something at the heart of the device too, but the more he stared at it – or her, Ulalliall – the more it seemed to shimmer and shift before his eyes, as if determined not to be seen.

'Come on!' Helfigor said. 'We've got to talk.'

'Indeed,' Parsifoe replied frostily. 'Bring Ulalliall up to the forty-eighth floor, children.'

The two wizards headed up a broad, crumbling staircase of yellow stone. Runcie, Mariam and Tigris took hold of Ulalliall, who was the size of a washing machine, and tried to lift her.

'She weighs a ton,' Runcie groaned. 'We'll never do it.'

Mariam found a splintery plank, laid it up the steps, and they began to slide Ulalliall up it. That was easier, though it still took them an hour of brutal labour to heave her up to the top, with Ulalliall whining and abusing them every step of the way, and more than once Runcie was tempted to topple her over the edge. Tigris didn't open her mouth once, as if too ashamed. Runcie didn't speak to her either, for he didn't know what to say or, indeed, what he thought of her.

But all that was behind them. They'd scrubbed themselves in hot baths until their skin shone, and put on clean clothes while their filthy gear was boiled in the coppers downstairs. Now Runcie and Mariam were sitting in a pair of worn leather armchairs in a large chamber on the top floor, the fiftieth, close by a crackling, resin-scented fire. Tigris sat well back, as silent as a ghost, but Runcie wasn't paying her any attention.

Here he felt safe at last, for the protection spell which had guarded Thorasdil for a thousand years had been racked up another notch and he wasn't even going to think about tomorrow. He sighed and turned so the blissful warmth could ease the aches down his other side. All he needed to make the night perfect was a hot dinner and a long night in a comfortable bed.

The chamber was the size of a school refectory, though its only furnishings were their three armchairs, plus a sideboard, table and chairs over near the door. The two side walls were covered in moth-eaten tapestries so dusty and threadbare that Runcie couldn't make out their design. The slate flagstones were bare except for a grubby carpet in front of the fire, speckled with burn marks from flying coals.

'I wouldn't mind going to school here,' sighed Mariam. 'As long as I didn't have to learn magic,' she added hastily.

'I'd love to be taught magic, if only I had the talent,' Runcie said. 'What about you, Tigris?'

Tigris was staring at the floor. 'I never wanted to study magic anyway,' she said, almost inaudibly.

'But you're so good at it,' said Mariam.

'It – it runs in the family. My mother and father are both magicians – she's a Second and he's a Third – and my two brothers are prentices.'

'That must be so exciting,' said Runcie, plunging into a daydream where he was part of such a family. Even *having* a family was a beautiful dream.

'But I don't want to be a magician,' said Tigris. 'Ever since I could walk, all I wanted was to be an acrobat.'

'Wouldn't your parents let you?' said Mariam.

'Mother refused to allow it. It's not a respectable profession. She said I'd be disgracing the family name.'

'When you grow up –' Runcie began.

'Acrobats start training when they're six. Besides, you know I don't have any choice.'

Runcie and Mariam exchanged glances, still unsure whether Tigris's loyalties lay with them or Thandimanilon. Or Sleeth, for that matter. Unfortunately, Tigris noticed. She lowered her head again, looking desperately unhappy.

The door creaked and Parsifoe appeared, carrying a heavy tray. Runcie's mouth watered. After the delicious food he'd had previously, he couldn't wait to try hers.

'You've all been working so hard, children, you deserve a treat,' she said, setting the tray on the carpet and removing the battered tin covers with a flourish. 'Cook scoured the larders for our best, and here it is.' She looked at them expectantly.

'Thank you, Parsifoe,' they said dutifully.

Runcie inspected the steaming dishes, but none smelt the least bit appetising. A chipped oval platter contained cubes of some grey meat that looked as if it had been boiled in dishwater. The pickled vegetables must have been a decade old, for they were quite transparent. And the rubbery mass of rice was so overcooked that it would have to be hacked out with a knife, while a bowl of green sauce looked unnervingly like pond scum. Still, he reminded himself, Gorbal's Premium Sausage had looked and smelt far worse.

'Tuck in,' said Parsifoe, the smile fading. 'There's my favourite dessert to finish up with – stewed bogberries and slubbily custard.' She raised the cover of the last dish.

326

'Ooh,' said Tigris unconvincingly. 'Thanks, Parsifoe. That looks . . . delicious.'

The horrid brown and yellow streaked mass could have been scraped from the bottom of Sleeth's compost heap. Parsifoe's anxious eye fixed on Runcie so, taking a plate, he spooned one-third of the meat, the vegetables and the sauce onto it. Mariam and Tigris did the same, avoiding each other's eyes.

Spearing a piece of grey meat with his fork, Runcie took a bite. It was like chewing on a chunk cut out of a tractor tyre, except it didn't taste nearly as good. 'Mmm,' he said. 'Thanks, Parsifoe. It's really yummy.'

Her smile had gone. She nodded stiffly and turned away.

'Is that the best you can do?' hissed Mariam. '*Really yummy!*'

'You wait till you try it.' His teeth were making no impression on the rubbery cube. 'I'm starving and it still tastes horrible.'

'I'm sure she's done her best,' Tigris said. 'She hasn't got two coins to rub together and the moneylenders are after her.'

Runcie had unpleasant memories of the stallholders chasing her in Pellissidan. They stared grimly at their plates. 'It feels more like the Last Supper,' said Mariam, but set to.

By the time he pushed back his half-empty plate, Runcie's good mood had evaporated. The food lay in his belly like a sandbag and he could only think of tomorrow. Parsifoe and Helfigor came in and sat at the table with their plates, though Parsifoe looked angry and Helfigor defensive, and he kept quaffing from his flask.

'What do you think they're on about?' Runcie asked, picking bogberry fibres from between his teeth.

'Getting rid of me,' Mariam said gloomily. A piece of firewood popped, shooting sparks at them and filling the air with a resinous scent that helped to mask the lingering smell of dinner. She flicked a spark off her sleeve.

'What do you mean?' He kicked an ember off the smoking carpet.

'They'll have to do *something*, because of my Re-sighting.' She shivered. 'That was the weirdest feeling. I was actually there.'

'We saw,' grinned Runcie, failing to recognise her mood. 'You were sweating like a pig.' He snorted like one.

'I was *perspiring*,' Mariam said acidly. She glared down her long nose at him.

'Sorry. Was it like having your mind taken over?'

'It was horrible – people were dying all around me. I don't want to think about it.'

No one spoke for a while. Parsifoe had thrust her plate aside and was leaning across the table to Helfigor.

'What do you think we should do, Runcie?' asked Mariam.

He sat up. She was asking *him* for advice? Things *had* changed. 'I don't suppose you can tell what they're saying, Tigris?'

'Eavesdropping spells are strictly forbidden to prentices,' she muttered.

'But you do know how?'

Again Tigris flushed. 'Er, yes. Jac taught me, back when we were friends.'

'Please, Tigris,' said Mariam. 'They could be talking about my life.'

Tigris bit her lip, then nodded. 'Just this once.' She made curving motions with her hands, shaping a pair of giant ears, spoke a spell so quietly that Runcie didn't catch a word of it, then put her hands to Mariam's ears.

'Can I hear too?' said Runcie.

She put her hands to Runcie's ears and then, with a deeper flush, to her own.

Tigris really is a *good* person, thought Runcie. She always wants to do the right thing. But to save her sister, betraying Mariam to Thandimanilon probably *was* the right thing, so how could he ever trust Tigris?

'How long do we have?' Helfigor said clearly in Runcie's right ear. Runcie jumped, for he could feel the wizard's breath as he spoke.

'A day at most,' said Parsifoe, her breath tickling his left ear. 'I'm afraid, Helfigor. I'm not sure the protection can withstand an assault by two First Order wizards. I should never have brought Mariam here. What the devil were you doing anyway, taking so long? I hope you weren't up to your old tricks again.'

Helfigor looked shame-faced. 'You never let up, do you. One little mistake . . .'

'Little!' cried Parsifoe. 'We're still paying –'

'All right! Tell the whole world, why don't you?' He had a green crystal rod in his right hand and began smacking it into his left. The magnified sounds hurt Runcie's ears. 'Where else could you have taken her, anyway,' he said pointedly, 'without being arrested and having Ulalliall seized?'

'Ulalliall's mine by right, I keep telling you.'

'And I believe you – though thousands wouldn't.'

'My grandmother's family was defrauded by Clan Mummery and reduced to beggary, as you well know! I swore I'd make up for it, and I've devoted my whole life to mastering magic –'

'Yet you only rose to the Second Order,' Helfigor said cuttingly.

Parsifoe gritted her teeth. 'Well, at least I got there honestly. At least I haven't wasted a brilliant talent in drink and dissipation.'

'I like to drink.' He took another slug. 'It helps me to forget –'

'– that you abandoned your noble ambitions for a life of vice!' But then she said softly, 'Helfigor, let's not quarrel again. We need you, for if I fail here, not only will these innocent children die, but the world will have lost its last chance to turn back the Cybale.'

He gave her a meaningful look. 'You haven't mentioned the other alternative.'

'Giving Mariam up?' cried Parsifoe. 'Letting them win?'

Helfigor studied the contents of his fork, grimaced and dropped it on his plate. 'Perhaps it would be better if you did. If you can't fight them . . .'

Beside Runcie, Mariam sucked in her breath. He reached out and took her hand, and she squeezed it so tightly that it hurt.

'Considering you risked your life for those children –' snapped Parsifoe.

330

'It's mine to risk. But had I prentices, and a sworn duty to protect them –'

'How could I throw her to that wolf? Besides,' Parsifoe glanced at the children and lowered her voice further, 'there's more at stake than the fate of one child.'

'More than you know. I've been in contact with the Night Watchers. Nightland's resonances used to be no more than bad influences, but suddenly they've burst through in the Sodden Wastes in great seeps of malignity that every foul force on Iltior is flocking to.'

'What do you mean, *seeps?*' she cried

'I'm told they're like poisonous bogs, oozing foul miasmas, and once they touch you, all your hopes and dreams are corrupted – Ugh!' He shuddered. 'That's all I know.'

'Why haven't I heard about this?' Parsifoe said uneasily.

'They only appeared a few days ago. Look what's happened since the children came, Parsifoe. Three ghasts, showing unheard-of strength, went close to destroying a First Order wizard, then broke free. Next a ghoolwyrm reappeared from the past, *with live eggs*, and now the Cybale, a powerless group of cranks for a hundred and fifty years, have only to locate their Citadel of Magic to threaten the fabric of the world. Iltior's long, fragile peace is coming to an end, old friend.'

'Did you tell the Night Watchers about Wyrmhilte?'

'Of course, but she'll be gone before they can get there. And don't be fooled by her present weakness. As soon as she relearns the great wyrm magics, she'll be a mighty opponent – one that humanity forgot how to deal with thousands of years ago.'

'And the ghasts?'

'I mentioned them too, though I'm not sure anyone believed me.'

'Who listens to Stick-at-Nothing Helfigor or Paltry Parsifoe?' she said gloomily. 'The councils think we're deluded.'

'And that's just what Lars wants them to think. This battle, this *war*, is way beyond our strength, Parsifoe. We may as well give in now.'

They looked at one another. 'But we're not going to,' said Parsifoe. 'Are we?'

'We fight to the very end, no matter how bitter.'

After a long pause, Parsifoe said, 'If Lars locates Anthrimorie, he'll soon tunnel in to find the Citadel of Magic, and then all the scoundrels in Iltior will flock to his banner.'

'He's not clever enough to control them.'

'Even worse! Some cunning villain will overthrow him and step into his shoes. The change has begun, Helfigor, and this is our last chance to reverse it.'

'Even so –' said Helfigor.

'I blame myself for not realising what these children were, and for letting Thandimanilon take them from me. There's only one way to make up for that folly.' There was a long silence. They stared into each other's eyes, then Parsifoe went on, 'And since you've spent so much of your life in low dives, carousing with all manner of scoundrels and ne'er-do-wells, I thought you might know a sneaky way to *create* one.'

'What are they talking about?' said Mariam. 'Create what?'

'Shh!' said Tigris, 'and you might find out.'

Helfigor looked shifty. 'Er, I don't think so –'

Parsifoe put her head in her hands. 'Then we're done for –' But then her grey head snapped up. 'Helfigor?' she said in a low, dangerous voice. 'You know something. *Don't you?*'

He put on a puzzled expression. 'What are you talking about, my darling?'

'How dare you try to butter me up, you ugly old villain? Out with it.'

'That would be betraying something I learned in confidence,' he muttered.

'Whose confidence matters more – your *darling's,* or some defrocked sorcerer you get drunk with while neglecting your responsibilities?'

Now he looked really embarrassed.

Parsifoe's eyes narrowed to slits. 'It'd better not be a woman!'

Helfigor gave her a sickly smile.

She raised her knife. 'You can die more horribly at my hands than you can at Lars's,' Parsifoe said savagely. 'And you will, if I ever find out you've been seeing –'

'It's not like that,' he said in a low voice. 'What do you take me for?'

'I won't say – the children's eyes are straining out of their heads as it is. But when this is over –'

'All right!' he hissed. 'But I warn you, if we make one there'll be consequences.'

Runcie and Mariam exchanged glances. 'And we're relying on these two second-rate, bickering fools to save us?' said Mariam.

'*Dimensional* gates are First Order magic,' Helfigor went on. 'Even if we got one to work, think of the penalty. Being chained upside down to the North Face of the High Ghool, with the eagles tearing at my kidneys, isn't how I'd planned to spend my declining years.'

'Nor mine,' Parsifoe said grimly. 'But what else can we do, save give Mariam up?'

'No!' Runcie cried involuntarily.

Parsifoe broke off, staring in their direction. Tigris began talking animatedly about the gown for her Fifth Order Bestowal Ceremony, and shortly Parsifoe resumed, in a lower voice. 'We're all alone, Helfigor. Our allies won't dare take sides against First Order wizards.'

'It's the gate, then, and the eagles take my kidneys if we're caught.' Helfigor's face had gone a sweaty grey. 'I quail at the thought of attempting a *dimensional* gate. Ordinary gates hurt me cruelly, even with my staff. This rod doesn't feel right.'

He scowled in Runcie's direction. Runcie ducked his head, his cheeks burning.

'It's the best I can give you!' Parsifoe snapped. 'You'll have to wait till your staff is repaired. I can't believe you let a magick-less kid damage it.'

They rose together and came across to the children. Helfigor waved his hand and Runcie's ears popped. 'You won't need that any more,' the wizard said coldly.

'Sir?' said Runcie, trying to play dumb.

'Will you, Tigris?' Helfigor said.

'No, Helfigor,' she said quietly.

'Get yourselves to bed now,' Parsifoe said kindly, as if they'd done nothing wrong. 'Tomorrow's going to be a big day.' They stood up, wondering where to go, but she went on, 'And since it could be their last night together . . .'

'We could sleep here,' said Mariam. 'By the fire.'

Parsifoe nodded. 'You'll find blankets in the airing room down the hall. Good night, children.' She looked as if she wanted to say something more important, but in the end just added, 'Sleep well,' and the wizards went out.

Runcie pulled his armchair closer to the fire. Mariam drew hers in beside his. 'Suddenly I don't feel secure at all. And after what Thandimanilon did to me last time . . .'

'What did she do, anyway?'

Mariam, staring at the flames, just shrugged. 'You know what I'm like.'

Runcie wasn't put off so easily these days, and there was another way to find out. 'You said Tigris helped you.' He gave Tigris a cool stare, hoping that she'd feel guilty enough to tell him.

'After you were thrown out,' said Tigris, 'Mariam knocked Thandimanilon down and sat on her, demanding that she bring you back.'

'You *sat* on Thandimanilon?' gasped Runcie. 'It's a wonder she didn't kill you.'

'She was so furious she was going to use Mimsy Norn's

Inside-Out Spell,' said Tigris, 'but luckily Heunch came back and stopped her. He put Mariam in the stocks and made the other girls throw rotten food at her all day.'

'You spent the day in the stocks because of me?' said Runcie.

'It was worth it,' grinned Mariam. 'You should have seen proud Thandimanilon's face when I rubbed her nose into the floor.'

Runcie would never understand her. He'd never have a more loyal friend either.

As soon as the lanterns were blown out, Runcie began to worry about tomorrow, and whether these two quarrelling wizards could protect them. After several restless hours he gave up trying to sleep. The fire had died down to orange coals that gave forth a cheerful crackle every now and again, but it didn't help. He felt very small and helpless.

'Mariam?' he said quietly. 'Are you awake?'

'Yes,' she said at once.

'I'm scared.'

'So am I. By this time tomorrow we could be –'

'Don't say it,' he said hastily. 'Let's talk about something good.'

'I can't think of anything good, Runcie,' she said with a catch in her voice.

'Well, it has been a great adventure. And Tigris is really nice, despite . . .'

Mariam didn't answer. Runcie could hear her heavy

breathing. 'And Parsifoe and Helfigor are all right, *really*,' he went on. 'They're doing their best.'

'Somehow that makes it worse.' Mariam said, rolling over in her blankets and staring at the patterns flickering across the ceiling.

Runcie was doing the same when something occurred to him. 'You know that Earth affects Iltior through resonance, Mariam?' They'd discussed this on the way to Thorasdil.

'Mmm,' she said.

'And Helfigor said that our two worlds are linked. So, surely, to maintain the balance, Iltior must also affect Earth in some way.'

'I suppose so, but how would you tell? People on Earth have so many mad ideas, a few more resonating from Iltior aren't going to make any difference.'

It only reassured him for a moment. 'But what if the link from Iltior to Earth isn't through resonance at all?'

'I'm really tired, Runcie.'

'Magicians don't know where their magical *quintessence* comes from, and they don't care,' he said, thinking aloud. 'But what if they're drawing it from Earth?'

She shot up, cast a swift glance at Tigris's sleeping form, then lowered her voice. 'So *that's* why our appliances are acting up! And the power stations. And that's why Iltior's wizards only discovered *steady quintessence* recently – power stations haven't been invented all that long.'

'It's got to be. Remember how pleased Thandimanilon was when you told her? What if the Cybale *do* know where *quintessence* comes from? They might be able to attack Earth by simply taking all its power. And since they use magic, not science, no one on Earth would know what was happening.'

Mariam looked horrified. 'But our whole world relies on power. If it suddenly vanished . . . planes and trains and ships would crash; hospitals couldn't operate; the food would go bad. Nothing would work and millions of people would die! It'd be like being thrown back to the Dark Ages. We've got to get home and warn the authorities.'

It seemed absurd that Earth, with all its power, weapons and technology, could be at risk from primitive Iltior, but it was. And, no matter how enchanting Iltior was, it had to be stopped.

'And Runcie,' she whispered, 'we can't talk about this to anyone. No one from Iltior will be on our side.' She was silent for a while, then added, 'Of course, after tomorrow . . .'

'I know. But, as Dad used to say, you've only failed when you can't find the courage to do what you've got to do.' Only now did he understand what that meant, and it reminded him of his biggest failure. He was afraid to keep digging, in case he stumbled upon something nasty about his father. Did that make him a hypocrite as well as a coward?

Neither spoke for some time, then, as Runcie was dozing off, she said, 'Runcie?'

'Yes, Mariam?'

'If we never see each other again –' she made a tiny choking sound, '– I'm glad I met you. I'm even glad you brought us to Iltior. It's been worth it.'

Runcie couldn't think of anything to say, though it warmed him more than the fire.

'And I hope you discover the truth about your father.'

He lay there, listening to her steady breathing. The truth seemed further away than ever. If anyone did know, it would be Lars Sparj, but how could Runcie get the truth out of him? Dare he even try?

CHAPTER 26

Ulalliall's Lament

Runcie woke with a start. It was still dark and a gale shrilled around the tower. The wind was always whistling on Iltior; unless it was howling. He sat up. Mariam lay wrapped in her blankets like a caterpillar in a cocoon, with just the tip of her dark head sticking out. Tigris, further away from the dying fire, had kicked her blankets off and both girls were sound asleep.

What had woken him? He vaguely remembered a bright flash and streams of coloured particles like fireworks. Closing his eyes, Runcie could still see the faintest afterimage there. What if it was Lars Sparj?

He went across to the narrow window, whose hundreds of little panes were shaped like hexagons, expecting to see a furious storm outside, but looked out on a moon-touched sea and, in the heavens, the red moon and white stars peering down between scudding clouds.

The floor trembled gently. Runcie supposed it had to do with Parsifoe's dimensional gate. He was heading back to his blankets when he felt a momentary dizziness, then his stomach heaved and bubbled. It stopped after a few seconds but as soon as he lay down the sickness began to come and go in waves. Wiping away icy sweat, he went out to the stone stair and looked down. He didn't see anything, but a cascade of sparks flashed across his inner eye and a ring of bright light began to pulse. It *was* magic, and powerful magic at that. What were they up to?

Runcie began to creep down the crumbling stairs. It was pitch dark here, save for an occasional moonbeam when he went past one of the salt-crusted windows. On the next floor he tiptoed around, opening each door carefully. All the rooms were in darkness.

'Who's there?' foghorned an angry voice. 'And what are you doing, creeping about in the middle of the night like some pint-sized burglar?' It was Ulalliall. Runcie was tempted to run, but if he did she'd raise the roof, so he opened the door and went in.

'It's me, Runcie,' he said softly to the dark. 'I didn't mean any harm.'

'Boys!' sniffed Ulalliall. 'What are you doing out of bed? Up to mischief, I'll warrant.'

'I'm not,' cried Runcie. 'I couldn't sleep. I – I'm too worried about tomorrow.'

'Quite rightly. You're going to come to a sticky end, and good riddance –'

She broke off. Runcie heard a sound like gears whirring, then a loud sniffle. After what Tigris had said in the ice cavern, he understood Ulalliall better now. 'What's the matter?'

'Can't you tell?' she hissed. Ulalliall gave another sniffle, followed by a choking sob. 'Just look at us.'

'Are you lonely? Do you, er, miss the company of other transportals?'

'We miss the times when we were the greatest on Iltior, and all the youngsters would gather around to hear our tales. Not a one spoke without our say so. Respect, that's what we miss. And dignity.'

Runcie let out a little sigh. He'd not thought much about transportals before, but they were marvellous devices – half mind and half machine, and age old.

'You must know lots of stories,' he said wistfully, remembering how he'd sat on his father's lap by the fire, listening to Ansie's magical tales.

Ulalliall snorted. 'We're 3,062 years old, you little twerp, and we know the entire history of Iltior from that time to this. We lived that history; helped shape it too, but does anyone care? We're stuck with a lousy keeper who wouldn't have made the Third Order in the good old days, and used to carry vegetables and firewood like a vulgar porter-portal. We're neglected, forgotten and falling to bits!'

'I care,' said Runcie. 'I'm really interested in old machines –'

'We're not an *old machine*, you foul-mouthed little brat. We're an ancient, venerable transportal and don't you forget it.'

'Sorry. I'd love to hear all about your, er, *life*. And your tales of ancient times –'

Before he could finish, Ulalliall was off, painting him a picture of the early days when she was the first transportal in the world, the ghoolwyrms had just been vanquished and everyone was full of hope. She was a marvellous tale-spinner. The whine disappeared from her voice and Runcie listened, captivated, as a moonbeam touched the window and crept across the floor.

But then came the Wizard Wars, dark and desperate times when conflict over magic blazed across Iltior and it seemed that everything people had fought for, for so long, would be lost. Wizards had even used transportals in battle as though they were common chariots, and Ulalliall's voice grew high in outrage as she recounted the tragic destruction of dozens of transportals, old friends as well as youngsters on their first journeys.

But the times after that proved darker yet, when the Cybale routed the magicians, destroyed many transportals and enslaved the rest, along with most of the people of Iltior.

'Even you, Ulalliall?' Runcie asked softly, for she had fallen silent.

'Even us,' she said. 'For a while, at least. Ah, what a hideous time that was.'

'Were you rescued after the Cybale fell, then?'

She snorted. 'We escaped, boy, all by ourselves.'

'But don't transportals need a wizard keeper to work the spell?'

'*We* aren't like other transportals. We learned to work the magic by ourself. We escaped, and we were the mainstay of the resistance for 227 years. The Cybale hunted us ruthlessly, but we were too clever for them.'

'I'd love to hear that tale,' said Runcie.

'Humpf! We may tell you, one day, if you mind your manners. You're not as bad as we thought, Runcible Jones. We could grow to endure you. Get to bed. You're yawning and that's disrespectful.'

'Ulalliall,' Runcie said as he got up, 'can I ask you something?'

'Ask what you like, but there's no saying we'll answer.'

'Do you know who killed my father, Ansible Jones? I've asked everywhere, but no one knows. Or will tell me, at any rate.'

'Never heard of him. The affairs of ordinary humans are beneath us.'

Runcie suddenly felt very small and insignificant. He yawned, quickly covered his mouth, and said 'Thanks anyway, Ulalliall. Er –'

'What is it now?' she snapped.

'That was the most marvellous tale I ever heard.'

Outside, he felt wide awake and his legs were restless, so he headed down the stairs, flight after flight, endlessly recycling his fears of tomorrow. Runcie reached the ground floor feeling even more helpless, and then had to climb all the way back up.

What a strange place Thorasdil was. Runcie wondered who had built it, and why. The tower was monumentally tall and ancient, but most of its chambers, though filled with worm-eaten furniture and soot-stained tapestries, were unused, for Parsifoe's college only occupied the top five floors.

When nearing the top an hour later, he noted a flickering stream of light coming through the keyhole of a chamber on the far side of the tower. Creeping across, he put his eye to the hole.

Helfigor and Parsifoe were at either end of a long table. Helfigor was standing, waving the crystal rod as he chanted a spell. The two halves of Tawcryffe, held in place by callipers, and joined by a black and bubbling clot, hung from the ceiling. A black bat clung upside down from a hatstand behind him. Parsifoe sat in a high-backed, carved chair, holding a quill pen whose white feather extended over her left shoulder. An ivory wizard's baton lay on the table beside her, and something large and curved in the middle, under a canvas. Her grey head was bent over a parchment, checking what she'd written.

She raised one finger and Helfigor went still, looking at the parchment. Parsifoe nodded, dipped her nib in the inkpot and wrote several careful words.

They were doing magic but it wasn't as interesting as Runcie had expected. He was about to go up to his blankets when Helfigor snapped the crystal rod upwards, whereupon the covered object let out a furious squawk.

'That's right, use us like any old bit of machinery. Don't have a thought for our feelings, or our dignity, oh no! It's not enough that you . . .'

345

It was Ulalliall again. Runcie smiled. He was developing a fondness for the querulous old transportal.

'Shut up, transportal,' said Helfigor. 'Darkness is gathering and we don't have time for your shenanigans.'

'Are you going to let him speak to us that way, keeper,' cried Ulalliall, 'after all we've been through?'

'Not now, Ulalliall, please,' said Parsifoe in a bone-weary voice, 'or we'll never get it done.'

'All right! We won't say another word.' The transportal added, slyly, 'Even though –'

'Splendid!' said Helfigor. 'Can we get on?' He raised his rod.

Parsifoe began to read from the parchment. The words sounded similar to those the intruder had spoken in Runcie's room at the Nightingales'. The air shimmered and strange shapes formed in his inner eye, like green doughnuts joined together, with yellow lines running around them, and white speckles across their surfaces. One of the speckles grew into a circular pore and light sprayed through it. Another useless vision. Runcie was heartily sick of them.

When it cleared, Helfigor was slumped over the table. 'We're not going to do it, are we?' His voice had developed a nagging rasp. 'We simply can't find enough *quintessence.*'

'How long do we have left?' said Parsifoe without raising her head.

'Hours, at most.'

'Transportal?' said Parsifoe.

Ulalliall didn't answer.

'Ulalliall?'

'*He* told us to shut up,' Ulalliall said sulkily.

'He didn't mean it,' Parsifoe said with breathtaking insincerity. She glared at the wizard. 'It's just his way, the old curmudgeon. Secretly, Helfigor thinks you're a national treasure.'

'You can't get around me that easily,' Ulalliall said, though smugly. 'What do you want?'

'I don't suppose you know anything about dimensional gates?'

'Nothing I'd tell you,' said Ulalliall. 'They're far too dangerous. Only a fool –'

'I thought so,' said Parsifoe. 'Oh, what was it you were talking about earlier?'

'Don't know what you mean,' mumbled Ulalliall.

'You said, "Even though –".'

'Nothing. We don't know anything. We're just a useless old piece of junk.'

'Oh, don't start that again,' groaned Helfigor.

'Will you be quiet!' snapped Parsifoe. 'Ulalliall, do you know another way to make the gate?'

'No,' said Ulalliall.

'Then what were you on about?'

'Why is that lout of a boy peering through the keyhole?'

Runcie turned to run, but thought better of it. He'd sooner take his medicine now than lie awake waiting for it. But worst of all, as the door swung open and Parsifoe dragged him in by the ear, was the sniggering coming from beneath the canvas. It felt like a betrayal.

Parsifoe flung Runcie into a chair and stood over him like a plump little thundercloud. 'How dare you spy on magicians' work, you wretch?'

'Or has Lars got at you?' roared Helfigor, clouting him over the ear. 'Are you doing his business? Betraying your friends?'

'No!' Runcie rubbed his stinging ear. The black bat was standing upright now, those enormous eyes on him as if to read his mind and whisper what it found there. Runcie, shuddering, wasn't sure he wanted a mindsake after all.

'If you're in the pay of the enemy, boy, after all we've done for you –'

'It's nothing like that. S-something woke me,' gabbled Runcie, desperate to get an explanation out before they inflicted some dire punishment on him. 'It was a kind of sick, dizzy feeling, like going through a gate. I was afraid it might be the enemy.'

'Worthless child,' muttered Helfigor. 'He can't do a scrap of magic, yet squeals like a pig when anyone else uses it.'

'But then,' Runcie added hastily, since that didn't explain why he'd been spying, 'I looked in through the keyhole and what you were doing was so interesting that I couldn't tear myself away. I've always been fascinated by magic.'

'An odd preoccupation, in the circumstances,' Helfigor said cruelly.

'Kids see magic as the easy way out,' said Parsifoe. 'Just wave a wand and you can have whatever you want, without working for it. But magic isn't easy, Runcie, and it should never be wasted. It requires unrelenting discipline, plus year upon year –'

'Not to mention *talent*,' Ulalliall interrupted pointedly. 'Which this little thug has none of. Not an iota. Not a –'

'Enough, transportal,' Helfigor said wearily. He gazed at Runcie. 'Unfortunately she's right. You don't have a talent for magic, do you?'

'No sir,' Runcie said forlornly. 'And I used to dream about it so much, because of Dad . . .' To Runcie's horror, tears welled in his eyes, forming faster than he could wipe them away.

Parsifoe looked puzzled. 'What about his father?'

Runcie explained, haltingly. 'I don't suppose you know anything about Dad?'

'I've not heard his name before, lad.'

'Let's get on,' said Helfigor.

Parsifoe peered into Runcie's eyes. 'Has he been tested for magic, *thoroughly*?'

'I checked once, when he was asleep. *Nothing!*' he said in tones that crushed what remained of Runcie's dreams. But then Helfigor lowered his voice and said, 'though he does know about *science*.'

'What?' Parsifoe ran to the door, checked outside, then bolted it and thrust her handkerchief into the keyhole. She peered up the chimney too, before coming back. 'You'd better explain.'

Helfigor whispered in her ear. Runcie's stomach churned. He had a feeling they were going to ask him something unpleasant.

'The penalty for using *science*–' Parsifoe's mouth puckered.

'It can hardly be worse than being slain by two First Order Cybale wizards.'

'I suppose you're right,' she said heavily. 'Though to sink so low as to use science, when my wizardly ambitions were once so noble . . . And even if we do succeed, it's going to hurt a lot. Very well, have you still *got it?*'

Helfigor took hold of the ornament dangling from his left ear, twisted, and what looked like a little paper cylinder slipped into his hand. He made a pass over it with the rod, and the cylinder grew and became a roll of paper tied with string. He unrolled it on the table.

Runcie leaned forwards. It looked like an article cut from one of his mother's science magazines. It was mostly words but there were several coloured diagrams and charts. He tried to read the first page upside down but Helfigor covered the beginning of the article with his hand.

'Better that you don't, Runcie. Then, when . . . *if* you're tortured you can say truthfully that you don't know anything.'

Parsifoe began to say something but the wizard hastily shook his head, continuing, 'Runcie, we think this paper might be able to show us another way to make a dimensional gate – with *science*. Unfortunately, since travel to your world is so difficult, we're not sure what the article means.'

'But before the wyrm came,' said Runcie, feeling that Helfigor was being something of a hypocrite, 'you said that science was rightly banned.'

'I'm not taking lessons in morality from a Nightlander!' Helfigor snarled, red-faced.

Runcie backed off. 'What do you want me to do?'

'Just explain the meaning of a few words.'

'Where did the article come from?' said Runcie.

'It . . . er . . . fell into my hands. No need to worry about that.' Helfigor ran a battered fingernail down the first page. 'Ah, here's the first. What does "quantum tunnelling" mean?'

'I have no idea, sir,' Runcie said after a decent pause.

'Really?' Helfigor looked disappointed in him, but continued down the page. 'What about "Planck length"?'

Runcie shook his head.

Helfigor scowled and turned the page. 'Negative vacuum energy?'

'No, sir.'

'Six-dimensional manifold?'

'No, sir.'

'The Duality of Dualities?'

Helfigor was looking so ferocious that Runcie couldn't meet his eye. 'No, sir.'

'Stable configurations of space-time?'

'I'm afraid I've never heard of any of those things before,' said Runcie.

'Why the devil not?' cried the wizard, as though Runcie had let the side down badly. 'The other day you were boasting about how good you were at science.'

'I didn't boast,' Runcie said with as much dignity as he could muster. 'And I *was* good at the science we did in primary school. I . . . I think that article must be very advanced, sir . . . It would be like Tigris casting a First Order spell.' He couldn't resist adding. 'Or even *you* doing one, sir.'

Parsifoe snorted, then tried unsuccessfully to hide her grin behind her hand.

'I don't know what you're laughing about,' Helfigor snapped, as black as a thundercloud. 'This was our last chance and it's come to nothing.' He scowled at Runcie. 'Clear out, boy, and don't come back or, by the powers, you'll regret it.'

As Runcie scurried for the door and drew back the bolt, Parsifoe said, 'Let's have one more try, Helfigor. If that fails, then I don't know what we're going to do.'

CHAPTER 27

Waves of Magic

'What was that?' Tigris said shrilly, right in Runcie's ear.

He had finally fallen asleep not long before dawn, and had been deep in one of his favourite dreams. It involved the glorious food Thandimanilon had given them in Miluviand – tables creaking under the weight of it – and strings of Gorbal's Premium Sausage the length of mooring cables. He groaned.

'Shh!' said Mariam.

Runcie sat up, hastily wiped a thread of drool off his chin and pulled the blankets around his shoulders. It was light outside but he couldn't hear anything except the incessant whistling of the wind. Then, very faintly, came a dull rumble and the tower quivered.

'Did you hear that?' Mariam said.

Tigris's eyes were very wide. 'They've come!'

A distant *boom* was followed by a shudder, and a vase containing a few long-dead flowers slid off the mantelpiece to smash on the floor beside Runcie. Smelly brown water splashed his face. He wiped it with his sleeve.

Tigris scurried to the window. 'I can see something out there.'

'What?' said Mariam, running after her.

'I'm not sure. It's foggy.' Tigris rotated the lowest set of panes open, then swayed out of sight as something dark shot past, so close that it blocked out the light. Clammy fog billowed in, netting Mariam's wild hair with tiny drops.

Down below, a bell clanged. Youthful yells echoed up the stairs and a child began to cry.

'Prentices?' came a young woman's voice. 'Go back to your dormitories. There's nothing to worry about.'

'Why do grown-ups say such dumb things?' Mariam muttered.

A louder boom was followed by a heave like the deck of a ship moving. The window crashed shut.

'We'd better go down,' said Mariam. 'We might be able to help.'

'I don't see how,' said Runcie. His chest felt so tight that he could hardly breathe.

Someone came running up the stairs, panting. It was a tall young woman, rather thin and freckly, wearing green robes tied at the waist with a yellow tasselled cord. A pair of silver-rimmed spectacles were perched on top of short, neat brown hair.

She staggered up the last few steps, red in the face, then gasped, 'Come down to the dormitories at once. Didn't you hear the bell?' She turned and began to stumble down.

'What's happening?' Mariam demanded.

The young woman stopped on the landing below them, trying hard to appear in control. 'Don't worry – it'll be all right.'

There came a louder boom, and a wedge of stone the size of an atlas flaked off the wall above her, crumbling to fragments as it hit the steps. The prentices began to scream. The young woman fled.

'I'm not going to be locked up with a bunch of screaming kids,' said Mariam. 'Coming?'

After getting into such trouble last night, Runcie was reluctant, but he didn't want to be locked away either. He followed Mariam and, after a brief hesitation, so did Tigris.

The dormitories were on the forty-sixth level. As Mariam approached the level above, she ducked below the rail. 'Get down. That teacher's counting the kids in.'

'She'll be watching for us,' said Runcie.

Mariam shushed him. 'Quick! She's gone in.'

They scurried down, across the landing and down again. Two prentices waiting outside the door stared at them curiously, then one boy yelled, 'Miss! Miss! Some funny-looking kids are going downstairs.'

'Run!' said Mariam. They bolted down the stairs.

'Children!' cried the teacher. 'Come back here at once.'

They kept going down another four or five floors, before collapsing in a heap together, laughing, even Tigris. 'She won't come after us,' said Tigris. 'She can't leave the prentices by themselves.'

'I don't know why we're laughing,' said Mariam.

'Because it's better than screaming,' said Runcie. The coming battle wasn't just over Mariam. It could change the fate of both worlds.

They found Helfigor and Parsifoe on the lowest level, near the outer door. It was made of foot-thick timber reinforced with iron bands, which they'd barricaded with stout beams and even stouter spells, but water was pouring in underneath.

Helfigor heaved a sandbag against the gap. He looked as if he'd been up all night. 'What the blazes are you doing here? Didn't you hear the bell?'

'We came to help,' said Mariam.

The wizard scowled at her. Mariam thrust out her jaw defiantly. 'Bah!' he snorted. 'All hands to the pump, I suppose. Hump those sandbags.'

Runcie and Mariam caught hold of a sandbag and began dragging it across to the door. Something thumped against the outside, sending a surge of water in, and the tower shuddered.

'Is it Lars Sparj?' said Runcie.

Parsifoe nodded. She looked even worse than Helfigor – all pallid, red-eyed and saggy. Trying to make the gate had taken a lot out of her. 'See what he's up to.'

Runcie scampered up to the unglassed slit window and peered out, right into a stinging burst of spray. He wiped his eyes. The fog had blown away, though the sky was as leaden as ever. Something shot past, curving in a tight circle around the tower – a sleek black transportal shaped like a shark.

'He's going around,' said Runcie. 'Oh, just look at *that*!'

A wave began to swell in the wake of the transportal, steepening as it curved towards the rocks and rising until it towered as high as his head. That had to be magic. Down it crashed over a long stone jetty, exploding in spray that blocked out the world like a violent fog.

Runcie ducked as the deluge thundered against the base of the tower. Something went *bang-bang* on the door, like a giant demanding entrance, and water squirted underneath so powerfully that it tumbled the sandbags out of the way.

'How are we doing?' Helfigor croaked, splashing through knee-deep water. Lengths of wood, boxes and barrels bobbed on the surface and the core-less shell of Ulalliall, in the corner, was floating, coiled end low in the water. Runcie began to come down the steps.

'The door holds,' said Parsifoe, circling it with her wizard's baton to reinforce the spells that held it fast, like layer upon layer of web. 'But only just.'

Mariam, who had been washed off her feet, spat out a mouthful of dirty seawater. She looked like a drowned rat. 'Can Lars get in up top?'

'Not so easily. A *protection* spell was bonded to the tower when Irascible the Third built it, more than a thousand years ago, and the spell has never been breached. Indeed, though Thorasdil has been besieged more than twenty times, it's never been taken by force.'

'But it's twice been taken by treachery,' grunted Helfigor

as he slammed a sandbag against the door, sending water everywhere.

Without thinking, Runcie looked at Tigris, who started. He turned away hastily but the damage had been done. Tigris gave a little, despairing cry and covered her face with her hands.

'No stronghold is impregnable if the enemy is strong or cunning enough,' Helfigor went on. 'Runcie, stay on watch. What's he's doing?'

Runcie returned to the window, mortified. 'He – he's coming around again, closer this time. I can see him standing on the platform.' He swallowed hard. Lars Sparj was a huge man, handsome in a grim sort of a way. His black hair was flying in the wind and his cloak billowing out behind him, displaying its crimson lining. His moustaches stuck out like wires, their waxed points as sharp as needles. He turned as the transportal shot past and looked into Runcie's eyes. *Open the door, boy.*

Runcie almost fell off the stairs. It was as if Lars were trying to control him.

'What's he doing?' Helfigor rapped out.

'He's gone past. There's no wave this time.' Runcie swayed, feeling a compelling urge to push the wizards out of the way and slip the bolts of the door. What was the point in fighting on? They could never defeat such powerful sorcerers.

'That's bad,' said Parsifoe. 'What's the matter, lad?'

'He looked right into my eyes,' said Runcie. 'I – I –'

'Avoid his eye,' said Helfigor. 'It's part of his magic, even from that distance.'

Runcie fought the urge, as he had Thormic's compulsion, and it faded, though he felt even worse now. Who was he to judge Tigris, when he could be swayed so easily? 'He's gone. No, he's turning, curving around the other way. The wave is rising again.'

'A good strategy,' said Helfigor, 'to pound us from the other direction. It'll weaken the structure faster.'

'The wave is rising higher than before, sir. And steeper . . . Much steeper,' Runcie whispered. 'Get ready. It's breaking over the jetty. Here it comes . . . *now*.'

Parsifoe's baton was going furiously. Helfigor heaved another sandbag against the door. Tigris and Mariam were about to drop theirs in place when the wave struck the door like an explosion. Blades of water burst in around the sides and top, shooting across the room with such force that they scoured grime off the far wall. With an almighty crack, the bars that reinforced the door were torn out of their sockets, then the door burst open, throwing the girls and Helfigor halfway across the room.

Parsifoe, who had been standing to one side, gasped and clutched at her heart. She stood there for a moment, bent double, but rallied, raised her baton and, with a sweep of her hand, the door slammed.

Helfigor pushed himself to his feet, drew his crystal rod and stood beside her. Mariam splashed back to the door. She had a bruise on her forehead the size of a peach but her eyes were shining. Runcie would never understand her.

'Watchman, report!' snapped the wizard.

'He's coming around again . . .' Runcie tore his gaze away from the window, realising that he hadn't seen Tigris get up after the wave.

'Come on,' said Helfigor. 'What the blazes . . .?'

'Tigris!' Runcie hurtled down the steps and churned through the water, crashing into floating crates and planks. He had a vague memory of her being thrown through the air, towards the far corner. The water was almost up to his waist here. He dived under the bobbing transportal, eyes closed, and felt around. Nothing. Coming out next to the wall, he turned and dived again. Was that an arm? He traced it along. Yes, Tigris was caught under a crate. He took hold of her coat, wriggled her around and heaved her to the surface.

'She's not breathing!' He looked around frantically for somewhere to lay her. He'd often seen people resuscitated on TV, though Runcie didn't know how to do it.

'Just hold her up,' said Parsifoe.

Runcie held Tigris. Parsifoe pulled her jaw down, thrust the baton into her mouth and whispered, 'Deluge, Degurge!'

Water erupted from Tigris's mouth onto the front of Parsifoe's gown. 'Degurge!' Parsifoe repeated, but only a few trickles of watery vomit came out.

Tigris gave a gasping shudder, steadied herself on Parsifoe's arm and gasped, 'Thank you.'

'Runcie saved you,' said Helfigor. 'Well done, lad. It's easy to miss a fallen comrade in the thick of the action. Now, back to your watch.'

Runcie limped up to the window; he'd cracked his knee on something. Tigris was staring at him and there were tears in her eyes, but he didn't have time to wonder about them, for the transportal was cruising around again. Thandimanilon stood beside her hawk-faced consort with her hair blowing in the wind, and she looked extraordinarily beautiful. Beautiful but deadly, Runcie reminded himself before he fell under her spell. Her head was thrown back; she was wild with glee and revelling in her wickedness. And then someone moved behind them and there, wearing a black, crimson-lined cloak like a miniature Lars, stood Jac Sleeth, looking as cool and focussed as a wizard. Runcie was overcome by helpless fury. Sleeth was a nasty, treacherous little brute. What would he be like as a First Order wizard?

'Report!' shouted Helfigor.

'They're inspecting the damage,' Runcie said. 'They look pleased.'

'Well they might be,' said Helfigor. 'The tower can't take many more blows like that. They'll back off now.'

'Why?' said Runcie.

'They want their quarry alive and whole, plus any other treasures they can gather from our fall. And there's nothing we can do to stop them.'

And then Runcie had a wild idea. 'I think there might be, actually.'

'Really, boy?' said the wizard, less sarcastically than usual. 'You astound me. What can you possibly come up with that we mighty have failed to think of?'

'Science,' said Runcie as boldly as he dared.

The wizards exchanged glances. 'We've been down that road,' muttered Parsifoe.

'Just listen, please,' said Runcie. 'Have you any oil?'

'There's barrels of the stuff in the west cellar,' said Parsifoe. 'We use nut oil for cooking and distilled naphtha for the lamps. There could be a barrel or two of black oil, too, though I don't see what use oil could be.'

'Oil calms troubled waters,' said Runcie. 'It used to be poured onto the sea so shipwrecked sailors could be rescued. I've read about it in storybooks.'

'Storybooks!' Parsifoe sniffed. 'Anyway, we don't have enough.' She turned back to the door, wearily raising her ivory baton.

'But if you were to spread it with magic . . .' said Runcie, aware that he didn't know what he was talking about.

'Yes,' Helfigor mused. 'I see a way that the effects of a little oil might be magnified to frustrate Lars's wave magic.' He let out a snort of laughter. 'And best of all, since my magic would be based on *science*, he'd never know how I did it. Tigris, how are you feeling?'

She was clinging to the bottom of the stair rail. 'I'm . . . a little faint, sir.'

'Take Runcie's place on watch. Runcie, come with me. Parsifoe, if you and Mariam could be ready with the door when we bring the barrel. We won't have much time.' He watched Tigris drag herself to the window. 'Any waves yet?'

362

'No, but it won't be long.'

Runcie followed Helfigor through an archway into another chamber, where the wizard conjured finger-light to read the markings on the crates and barrels. 'Wax, honey, tallow. Wine,' he bent his nose to the barrel, 'gone sour – what a tragic waste. Wine, Madeira – that takes me back. I remember a night that lasted for four days. Ah, to be young and carefree again –' He broke off, shaking his head, and hurried into the third chamber. 'This looks more like it – black oil. Give me a hand, lad. Look sharp, now.'

They floated the barrel out, manoeuvring it through the debris-clotted water.

'Watcher, report!' called Helfigor.

'The transportal is starting to circle,' said Tigris. 'They're laughing.'

'I'll bet they are. Open the door, Parsifoe.'

'You'd better be quick! If the wave catches us before we've redone the spells –'

'We've no choice.'

Runcie and Mariam started heaving the sandbags away. Parsifoe had just cracked the heavy door open when Tigris yelled, 'They're starting. The wave –'

'Stop!' Parsifoe banged the door closed.

Helfigor hesitated, then cried, 'No, it's our last chance. Come on. Don't look into his eyes, Runcie.'

Parsifoe, white-faced, swung the door open. Runcie and Helfigor floated the barrel through on the outrushing water and began rolling it down the winding path towards the stone jetty, which was pocked with holes where huge stones had been torn out.

The transportal was well out to their left, spiralling in around the tower with the wave rising behind it. 'It's not as big this time,' said Runcie, trying to reassure himself.

'Lars is trying to sucker us. It can grow quickly if he wants it to.'

'He's seen us. He's turning our way.'

'Faster!'

He heaved with all his heart but, as the barrel bounced onto the jetty, Helfigor turned his ankle and Runcie couldn't hold the barrel steady. It spun right and dropped into a hole. Helfigor cursed and heaved at it, but it was stuck. 'Come on! What's Lars doing?'

'He's racing now,' said Runcie. 'Oh, look!' The wave was growing rapidly, swelling like a tsunami.

He heaved uselessly at the barrel, sure he was going to die. Helfigor bent, wrenched it out and sent it rolling down the long jetty. Runcie held his breath, expecting it to fall into another of the many holes but, with skilful flicks of his crystal rod, Helfigor managed to spin the barrel around each one.

'Run to the door, boy!' he snapped as the wave rose until it blocked out a quarter of the sky.

Runcie didn't move. The barrel still had to be opened, surely?

'Run, you bloody fool!'

Runcie darted back up the path, looking over his shoulder as Helfigor, with a flourish that lit up the crystal rod like an emerald, burst the barrel into staves and hoops. Black oil poured off the end of the jetty and he directed it into the path of the monster wave, then sent it curling into an arc around the tower. But it couldn't work in time – the wave was roaring towards him; it was going to sweep him away.

The transportal suddenly turned and zoomed high. 'What's he doing?' said Helfigor.

'Come on!' screamed Parsifoe.

Runcie bolted up the winding path, bounding over the potholes. Helfigor was trotting backwards, still directing the oil. The towering wave hit the magical slick and seemed to hesitate. Runcie gained the door but Helfigor, still halfway down the jetty, caught his heel in a pothole and fell sprawling. Parsifoe gave an anguished cry.

The oil-coated wave smoothed out, dropped, then collapsed at the edge of the rocks. It wasn't going to smash through the door, but the surge could still sweep the wizard away. Runcie turned back.

'Runcie, no!' screamed Mariam.

The transportal reached its zenith, tilted over and raced towards Helfigor. If Lars caught him, Parsifoe would be forced to give up Mariam. Runcie had to do something.

He'd just taken off when he cracked his shin on a broken crate outside the door. Wrenching off a board, he put it behind him, praying that Lars Sparj wouldn't take any notice of a kid who had no magic. Lars glanced in his direction but Runcie didn't duck in time. Their eyes met.

Bring your little friend to me.

And how he wanted to. Suddenly, taking Mariam down to Lars seemed the right and only thing to do. And she was at the door, close by, looking anxiously out.

Bring her.

No, fight him every step of the way. Runcie tried to turn away but his feet took one step towards Mariam, then another, and he saw the dawning horror on her face, that he was going to betray her. 'No,' he gasped.

You can't fight a First Order sorcerer, Nightland brat. Bring her now.

Runcie closed his eyes, defying Lars for all he was worth, but his feet kept moving towards Mariam. How could he fight the compulsion? Think!

Of course – Lars could be mixed up in his father's death. Such a surge of fury went through Runcie that he almost blacked out. 'Go to hell, you stinking, murdering scum!' he shrieked, using every ounce of his hate and rage to fight his enemy.

The compulsion faded and he whirled. The transportal now hovered beside Helfigor and Lars was striding down the steps. Runcie ran forwards and hurled the heavy board at him. It spun through the air, caught Lars in the face and knocked him into Thandimanilon in a tangle of arms and legs. She slammed into the wall of the transportal, which veered sharply to the right and would have crashed into the tower, had Sleeth not jerked it away.

Lars Sparj sat up, pointed a long finger at Runcie and coils of light corkscrewed through the air at him. Helfigor desperately swung his rod into the path of the spell, sending most of it flashing back the other way to hit Thandimanilon in the chest. She went down a second time.

Unfortunately the crystal rod hadn't completely blocked Lars Sparj's attack. One corkscrew of light twisted into Runcie and he fell, his muscles so twitchy from millions of pinpricking electric shocks that he couldn't move.

CHAPTER 28

Cast Aside

Parsifoe and Mariam carried Runcie inside, laying him on the landing by the slit window. Helfigor limped in after them, holding the still-glowing crystal rod in a smoking sleeve. Though Runcie could see and hear them, he couldn't even blink. His staring eyes were already dry and itchy; and what if he were paralysed?

'You'd better try the gate again, Parsifoe,' Helfigor said quietly.

'You can't defend the door alone.'

'With Runcie's magicked oil, I can hold back the waters until nightfall. But Lars won't wait that long. The instant he recovers, he'll start planning another attack.'

'Can we strengthen the protection further?'

Helfigor looked down at Runcie. 'Yes, though everything takes time – including saving the boy. If we do one, we may not be able to do the other.'

Chills swept up Runcie's arms. For everyone else's sake, they'd have to let him die.

'You've got to save him!' Mariam's face crumpled up. She took hold of the wizard's hand. 'Please, Helfigor.'

Helfigor exchanged glances with Parsifoe, then drew her aside. Runcie couldn't hear what they were saying, though, judging by the despairing look on Mariam's face, they were preparing to sacrifice him for the greater good.

'Runcie's done everything for us,' said Mariam, shaking him. 'And he saved your life. You've *got* to do something.'

After a long pause, Helfigor said, 'I – I'll try my best. If you can get the gate working, Parsifoe . . . well, do whatever you can.'

'And if I fail again?' said Parsifoe.

He just shook his head. She trudged up the stairs. A pale Tigris followed, with more than one backward glance at Runcie.

'What's the matter with him?' said Mariam.

'I'm not sure,' Helfigor said heavily. 'I don't know how much of Lars's spell got through.'

Mariam took Runcie's wrist in her hand and pressed it to her cold cheek. She must have thought he was unconscious.

'Reckless little fool – how could he think to take on *Lars*?' Helfigor shook his head in wonder. 'But if he hadn't acted . . .' He bent over, passed his callused hands back and forth over Runcie's face, peered into his eyes then touched the rod to Runcie's forehead.

Runcie felt drowsiness creep over him, though his gritty eyes remained open. Helfigor closed them with his thumb.

'He doesn't look any different,' choked Mariam.

'It's not easy to bring them back from such a spell,' said

Helfigor, heaving the semiconscious boy over his shoulder. Runcie, almost asleep, barely felt it.

Runcie opened his eyes and sat up, carefully, for he had the most desperate headache. He was lying on the floor of the chamber where Parsifoe and Helfigor had been doing magic last night, though Ulalliall was gone from the table. The far window was dark. Night had fallen.

'Runcie!' Mariam fell to her knees beside him. 'I was so worried.'

'But they *did* break the spell?' he said anxiously.

'They think so . . .'

'What is it?' His head gave a vicious throb.

'It was a First Order spell, so they can't be sure.'

'Great!' said Runcie. 'I suppose I'll be walking down the street one day and my nose will drop off, or something.'

Mariam giggled. 'They felt *pretty* sure the spell was gone, but –'

'What is it?'

'It took all day, and they didn't get time to strengthen the protection.'

'Oh,' he said dully.

'Runcie –?' Mariam began.

'Mariam,' he said, thinking to forestall her. 'I'm really sorry. I – I –'

'What for?'

'When I looked into Lars's eyes, he ordered me to bring you . . . and I was going to.'

'It was a spell, you dill. A compulsion.'

'I know, but I really *wanted* to.'

'But you fought it, and then you saved us all.'

'I was sure you'd despise –'

'Go back to sleep,' she said crossly. 'Your brains are still addled. Everyone thinks you're a hero, Runcie. Even me.'

He began to lie down, but sat up again. 'What's Lars up to?'

'Planning a different attack. Hey, are you all right?'

Runcie's head was spinning. 'I think I'll have a little rest. Wake me when –'

The crash shook the tower like an earthquake, shattering every pane in the window and sending fresh agonies gouging through his head. His skull felt like a pumpkin dropped from the top floor.

Mariam jumped up. 'Stay here.' Her feet clattered down the steps.

Stay here! He couldn't even sit up. More crashes and bangs came from below, as if a door were being smashed in. Children screamed, then all went ominously silent. Runcie lay there, grateful to be alive and knowing he owed it to Mariam. But if Lars got in, he'd go straight for her, and she'd known that when she'd pleaded for his, Runcie's, life. How could he ever repay her?

Shortly there were running footsteps on the stairs and she appeared, panting. 'Lars catapulted a boulder through the wall of the tower, drove the transportal in and he's taken the prentices hostage.'

More pain speared through Runcie's head. 'What's Helfigor doing?'

'He and Parsifoe are trying to fight back from the floor above – two below here – but they're looking pretty grim. I'm scared, Runcie. Lars says he'll only give up the hostages in exchange for me. Parsifoe will have to agree.'

The pain spread to his chest. 'Unless Helfigor can do something really clever to turn the tables.'

'On *two* First Order wizards? Besides, he won't risk the lives of Parsifoe's prentices. And I wouldn't ask him to,' she added staunchly. 'I really wouldn't, Runcie. No matter how terrified I was.' Her bottom lip trembled.

Runcie's heart went out to her. 'Help me up.'

She started to heave him to his feet but let him down again, eyes narrowed. 'Why?'

'We agreed we wouldn't be separated. If this *is* the end, I'm spending it with you.'

'Lars tried to kill you this morning, Runcie. If he sees you . . .'

'If he *really* wants to kill me, there's nowhere I can hide. Come on.'

She helped him up and they crept halfway down the broad stone staircase, to where an untidy wall of tables, chests and chairs blocked off the landing. Helfigor and Parsifoe were crouched behind the barrier.

'Where's Tigris?' said Runcie.

'She's busy upstairs,' said Parsifoe. 'Shhh!'

Runcie peered down. The left half of the floor below was an

open common room littered with rubble and overturned furniture. In the middle of the central wall a large, panelled door led to the dormitories. A ragged hole gaped in the outside wall to their left, and about thirty feet away Lars Sparj's black transportal sat on the floor. There was no one in sight, though just inside its shark mouth a battlefield diorama stood on a plinth. It was a clockwork automaton playing the same attack – the fatal charge, the lopped heads and impaled bodies, the desperate rout – over and over in bloodcurdling realism.

'What's that for?' said Runcie.

'It's a magnificent toy for Lars's amusement,' Helfigor said wearily. 'But an historical lesson too, for it replays the ruinous defeat of the wizard army, through treachery, which gave the Cybale control of Iltior in ancient times.'

Runcie tore his eyes away, swallowing hard. It looked as though history was about to repeat itself. 'Did you make the gate?'

'Yes,' said Parsifoe. 'But we can't summon enough *quintessence* to make it work.'

'Lars is still in the dormitories,' said Helfigor. 'With Sleeth.'

'What's Lars going to do to me?' said Mariam with a catch in her voice.

Runcie felt even worse now. He wriggled around the edge of the barrier and studied the floor below. There was no sign of Thandimanilon, which was odd.

'He hasn't got you yet,' Parsifoe said unconvincingly. Her face was blotchy, her jowls sagging. Making the gate had worn her out and it didn't look as if she had anything left.

'But he will.' Mariam sounded more grown-up than either wizard. 'So what happens after he's got the secret?'

'He might kill you to cover up his plans,' said Parsifoe in a deathly voice. 'What am I to do? Send you to your fate, or let him take my prentices instead?'

Runcie squinted into the darkness inside the transportal, thinking that there had to be a way. He could just make out Thandimanilon, right up the back. She was sitting, no, *lying* in a chair, and that made no sense, unless . . .

'Thandimanilon is lying down,' he hissed. 'I think she's ill.'

In a rush, Helfigor and Parsifoe were beside him. 'The lad's right,' said Parsifoe. 'She's always had a frail constitution.'

'The ghasts nearly killed her the other day,' said Mariam. 'And Lars's spell struck her down this morning. Parsifoe –' Her eyes were shining.

'Come on,' said Parsifoe to Helfigor. 'Stay back, children.'

The two wizards crept down, keeping close to the banisters.

'Keep watch,' Runcie heard Helfigor whisper. 'Lars is tougher than he looks.'

'So am I.' Parsifoe sighted along her baton at the door to the dormitories.

Helfigor scuttled to the transportal. Thandimanilon groped feebly for her staff but he grabbed it first and touched it to her heart. Shortly she shuffled out, hands on top of her head, and lurched up the stairs. Helfigor helped her over the barrier and she slumped to the steps. Her skin was so pale that Runcie could see the blood moving sluggishly beneath it.

Helfigor bound her hands and tied a rag across her mouth to prevent her speaking any spell, though there seemed little danger of that. Thandimanilon just laid her cheek on the cold steps and closed her eyes.

'Let's get on.' Helfigor stood up, raising his voice. 'Lars, we've got Thandimanilon. Come out.'

After a minute, a small blonde girl, about ten, appeared at the dormitory door, then a nuggetty, curly-headed boy of eight, both walking stiffly as if bespelled. Lars followed them out and said, 'Stop!' They stopped at once.

Looking up towards the barricade, he smiled, and with his red mouth and sharp teeth he looked like an angry wolf. A bloody welt ran from his right cheek up into his hair. Points of light reflected off his monocle as he moved. 'What do you want?'

Just the sight of him made Runcie shake with rage, but he controlled it. He had to *know*.

'We have Thandimanilon,' said Helfigor. 'We're prepared to give her up in exchange for the prentices, your immediate departure, and compensation for damage and distress.'

'An obvious tactic,' sneered Lars, 'but what can you expect from a man who only made the Second Order by cheating?'

Helfigor tried to ignore the taunt, though his throat quivered. 'Don't mess us about, Lars.'

'My call has gone out,' said Parsifoe feebly. 'I have friends in high places –'

'Not as high as I have. I've ordered that there be no interference.' Looking over his shoulder, Lars rapped, 'Come!'

Shortly the rest of the prentices appeared, twelve children walking in two lines of six, led by Sleeth. The youngest looked about six, the oldest no more than fourteen. They stiffly climbed the steps into the black transportal and sat down at the back in rows. Several children were crying. Sleeth stood in front of them with his arms crossed.

Lars strode to the transportal, raised one be-ringed hand and the transportal lifted off the floor.

'What's going on?' Parsifoe and Helfigor exchanged puzzled looks.

Lars laughed mockingly. 'You've got nothing to bargain with.'

'We have Thandimanilon.'

'You're welcome to her.'

With a muffled wail, Thandimanilon staggered to her feet, holding out her bound hands to Lars like a beautiful, tragic statue. A single, diamond-bright tear made its way down her cheek and, despite her wickedness, Runcie was moved. He reached up and pulled the gag down so she could speak.

'Lars?' she whispered. 'Lars, tell me this is a joke.'

'I never joke.' Lars Sparj inspected her without a flicker of compassion. 'You have everything I could wish for in my consort,' he said brutally, 'except the thing I require most of all – vigour. You're frail, Thandimanilon, and I despise you for it. You're not worth a groat to me.' He turned to Parsifoe. 'Render Mariam up to me and you may have back your prentices. Fail me and I'll take the appeal directly to their parents. Once I've given them one or two bodies to put back together, the rest won't hold out on me.'

'You're a monster,' Parsifoe said savagely. 'A brute.'

'I'm Cybale to the tips of my moustaches and I'll not rest until we've been restored to our rightful place on Iltior. I *will* have Anthrimorie's location out of this child from Nightland, one way or the other.'

No one said anything. Mariam was trembling, almost imperceptibly, and her earlier words came back to Runcie. He couldn't let it happen. Edging closer, he caught her hand. 'It'll be all right,' he said softly. 'Helfigor and Parsifoe aren't finished yet.'

Mariam pulled free, turning to face him. 'Thanks Runcie, for everything.'

'No,' he said numbly. Surely she wasn't giving up without a fight?

A shudder racked her from head to toe, then she grew eerily calm. 'It's over. We don't have anything to fight with.' She tapped Parsifoe on the shoulder.

'Please, no,' said Parsifoe, who had aged twenty years. 'I can't bear for you to say it, child.'

Mariam's hand shook but she steadied it with an effort of will. 'I'm going to say it. I can't stand the waiting.' She stood up and called out, in a carrying voice, 'Lars Sparj, I'm coming down. Send out the prentices.'

Pushing past them, she slowly made her way down the stairs, walking with the dignity of a princess, her back straight and her head held high.

Parsifoe put her hands over her face and wept.

CHAPTER 29

The Nyssitron

Runcie watched Mariam go, a scream building up inside him. The world didn't make sense any more. His best friend was walking to her doom and no one was doing anything about it. And what was the matter with her? She must have a death wish.

He was so overcome by rage that the blood seemed to be boiling in his head. He couldn't think straight – he only knew that he had to do *something*. He flexed his knees, preparing to hurl himself at the enemy no matter the consequences, but as he came upright a pair of bound hands were lowered over his head and Thandimanilon drew him back against her.

'No, Runcie,' she said softly. 'You can't do a thing and he'll kill you if you try, for thwarting him earlier. Lars avenges the least affront to his dignity, to the last drop of blood.'

'I can't stand by,' said Runcie, twisting around to look up at Thandimanilon's drained face. 'I just can't.'

'You must, for if you fly at Lars, Mariam will go to her fate knowing you died because of her.'

'But . . .'

'Stay, Runcie; this tale isn't yet played out.' Thandimanilon cocked her head, though he could hear only Mariam's slow footsteps on the grit-covered floor.

She reached the foot of the transportal's steps. The prentices were assembled at the top. 'Send them down first,' Mariam said.

'Come up,' grated Lars Sparj.

'How do I know I can trust you?'

His eyes flashed. 'I'm a man of my word, Nightland brat!'

'You abandoned Thandimanilon, *Iltior scum*! And you're prepared to kill children.'

Even Thandimanilon gasped at Mariam's recklessness. Lars flushed, then said pompously, 'A Cybale's word is his bond, his honour, his *life*.'

But as he turned to the children, Runcie made out an eerie wailing that sent a shiver up his spine, and zigzags of colour flashed through his inner eye. Someone was using great magic, not far away.

Mariam backed away, crying, 'What are you doing?'

Lars ran straight past her to the hole in the side of the tower, peered out into the night then threw himself backwards. 'Into the transportal, quick!'

With a spine-tingling screech, a dark spinning shape shot past the hole and began to circle the tower, once, twice, three times. A shockwave reverberated in each time it went by, shaking plaster down from the ceiling.

'It's a *nyssitron*,' Helfigor said in wonder. 'A transportal automaton. Who could have made such a deadly device?'

'And it's broken the tower's protection,' Parsifoe whispered. 'Helfigor, there's nothing left.'

He stared at her. 'But . . . that's not possible. The spell's lasted a thousand years.'

Lars Sparj was thumping up the steps of his transportal. It lifted, curved towards Mariam, he threw a white lasso over her head, pulled it tight around her middle and heaved her in.

But before he could get away, an appalling screech began above them, as if hardened cogs were grinding through the tower wall. Chunks of rubble bounced down the stairs, followed by billowing clouds of dust. The prentices screamed and stampeded to the back of the transportal. The screeching grew louder as the nyssitron attacked the floor above. With a deathly glance at the ceiling, Lars Sparj gripped his staff and began to murmur the transportal's dematerialising spell.

'He's surely not going to jump to *between* from inside the tower?' whispered Parsifoe. 'It could bring it down on our heads.'

'Maybe that's the idea,' said Runcie.

Lars was only halfway through his spell when the nyssitron tore through the ceiling above the door to the dormitories and slid sideways to hover, rocking in the air, between Lars's transportal and the hole in the far wall. It was smaller than a transportal, only the length of a car, and dark grey but shiny, for not a speck of dust clung to it. Shaped like a metal starfish, it had a domed and embossed central disc from which five stubby metal arms radiated, each studded with whirring cogs along the sides and end – teeth that had ground through stone as if it were plaster.

A lustrous dome on the disc flipped back, revealing a seated man wearing a coarse-meshed wire mask that revealed more of his face than it covered. Bushy grey whiskers hung a foot below the bottom of the mask, while the longest moustaches Runcie had ever seen sprouted through the sides, where their ends were trained into multiple coils each large enough for an egg to pass through. The man was grinning broadly, showing a gap between his front teeth, and his brown eyes twinkled.

'Lord Shambles!' gasped Lars, his stiletto moustaches drooping. He cracked his staff and, with a roar that shook Thorasdil to its foundations, the transportal vanished.

Shambles raised both fists; a bolt of lightning crackled between them and his Words of Command rang out, 'Turn Back, Treacherous Transportal!'

The shark transportal snapped into being, first its rear, then the front. Bubbles formed on Lars's lips as he strained to get away, and Runcie was sure he would. How could such a powerful sorcerer be defeated? Lars let out a grunt, the staff bent in his fist and whirlpools of mist formed at either end. The transportal started to fade but Shambles drew his fists apart with another crackle of lightning and Lars groaned and slumped to the floor, cast down in a few seconds of overwhelming power. Parsifoe had been right. He'd just opened the way for a more cunning villain.

Helfigor made an incoherent sound in his throat. Parsifoe gasped. Thandimanilon slumped, all her weight coming down on Runcie's shoulders. The only one untroubled was Sleeth, who stood facing the nyssitron with a look of dreadful anticipation.

'I overestimated you, Lars.' Shambles had a hearty, booming voice. 'Did you really think you could keep this priceless child *from me?*'

Lars pasted on a sickly smile. 'I didn't want to mention it until I had her.'

'Liar!' said Shambles. 'I gave you what you needed to rise to the First Order –'

'And I'm most grateful, Lord.' Lars's squirming would have delighted Runcie, had he not been terrified of Shambles.

'– and I told you I'd come for repayment. This is your day of reckoning, Lars.'

'But Lord, I'll give you anything else. *Everything* else.'

'So the Nightland girl *is* worth it,' said Shambles. 'Why?'

Lars's face contorted before he was forced to admit, 'She's a Re-sighter, and she's seen where Anthrimorie lies.'

'Is that so?' Shambles surveyed Mariam from head to toe in a way that made Runcie's skin crawl. 'Splendid. I'll soon have it out of her, and more besides.' He turned back to Lars. 'I could almost forgive your petty treacheries, Count Sparj, but what I can't forgive is incompetence.'

'Lord?' said Lars.

'You were so dazzled by the gold, you missed the diamond lying beside it.'

A chill closed around Runcie's heart, for Shambles was now staring right at him. He'd known who they were all along.

'Runcible Jones, the Nightland boy. He's the one who set all this in motion, fool!'

'But he hasn't a scrap of talent,' said Lars.

'He's the Mover, imbecile. Without him, the changes won't go the right way – my way. He's worth more to me than she is, but I'll have them both. You, boy, come down.'

Now, *now* Runcie knew what Mariam had been going through all this time. He stood up, feeling the numbness spreading along his limbs and knowing that no one could help. He was going to suffer whatever terrible fate Lord Shambles had in store for him.

'Don't!' shouted Parsifoe and Helfigor together. 'Stay low, Runcie,' added Parsifoe. She nodded jerkily to Helfigor and, standing shoulder to shoulder, they raised baton and crystal rod together.

Shambles lifted his right fist. Metal studs glistered at the knuckles and a buzz-saw of sound blasted Parsifoe's baton up the stairs. Helfigor's rod went spinning out the hole in the wall.

'I could crush your little prentices just as easily, Parsifoe,' said Shambles. 'Don't interfere. Runcible Jones, come down.'

Runcie moved forwards but was brought up by Thandimanilon's bound hands, which still rested loosely in front of him. For some odd reason, he found the contact comforting. As Shambles's gaze ran chillingly up to her, Thandimanilon lifted her hands over Runcie's head and rested them on his left shoulder.

'You show sense, at least,' Shambles said.

'I know who my friends are,' Thandimanilon said in a husk of a voice.

She sounded on the edge of collapse. If she hoped to survive, she had to do Shambles's bidding. Butthen Thandimanilon bent and said, so softly that Runcie could barely make out the words, 'Don't move until I say so, then run for your very life.'

'Run where?' he breathed, feeling the faintest, absurd flowering of hope.

'Up to Parsifoe's dimensional gate. I can feel its potential, even now.'

'But what about Mariam?' said Runcie.

'Come down, boy!' bellowed Shambles. 'Every delay earns you an excruciation.' He chuckled merrily.

'I can do nothing for her, alas,' Thandimanilon whispered.

Runcie choked. 'Please, please try.' But as he spoke, he felt her skin grow cold, as if all the blood had drained away. He'd asked more than anyone could give.

She lifted her wrists off his shoulder, as if to spare him her torment, but an involuntary cry escaped her. 'What's the gate key, Parsifoe?'

'A scrap of parchment,' said Parsifoe. 'It's on the little table beside the gate.'

'You know what to do with it, Runcie?' said Thandimanilon.

He nodded jerkily, knowing that it didn't matter. She could barely stand up.

'Come, Runcible Jones,' Shambles roared. 'Don't be shy.'

Runcie looked wildly around the chamber. Mariam was between the transportal and the nyssitron, the white rope still around her middle. Lars Sparj clung to one of the shark teeth, staring blindly out as if trying to understand how his plans could have gone so wrong. And Sleeth stood before the prentices like a shepherd with his flock, wearing that crooked grin. When Thandimanilon and Lars Sparj fell, Sleeth would pledge himself to the stronger master in an instant, and Runcie despised him for it.

Thandimanilon gave Runcie a little push. He took one step down, two . . . Thandimanilon raised her bound hands, said softly, 'Clockwork Cogwheels, Clash!' and thrust her arms out.

The room went dark for a second. A halo of luminous dust sifted from the hole in the ceiling and the whirring cogs on the arms of the nyssitron made a chattering sound as they clashed. Shambles shot upright, his hair standing out in all directions and lightning streamers wavering off his mask. Then the automaton's gears ground together and it fell out of the air sideways, slamming into the floor so hard that the cogs tore chunks out of the stone.

'Run, Runcie!' Thandimanilon cried. 'Mariam, to the gate.'

Mariam flung off the rope and bolted for the stairs, taking them three at a time.

'Can't be as wicked as I thought,' Thandimanilon said with a feeble smile, then collapsed on the steps.

Runcie knelt by her. 'Thank – are you all right?'

'Just go.'

'Fly!' Parsifoe hissed, 'and don't look back.'

Runcie didn't move. He had to know. 'Thandimanilon, did Lars kill Dad?'

'No, Runcie, but I don't know who did.'

Mariam vaulted the barrier, wrenched at Runcie's wrist and he stumbled behind her up the rest of the stairs. He turned at the top but Thandimanilon hadn't moved. Had she given her life for them?

'Come *on*,' said Mariam.

The nyssitron was already rising. She raced around the corner and Runcie staggered after her on numb feet. This floor was an open chamber whose roof formed a series of vaults supported on large rectangular pillars. The only illumination came from a glowing flask next to the stairs, which cast swathes of dim light and deep shadow across the chamber. The air was filled with swirling dust and a ragged hole gaped through the outer wall, matching the one chewed through the floor. The stone floor was littered with broken furniture and rubble.

'Where's the gate?' Mariam looked around frantically as the nyssitron squealed up the stairs, chewing grooves in the stone wall and smashing the banisters on the other side.

'Here,' called Tigris from one of the pillars near the hole in the wall. She was coated in dust from head to foot and her eyebrows and eyelashes stood out like fine grey wires.

Runcie made out a structure to the left of the pillar. At either end of a large oval base of brass, two thick black rods rose halfway to the ceiling. Mounted between them were five iron hoops, each the height of a tall man, attached to each other by their outer edges to form an upright cross three hoops high and three wide. They were rusty, though, and the structure listed to the left.

'Is that *it*?' said Runcie.

'Just go through,' snapped Mariam.

'We have to open the gate first. Where's the parchment?'

'It was just there, on the little table –' Tigris looked around frantically. The table lay upside down but the parchment was nowhere to be seen. 'I'm sorry!' she cried. 'It must have blown away when the nyssitron tore through.'

They ran around, frantically searching for the parchment. 'Here it is.' Mariam pulled it from under a chunk of plaster and dusted it off. 'Now what?'

'Read it aloud,' said Runcie. 'At least it's written in letters, not some weird glyphs.'

Mariam began to sound out the words, awkwardly. '*Fla-myr ghiss-pie* . . .'

'That doesn't sound right,' said Runcie. 'Give it here. I've done this before.'

'I remember,' she said grimly.

'Take my hand. I'll read the gate spell and we'll go through together.'

'Which hoop?'

'The lowest one, I suppose. We'd have to climb up to get through the others.'

'He's coming!' cried Tigris.

The nyssitron was clattering sideways up the stairs, its iron cogs chewing the stone to powder, and Lord Shambles braying with laughter as if revelling in the destruction.

Runcie whacked dust off the parchment. 'I've got to get it right.'

'Runcie?' Tigris said hesitantly.

'Yes?'

She threw her arms around him. 'Thank you.'

'What for?' he said stupidly.

'You've helped me in so many ways; and you saved my life, even though I betrayed you both.'

'Surely you didn't think I'd let you drown, after all we'd been through together?'

She bowed her head, saying nothing.

'Just read the damn thing,' Mariam said gruffly, pulling him out of Tigris's embrace.

'It's turning this way,' said Tigris. 'He'll see you in a minute.' The despairing look reappeared, but she shook it off and took a deep breath. 'Mariam, give me your coat.'

'What for?'

'Just do it, quick!'

Mariam took her coat off. Tigris put it on, pulled the hairpins out of her hair and shook it free. Scooping up handfuls of dust, she rubbed it into her hair. She looked a bit like Mariam, from a distance. 'Get down!' she said, pushing Mariam to the floor. Runcie flattened himself beside her.

Tigris ran wildly across the room, pretending to be in a panic, passed in front of the nyssitron then doubled back and bolted for the stairs to the floor above. After a brief grinding of cog wheels, the nyssitron followed.

Runcie watched it go, afraid for her, but he couldn't waste the chance. He began to read from the parchment, but stumbled over the last few words. He read the gate spell again, trying to mimic the tones used by Lars that night at the Nightingales'. Nothing happened.

Three times. It has to be said *three* times. Runcie read the words a third time but felt nothing. 'It's because I'm useless at magic,' he said miserably.

'Let's go through anyway,' said Mariam, looking anxiously up the stairs. 'You never know . . .'

She didn't believe in him either. They went through the lowest hoop together but it felt no more magical than walking through a door.

'Get Parsifoe,' hissed Runcie. 'Find out what we're supposed to do.' She dashed off. He studied the words. Perhaps he'd been pronouncing *throppmyr* wrongly.

Shortly Mariam came running back with Parsifoe plodding behind her. 'Speak the words,' panted Parsifoe.

Runcie did so. 'That's right,' said Parsifoe. 'And you said them three times?'

'Yes, and we went through the lowest hoop.'

'It's always the middle hoop,' said Parsifoe. 'Surely –?'

'No, we *didn't* know,' snapped Mariam, swinging herself up to stand in it. 'Come on, Runcie.'

'Do I need to say the words again?' said Runcie.

'Not if the gate's been activated . . .' Parsifoe didn't sound convinced. 'Give me the parchment.' She read the spell.

The nyssitron was crunching down the stairs, though they couldn't see it through clouds of dust. Runcie climbed up, clinging precariously to the other side of the gate. 'I can't see anything,' he said as Helfigor came staggering across.

'What do you mean, *see* anything?' said Helfigor roughly.

'I always see stuff when strong magic is used. Sprays of coloured light, weird shapes –'

'He's coming!' yelled Mariam. 'Are we going through or not?'

Runcie took a deep breath. 'I'm ready.'

She reached out her hand, he took it, and they jumped together.

CHAPTER 30

The Rotting Curse

There was no wrenching sensation, no dizziness, no nausea – they simply landed on the gritty floor on the far side of the hoop. Runcie didn't bother to get up. They'd failed, and all the courage, all the sacrifices had been for nothing.

The nyssitron was settling to the floor, crushing the rubble to powder. The hood rose and Shambles laughed mockingly. Tigris sat beside him, her sad face twisted as if her skin were trying to pull away.

'Come quick, children,' Shambles said. 'Any more tricks and the prentices die, one by one. Lars,' he boomed down the stairs, 'bring the transportal up.'

Runcie and Mariam edged out from behind the gate and shortly the shark transportal came creeping up, tilting sideways to negotiate the turn of the broad stairs. The prentices fell in a jumble against the lower wall, but not one made a sound, though Runcie could see the whites of their eyes. The air above Lars shimmered with his fury.

Sleeth stood upright as though his feet were glued to the floor, staring at the nyssitron. The transportal straightened and settled beside it.

'Get in the transportal, Mariam and Runcible,' said Shambles.

'What about the prentices?' Helfigor said thickly, as if his tongue filled his mouth.

Shambles chuckled. Everything seemed to amuse him. 'Because you resisted, I'm taking them too.'

Mariam, now walking like a robot, went across. Runcie tried to fight Shambles's will as he'd previously fought Lars's, but his feet followed her, one step, two, three and inside. They were done for.

Sleeth, standing before the silent prentices, wore the oddest half-smile, as if he'd just realised where his true destiny lay. He proceeded down the steps, head held high, his cunning eyes fixed on Shambles.

'Take them to my tower,' said Shambles to Lars.

'Just a moment!' Sleeth arrogantly held up his hand.

'Go back with the rest of the prentices, boy.' Shambles didn't bother to look at him.

'I don't think you realise who I am,' said Sleeth.

'I couldn't give a damn who you are.'

'But I know who you are. Who you *really* are.'

Shambles turned sharply, his multi-coiled moustaches quivering. 'You intrigue me. Pray, who am I?'

'You're a monster.'

'Insults can't move me, boy. I've heard them all in my time.' Shambles's voice had gained a steely edge, however.

Sleeth's right hand shook, but he managed to quell it. 'You're a stinking, treacherous liar. A vicious mongrel. A man utterly without honour.'

The coils of Shambles's moustaches sprang out like dagger blades, then slowly rolled up again. 'If you were a man I'd call you out for that last insult, but nothing any lout of a prentice can say matters to me. Get back in the transportal.'

'Your true name, your *secret* name –'

A blast of sound erupted from the nyssitron, so loudly that the prentices fell down, clutching at their ears. Runcie and Mariam did too.

Sleeth had clapped his hands over his ears as he spoke, but the odd smile remained fixed to his face. The instant the sound cut off, he shouted, '*Skirrlydoun!* Your secret name is Skirrly-doun.'

Shambles reeled, then pulled himself to his feet with a peculiar mechanical motion. Tigris tried to slip over the side but he held her back. 'You've just signed the death warrant of everyone in this chamber. But before I deal with you, who are you?'

'You don't recognise me,' said Sleeth, 'yet your face has lived in my nightmares since I was old enough to have them. I'm going to bring you down, Lord Shambles. *Skirrlydoun.* I've come to avenge my father and all my clan.'

Shambles peered at Sleeth, then took off the wire mask to squint at him, as if short-sighted. He looked puzzled.

'My name is Sleeth!' Sleeth said softly. 'Jac Sleeth. You slew my great-uncle Mahan and, after him, every adult man in Clan

393

Sleeth, out of sheerest malice. You cursed my father, Croome, making his life a living death from which he cannot escape. You made me, and now I'm going to rid the world of you.'

'Ah, Clan Sleeth,' said Shambles, who had regained his composure. He grinned broadly, twisting a coil of moustache around a yellow-stained middle finger. 'One of my finer revenges. I reprise it every night before bed – the blood and torment help me sleep. But tell me,' he said curiously, 'how did *I* make you?'

'My mother conceived me for a single purpose: to become a wizard of the First Order who could remove the curse from my father.'

'Ingenious,' said Shambles. 'Cunning, too. I've heard of you, Jac Sleeth – the most brilliant prentice in twenty generations, some say. And her plan might even have worked, *had you kept to it.* But you've doomed your father now and you'll have the rest of your childhood to regret it.'

'I'm going to destroy you,' Sleeth ground out.

'Run away, little prentice,' sneered Shambles. 'Brilliant you may be, but you're not the match of a Third Order wizard yet. Why, slatternly old Parsifoe could take you down with one hand. Come back when you're fully grown, if you dare, and I'll mete out the fate I've dealt to the rest of your male line.'

'Damn you!' cried Sleeth, furious that he wasn't being taken seriously. 'I'll show you.'

Shambles threw back his head, roaring with laughter. 'Go on, little wizardling.' He spread his arms wide. 'I'll even allow you the first strike.'

Sleeth went into a boxer's stance, fists held out in front of him, the left a little advanced, and began to mutter words that Runcie didn't know.

'Speak up,' jeered Shambles. 'You have to shout the Batterer to have any effect. Even a lowly prentice should know that.'

Sleeth cried, *'Flimminth, Skirrlydoun!'* and snapped his splayed fingers back and forth. His stubby bone wand slid from his sleeve into his left hand. *'Flass! Flooet!'*

Shambles's smile faded, though he dismissed the spell with a wave of his hand. 'Not the Batterer at all. The Bruiser?'

'It's a forgotten spell,' said Sleeth, panting but now eerily calm. 'It's Morgentroy's Recurring Rotting Curse and it's got you – *Aaaaah!*'

Shambles had clenched one studded fist and Sleeth doubled over, spitting blood. The bone wand clattered to the floor.

'Not a skerrick got through –' said Shambles. He rubbed at the tip of his nose, then looked down in disgust at the purply-brown sludge on his fingers.

A bubbling patch spread up his nose, then onto his right cheek, and a disgusting smell wafted across the chamber. Runcie gagged; behind him he could hear children throwing up. Shambles lunged sideways, raised an extravagantly embossed bronze staff and chiselled a cloverleaf symbol in the air with the tip. A green blob appeared there, swelling like a piece of bubblegum. Reversing the staff, Shambles pressed the blob flat against his face and mumbled a lengthy spell.

'What does Skirrlydoun mean?' said Mariam.

To Runcie's surprise, Lars answered. 'A wizard's secret name is the key to his magic, but it's also a protection against the one terror he could not bear to face. Skirrlydoun, a magician who lived in ancient times, was the most handsome man in the world . . .'

'Shambles isn't good looking,' said Mariam.

'He was when he was young. Handsome and vain. By our secret names are we revealed.'

Shambles whipped the blob away and felt his nose, which was whole again. 'Not a bad effort for a prentice,' he said to Sleeth. 'I commend you for sneaking the curse through my defences, though it took little effort to remove it.'

'But you *haven't* removed it.' Sleeth wiped his bloody mouth on his sleeve then stood up, smiling redly through the pain. The bone wand was back in his hand and he looked serene, doing what he was born to do. 'It's Morgentroy's *Recurring* Rotting Curse, I said. It'll keep coming back until the day you die, but never kill you. Even when you're rotting to pieces, I want you to know what's happening to you – and dread how long you still have to endure it.'

'Absurd!' But Shambles looked down at his legs, inside the nyssitron, and let out a gasp of horror. 'Lars, assist me!'

Lars Sparj's aristocratic face bore a look of the most profound disgust, then he broke. The shark transportal lifted, spun on its axis and raced for the hole in the wall. He would have escaped had not Mariam sprang forwards and swept the battlefield diorama off its plinth. The glass dome shattered and the automaton broke apart, little marching wizards and soldiers scattering in all directions. Lars cried out and the distraction gave Shambles his chance.

He shook the bronze staff, stopping the transportal so suddenly that the prentices, and Runcie and Mariam, went flying out onto the floor. Lars, moaning, drove it on, and as it lurched forwards Runcie thought it was going to grind right over them. Parsifoe came running out but it stopped just short of Mariam, then the children scrambled out of the way.

Lars began another spell; Shambles matched it. The transportal shook violently. Its black metal skin puckered, tore with a series of shrieks, then the curved top and sides began to curl off in strips like orange peelings. Coils of floor sprang up, twanging a merry tune against Lars's boots, whereupon the transportal simply fell to pieces. Lars Sparj stood in the ruins in disbelief.

'Attend me, Lars!' ordered Shambles, panting. 'You too,' he said to Tigris.

Black with rage and humiliation, Lars stalked across and, after much straining, he and Tigris managed to lift Shambles out of the nyssitron. Mariam choked and clutched at Runcie's shoulder.

'What is it?' said Runcie.

'You can't *see*?' Mariam turned to Parsifoe.

'See what, child?'

'The way he really is! Parsifoe, I know what his secret name protects.'

Shambles looked perfectly normal to Runcie. He followed Mariam, though he didn't catch what she said. Parsifoe whipped her baton from a pocket, gripped it in both hands like a sword and her voice rang out in the spell, 'Skirrlydoun, Revulsion be Revealed!'

The air shivered like a mirage and Runcie did see. His stomach heaved; the prentices gave a massed gasp and several of the smaller ones began to scream in terror. A putrid stench oozed across the room and Lars Sparj retched. Tigris scuttled into the shadows.

Above the waist, Shambles was a normal man, but below it he was a monster whose hips, legs and feet looked as though they'd been magicked into rubber, then twisted into impossible positions before being restored to flesh and bone again.

Letting out the most hideous cry, Shambles drew *quintessence* into his staff so hard that it melted a fuming pit in the floor. Parsifoe's baton burst asunder, embedding splinters of ivory in her cheek, then Shambles's illusion was back and he was a normal man again, save for the haunted look in his eyes.

'*Not* out of malice,' Shambles said softly, as Sleeth stared at him. 'The great-uncle you idolise did this to me with an incompetent duel-spell, just to cut me down to size. I *was* a vain man, once, but is that a crime? Now look at me. Each day the unbreakable spell twists me a little further. The pain is unbearable, but that's the least of my agony. For making a monster out of me, I vowed to wipe out Clan Sleeth to the last adult male.'

'Liar!' cried Sleeth. 'Your clan has hated mine since Athanor Sleeth burned the last maps of Anthrimorie eight hundred years ago, to stop your power-crazed ancestors getting them.'

'Well, soon I'll have Anthrimorie's secrets anyway. And you! Lars, uncover my feet!'

Lars Sparj, gagging, began tearing off the lumpy leather bags that covered Shambles's feet. The fury in Lars's eyes was dreadful to behold. Someone was going to pay for this insult but, unfortunately, Runcie didn't think it was going to be Lord Shambles.

'Aaargh!' Shambles cried as the illusion cracked again and his misshapen flesh and protruding bones were revealed. A purple-brown stain covered his right foot.

'Hist!' The sound came from somewhere behind Runcie.

'Helfigor's waving at us,' whispered Mariam. 'Come on.'

This time Shambles seemed to be struggling to draw enough *quintessence* to restore his illusion. They edged into the shadow behind a rectangular pillar, where Helfigor had retreated with Parsifoe and Tigris.

'Runcie,' said Helfigor urgently, 'you said something earlier, about *seeing* things. What did you mean?'

'Whenever I've gone through a gate,' said Runcie, 'and sometimes when great magic has been done, I've seen lights and colours and stuff.'

'What do you mean, *lights and colours and stuff*?'

Runcie explained as best he could, whereupon Helfigor and Parsifoe went into a huddle, glancing back at him all the while.

'Have you ever done anything with it?' said Parsifoe, whose cheek was dotted with flecks of blood.

Cries of disgust erupted from behind them. Runcie hoped the curse removal was going badly. 'Of course not. I can't do magic.'

'But Runcie,' said Tigris, 'remember when we were in Wyrmhilte's cavern and I tried to boil her tears, but she cut off my *seeing*. I couldn't draw *quintessence* until you did something and suddenly there was more than I could ever use.'

'I saw this thing like a vast glowing balloon wall,' said Runcie. 'I focussed on one of the little pinpricks in it and tried to see through, but I didn't do anything.'

'That's the Art of Seeing, you nitwit,' Helfigor said gruffly. 'It's the first of the Four Basic Arts of Magic. Do you mean to say that you've been *seeing* all this time and you didn't think to tell anyone? Idiot boy, you deserve a swift kick up the backside.' The wizard's eyes were shining, though.

'Thandimanilon told me I didn't have any magic,' said Runcie, his heart singing. 'Everyone said I was rubbish at it.'

'You must have a new kind of talent. Parsifoe,' Helfigor said urgently, 'we'd better have the Helm and the Ocular, just in case.'

'They're up in the top chamber,' said Parsifoe. 'Tigris?'

'I'll get them.' Tigris darted into the shadows, dusty hair flying.

'What are we going to do, sir?' said Runcie to Helfigor.

'Shambles spoke truly, lad. We can't draw enough *quintessence* for a dimensional gate.'

'Then what's the good of it?'

'If you can *see* so powerfully, without any training, you must have a strong talent, though whether it'll come to anything is another matter. It might just make the difference. You'll put on Flibbermal's Clarifying Ocular, which will help you envision a source of *quintessence* more clearly. Parsifoe will wear Henrietta's Helm of Identification, and thus see what you're seeing. If you can find a strong source, she'll pour *quintessence* into the dimensional gate and . . . let's hope it works.'

It sounded so simple, but nothing ever was, on Iltior. 'And if it doesn't?'

Helfigor eased his head around the pillar, peering in the direction of the nyssitron for a moment before ducking back. 'Our fate will be sealed. We all heard Shambles's secret name. Skirrlydoun indeed!' he snorted. 'He can't allow us to live.'

'Can't he take another name?' said Runcie. 'Surely that's easier than killing us all?'

'It's not hard to kill people. If you've done a lot of it, as Shambles has, you can take a life without a thought. *And* sleep like a baby afterwards.'

'Erasing an old secret name and creating a new one is a long, painful process,' said Parsifoe. 'And between names, Shambles would be terribly vulnerable. It's safer to kill us all, though he wouldn't do you two in straight away,' she said to Runcie and Mariam.

'That's comforting,' Mariam said sarcastically.

'Is there any sign of Tigris?' asked Parsifoe.

'Not yet.' Helfigor looked anxiously at the stairs.

'Ha!' boomed Shambles. 'It's broken. And now, my lad, *for you.*'

Runcie put his head around the pillar. Shambles was back in the nyssitron, unblemished though rather shrunken. Breaking the curse, and restoring his illusion, had weakened him.

'You can't kill me.' Sleeth was shaken but defiant.

'Really?' grinned Shambles. 'Why ever not?'

'Because you swore an oath before you murdered Great-Uncle Mahan.'

'Why, so I did,' said Shambles, pulling at his whiskers. 'I vowed that I'd harm no beardless boy of Clan Sleeth. A sorcerer's word is his bond and I hold to mine, no matter the provocation.' He gave Sleeth an evil smile. 'I also swore that I'd suffer no *adult* male of your line to live, save in endless death agonies. Nor shall I. You're spared for the moment, Jac Sleeth, so there's no point killing the others to protect my secret name. I could do it just for fun, though . . .' He considered, hand on chin. 'No, my name must be changed, no matter what it costs me.'

He threw back his head and let out another of those hearty but chilling guffaws. 'But I'll extract the cost of all that pain from you, when the time comes.'

Shambles raised the mask high in one hand then lowered it over his head, like a judge about to pass the death sentence on a criminal. His coiled moustaches popped out between the wires, quivering like clock springs, as he intoned, 'On the day your true beard-growth begins, Jac Sleeth, I shall deem you a man, and that day marks the first day of your death. For what you've done to me today, and all the pain you're going to cost me, your death agonies will be my final work of art against Clan Sleeth. Until that day, begone!' The mask turned right, then left, searching the ruined chamber.

Sleeth's cunning eye did too, as if calculating how he might earn back favour.

'Find Mariam and Runcible,' said Shambles, 'and I'll commute one of your excruciations to simple agony.'

Sleeth considered for a moment, nodded, and turned into the gloom in the direction of Runcie's hiding place, limping heavily. Runcie moved further into the shadows.

Parsifoe caught him by the arm, hissing, 'Get to the gate.'

'Tigris isn't back,' said Mariam.

'She's coming.'

It couldn't work, Runcie knew it. Even if Tigris got there with the magical ocular, there wouldn't be time to learn how to use it. They were about to make their dash for the gate when Sleeth's darting eye fixed on them. Runcie clenched his fists and prepared to do battle. At least Mariam might get away.

'Don't come any closer,' he said when Sleeth was ten feet away. 'Or I'll –'

'You'll what?' grinned Sleeth. 'You're in my power.'

Runcie knew it but he wasn't going to give in. 'Yeah?' he said weakly.

'I don't like you, Runcie. There's something about you that really irritates me.' Sleeth moved out of Shambles's sight and

403

lowered his voice. 'But I loathe Shambles with all my being and I'll do anything to thwart him. Get going. I'll cover for you.'

Runcie looked up at him, sure it was a trick.

'Just go,' Sleeth said quietly. Looking as if a weight had been lifted from his shoulders, he walked a few yards then ran away from the gate, shouting and pointing to the shadows on the other side of the chamber.

Every eye followed him. Runcie and Mariam scuttled to the gate but, unfortunately, Tigris wasn't there.

'Ready?' said Parsifoe, holding the parchment out in her right hand.

'But Tigris . . .'

'We'll have to try without her.' She began to read.

Runcie closed his eyes and tried to visualise the balloon-like wall which he must see through to find *quintessence*, but saw nothing. He could hear Mariam's heart pounding. To his left, Parsifoe began the second reading. The words on the parchment were glowing now but, by the time she'd finished, all he'd seen were a few pink flashes and green streaks. A commotion began on the other side of the room and he opened his eyes. Tigris was hiding in the shadows along the wall, waiting until Shambles was looking the other way. Lars sat in the ruins of his transportal, head in hands. Nearby, the little clockwork wizards and warriors were replaying their battle in the rubble, the wizards desperately trying to rout their treacherous enemy, though the outcome was always the same: the wizards bloodily routed.

'Anything?' said Parsifoe. Henrietta's Helm came flying through the air and she caught it in her left hand and put it on. It was like a dunce's cap made out of green vinyl, with squiggly symbols around the base. Runcie and Mariam exchanged glances. It didn't look very magical.

'Not much,' Runcie replied.

'Then all rests on the third reading.'

Or *nothing*, Runcie thought.

'What if he follows us?' said Mariam.

'Once a *dimensional* gate is closed,' said Parsifoe, 'that is, one between Iltior and Nightland, it seals the dimensions against all other gates. For a month or two, anyway.'

'Aha!' roared Shambles. The nyssitron crunched in the direction of the gate, then stopped. 'Oh, this is priceless,' Shambles guffawed. 'There's not a glimmer of *quintessence* in your gate, Parsifoe. It's even more pathetic than your absurd transportal.'

The rubble behind Runcie quivered, sending up a little cloud of dust. Sleeth came walking towards Shambles, wearing that crooked half-smile.

'I'm going to double your excruciations for that little sally,' said Shambles, wearily removing a patch of rot from his forehead. His head drooped but he forced it upright.

Sleeth went into that boxing crouch as if to deliver his Rotting Curse again. 'Skirrlydoun –'

Shambles threw up his staff and Tigris seized the moment to toss Flibbermal's Clarifying Ocular to Runcie. He caught it. It was like a snorkeller's face mask, except that in front of each eye a series of thick glass discs protruded outwards like stepped pyramids. He pulled it over his eyes and wrenched the straps tight. 'How do I use it?'

'Just close your eyes and try to *see*,' said Parsifoe.

He closed his eyes. 'Do your best, Runcie,' said Mariam.

As Parsifoe began to speak the words on the parchment for the final time, Runcie's inner eye lit up and the curving wall was there, scattered with pinpricks of light. He tried to focus on one, but it disappeared. He attempted another; it faded away. The third pinprick was smaller but brighter and he managed to keep hold of it, using the ocular like a microscope. And then the pinprick grew to a hole that became a well of radiance, expanding until it blocked out all the world. Runcie could hardly breathe. Had he finally done it?

Parsifoe sang out, 'It's working!' Tearing the ocular off, she thrust the parchment at Runcie's hand. 'You'll need this *between*. Climb up, and *say it right.*'

Before he could take it, Runcie heard a gasp from the direction of the stairs. Thandimanilon had dragged herself to the top and was staring at Lars's slumped figure, her eyes shining with a sickening, hopeless love that he certainly didn't return. She reached out with one slender hand towards Mariam, opening her fingers in the shape of a flower, and intoned, 'Remove Re-sighting to Gelatinous Globule.'

Plop. Mariam's head was enveloped in a transparent yellow membrane that began to wobble in and out like a jellyfish. Her eyes went wide, her fists clenched, then she opened her mouth and screamed just as she had during her panic attack *between*, though no sound came through.

'What's *that*?' cried Runcie.

'It's Torgsted's Transcendent Recollection Encapsulator,' said Helfigor. 'A risky spell at the best of times.'

'Is Thandimanilon stealing Mariam's memories of Anthrimorie? For Lars?'

'So it would seem. But he still won't take her back.'

This was going to go really bad, and it was his fault. Mariam's silent screams reached a crescendo as the envelope collapsed into a jelly-globule the size and shape of a lemon, floating above her head. Thandimanilon drew her spread fingers through the air and the globule wobbled towards her. She caught it and passed her hands over it until it shone with a soft green light. Shambles watched, slumped in his seat. His struggle to keep the curse at bay seemed to have greatly weakened him.

'What happens now?' said Runcie. Mariam was crouched down, rubbing her forehead, the panic gone.

Parsifoe answered. 'Whoever breaks the globule on his forehead will know the secrets of Anthrimorie.'

'And not even Torgsted's spell can extract them a second time,' said Helfigor.

'What if we smash the globule?' said Mariam, looking better.

'It would let the memories loose for any magician with the strength to seize them. Unfortunately, the only strong magicians here are bad ones.'

'And then it's all over.'

'We need time,' said Helfigor. 'We're gaining strength, and Shambles is weakening as he fights the two curses. Once the Recurring Curse begins to overpower him, he'll have to flee to his tower and use his greatest magic to break the spell. But not yet. He's still stronger.'

'Can't you use his secret name against him?'

'We're trying, but he's on his guard now.'

Runcie's heart began to pound. He'd had an idea to gain time, though he wasn't sure he had the courage for it. He felt utterly exhausted and the only parts that didn't hurt were his numb legs. He just wanted to lie down and never get up again, but he had to fight on.

Thandimanilon finished rubbing the globule, turned towards Lars, her eyes alight, and tossed it hard and high. Lars jumped up and Runcie took off. He sprang and, as the luminous globule wobbled overhead, stretched up with both hands as high as he could reach, snatched it out of the air and bolted into the shadows.

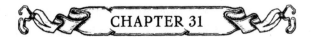

CHAPTER 31

Stolen Memories

Runcie could hear the nyssitron's battered cogs grinding as it turned towards him. There was only one way to gain the time they needed, but if his bluff was called he was doubly doomed. No time to think about that. Turning away, he raised his hand as if to crush the globule against his forehead, but instead dropped it down the front of his shirt. Then he doubled up, clutching his forehead in pretended agony, and waited to be taken.

'Damn you!' Shambles's voice shook. 'I don't have time for this.'

The globule was sliding around inside Runcie's shirt like a slippery, stinging jelly, as if it wanted to betray him. He'd never get away with it – he couldn't possibly fool the greatest sorcerer in the world. Or could he? Runcie turned and peered through his fingers. Shambles's forehead and cheekbones were dotted with spreading rot.

Helfigor made a sudden move towards him but Shambles swung his staff in a circle, crying, 'Immobilise Iltiorians, Immediately!' and straining so hard that one of his front teeth snapped.

With a feeble clap of thunder, the rest of the room went still.

Shambles hung over the side, his mouth gaping, and for a second Runcie thought the sorcerer had immobilised himself as well, but then Shambles grunted and raised his head. Runcie prayed that the spell had taken the last of the sorcerer's strength, but shortly he pushed himself upright and the nyssi-tron came jerking across.

Shambles looked Runcie in the eye. 'This curse, like the one that maimed me, comes from the era of the Cybale, so I must have those memories. Your friends are paralysed; neither can your enemies intervene. It's just you and me, Runcible Jones, and you will tell me where Anthrimorie lies, won't you?'

'No,' said Runcie, sick with terror. 'I won't.'

Shambles reversed his staff, exhaustedly banished the rot and stared at Runcie from under hairy eyebrows. 'Why not?'

'Because you're evil.'

'You judge me too harshly. Revenge sustains me through the torment of my daily existence, but it doesn't control me. I'd give it up in an instant, and yes, even lay the hand of forgiveness on Clan Sleeth, if they could give me my body back.'

'You're trying to destroy Iltior,' Runcie said weakly.

'I love Iltior with all my heart and my highest wish is to defend it, from *all* its foes. Indeed, who else can? Not your incompetent wizards nor the fanatical Cybale. The ghasts are rising, Runcible Jones, and wyrms have come back from extinction, while our magic has declined since they were first defeated. Only the strongest leader, with all Anthrimorie's secrets at his disposal, can hope to defeat them now.'

Runcie hesitated. How could he tell? Bad people could also act from good motives. Maybe Shambles *was* the only one strong enough. It didn't feel right, but Runcie's feelings weren't always reliable. No, but he could judge Shambles on what he'd already seen of him. He wasn't just bad, he was malicious and cruel and if he got ultimate power he'd be far worse.

'No!' Runcie said firmly, trying to banish his self-doubt.

Shambles was regarding him with more interest now. 'You show unexpected resistance for a Nightlander. What moves you, boy?'

After all that had been done to his family, Runcie believed most strongly in fairness and justice, so he said, 'Treating people the way I'd like them to treat me.'

'A noble fool,' sneered Shambles. 'Fairness signifies nothing but weakness. Besides, I didn't ask what you most believed in. What do you most *want* in all the world?'

Runcie wasn't fool enough to reply. He couldn't look directly at Shambles in case the sorcerer read his deepest desire on his face, or tried to compel him as Lars had nearly done. He kept his eyes fixed on the dusty floor, though he couldn't avoid a quick sideways glance at Mariam, who had come creeping across.

Shambles's eyes touched on Mariam, then swung back to Runcie. 'You've been through a lot together, and she's your dear friend, so if I were to threaten her . . .' Runcie blanched but the sorcerer went on. 'I don't have the time, and I still have need of her. Besides,' Shambles gave a gap-toothed grin, '*she's* not what you want most deeply, is she?'

Runcie didn't answer; didn't look up. He just kept thinking, Skirrlydoun, Skirrlydoun, as if the sorcerer's secret name might help to defy him.

'Who would know?' said Shambles. He inspected the paralysed watchers, one by one, then settled on Sleeth. Pointing his staff, he uttered a truth spell, 'Speak, Slippery Sleeth!' Sleeth shook violently, cursing the sorcerer's name, but came to him, feet dragging. Shambles pressed the tip of his staff against the boy's throat and Sleeth began to talk in a ragged voice, as if every word were being gouged out of him.

Shortly Shambles turned back to Runcie, bestowing that unnerving smile on him again. 'I can send you home afterwards. You want that desperately, don't you? Your mother must be going out of her mind at your disappearance.'

Runcie tried to resist but his head nodded, jerkily. His plan was failing. Shambles wasn't weakening quickly enough, so what was the point? Even if he held out here, back at Shambles's tower he, Runcie, would soon be broken.

'I'll even give you the gold to get her out of her dungeon,' said Shambles.

'You can't bribe people out of prison on Earth,' said Runcie.

'Of course you can. With me on your side you can have whatever you want, Runcible Jones. Well, boy? Don't you care about your mother's fate?'

It felt as if fishhooks were being dragged through Runcie's heart. He could imagine, as clearly as anything, what Millie must be going through because of his broken promise. She would be dwindling daily, perhaps going mad, and he desperately wanted to help her. But did he want it more than *anything*?

'Mum taught me the difference between right and wrong. The end doesn't justify the means, and she wouldn't want all Iltior to suffer just to save her.' He'd said the words but Runcie wasn't sure he could hold to them.

'I'm not asking her,' said Shambles. 'I'm asking you.'

Runcie swallowed and his dry throat hurt. Skirrlydoun, Skirrlydoun. 'No.'

'No?'

'No,' Runcie rasped.

'What a worm you are,' Shambles said incredulously. 'Does clan loyalty mean nothing to you?'

Runcie just shook his head. He didn't dare speak. He wanted to die.

'I thought you might say that,' said Shambles, chuckling mechanically. 'And so, we finally come down to it. The ultimate question. Are you ready?'

Cold dread spread through Runcie, down to the tips of his toes. Shambles had been playing with him. All this time, he'd known the one offer Runcie couldn't refuse. He looked up and the sorcerer's gappy grin stretched from one side of his face to the other.

'Tell me where Anthrimorie's treasures lie,' Shambles said, 'and I'll tell you what happened to your father. *And why.*'

Runcie screwed his eyes shut in a desperate attempt to stop the scalding tears leaking out. That was a test in itself, and if he couldn't hold tears back he had no chance of besting this vicious and deadly opponent. His eyes were burning, and the effort was making his head throb, but he would not cry. Never give in. While he held out, there was still hope. Skirrlydoun!

But Runcie wanted to give in more than anything. He remembered his tall, untidy father sitting in the folly with that endearing cheeky smile, and all the wonderful memories of Runcie's childhood welled up. He had to turn his back on them before he began to bawl.

'Well, boy?' said Shambles.

This was it. Everyone had their price and Shambles had found Runcie's. The truth about his father was the one thing he couldn't refuse – he'd been searching for it far too long. And if he didn't find out, all the suffering he'd caused his mother, to say nothing of the turmoil on this world, would have been for nothing.

Shambles crowed, and Runcie knew that his struggle had shown on his face. But not only that – his choice had too, *that he was going to give in.* He had to. And how could anyone blame him? He was just a kid up against the most powerful sorcerer in the world. Even Millie would make this choice. She still loved his father, and her need to know the truth was so over-whelming that of course she would pay the price.

'Imagine if you could set her mind at rest,' said Shambles, as if Runcie's thoughts were printed on his brow. 'No son could give his mother a greater gift.'

Runcie couldn't hold out any longer. He opened his mouth to

tell Shambles that he had the globule in his shirt, to betray Mariam's trust and put this whole world within Shambles's grasp.

Then his eyes met Mariam's, she shook her head and Runcie stopped. She would never give in. She would curse Shambles and attack him in any way she could, even at the cost of her own life. But he wasn't that strong. Ansie, he thought, Dad! His eyes flooded and this time nothing could hold the tears back. Dad, at last I'll know you.

'Come on, boy,' growled Shambles, rubbing his whiskery jaw.

It couldn't get any worse than this. The words were about to burst forth when Runcie saw a large patch of corruption growing below the sorcerer's bottom lip, and it helped him find another scrap of defiance. Don't give in! Shambles has put me through this, not just to find Anthrimorie, but for the pleasure of tormenting me. He set it up deliberately so I'd have to chose, which proves he's a monster, and he'll corrupt Iltior just the way Sleeth cursed him.

Runcie's life had been one injustice after another – Millie going to prison for having the book, his father's name being destroyed, Grindgrim setting the bullies on him so he'd repudiate his parents – so how could he inflict a worse injustice on Iltior? He couldn't, no matter what. But ah, Dad, Dad . . .

'No,' he croaked, faintly and indecisively.

'What's that, boy?' said Shambles, the smile fading.

Runcie clenched his fists, summoned every last vestige of courage and shouted, 'I'll never tell you, not even for the truth about Dad. Not for any reward, *or at any price.*'

'You little swine,' cried Shambles, all composure gone. He rubbed furiously at his chin, then looked down in disgust at the clots of hairy, rotting flesh quivering on the back of his hand. 'Speak now, or pay *forever*.'

Runcie said nothing.

'I'll tell you anyway,' the sorcerer snarled. 'Your father was a base, lying scoundrel who hated you both.'

'No,' whispered Runcie. 'Dad was a hero.'

'Only to a lonely seven-year-old boy. In reality, he was a reckless, selfish fool.'

'Did you know him?' Runcie couldn't keep the eagerness out of his voice.

'No, but I interrogated the Night Stalkers who . . . he dealt with.'

'Anyway, Dad wasn't selfish. It was just that his work meant everything to him.'

'More than you or your mother did, certainly. Search your memory, boy – you know it in your deepest heart.'

For once in his life, Runcie tried *not* to think, but he couldn't help remembering that his father hadn't had time to see him in the disastrous school play, or visit him in hospital after he'd fallen out of a tree and broken his leg. He recalled the mysterious disappearances that had so infuriated Millie, to say nothing of the times Ansie had spent their last pennies on champagne or extravagant birthday presents, with no thought for tomorrow . . .

'Dad wasn't perfect,' he said faintly. 'No one is. But he still loved us.'

'No, you got in his way, always wanting attention, taking time he couldn't spare from his work. Preventing him from finishing it.'

'But Dad did finish it. I saw his book.'

'He only finished the first book,' said Shambles. 'Thankfully the other four were incomplete when he died.'

'Dad was writing *five* books?' Runcie couldn't take it in.

'He had to escape. That's why he tried to fake his death, to get away from you and your mother.'

Shambles's words hit Runcie like a brick wall collapsing on him. 'You're lying.' He put his hands over his ears but nothing could block out the betrayal. 'Shut up!'

'*I'm* not the liar. Your father hated your mother for bringing you into the world, and despised you for the magickless little worm you are, so unworthy of his talents.'

'I don't believe you.' Runcie hurt all over, as if he'd been beaten up. What kind of a man would tear down everything good about a kid's family, simply out of malice? 'You're a filthy liar!' This was worse than his father merely being bad; it was a negation of Runcie's whole life. He couldn't stand to hear any more, yet he couldn't bear not to know, either. He took his hands away; he couldn't hold out a second longer. 'What happened to Dad?'

'He tried to escape through a Night Stalker's gate, but Ansible made the biggest mistake of his reckless life . . .' Shambles rubbed more hairy clots off his chin. There was nothing hearty about his smile now; it was as corrupt as the flesh bubbling off his face.

'What happened?' Runcie screamed. 'Where was he going?'

'You know the price.'

This was worse, far worse than before. Runcie's need to know the truth, no matter how awful, was so all consuming that he would have given up anything or anyone – even Mariam; *even his mother* – to satisfy it.

But as he was about to reach inside his shirt for the globule, something about the look on the sorcerer's face gave him pause. Shambles was truly evil, utterly base, and therefore, whatever his answer, Runcie could never be sure if Shambles were telling the truth or lying through his grey teeth. And in that case, there was no point paying the price.

'I don't believe you,' said Runcie. 'So I'm not going to tell you anything.' He said it with the most desperate feelings of regret and loss.

Mariam was jerking her head at him. He flicked his eyes that way. Parsifoe must have broken the paralysis spell, for she was signalling with one hand towards the gate, which was shimmering faintly.

'Then you've doomed all your friends, and back in my tower I'll tear the secret out of you anyway,' raged Shambles. 'And once I've gained the treasures in the Citadel of Magic, I'll fashion resonance into a weapon and hurl it back into the black hearts of its creators.' He turned to Parsifoe.

'Paltry Parsifoe,' Shambles sneered. 'Trans-dimensional gates are one of the greatest of all magics, beyond most First

Order wizards. How could you, a slovenly fool who barely scraped into the Second Order, think to use one? You could never draw enough *quintessence* to open it.'

Parsifoe reeled and Runcie felt for her. She *was* plump, plain and dowdy, untidy and crotchety. Her clothes always had food stains down the front and nothing she owned seemed to work very well, but her heart was in the right place and that was the only thing that mattered.

Shambles began to grind the nyssitron towards Runcie, but as he did, Sleeth pointed his wand and choked, 'Recurring Curse, Recur, Skirrlydoun!'

The rot exploded across Shambles's face and Runcie stumbled towards the gate.

'Is it ready, Helfigor?' panted Mariam, who had reached it first.

'Forty seconds,' said Helfigor. 'More or less.'

'Where are we going?' Runcie said numbly. He felt shattered, despairing, lost. Mariam put her arm around him but it didn't help. Nothing could.

'You're going home,' said Helfigor. 'So we can stop the mischief you began by coming here, before it's too late. Climb up.'

The nyssitron was moving jerkily. Shambles had the staff against his face but this time the curse was taking longer to remove. Mariam climbed onto the central hoop and crouched there, hanging on with her left hand and extending her right down to Runcie. He clambered up. Parsifoe handed him the parchment, which was smoking at the edges.

'Twenty seconds,' said Helfigor.

The nyssitron was gathering speed now. They couldn't do it anyway; the gate wouldn't open in time. Besides, the truth about Ansie lay here, not at home. The awful, unbearable truth . . .

But when Shambles was just seconds away, a thick coating of dust blasted off the nearby rubble, revealing Ulalliall's orange glass dome. Triple cones of brilliant light burst forth from it, and Runcie, dazzled, lost his grip and fell.

The light focussed on the racing nyssitron, which began to spin. Shambles let out an uncharacteristic squeal of terror as it corkscrewed across the flagstones and slammed into the wall, throwing him out onto the floor. The nyssitron skidded along the wall to the hole, hung on its lip, its cogs chewing more stone out of the wall, then fell through.

Shambles rolled over, spitting dusty blood and wailing, 'My precious nyssitron!'

'Parsifoe *is* a weak, slovenly keeper,' foghorned Ulalliall, 'the least we've ever had. But we won't hear her insulted by an upstart like you. Revulsion be Revealed, Skirrlydoun!'

As the illusion vanished, Shambles's lower body twisted grotesquely. He lay on the floor, forehead and eyes covered in blood, clutching his staff. With a supreme effort, he managed to restore the illusion, though doing so left him so weak he couldn't get up.

'The gate's ready!' said Helfigor. 'Go!'

'Runcie?' Ulalliall said softly. 'Come closer. We've something to tell you.'

Runcie hesitated, wondering if it was another of her malicious tricks, but something in the tone of her voice drew him across. He knelt beside her. 'Yes, Ulalliall?'

'We're sorry for sneaking on you last night,' she said in the oddest whisper, as if she'd never apologised before. 'It was unworthy of us, especially –'

'To the gate, Runcie!' shouted Helfigor. 'He's stirring.'

Shambles wiped the blood from his eyes with his forearm. He looked even more shrunken now, and his skin hung in baggy folds from all the magic he'd drawn from himself, but he wasn't beaten yet. Runcie's mouth went dry. He wanted to run, but this could be important.

Ulalliall said wistfully, 'You were kind to a cranky old transportal, no matter how meanly we treated you. You listened, *and you cared*, so we have a gift for you.'

'That's not necessary –'

'We talked to Lars's transportal earlier – Ah, that was tragic! – about your father. We've never broken a transportal's confidence before, but since he's no more . . .'

Runcie's heart began to beat very fast.

'Lars doesn't know what happened to your father, and Shambles will never tell you, but a witness was there when the deed was done. Find Ursia Muddlestone, pay her price, and you'll learn what you need to know.'

'Who is she, Ulalliall?'

'A lesser wizard from the Isles. A Navigator.'

'But why was Dad killed?'

'His book said that anyone on Nightland could learn magic, *and told how*, and that threatened Iltior's survival. The book had to be destroyed and your father silenced.'

'But –'

'That's all Lars's transportal knew. Fly, Runcie.'

Runcie ran, darted back and planted a kiss on Ulalliall's glass top. 'Thank you.'

He thought he heard a teary sigh, then the gate hummed and its central hoop was filled with metallic fluid, like swirling mercury.

But before he could climb up, Shambles came to his knees and forced that eerie smile. 'No you don't. I still have one last weapon.' He pointed at Ulalliall and *quintessence* flashed from one of her greenstone posts into his staff, before she could stop it. Now directing it at the gate, Shambles gasped, 'Extinction Escapee, Emerge Enthralled!'

Black light fountained from the staff tip and the gate shook violently. Mariam yelped and sprang down as the interior of the central hoop glowed the colour of Iltior's ruddy sun, before turning ice green. With a wild screech of out-rushing air it went the colour of midnight and something gigantic, all fangs, claws and thrashing tail, exploded backwards through it like an inflated balloon being forced through a wedding ring.

Wyrmhilte turned a somersault, her claws screeching on the stone floor, then landed on her feet, kicking and squealing. Her head darted this way and that, scanning the room with those enormous golden eyes, and she lunged at Shambles.

'Heel, wyrm!'

Wyrmhilte was still battered and bruised, and her left shoulder hung limply, but she dragged a spangled crystal baton from her jerkin and thrust it at Shambles. For one mad second, Runcie hoped she'd fall upon the sorcerer and devour him.

'You're not dealing with *Lars* now.' Shambles swung his brazen staff forward, like casting with a fishing rod, and Wyrmhilte stopped as if she'd hit a wall. Her baton fell and broke in two. Evidently she'd not re-learned the great wyrm magics yet. 'Kill Helfigor and Parsifoe!' gasped Shambles. 'Seize Mariam and Runcible, then bow down so I can ride you home.'

Wyrmhilte looked outraged, as if being ridden was the greatest insult of all. She blew out a great gust of ice-breath, covering Shambles with frost. He slowly set rigid and Wyrmhilte didn't move either.

The gate turned quicksilver again. 'I have it,' shouted Helfigor. 'Get going!'

Runcie climbed up. Mariam was already at the gate.

'Come on.' She caught his arm.

But Runcie couldn't leave without saying goodbye. 'Thank you,' he said, and his eyes grew hot as he looked from Helfigor to Parsifoe. They *were* second-rate wizards, but they, and Tigris, had given everything for him. Even his enemies, Thandimanilon and Sleeth, had helped him, to say nothing of Ulalliall. 'Farewell.'

'Oh, for pity's sake clear out,' snapped Helfigor. 'We're sick of the sight of you.' Parsifoe spoke sharply to him, whereupon

Helfigor gave her a sheepish smile and drew something from his pocket. 'A parting gift to remember us by.'

He tossed a little book at them. As Runcie caught it, one-handed, from the corner of his eye he saw the frost evaporate off Shambles. He thrust the book into his pocket.

'Get them, thrall-wyrm,' croaked Shambles, and Wyrmhilte, now seemingly under his control, sprang towards the gate, claws extended.

Runcie let out a squawk and tried to jump through, but his numb foot slipped and he fell the other way. Mariam threw her arm around him, catching him just in time but, to Runcie's utter horror, the globule of memories was squeezed up inside his shirt and shot out the back of his collar, high in the air. How could he have forgotten it was there?

It flew up and up and up, hovered in mid-air for long seconds, surely by magic, then began to fall as slowly as thistle-down.

'Why, you cunning little devil,' Helfigor said.

Lars Sparj hurled himself for his staff. Sleeth ran towards the gate. Wyrmhilte changed course abruptly, her cracking wings sending dust swirling up into everyone's faces as she beat a path upwards. Shambles, on his knees, was desperately working his staff, though it wasn't clear whether he was controlling the wyrm or trying to draw the globule to himself.

Runcie watched it fall, knowing all his efforts had been for nothing. He wasn't sure what was worse: that Lars should get the secret, or Shambles, or Wyrmhilte. No, surely even

Wyrmhilte was better than Shambles. Runcie had sensed some nobility and greatness of purpose in her, but there was none whatsoever in Lord Shambles.

The jelly globule drifted towards Sleeth, only to be caught by the pull of Lars Sparj's magic and jerked in his direction. It skidded away towards Shambles, but turned again, bobbing and darting as it fell within the magical influence of one sorcerer then another.

It drifted back and forth above the gate, losing height ever so slowly, while Runcie tried to think of something he could do to make up for his blunder. But this time there was nothing anyone could do. Without rod or baton, Parsifoe and Helfigor were outclassed, so it was just a question of which enemy got it first, and whether Shambles still had the strength to take it from them.

Then something happened that no one could have anticipated. Tigris ran to the gate, caught hold of the lowest ring and flipped herself up onto the second. She swung around through the gate, holding tightly so it wouldn't take her, passed back through the upper hoop, spun in the air and caught hold of its top. Flipping herself up backwards, she somersaulted through the air and landed, feet together, on the very top of the upper ring, twenty feet above the floor.

Runcie wanted to clap – she would have gained a perfect ten at the Olympics. Tigris balanced for a second, held out her right hand and the glowing globule settled into it. But then she just stood there, staring at Thandimanilon and surely thinking about the unpaid clan debt. Don't give it to her, Runcie prayed, as Lars's face lit up.

The magicians halted, each evaluating this new opportunity, or threat. Wyrmhilte hovered, her great wings beating slowly. Each leathery flap swirled more dust into the air until the chamber was thick with it. Shambles, white as paper, clung shakily to the wall.

'Tigris!' cried Sleeth, reaching up to her with shining eyes.

Her face softened and Runcie felt sure she was going to give it to him, but she said sadly, 'No, Jac. I can never trust you again.'

'Here, Tigris,' said Mariam softly.

'But if I don't pay the debt,' said Tigris, 'Thandimanilon will take my little sister.'

'If you give it to her,' Runcie pointed out, 'and Lars gets it, what will happen to your family then?'

'Besides, they're *my* memories,' said Mariam.

Tigris held out her other hand and, with a little wrench, *envisioned* her yellow frog mindsake there. She looked from one hand to the other. The frog opened its mouth, gave an audible croak and vanished. She nodded to herself and turned to Thandimanilon.

Thandimanilon had her hand out towards Tigris but she was staring at Lars. Runcie didn't understand how she could love such a monster, and suddenly he saw the solution.

'Helfigor,' Runcie hissed, 'remember when we were talking about good and evil the other day?'

'What of it?' Helfigor said absently.

'Put the question to Thandimanilon.'

'Ah,' said Helfigor, then rapped out, 'This is your moment of truth, Thandimanilon. Our lives are fashioned from the choices we make, and you're standing on a knife-edge. Lovably wicked you may be now, but the wrong decision will plunge you into the abyss of evil and there's no climbing out again.'

'After your base existence, you dare moralise at me?' snapped Thandimanilon, 'Besides, you don't know what you're asking.'

'After my base existence, I know *exactly* what I'm asking. To condemn a little child –'

'Enough!' The whole room was still now, even Shambles. Again she looked at Lars, who pasted on an unconvincing smile.

Thandimanilon smiled back, lovingly, and reached out her slender arm to him, but after a moment she shivered, drew back and the smile faded. She turned to Tigris.

'Faithful prentice, I now know that you helped to save my life, *and* did your best to hinder Sleeth's escape. Though you had to suffer the most bitter choice of all, you did your duty by me, and your family, even at the cost of friendship. But set against that, you aided Mariam in her escape, and had you not done so, I might not have lost Niddimaun. For that reason I cannot forgive the clan debt and set you free, as you so desperately desire.

'But I will halve the debt, and take you back to repay the

remainder. And –' she gripped the top of the stairs with her other hand, steadied herself and added, '– your little sister is safe, whatever the future holds.' Thandimanilon tried to smile, but couldn't. 'Thus is my bitter choice made. You, Tigris, must make your own.' She slumped to her knees.

Still Tigris hesitated, until Lars took in what Thandimanilon had done to him. He let out a bellow of rage and the room went mad.

'Get the globule, thrall-wyrm!' choked Shambles, his skin hanging off in folds.

'Do the spell again, Parsifoe,' cried Mariam.

'Revulsion be Revealed, Skirrlydoun!'

Shambles collapsed onto his twisted knees. Wyrmhilte broke free of his spell, rotated in the air and cracked her wings so hard that he went skidding across the floor. He sat up, covered in rot, that look of horror on his face once more. Suddenly he broke, stabbed his staff at the floor and steam burst up from it. By the time it had dispersed, Shambles was gone.

But it wasn't over yet. Lars, free at last, was racing towards them, swinging his staff to blast the gate to smithereens, and there was no way to stop him.

'Helfigor!' screamed Mariam, pointing to the clockwork armies.

He acted at once. Stooping, he snatched a segment of Wyrmhilte's broken crystal baton and bowled it underarm across the floor, scything down the soldiers like ninepins. 'There's your real enemy!' he roared, pointing, and the clockwork wizards, free at last, swarmed after Lars, attacking his calves and shins with their tiny swords and staffs.

Lars, mad with pain and fury, began to kick and stamp them to pieces, and it was enough. Tigris, giving him a look of deepest contempt, thrust the globule into Mariam's upraised hand.

'It can't be destroyed, Mariam,' said Runcie.

'I know,' she said softly, looking quite calm, almost relieved. 'Nor released again. That's why I'm doing the only thing that can be done with it.'

Mariam raised her hand and, as the whole room stared in disbelief, she crushed the globule against her forehead. Its contents disappeared with a zipping sound and Runcie felt little flares of pain everywhere the globule had touched him. Mariam was swaying, hands clutched to her head, keening in agony. He steadied her, then suddenly his pain was gone.

Mariam straightened up, giving him a weak smile. 'There – the memories can never be stolen again.'

'Nobly done, child,' said Parsifoe, who had tears in her eyes. 'Now fly, so we can seal the gate. And fare well.'

'Farewell,' Mariam and Runcie said, then, as Wyrmhilte turned to the gate, they jumped.

Parsifoe tore off the helm and that was the last they saw of Iltior. The gate, the room, friends and enemies alike, all vanished like smoke.

CHAPTER 32

The Book of Magic

This time they fell into something the colour of orange cordial which felt like a warm sea, though Runcie could breathe. They drifted slowly around, then stopped, *between, nowhere*. His heartbeat came back to normal and he turned to Mariam.

She gave him a weak smile. 'We did it, Runcie. It was impossible, but you never gave in, and we beat them.'

He smiled back. 'We did. How did you know Shambles's weakness?'

'As soon as he was lifted out, I could see the real him beneath his illusion, and since Lars had told us what Skirrlydoun meant, it was obvious. What could a vain man fear more than becoming grotesque and being mocked for it?'

'And that's why you asked Parsifoe to break the illusion.'

'So Shambles would use up his strength restoring it and fighting Sleeth's curse, rather than attacking us.'

He took a deep breath. 'Do you think it's over, truly?'

'No,' she said. 'Lars and Shambles will keep trying, but all Iltior will soon know what they're up to. It's out of our hands.'

He'd made up for coming here, at least. The relief was so overwhelming that for a moment he couldn't draw breath, but then all that Shambles had said about Ansie struck home and Runcie couldn't hold back any longer. He broke down and wept for all those wonderful memories, now sullied, and all his hopes for the future. Everything good – family, hopes, dreams, to say nothing of his longing for magic – had been destroyed.

'He's ruined everything I cared about,' Runcie said when there were no tears left. He wiped his sore eyes. 'What am I supposed to do now?'

'Shambles is a stinking liar,' said Mariam. 'I'm sure your father loved you both very much.'

'How am I supposed to tell?' Runcie sniffled. Mariam offered him a dusty handkerchief and he wiped his nose. 'Shambles was right about Dad being selfish. Lots of times he wasn't there for us, because of his work.'

'Sometimes work has to come first. With parents like mine, I should know!'

'But he said Dad was a fool and a scoundrel, so I can't even believe in his work any more.'

'That's got to be a lie. If your father hadn't done something brilliant, why was his book banned? And why did Lars make such a painful journey looking for a copy?'

Runcie wiped his nose again. 'That's true, but –'

'And since Shambles lied about that, he probably lied about everything. But even if there is some truth in his story, I'm sure your father did what he did for a good reason . . .' Her eyes lit up. 'Runcie, what if your dad knew about the threat from Iltior – about them taking our power? The magic he discovered could be the only way to save Earth.'

'But everyone says Dad was bad.'

'Of course they do, because his book is a threat to Iltior. That's why they want to destroy it. But what's bad for Iltior is good for Earth, isn't it?' Her eyes were glowing now. 'Your father's work could save our world, Runcie.'

Runcie's stomach took a great swoop, then the warmth of a vast relief spread through him. '*Of course* that's what he was doing, and I'll bet there's another copy of his book – or books – hidden somewhere. Thanks, Mariam.'

They revolved in the air a few times, then he went on, 'I only kept the parchment to find out about Dad, yet after all that's happened I hardly know anything about him.'

'Well, you know he's got a talent for magic, and so have you.'

Runcie let that pass unchallenged. 'But –'

'And he kept on with his work even though the whole world was against him, which proves he's absolutely determined. Just like you.'

Runcie smiled briefly. 'But his work tore our family apart and put Mum in gaol.'

'No, that happened because the Night Stalkers bribed Earthly politicians to pass laws against magic. Anyway, your mum *chose* to keep his book after he died. Trust your feelings, Runcie. Look at the good as well as the bad.'

432

He thought about that. Ansie had been so patient with him in the folly. He'd made time for Runcie whenever he could, and had never been cross with him, even when Runcie had broken a table full of precious equipment. And Ansie had spent ages telling him stories about magic and other worlds, and therefore, whatever the reason he'd attempted to use a Night Stalker's gate, good or bad, it can't have been to escape from his family.

'You're right. Dad wasn't perfect, but Mum and I can be proud of what he achieved. Though I still don't know who killed him.'

'You'll have to come back when you're grown up, and look for the Navigator.'

'I *will*!' Runcie studied the crumpled parchment. 'And then I'm going to bring the murderer to justice.'

'But not now,' she said hastily.

'Of course not.' He looked up as she drifted overhead. 'But why *did* Mum keep a copy of his book, after he died?'

'Because she still loved him, and his work was all she had left?'

'That's a nice way of putting it.' Runcie smiled, then, realising that the parchment was smoking, let go of Mariam to beat it out.

She snatched for his hand, crying, 'Don't do that!'

'What's the matter?' he said thoughtlessly.

'We're in the middle of a gate, you idiot! We could end up anywhere. Or *nowhere*.'

'Sorry.' Runcie rubbed his eyes. 'I can't take it all in.'

'Me either.' She studied him. 'But you've certainly changed.'

'Really?'

'You used to be such a timid little thing –'

'Well, thank you very much!'

'I'm praising you, you boofhead. You were scared of everything and full of self-doubt. You thought too much, but never *did* anything about your problems. And you so idolised your father that you could never live up to what you thought he'd expect –'

'Hey!' he said, miffed because she was spot on. 'Do you call that *praise?*'

Mariam laughed. 'I'm setting the scene for your future triumphs. And now look at you – standing up to Shambles all by yourself. You're amazing.'

'Really?' he repeated, very pleased and hoping she'd go on.

'Yes, you are. And when he gave you that impossible choice, it was just brilliant the way you found a way out so you didn't have to compromise your principles.'

If only she knew. But then, Mariam was his dearest friend and he couldn't deceive her. She had to know the truth, no matter what she thought of him. 'But I did,' he said softly.

'What are you talking about?'

'I *did* make a choice. I – I – you'll despise me for this.'

'If you've got something to say,' she said crossly, 'just say it. Don't tell me what I'm going to think, all right?'

'Sorry. But I had chosen, Mariam. I chose to go against everything I believe in. Even though giving Shambles the memories could start an unjust war, I was going to do it. I had to know the truth about Dad. I couldn't bear not to. So now you know.' Runcie turned away, sure she'd be disgusted with him.

'But you didn't give the memories up,' she said after a long pause.

'I was going to, and that's just as bad, isn't it?'

'How would I know? No, of course it's not. Anyway, you *didn't do it*, so it doesn't count.'

Runcie had to think hard about that. He'd made a terrible choice, and it was only by good luck that he'd gotten away with it, but no matter which way he turned the choice around he couldn't tell just how bad it was. His head was starting to hurt so he quickly changed the subject. 'You've changed too, actually.'

'Me?' she snorted. 'How?'

'You used to be really rude and arrogant and selfish. You're much nicer now.'

'Thanks, I think!'

'And you're so brave.'

'I have a reckless streak,' she said offhandedly. 'I was just doing what I always do, so it wasn't brave at all.'

It was far greater than anything I did, Runcie thought. 'That's not true. You've got a wonderful, noble streak. It was like Joan of Arc or someone, the way you gave yourself up to save Parsifoe's prentices. I couldn't have done that – I was thinking about myself all the time.'

She waved a hand. 'I really don't want to talk about it, Runcie.' All the same, she looked pleased. 'No one ever said nice things about me before.'

'And as for taking back the memories . . .'

'I don't know why I did that. It was just, well, they were *my* memories and I didn't see why anyone else should use them for some evil purpose.' She thought for a moment. 'So once Parsifoe and Helfigor have sealed the gate, and no one can come to our world, we'll be safe, won't we?'

'Of course,' he said absently. For a month or two, anyway.

Mariam wiped her watering eyes on her sleeve. 'I never thought we had a hope, and suddenly, it's over. We'll never see Tigris again. Or Helfigor or Parsifoe. Or Ulalliall.'

Or Sleeth, he thought. Or Shambles, Lars Sparj or Thandimanilon. The good, the bad or the joyously wicked. 'I suppose not.' He couldn't take that in either. 'I've never known anyone like Tigris before.'

'Nor I,' said Mariam. 'My life was really horrible until we went to Iltior. Now Iltior's gone. We're going home.'

Home! That made him feel misty-eyed too, though the thought of returning to the Nightingales, and Grindgrim Academy, did not. But he was alert enough to notice that Mariam said it as if it were a prison sentence. 'It's not all bad . . .'

'At least you'll be able to visit your mum. She must be out of her mind.'

He couldn't bear to think about what his broken promise had done to her. 'And you'll be able to see your folks. You must have missed them.'

'Of course I've missed them,' she said snappily. 'They're my *parents*! But what am I supposed to tell them? That I just popped through a gate to another world, to learn about magic and have a few dozen near-death experiences? They'll do their nuts, Runcie. And then . . .'

'What?' said Runcie, fear curling around his heart.

'I won't be going back to Grindgrim. They'll send me far away this time.'

'But surely . . .?' Runcie began.

'Fulk will have told everyone how we magically disappeared, and that'll be the end. That's why I was sent to Grindgrim in the first place.'

'What do you mean?'

'I did magic at my posh school and it turned out really badly.'

He just gaped. '*You* did magic?'

'You don't have to act so amazed,' she said stiffly.

'But you've always been so against it.'

'That's *why* I'm against it.'

'What did you do?'

'I'm not saying.' Mariam had gone brick red.

'Oh, come on,' said Runcie, more forcefully than he would have been capable of a week ago. 'I've owned up to *my* worst failings.'

'All right!' she said, so furiously that he wondered if she entirely appreciated the new, bolder Runcie. 'If you must know, I used a spell on the headmistress.'

'What spell?'

'Oh, just some nonsense my old granny taught me.'

'Yes?' persisted Runcie.

'You really are very irritating, you know. I liked the timid you so much better.'

He just grinned. 'Why?'

'The headmistress was a vicious old toad who was always picking on me.'

'And?'

'I used Granny's Toad-Mind spell on her. How was I supposed to know that it was a real spell, and I could work it?'

'Do you mean to tell me you turned the headmistress of the best school in the country into a *toad*?'

'Of course I didn't. I'm not a magician. It just made her *think* she was a toad.'

'What did she do?'

'First she licked all the dead flies off the windowsill, in a meeting of the Board of Governors. Then she hopped out the window and down to the school pond, gobbling up insects and slugs. It was the most grisly sight. She had cockroach legs stuck between her teeth, and grasshopper guts hanging off the warts on her chin.' She managed a smile.

'I can imagine,' Runcie chortled.

'But then she tried to jump onto a lily pad.'

Runcie, wishing it had been the malicious headmaster at Grindgrim, laughed until his sides ached. 'I'd love to have seen that.'

Mariam wasn't laughing now. 'If the governors hadn't gone after her, she would have drowned. She's still in a locked ward in the infirmary, in a strait-jacket, completely mad. *That's* why I was expelled.'

Suddenly he understood what had been behind her reckless defiance all this time, and her noble self-sacrifice too. 'Is that why you do such mad, brave things?'

'To punish myself, you mean? I don't think so, but I feel so guilty, and I've got to make up for it. One stupid mistake wrecked her life and changed mine forever. She *was* nasty, but she didn't deserve that.'

'I don't think any the less of you for it,' he said quietly.

'I was lucky I didn't end up at Ruersham Correctional. It cost Mum and Dad most of their fortune to hush it up, which is why I was on a good behaviour bond at Grindgrim. Now everyone knows I disappeared magically, *with you*, and it'll cost them what money they have left. Mum and Dad will blame you, Runcie, and they'll do everything in their power to ensure we never see each other again.'

She stared at the orange cordial sky for a while, before adding, 'even if they have to send me to the other side of the world. I'm afraid – I don't want to go home. What am I to do?'

He didn't have the faintest idea. 'Well,' he said carefully, 'we can't stay here.'

'Why not?' she said, unreasonably. 'I like it here. There are no teachers, no parents, no homework . . .'

'Nothing to eat or drink. Nowhere safe to sleep. Besides, we've got to alert Earth about the threat.' He had no idea how they were going to do that, since no one would believe their story. And after that, he was going to look for Ansie's book. Runcie looked down at the parchment. 'I've got to read the words, Mariam.'

'Can't you wait a bit longer?'

'What if Shambles didn't go home, but *between*?' Runcie thought he caught the faintest disgusting whiff of Sleeth's Rotting Curse. 'Besides, the spell on the parchment might not last. The words are fading.'

'Oh, all right! I get the message. Just do it.'

'Sor-ry!' he snapped, but at the look on her face he said, 'Mariam, let's not finish up like this. Please – you're my best friend. My only friend on Earth.'

It shook her out of her black state. 'And you're mine.' She snorted.

'What's so funny?' he said, thinking she was laughing at him.

'If someone had told me a month ago that I'd have a friend from Grindgrim, I'd have slapped her. But if she'd said I'd be best friends with a boy who wasn't even as tall as me, I'd have laughed until I choked.'

Runcie had to think about that for a while before deciding that it was, after all, a compliment. It made what was to come all the worse. He swallowed the lump in his throat. 'Promise you won't lose touch, Mariam. If your parents take you away, promise you'll find a way to contact me.'

'I promise,' she said. 'And you've got to do the same. Okay?'

'Okay, but I'm not going anywhere. You'll always know where to find me – in the alley between the school buildings, being beaten to a pulp by Fulk's bully boys. With no one to save me.'

Her eyes grew soft. 'I'll always be with you, in here.' She tapped him in the middle of the forehead. 'Besides, after the people we've dealt with on Iltior, Fulk will be putty in your hands. It's what's inside that counts, and no bully can touch that. You're not a victim any more, and bullies only pick on victims.'

'Yeees,' he said, thinking that they also *created* victims by constantly picking on them. No – damn them! He'd fight the whole school if he had to. They might cow him but they'd never break him.

'And there's one more thing.'

'What's that?'

'You've got magic in you, Runcie. That's what you always wanted, isn't it?'

'But I was holding your hand both times I opened a gate, so it's got to be your magic.'

'Well, maybe you can't *use* magic, but you can see where it comes from. And you saved our lives that way.'

'True,' he said slowly. 'Whoopee!' He threw his arms in the air.

'Don't do that!' Mariam grabbed his wrist with one hand and snatched the drifting parchment out of the air with the other.

'Sorry.' Runcie couldn't stop grinning. 'And you've got real magic, Mariam.'

'That's what I'm afraid of,' she muttered, 'but I suppose there's a good side to it. Hey, what's that book anyway?'

He'd forgotten about it. The cover said, in spidery black writing, *The Four Basic Arts – A Primer*, by Lugitroyd Melvinion Helfigor, Wizard Second Order (conceded), Third Class. 'It's a book of magic. Do – do you want it?' He was praying, selfishly, that she wouldn't. If he did have a talent for the Art of Seeing, maybe he could learn the other Basic Arts as well. And if he could find Ansie's book . . .

'No way!' said Mariam. 'Not in a million years. Mum and Dad would burn it, anyway.' She glanced at the orange void, then said thoughtfully, 'but if I *did* want to look at it one day, I'd know where to find it, wouldn't I?'

He grinned. 'Of course. It'll be behind the loose brick in the wall, under my bed at the Nightingales, at 13 Thirteenth Avenue.'

'All right. Read the parchment, Runcie. Let's go home and face the music.'

Runcie sniffed the air. Was that the faintest smell of diesel fumes? Once more his eyes pricked. Whatever else Earth was, foul or fair, it was home as Iltior could never be.

'Let's go home.' Holding the writing up, Runcie began to recite the glowing words.

The end of

Runcible Jones: *The Gate to Nowhere*

Runcie's and Mariam's story
continues in book 2

Runcible Jones: *The Buried City*

About the author

Ian Irvine was born in Bathurst in 1950, and educated at Chevalier College and the University of Sydney, where he took a PhD in marine science.

After working as an environmental project manager, Ian set up his own consulting firm in 1986, carrying out studies for clients in Australia and overseas. He has worked in many countries in the Asia-Pacific region. An expert in marine pollution, Ian has developed some of Australia's national guidelines for the protection of the oceanic environment.

Ian Irvine lives with his family in northern New South Wales. His previous fantasy quartets, *The View from the Mirror* and *The Well of Echoes*, have been published in ten countries. He is currently working on the first book of his new Three Worlds trilogy, *Song of the Tears*, after which he will write *Runcible Jones 2: The Buried City*.

Ian can be contacted at ianirvine@ozemail.com.au

His web site is www.ian-irvine.com

ALSO AVAILABLE FROM PENGUIN

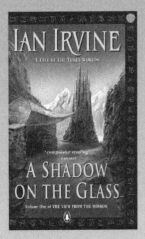

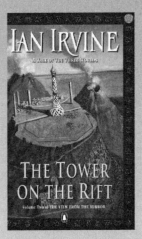

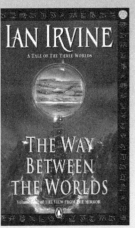

THE VIEW FROM THE MIRROR QUARTET

Volume One A SHADOW ON THE GLASS   **Volume Two** THE TOWER ON THE RIFT

Volume Three DARK IS THE MOON   **Volume Four** THE WAY BETWEEN THE WORLDS

ALSO AVAILABLE FROM PENGUIN

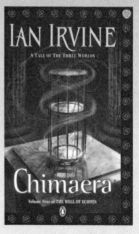

THE WELL OF ECHOES QUARTET

COME EXPLORING AT

www.penguin.com.au

AND

www.puffin.com.au

FOR

Author and illustrator profiles

Book extracts

Reviews

Competitions

Activities, games and puzzles

Advice for budding authors

Tips for parents

Teacher resources